FLOWER
NET

ALSO BY LISA SEE

On Gold Mountain

LISA SEE

FLOWER NET

For Debbie —
Thank you for
your kind words!

Lisa See

HarperCollins*Publishers*

HarperCollins books may be purchased for educational, business, or sales promotional use. For information please write: Special Markets Department, HarperCollins Publishers, Inc., 10 East 53rd Street, New York, NY 10022.

FIRST EDITION

Designed by Ruth Lee

Library of Congress Cataloging-in-Publication Data

See, Lisa.
    Flower net / Lisa See. — 1st ed.
      p. cm.
    ISBN 0-06-017527-3
    I. Title.
   PS3569.E3334F58   1997
   813'.54—dc21   97-10677

97 98 99 00 01 ❖/RRD 10 9 8 7 6 5 4 3 2 1

For my husband,
with love

Acknowledgments

I wish to thank Richard Drooyan, Nathan Hochman, Nora Manella, and Carolyn Turchin who shared with me their experiences of working at the U.S. Attorney's Office over the years. I am also grateful to Special Agent Dan Martino of the FBI, agent George Phocus of the U.S. Fish and Wildlife Service, Ken Goddard of the U.S. Fish and Wildlife Forensics Laboratory, and Deborah Mitchell of U.S. Customs for their stories and expertise. In addition to those listed above, I am thankful for the work of the World Wildlife Federation and Traffic, both of which keep a vigilant eye on the trade in endangered animals and products made from them. Their publications bolstered several first-person accounts, as well as helped me to understand what I had seen in herbal markets, an herbal medicine institute, and a bear farm in China.

Although I had heard many legends of the real Liu Hulan, it took the fine folks at UCLA Special Collections to locate two books on her: *Stories from Liu Hulan's Childhood* (Chen Li) and *Liu Hulan: Story of a Girl Revolutionary* (Hsing Liang). On the other hand, much has been written about the Cultural Revolution, and I am particularly

indebted to the memoirs of Rae Yang, Anchee Min, and Zhai
Zhenhua. I have long admired historian W. J. F. Jenner's insights
into the history and culture of China. Du Xichuan and Zhang
Lingyuan's survey of China's legal system, as well as A. Zee's meticu-
lous account of the importance of bear paw in Chinese cuisine,
helped me keep my facts straight. I also want to acknowledge
Nicholas Eftimiades for his research into Chinese intelligence opera-
tions and Mark Salzman for his help with the title for *Flower Net*.
The watershed work of Nicholas Kristof and Sheryl WuDunn continues to be an inspiration to me.

For the bloody details, I relied on John Douglas's groundbreaking
research on serial killers, Dr. Werner Spitz's forensics knowledge, and
William Kleinknecht's *The New Ethnic Mobs* for additional background on the changing face of organized crime. Dr. Pamela
Maloney and Dr. Gretchen Kreiger offered invaluable information on
Chinese herbal medicine, while Sophia Lo helped me with my
Mandarin and other issues relating to the Chinese language. I am
likewise indebted to several people in Beijing and Chengdu who prefer to remain anonymous.

The wildlife trade, Chinese culture, and U.S.-Sino relations would
remain inaccessible and incomprehensible if not for the measured and
accurate reports of many journalists. These include: Marcus Brauchli,
Kenneth Zhao, Andrew and Leslie Cockburn, Christine Courtney,
Susan Essoyan, Seth Faison, Maggie Farley, James Gerstenzang,
Michael J. Goodman, Marlowe Hood, Evelyn Iritani, K. Connie
Kang, Jeff Kass, Elaine Kurtenbach, Jim Mann, Ronald J. Ostrow,
Richard C. Paddock, Rone Tempest, Paul Theroux, Patrick E. Tyler,
Xiao-huang Yin, and Fareed Zakaria.

At a very dark moment, Jessica Saltsman came in with a breezy
smile and lots of energy. She saved the day! Alicia Diaz also provided
me with peace of mind.

I am, as always, beholden to Sandra Dijkstra and the wonderful
people in her office for their indefatigable enthusiasm. They're the
best! Ron Bernstein was inspiring as he guided me through uncharted
waters. Larry Ashmead at HarperCollins and Alan Ladd Jr. were
exceedingly generous in their early support, for which I will be for-

ever grateful. Huge thanks must also go to my editor, Eamon Dolan. I didn't know editors could be so much fun or so funny. It's been an honor and a pleasure.

My deepest appreciation goes to my family. My mother, Carolyn See, my sister, Clara Sturak, and our good friends John Espey and Chris Chandler always provide sound—and loving—criticism. My sons, Alexander and Christopher Kendall, have been indispensable on issues of plot and gore. Finally, I need to thank my husband, Richard Kendall, for the access he provided me, for the trips to China and those karaoke bars, and, ultimately, for his kindness, loyalty, and strength. This book never would have been written if not for him.

FLOWER
NET

1

JANUARY 10
Bei Hai Park

Wing Yun held tightly to his granddaughter's mittened hand as he guided her in slow rhythmic glides across the frozen expanse of Bei Hai Lake just outside the burnished walls of the Forbidden City. On the opposite shore, Wing Yun could see the Beijing City Young People's Speed Skaters hard at their interval training. Behind the team, shrouded in a haze of coal smoke and heavy gray clouds, he saw the Five Dragon Pavilion and the Hall of Celestial Kings. Nearby, along the walkways surrounding the lake, old people swept last night's dusting of snow with bamboo brooms. Based on the solidity of the ice beneath the blades of his old skates and the way the air billowed and steamed with every breath he took, Wing Yun guessed that it must be –15 degrees Celsius. And this was as warm as it would get today.

Wing preferred to stay on this side of the lake just inside the main entrance to the park, where the old Round City curved around what had once been a fortress protecting the residence of Kublai Khan. Very close to shore and accessible by footbridge was Jade Island. In summer, Wing Yun liked to stroll along its covered pathways, stopping at the sheltered pavilions along the way. If it wasn't too hot or humid, he might climb to the top of the hill to the White Dagoba, an onion-shaped shrine built in the Tibetan style to honor the first visit of the Dalai Lama in 1651.

Wing Yun kept his granddaughter in the area near the loudspeakers. Old-fashioned dance music drifted across the frozen expanse. Here and there, twosomes tangoed and waltzed. Other young couples giggled together. A few even held hands, and Wing Yun thought, Ah, how life is changing. When I was young, no one, *no one*, could hold hands in public. Even now he wondered what the parents of these couples would think if they saw their children acting so brazenly in front of—well, in front of so many citizens. Nearby, families— mama, baba, grandparents, aunts, uncles, and many children— laughed and teased one another. They made picturesque tableaux, bundled in old-style padded blue jackets and brightly colored Western-style coats, mittens and mufflers. Many of the younger children—still struggling to find their balance—held on to wooden chairs outfitted with runners. Seated on these chairs, grandparents beamed as their grandchildren pushed them along.

Wing Yun was familiar with many of the skaters, but today, as usual, a few strangers tried this bit of exercise for the first time. He and his granddaughter had nearly been knocked over by two uniformed soldiers. Wing Yun didn't scold them as he might have. He could see they were just country boys, perhaps peasants from South China. They had probably never seen snow and ice before.

Wing Yun and Mei Mei had spent many days together here this winter. She was a good companion for him. She didn't mind quiet and often seemed as engrossed in her own thoughts as he was in his. Right now, he could feel her fingers moving inside her mitten. She wanted to skate out on her own, but he was reluctant to loosen his grip.

"Sing to me, Mei Mei," he said. "Sing me that song about the ice."

She looked up at him, and he had to push her scarf down so he could see her cheeks flushed pink by the cold. She smiled at him, then began to sing "Nine Nine," which recounted the nine phases of winter and cautioned the listener about the season's dangers. He could remember the song from his own childhood; it was familiar to anyone raised on the North China Plain.

"One nine, two nine: hands can't show," she began, her voice as crisp as the afternoon air. "Three nine, four nine: on ice go. Five nine, six nine: river willows seen. Seven nine: ice crack! Eight nine: swallows back."

Wing Yun joined in for the last line. "Nine nine and one nine more, oxen in fields encore." The last notes faded into the icy quiet, then Wing Yun asked, "What 'nine' are we in, Mei Mei?"

"Three nine, because the ice is good and we can skate."

"That's right. And what will happen at seven nine?"

"Grandpa!" she said indignantly. "I promise not to skate then. I always tell you that."

"I just want you to be careful," he said. "Now, do you think you're ready to go by yourself?"

A shy smile crept across her features, and he watched as she took a deep breath of anticipation. Then he pulled to a stop and released her mittened hand. With her narrow ankles wobbling, she edged out on her own. With each stride, she grew more confident.

"Don't go too close to the middle," he called out, though he knew that at this "three-nine" time in January it was perfectly safe. Still, his granddaughter slowed, then set off toward a deserted area of the lake near the shore. As Wing Yun followed, he noticed how few grooves there were here in the ice. Funny, he thought, how people like to stick together—the racing team so far away, the families gathered in groups near the main gate and no one in between.

Just as Mei Mei neared the bank, she lost her balance. Her arms flailed about her for a moment as she tried to regain her equilibrium. Then she fell forward, hard. Wing Yun hesitated. Would she cry?

The little girl sat up, stared at the ice before her, and began a high-pitched wail that cut through the romantic waltz music, the soft conversations of young lovers, and the jovial teasing of the family groups. Wing Yun skated quickly to his granddaughter. Once he reached her side, he, too, wanted to scream. Before his granddaughter, a man lay embedded in the ice. He stared up at Wing Yun and Mei Mei, wide-eyed but unseeing. He was a white ghost, a foreign devil, a white man.

*   *   *

Two hours later, Liu Hulan arrived on the scene. The atmosphere had changed dramatically since the body had been discovered. All of the skaters were off the ice and being held as witnesses in one of the pavilions on the shore. Local police guarded the perimeter of the crime scene. Within their loose circle, Hulan could see other men in plainclothes, some looking for evidence, others standing and talking to a citizen and a small child. At the very center of the circle, a man hunched over a dark shape lying next to a small mound of what appeared to be shaved ice. Liu Hulan sighed, pulled her scarf and the collar of her lavender down coat up over her ears, and set out across the ice.

She seemed oblivious to the ripple her arrival caused among the men. If they could have gotten their nerve up to say what attracted their attention to her, they might have pointed out that she was too beautiful for her job, that she dressed differently from other women they knew, that she was vain, that she always held herself apart. In just a few answers the men would have moved from the hazardous territory of sex to the safe realm of political criticism that they knew so well.

It would have been easy to attack her on her physical presentation, except that she didn't seem particularly interested in the Western-style fashions that had been available in the city in recent years. She preferred to wear pre-Revolutionary clothes: long skirts tailored to fit her sleek shape and cream-colored embroidered silk blouses of antiquated Chinese cut that crossed at her breast. In winter she added cashmere sweaters made in villages along the Mongolian border and dyed to soothing tones of coral, aqua, and winter white. These colors set off her complexion in ways that brought to mind all the time-honored descriptions of women in China: Her skin was as translucent as fine porcelain, as delicate as the rose petal, as soft as a good-luck peach.

Liu Hulan would have laughed at any such comparisons. She dismissed her beauty. She never wore makeup. She didn't perm her black hair, wearing it, instead, in a blunt cut that reached just below her shoulders. It was always slipping forward over her ears in silky waves. A few strands always seemed to stick straight out from her head as though electrified. More than one man had wanted to run his hands through them. But none of her male colleagues would have ever risked touching, even casually, Inspector Liu Hulan.

As she reached the circle, she held up her credentials from the Ministry of Public Security and was waved through. Walking these last few steps, she braced herself for what she would see. She had been with the MPS for eleven years now but still had not hardened herself completely to the sight of the dead, especially those who had died violently.

Fong, the pathologist, looked up from the body. "Another pretty one for you, Inspector," he said, grinning.

The victim, a young white man, had been laid on a clean white sheet. The workers, whose gruesome task was to chisel the body out of the lake, had done their job carefully. The corpse was still encased in a thin shroud of ice. His form was straight and flat. Only one arm twisted awkwardly away from his torso. His fingernails were dark purple. His eyes and his mouth were open. Everywhere else on the body, the icy shroud showed pure white, but here, in the victim's mouth—where his teeth appeared as horrible black pearls—as well as in his nostrils, the ice was tinged pink. Other than this, Liu Hulan could see no external signs of injury.

"Have you turned him over yet?"

"What do you think?" Fong retorted. "This is my first case? Of course I turned him over. I don't see anything, but that doesn't mean I won't find something when I get him back to the lab. I can't get all of the ice off of him out here without damaging the body. So we're just going to have to wait. Let him thaw out, then I'll know something."

"But what do you think?"

"Maybe he was drunk. Maybe he came out here on the night before the big freeze. Maybe he stumbled. Maybe he hit his head. I don't see any signs of this, but it's possible."

Liu Hulan thought about that scenario, then said, "He looks

pretty young to me. If he fell in the water, or even through the ice, wouldn't he have had the strength to pull himself out?"

"Okay, Inspector, lesson time," Pathologist Fong said, his voice sharpening. He never liked it when she questioned his expertise. He stood and stared up at her. He was several inches shorter than Liu Hulan, and he didn't like this either. "You take an average person. I'm talking about a man of average height for a foreigner, maybe five feet ten inches. He's wearing everyday clothes. In this case, I see he's wearing just jeans, a shirt, a sweater."

"So?"

"So, our average man here—dressed in street clothes and in good physical health—should be able to last about forty-five minutes in water that's less than about two degrees Celsius. Something kept him from fighting his way to shore."

"You think it's alcohol?"

"Could be. Could be a drug overdose."

"Suicide?"

"I can think of better ways," Fong said and grinned again as he squatted back down next to the body.

Liu Hulan bent over to get a closer look at the victim. "What's this blood in his mouth? Does that have something to do with freezing to death?"

"No, I don't know what caused that. Maybe he bit his tongue. Maybe he broke his nose in the fall. I'll let you know later."

"Does it bother you that he isn't wearing a coat? Could he have been dragged out here and dumped?"

"Everything about this case bothers me," the pathologist answered, "but if you're thinking murder, you're just going to have to wait for the results of the autopsy."

"One last question. Is it him?"

"I haven't been able to get in his pockets yet, but it sure looks like the photos they gave us." He jutted his chin over to the shore. "I've been waiting for you to get here. I think you'd better deal with them." Liu Hulan followed his gaze and saw a Caucasian couple sitting on a wrought-iron bench.

"Shit."

Fong snorted. "Are you surprised?"

"No." Liu Hulan sighed. "But I wish I wasn't the one who had to tell them."

"That's why the vice minister sent you."

"I know, but that doesn't mean I have to like it." As an after-thought, she asked, "How did they know to come?"

"Their son has been missing for over a week, and the victim appears to be the right age, the right race. The vice minister called you after he sent the car for them."

Hulan absorbed the political implications of this information and said, "I'll come down to the lab later. And thanks."

She looked at the body one more time, then over to the shore. The Caucasian couple would have to wait a few more minutes.

As she usually did at a crime scene, she began stepping backward away from the body. With each step, her view of the scene widened. Although digging out the body had been a difficult job, the workmen had meticulously kept the excess ice in one neat pile adjacent to the shallow grave. And although there had been dozens of people on the scene, the ice was so hard that it still appeared utterly smooth except for two sets of skate tracks. One set etched deep grooves, the other only lightly scraped the surface. Liu Hulan could see no signs of a struggle, no blood, or any other imperfections in or on the ice.

She turned now and walked briskly to where an old man and a lit-tle girl huddled together. The old man's arm was draped protectively over the child's shoulder. They were still wearing their skates.

"Good afternoon, uncle," Hulan said, bestowing a polite honorific on this stranger.

"We didn't do anything," the old man said. She could see he was shivering.

Liu Hulan addressed a guard. "Why do you have this man here? Why haven't you taken him inside and given him tea?"

The police officer's features twisted in embarrassment. "We thought . . . "

"You thought incorrectly." She refocused her attention on the pair before her. She leaned down until she was at eye level with the little girl. "What's your name?"

"Mei Mei," the girl answered through chattering teeth.

"And who's this?"

"Grandpa Wing."

Liu Hulan straightened again. "Grandpa Wing, *ni hao ma*, how are you?"

"They said we would be detained. They said we would go to jail. They said . . . "

Liu Hulan looked at the police officer, who lowered his gaze. "You must forgive the zealousness of my colleagues. They have been very rude to you, I'm sure."

"We didn't do anything wrong," the old man repeated.

"Of course you didn't. Please, don't be afraid. Just tell me what happened."

When the old man finished his story, she said, "You've done a good job, Grandpa Wing. Now why don't you take your grand-daughter home?"

The look of relief in the old man's eyes told her just how terrified he had been. "*Xie-xie, xie-xie.*" He thanked her again and again. Then he took his granddaughter's mittened hand in his and they slowly skated away.

She turned back to the police officer. "You! You get over to where they're holding the other skaters. I want them released immediately."

"But . . . "

"They obviously had nothing to do with this. And one more thing. I'd like you to make a self-criticism to your superior. When you're done, I'd like you to tell him that I do not wish to have you assigned to my cases."

"Inspector, I . . . "

"Get moving."

She watched his retreating back, regretting the need to maintain a cruel facade to protect her position and ensure her status at the ministry. Mao had said that women hold up half the sky, but Chinese men still held the most powerful positions in the workplace.

As Hulan began walking toward the shore, the Caucasian couple gradually came into focus. They were in their mid-fifties. The woman wore a mink coat and a matching hat. She looked frightfully pale, and even from a distance Liu Hulan could see she'd been crying. The man was, as newspapers customarily reported, extremely handsome. His face, even in the middle of a Beijing winter, was tan. His rugged good looks evoked the prairies and dry winds of his home state, where he had been first a rancher and then a senator.

"Good morning, Mr. Ambassador, Mrs. Watson. I'm Inspector Liu Hulan," she said in virtually accentless English. She shook hands with both of them.

"Is it our son? Is it Billy?" the woman asked.

"We don't have an identification yet, but I believe it is."

"I want to see him," Bill Watson said.

"Of course," Liu Hulan agreed. "But first I have a couple of questions."

"We've been down to your office," the ambassador said. "We've told you all we know. Our son has been missing for ten days and you haven't done a thing."

Liu Hulan ignored the ambassador and looked into Elizabeth Watson's eyes. "Mrs. Watson, can I get you anything? Wouldn't you rather wait inside?" As the woman resumed her weeping, her husband strode to the edge of the lake.

Hulan held on to Elizabeth Watson's hands for a few minutes and watched as she willed herself back to a seeming indifference. Speaking as the political wife she was, Elizabeth Watson said, "I'm sure you have your duties. It's okay, dear. I'm okay."

Liu Hulan rose and went to Watson. They stood side by side, neither speaking, just gazing out across the icy expanse to where the body had been found.

Without turning to face the ambassador, Liu Hulan broke the silence. "Before you identify the body, there are some things I need to ask."

"I don't know what more I can tell you, but go ahead."

"Did your son drink?"

The ambassador allowed himself a small laugh. "Inspector, Billy was in his early twenties. What do you think? Of course he drank."

"Begging your pardon, sir, but I think you know what I mean. Did your son have a drinking problem?"

"No."

"Have you ever known him to use drugs?"

"Absolutely not."

"Are you sure?"

"Let me put it to you this way, Inspector. The president of my country would not have appointed me to this post if there were drug problems in my family."

Good, Liu Hulan thought. Get angry. Get angry and tell me the truth.

"Was Billy despondent?"

"What are you implying?"

"I'm wondering if he was happy here. Often people in our expatriate community, especially the spouses and children of those who have been sent abroad, become lonely or depressed."

"My wife and son love China," he said, his voice rising. "Now I'd like to see if that person out there is Billy."

"I'll take you, but before we go, I'd like to explain to you what will happen. Our customs here may be different from what you're used to in America."

"I'm not accustomed to having my son die either in China or America, Inspector."

"Bill," his wife pleaded softly.

"Sorry. Go on."

"We'll be taking the body back to the Ministry of Public Security."

"Absolutely not. Mrs. Watson and I have been through enough. We want to take our son home for burial. We need to do that as quickly as possible."

"I understand your desire, but there are some things that are unexplained about your son's death."

"There's nothing 'unexplained.' He obviously had some type of accident."

"How can you possibly know that, sir? How"—and here she hesitated—"how can you be so sure that that *is* your son out there?"

"I'm telling you that *if* that's my son, I'm taking him home to Montana, where we'll bury him."

"I have to apologize again, because that's not going to happen anytime soon. You see, sir, I want to know why this young man—if he was your son—was out in the middle of winter without proper clothing. I want to know why he didn't simply swim to shore. We need to do an autopsy and determine the true cause of death."

"Let's just see if we're even talking about my son," Watson said then strode out across the ice.

As Liu Hulan and Ambassador Watson reached the circle, the human cordon parted and the pair walked through. Fong stood and stepped away from the body. The ambassador stopped, looked down, and nodded. "That's Billy." He exhaled heavily. Liu Hulan waited. Finally Watson spoke again. "I want my son. I want him fully clothed and untouched by you or anyone in your department."

"Ambassador . . . "

He held up his hand to silence her and continued. "I don't want to hear any of your bureaucratic nonsense. This was an accident. You and your superiors are going to treat this that way."

"I can't do that."

"You *will* do it!"

"Ambassador, I know this is painful, but look at your son. Something happened here."

Bill Watson returned his gaze to the frozen form of his son's body, seeing the open eyes, the ice-filled mouth and nostrils tinged with blood. The ambassador then looked up and contemplated the lake, the ancient buildings, the leafless willow trees. Liu Hulan wondered if he was memorizing this panorama as the last sight that his son had seen. Then Bill Watson addressed the group.

"This was an accident," he said in the even tones of a polished politician.

"How do you know that, sir? How can you be so sure?"

But he turned away and walked wordlessly toward his waiting, pale wife.

Liu Hulan called out after him. Her words seemed loud and harsh in the cold silence. "I'm not going to drop this, sir. I'm going to find out what happened to your son, and then you can take him home."

2

JANUARY 20

Los Angeles

ssistant U.S. Attorney David Stark, dressed in a conservative, pinstriped suit, flipped open his identification—though all the lobby guards knew him on sight—then bypassed the metal detector. He took the elevator up to the twelfth floor. He offered up a hearty "Good morning, Lorraine" to the woman who sat behind the bulletproof glass reception area. She looked at him wordlessly and pressed the buzzer to let him in. One day, he thought, one day I'll get a reaction.

David's office—recently painted in pale gray and decorated in the practical style favored by the government—faced west and was considered to have a great view. Usually that meant miles and miles of smog, but this morning the sky shone a bright Tiffany blue, scrubbed clean by a series of storms that had washed over L.A. during the last two weeks. Sitting behind his desk, he could see over buildings and roadways all the way to the ocean. To his right in the far distance, the San Gabriels glistened with a pristine capping of snow from last night's storm.

David had none of the framed diplomas and commendations that some attorneys hung on their walls, but details about his career and

13

personal life could still be deciphered in the few photos he kept on his desk—a law school graduation photo with his mom and dad, David on the steps of the federal courthouse giving a press conference. Yet another was from his last year as a partner at Phillips, MacKenzie & Stout. The photo, taken during the firm's annual gala, showed David in a tuxedo and his wife—his ex-wife—in a revealing burgundy cocktail dress.

David got right to work. He was between cases and took the time to catch up on mail and phone calls. He'd just gotten a conviction against a group of men caught smuggling heroin in from China. The FBI had impounded 1,200 kilos of the drug, which now would never make it to the street. David had also gotten good press coverage, which certainly wouldn't harm his career if and when he wanted to leave the government to go back to private practice. The buzz around the office was great, which, in turn, would mean more high-profile cases. All this was good, outstanding even. But the conviction was a disappointment too.

Since coming to the U.S. Attorney's Office, David had prosecuted drug, racketeering, and massive illegal immigration cases. He'd built a substantial reputation for the most federal convictions against Chinese organized crime, particularly against the Rising Phoenix, the most powerful gang in Southern California. But he'd never been able to tie the crimes to anyone high up in the organization.

In the meantime, the very face of organized crime continued to change in the United States. The Justice Department continued to pursue the Mafia, but today crime syndicates were multicultural. Some considered blacks and Hispanics—the Dominicans in particular—to be the new "royalty of organized crime." Others were fixated on the Russian Mafia and the Vietnamese gangs. As a result, the FBI had formed special squads to infiltrate, harass, and arrest each of these groups.

None was more entrenched or threatening to America's well-being than the triads. These Chinese gangs, what the Cantonese called *tongs*, had been in this country since the discovery of gold in California. But the traditions—blood oaths and secret rituals—and the organizations—hundreds of which had been established as the Chinese diaspora spread around the world—could literally be traced back for centuries. Like the Italians, the Chinese gangs had healthy international connections. They had glorious access to heroin coming through the Golden Triangle. From new immigrants, they drew a continual supply of foot soldiers to do their dirty work. Looking at the charts that lined his office walls, David could track what he knew of these activities in Los Angeles alone. He had reason to believe—but not enough evidence to make an arrest—that the Rising Phoenix was involved in casinos, bookmaking, loan-sharking, prostitution, extortion, credit-card and food-stamp fraud, illegal immigration, and, of course, heroin smuggling. All of this was supplemental to a wide array of legitimate businesses—restaurants, motels, copy shops.

At around two, the quiet of David's office was shattered when two FBI agents burst in. Jack Campbell and Noel Gardner had worked the Chinese gang beat with David for two years now. Campbell, the older of the two, was a lanky black man with a smattering of freckles across his nose and cheekbones. His partner, Gardner, was short, brawny, and at least twenty years younger. An accountant by training, Gardner was thoughtful and precise, letting the more personable Campbell do most of the talking.

"Last night's storm was the break we've been waiting for," said Campbell. "The *Peony* has drifted into U.S. territory. That makes her ours, my friend."

The *China Peony*, a freighter, had been languishing for a week just outside U.S. coastal waters, over two hundred miles off the California shoreline. The FBI had been tracking the ship because air surveillance had shown hundreds of Chinese crowded on the deck. After a few inquiries in Chinatown, David had surmised that the Rising Phoenix was behind this shipment of illegal immigrants. Once again, David found himself wishing for that little bit of luck that so far had eluded him. Maybe—out of all the people on board— he would find just one person to make the vital connection to the Rising Phoenix.

"The Coast Guard is sending a cutter out there," Campbell went on. "But I know we'll beat them if we go by chopper. So, what we want to know is"—Campbell looked over at his partner and smiled—"do you want to come with us?"

David didn't have to think about his answer.

Soon David was sitting in the backseat of a helicopter piloted by an FBI agent who gave his name simply as "Jim." Below, the ocean frothed with whitecaps. David heard the pilot's voice through the earphones. "We're going to be hitting some pretty bad air up here. The storm . . ." The rest faded into static. Within minutes, Jim's words became a reality as the helicopter trembled and jerked through rough winds. A dark mass of clouds hung on the horizon. Another storm would be coming through tonight.

An hour later, the turbulence had gotten so bad that David was beginning to wish that he'd stayed in his office.

"Hey, Stark, look! There she is," Campbell suddenly shouted through the earphones.

Peering over Campbell's shoulder, David saw the *China Peony* listing in the swells. As the chopper drew closer, he felt a surge of adrenaline. It was unusual for an assistant U.S. attorney to go out on busts, but he had found it useful to see exactly where things had happened and how people reacted when they realized they'd been caught. He'd accompanied Campbell and Gardner to garment factories in Chinatown, high-rise offices in Beverly Hills, and a few mansions in Monterey Park. The agents seemed to appreciate him as a shrewd observer, and there was always the hope that his presence when suspects felt most vulnerable would one day lead them to the top of the triads.

As the rotors slowed to a stop, Campbell and Gardner drew their weapons and stepped onto the *Peony*'s deck. When no one approached or seemed to offer any resistance, Campbell signaled an all-clear to David and he joined the agents. They cautiously made their way forward, unsure if they might still find a fully armed and combative crew.

Hundreds of Chinese clustered together on this upper deck. Walking along, David could see that the would-be immigrants—most of them men—had cooked over open fires. Small braziers sent up acrid fumes from smoldering coals. Some of the men sat on their haunches talking excitedly among themselves. Others lay stretched out on the deck's filthy surface, staring listlessly into space. Most of these people seemed beyond caring about what was happening to them. Only a few smiled weakly up at David in relief and gratitude.

"Jesus," Noel Gardner said. "They look like they haven't had food or water in quite a while."

"Find the captain," David said gruffly to the younger agent, who nodded and set off. "And, Jack, maybe you can call back to shore. These people are going to need showers, food, water, clothes, and beds. This is a big one, and we're going to have to handle it as diplomatically as possible." Then, as an afterthought, he called out, "Either of you guys bring Dramamine?"

"I didn't, but I'll check with the pilot," Campbell said.

David watched for a moment as Campbell lurched away, zigzagging along the deck. David grabbed a railing and continued forward. The *Peony* convulsed with each swell. Metallic groans rose from below as the ship rode the waves. David realized the ship was adrift.

From here on out, he hoped the case would be nuts and bolts. The immigrants would be remanded to the Immigration and Naturalization Service Detention Center at Terminal Island, where they would be interrogated. Rumors and gossip would spread quickly among the immigrants about what they would have to say to stay in America. Their best bets for asylum would be to claim involvement in the Tiananmen Square uprising or persecution stemming from China's abortion and sterilization policies. Out of the hundreds of Chinese David could see on deck, only a handful would be lucky enough to qualify for asylum. The rest would be deported. He felt sorry for them, but he wouldn't forget who he worked for.

David felt something pull at his pants leg. He looked down and saw a middle-aged man. "America?" the man asked in heavily accented English. Dehydration had caused his skin to hang slack on the bones of his face. "America?" the man asked again.

"Yes," David said. "Yes, you're here." Then he asked, "You speak English?"

"I speak a little. I am Zhao."

"How many are on this ship?"

"Five hundred, maybe more."

David let out a low sigh, then asked, "How long have you been at sea?"

"Almost three weeks," the man answered.

"Where's the crew?"

"Crew?"

"The men who work on the ship. Where are they?"

The Chinese man looked away. "They gone. They leave last night."

"I don't understand," David said. "How did they leave? Where'd they go?"

"The storm," Zhao said. He shifted his gaze away from David and out to the water. "It was bad. We were here like this—outside. We tie ourselves to"—the man struggled to find the word, gave up, and pointed to the railing. He brought his eyes back to David. "People wash away. I see it with my own eyes. Jie Fok—he was a farmer near Guangzhou. Some others too—I don't know their names."

"And the crew?"

"They are yelling. They are saying the ship is going down. And then this boat comes. We think it has come for us. But it is small. The captain, the others, they get in a saving boat."

"A lifeboat?"

"Yes, lifeboat. They get in that boat and they go down to the water. They have a rope to pull them to the other boat. Even so, I see some of those men wash away too. Then that other boat, it just goes away." Zhao paused. "You think we are going down soon? You think someone comes before the next storm?"

"Everything's going to be all right."

The man's eyes narrowed. "Every night another storm comes. This ship is going down."

David ignored this and asked, "Who did you contract with to come on this trip? What are the names of the crewmen?" But Zhao had turned away and was no longer listening. David stood up again and headed back toward the helicopter. Why would anyone expose himself to this danger, David wondered, and what sort of men would want to profit from this misery?

David knew the answers. The immigrants—like most immigrants—wanted freedom. These days, freedom was synonymous with money. The men and women on this ship were coming to America to make their fortunes. Since most of the immigrants didn't have money to begin with, they contracted with the triads—a free trip, room, and board in exchange for years of indentured servitude. These people would work in sweatshops and restaurants, as prostitutes and drug runners. Once they'd earned back their contracted price, they would be free. The problem was that it was almost impossible to meet their contractual obligations.

The triads, of course, were also motivated by money. A ship the size of the *China Peony* could carry about four hundred people in relative comfort. For this voyage, the boat had been loaded with five hundred passengers. Each of these people had contracted for an average of $20,000 apiece to get to the United States. Some—like Zhao—had probably agreed to pay back as much as $30,000 for the privilege of a seat on the deck in the fresh air. Less fortunate travelers would have agreed to between $10,000 and $12,000 to be crowded below. Altogether the gross revenues would total about $10 million.

The rub for the U.S. government was that this "catch" was insignificant. The INS and the State Department estimated that for every Chinese who came to this country legally, another three arrived illegally. At least a hundred thousand illegal Chinese crossed the border each year, by every means imaginable—from airplanes to fishing boats to freighters like this one.

As David considered all this, he realized there was something about the *China Peony*'s situation that didn't sit right with him. Why had the Rising Phoenix walked—sailed—away from $10 million?

He was halfway back to the chopper when Gardner found him.

The young man looked awfully green. "I know," David said. "The crew's gone. You tell Campbell?"

"Yeah, I told him. He's on the radio now."

"I need to talk to him. We've got to get these people off of this thing."

The men and women who clustered around the helicopter created an aisle as the two Caucasians approached. Campbell and the pilot sat in the chopper with the doors shut, both with their headsets on, both taking turns shouting into the radio and scribbling down notes. Every once in a while they would look at each other and grimace. Finally Campbell pulled off his headphones in disgust and opened the door.

"I've got nothing but bad news. The storm's coming in faster than the weather service expected. We can't take off because we won't beat the bastard back to shore. The Coast Guard won't be here until tomorrow morning. *They're* going back to the harbor! And I don't know about you guys, but I doubt this sucker will make it through the night."

This last bit of news sent Gardner to the railing, where he promptly puked. Campbell reached back into the chopper, then handed David a couple of Dramamine. "You'll have to swallow them dry. I don't think you want to drink any of the water on board—if there *is* any water on board."

David took the tablets and swallowed. Campbell went on. "Gardner's out of it for a while. So I guess that leaves you, me, and Jim here to work things out." Campbell's black face wrinkled into a broad grin. He held up the piece of paper with his notes. "Here are our instructions to keep this tub afloat. Let's see if they'll work."

By six, darkness had settled and rain had begun to spot the deck. David and Jack Campbell had found a few people—including Zhao—who spoke a smattering of English. These men were conscripted as translators. "We need to find someone who knows something about ships," Campbell told them. "Anybody—a sailor, a fisherman. Find them." Miraculously, they found an electrician and a mechanic. These two men—Wei and Lau—went below to see if they could get the engines started. Immediately they sent word back. The ship was in trouble; there was too much water in the bilge and the pumps were out.

For the first time, David went below decks, where conditions were even worse than outside. The air was thick, hot, humid, and eye-stingingly pungent. In the vast holds of the ship, David found dozens of people weakened by seasickness, lack of fresh water, and meager rations. Some of the men had vomited or defecated right where they lay. Most of the women were too weak to stand, let alone go out on deck to see what all the commotion had been about. A few people appeared delirious; others seemed to have fallen into a deep sleep. Adding to the misery was the strong sense of fear that permeated these dank rooms. These people knew they were finished; their dream of finding a new life in America was ruined.

Again, David had the feeling that there was something more here. These immigrants—at least the healthy ones—seemed more fright-ened than those he'd seen detained and deported in the past. Perhaps they feared the Rising Phoenix. The organization was known to be obsessed with retribution and brutal punishment. But this didn't make sense, because the profiteers themselves had abandoned their valuable cargo. Perhaps the immigrants were just afraid the ship would sink. *Just* afraid the ship would sink! David himself was terri-fied.

For the ship to stay afloat through the night, everyone needed to help. Some of the stronger men—those from above decks—wrapped pieces of cloth around their noses and mouths, then created a line from the first open-air deck down to the lowest part of the ship. Buckets were passed from hand to hand—slowly, painstakingly removing the water from the hold and throwing it overboard. Not knowing what else he could do, David took a place in the line.

As the sea became rougher, men fell ill and vomited where they stood. But no one left the line. The only relief came when every twenty minutes or so the line would rotate up. Those who had been at the very bottom would move twenty paces closer to the fresh air; those who were at the top took their turns down at the very bottom where the water—scummed with oil and who knew what else—

seemed never to diminish. No one spoke. The men—their faces set in tight lines of determination—grimly continued their work.

Every so often they heard the choke of the engine. It would catch for a moment, then fall silent again. The men only intensified their labor. After five hours, one hold had been emptied. The men showed David where there were others. He felt lost under here. The air was vile with oil fumes, human waste, and what David could only surmise were dead rats. Corners melted into darkness. Iron stairs seemed to go nowhere. Hallways ended abruptly. He would walk with a group of five or six, get partway down a hallway, then the group would break into loud, intense arguing. The men screamed at each other in their harsh voices, gesticulated wildly at David, and refused to let him pass. Zhao would finally speak a few words in English. "This is not the way. We go other way." And they would all turn around and go back the way they had come. It seemed to David that they were walking in circles, and yet, they had found five more holds that were waist deep in icy water.

Around midnight as the storm buffeted the *Peony*, the engine sputtered and came to life. Throughout the ship a collective cheer went up, but even this was short-lived. They still had so much to do. Within minutes, the pumps were started. Against their steady drone, David abandoned the men he'd been working with to look for Campbell. He found the FBI agent in the engine room. The older man was sweaty and grease stained, but neither his energy nor his humor had ebbed.

"You look like shit," Campbell said, and laughed.

For the first time, David looked down at his suit. Sometime this evening he'd taken off the jacket and left it somewhere. His shirt was smudged and a sleeve had a tear along the shoulder seam. His pants—wet with the fouled water from the hold—clung to his legs. David couldn't help but grin himself, but the moment of levity quickly dissipated.

"Okay, this is where we are," Campbell said. "We've got the engines going . . ."

"That I know."

"We've got the pumps going. Are they working? Can you tell?"

"Yeah, and they sure beat doing the work by hand."

"Wei tells me that if we keep the ship headed into the waves and everything else sealed up, we should be all right."

David looked at Wei. He was small—maybe five feet three inches—wiry and toothless. "If that's what he says, then we'll do it."

"Great. Get everyone below decks and—as they say in the movies—batten down the hatches."

It seemed like an easy enough job, but it turned out to be one of the most challenging of the day. Many of the immigrants—including Zhao, who had gone back to his old spot and was sitting with a tarpaulin around his shoulders—refused to leave the deck.

"Come on, Zhao," David insisted, shouting over the storm. Strong winds from the west pelted him with rain. "I need your help. We've got to get everyone down below."

"I stay out here the whole trip."

"You're going to die out here is what's going to happen." He motioned to the sea. Towering waves caused the ship to pitch violently. Every so often the *Peony*'s propellers could be heard as they rose up out of the water. "You're going to wash overboard."

"I make it this far. I make it to end."

David squatted. "I need you, Zhao. I need you to help me with the others. If you help me with them now, I promise to help you later."

The Chinese man considered. "How do I know if a white ghost tells the truth?"

David extended his hand for a formal handshake. "I always tell the truth."

By four in the morning, the worst of the storm had passed over the *China Peony*. Campbell had called to shore to say they were going to make it and to get off their asses and get a ship out here to tow them in, please. Here and there, men dozed. Others clustered in groups, smoking cigarettes, speaking in low voices. Gardner, still sick, was resting in the captain's cabin. Campbell had fallen asleep at a long table in the crew's galley, his head resting in the crook of his left elbow. His right arm swung at his side in rhythm with the ship's movements.

David lay on the top bunk in a cabin that must have been shared by four crewmen. He'd stripped off what was left of his clothes and had draped them over the end of the bunk to dry. Below him, two men gently snored. The helicopter pilot occupied the upper bunk across from him, but he'd turned to the wall. David stared at the ceiling, where a handful of postcards had been taped. Whoever had bunked here had been at sea a long time. One postcard showed a sweet-faced Chinese maiden posing before a colorful bouquet of carnations. Others showed Hong Kong Harbor, a neon-lit Tokyo street, the Golden Gate Bridge. David wondered wearily where that sailor was tonight. Had he washed into the sea when the crew had abandoned ship? Or was he in Chinatown, singing at a karaoke bar?

David closed his eyes and listened to the reassuring pulse of the engines. He could honestly say he'd never had a day like this before in his life.

In that stage between sleep and wakefulness, something started to edge in on David's consciousness. What was it they had been trying to hide from him down in the hold? He opened his eyes. He whispered, "Jim, you awake?" The pilot didn't move. David hopped down, slipped on his damp clothes, then quietly pulled open the heavy door and went out into the deserted hallway. He turned left and headed down a flight of stairs.

He paused to look at the immigrants. No one noticed him. He continued down another flight and down again. By now the stairs were little more than steep metal ladders. The air was humid and rotten, the hallway dimly lit. David closed his eyes and tried to think back, visualizing where he had been earlier in the day. There was a place where the men kept blocking his way. That was where he wanted to go. He passed the holds where they all had worked so hard. He turned a corner and found himself in a huge, deserted room with a ten-foot-high iron tank sitting against the wall. He had been there before, only to be led off in another direction time and time again.

He walked over to the tank and knocked on the side. It sounded hollow, but what did that mean? If the day had proven anything to David, it was that he didn't know anything about the sea or ships. The door was painted a drab green. Rust stains seeped from hinges and bolts. He tried the round crank. It moved easily in his hands. He turned once, twice, pulling hand over hand . . . .

A force pushed him back, and he fell to the floor. Water splashed over him for a moment, then spread out into a shallow puddle. An odor of decay filled the air. Next to David lay a mound of putrefying flesh. The body—human—was grossly swollen. The eyes and tongue protruded. The lips had pulled back, revealing black teeth. The skin—what was left of it—was covered in greenish black algae. The distinctive band of a Rolex glinted in the decomposing meat of the wrist.

David pushed away, sliding across the slippery surface of the floor. As he looked down, he saw on his chest something that looked like a glove. He tried to bat it away, but it stuck to his shirt. Then he realized what it was. The skin and fingernails of the dead man—woman?—had come loose and slipped off. Panicking now, David forced himself to look at the body again. The flesh from both the hands and feet *had* come off—like gloves, like socks.

That was enough to send David reeling to his feet. He staggered out of the hold and scrambled up the narrow staircases, paying no attention now to how much noise he made. Finally, he pushed through a last door and was on the deck. The rain was coming down hard and the ship still pitched relentlessly. David grabbed hold of the railing and threw up repeatedly.

But even as he was sick, even as one part of his mind recoiled at what he had seen, even as he wished that he could scrub from his body the horrible slime of that chamber, another part of his mind was already working. How was he going to find out who that person was? Shivering, his head hanging over the railing, his body soaking wet, David began to plot. Order an autopsy. Have Campbell call the

FBI—better yet, the State Department—to make inquiries about missing persons in China. Arrange for extra interviewers at Terminal Island. Because two things were certain: That watch did not belong to an ordinary immigrant, and the mass of illegals on board *knew* about the body.

3

January 21–22
Terminal Island

The next ten hours were a nightmarish blur. David could vaguely remember stumbling back to the galley and waking Jack Campbell. He could remember how smoothly the FBI agent responded, calming David down, getting him to explain what had happened, then going down again to that horrible place. He could remember Campbell sealing off the hold, leaving the body half floating in muck. David recalled the helicopter pilot bringing in a bottle of liquor dredged out of a first-aid kit and the feel of the harsh brown liquid as it slid down his throat. David desperately wanted to change clothes and sluice his body with seawater, but Campbell wouldn't allow it, claiming that evidence might be destroyed.

And then they waited. David could remember sitting out on the deck and watching as a cold, gray dawn rolled across the sky. Rain still lashed the deck, but the ocean had tamed to undulating swells. Finally Jim loped out to his helicopter and called to shore. David could remember Jim saying that the Coast Guard would be there in a few hours to tow them back to the harbor and that he was ready to fly back himself. Campbell had wanted David to go, but he'd refused.

After Jim and Noel Gardner left, Campbell and David began interviewing the immigrants.

Last night, David had worked side by side with many of these men. They had labored together to save one another's lives. This morning most would not speak to him, and none would meet his eyes. "I have that man *on* me," David said once in frustration, but nothing he said made any of them speak. Even Zhao turned away.

When they reached port late that afternoon everything moved rapidly. Officials from the INS and the Coast Guard boarded and spoke both in Mandarin and Cantonese over bullhorns. The immigrants gathered their few belongings and padded down the gangplank and into what looked like a gigantic warehouse. David was whisked away in an ambulance. All the while he resisted, repeating over and over, "I need to be there. Take me back." Finally, the paramedic clamped an oxygen mask over his face. At the hospital David was treated for shock and dehydration, then given a tetanus shot. With an FBI forensics expert on hand, David's clothes were removed, wrapped in plastic bags, and labeled. At two in the morning, he was released wearing hospital scrubs. David had never felt so alone as he did when he walked into his empty house. With considerable effort he figured out that he'd gone without sleep for forty-three hours. He showered, changed into sweatpants and a sweater, and fell into a fitful sleep.

He woke up abruptly at six-thirty in the morning, showered again—he thought he would never get the slime of that night off him—and went for a mind-clearing run around the Lake Hollywood Reservoir near his house.

Two hours later, as David stepped off the elevator and passed through the security door and into the halls of the U.S. Attorney's Office, he was immediately aware of a difference around him. Walking to his office, he nodded to a couple of secretaries, who assiduously looked at the floor as he passed them. He passed two young attorneys who worked in Complaints. They stopped talking when he came into view.

David poured himself a cup of coffee and went to the grand jury room, the only place in the courthouse large enough for Madeleine

Prentice, the U.S. attorney, to hold her weekly meetings. When he entered, a lull fell over the conversation. Then Rob Butler, Chief of the Criminal Division, cleared his throat. "Here's David. Back from his adventure at sea." The other attorneys laughed, but David sensed their discomfort. Still, he was grateful to Rob for just putting his story *out there*. It was as though Rob were saying, "We're not going to have gossip. We're not going to show jealousy. We're going to treat this case like any other." Madeleine echoed these sentiments by immediately launching into the meeting and asking for an update on current narcotics cases.

As David grabbed a chair and looked around the room, he saw that Rob and Madeleine's desire to keep his case out of the realm of the extraordinary might be hard to accomplish. Most of the other assistants in this room had been around long enough to get big cases, but none of them had ever been almost lost at sea or come in contact with a dead body.

One of the reasons David had left Phillips, MacKenzie & Stout was the comparatively collegial atmosphere the U.S. Attorney's Office offered. The attorneys—to a man, to a woman—had deliberately chosen to pass on the major firms' big salaries to work for government wages and go to court every day. The only true payoffs—aside from the sense of having done right—were good press and a possible judgeship. Clearly the former led to the latter. Yet there was a line that his colleagues didn't like to cross. They all—David included—made fun of attorneys who sought the limelight. At the same time, they admired those who could handle the press effectively. And so, today, as David listened to Madeleine and Rob query the other attorneys on their cases, he was fully aware of the weird combination of awe, jealousy, and distrust that floated around him.

Madeleine Prentice ran a manicured finger down her list. "What else have we got going to trial this week? Laurie?"

Laurie Martin, seven months pregnant, opened her file and began her summary. "On September fifteenth, Customs officials became suspicious when a woman, Lourdes Ongpin, stepped off her United flight from Manila wearing a raincoat. Although it isn't unusual for people to wear coats or sweaters while traveling, Customs thought that in this particular instance it was strange, since the temperature at LAX was about a hundred and five degrees."

According to Laurie, Customs began questioning the woman. Where was she planning on staying? Was she here for business or pleasure? As they were doing this, the inspectors noticed two things. First, the woman had a peculiar odor about her. Second, her raincoat seemed to have a life of its own. The woman was taken into an interrogation room, where inspectors found fifteen giant snails, weighing a pound or more apiece, sewn into the lining of her coat.

The other assistants fidgeted during Laurie's recital. They knew the way to make a name was by landing a conviction against a corrupt senator or a notorious drug dealer, not by going after penny-ante wildlife smugglers. Even though they were protected by international treaty, giant snails would never make page one of the *Times*.

Madeleine, with her sense of the dramatic, saved David's case for last. After his synopsis, Madeleine asked, "Do you think the murder is related to the Rising Phoenix gang, or did someone on the boat simply kill the man?"

"The triads have never shied away from murder. Can I tie them to this case? I don't know."

"It could be the break you've been looking for."

"That's right. If I can't get them on racketeering or immigration violations, maybe I'll get them on murder."

"I'd like to get the Justice Department, maybe even the State Department, in on this," Madeleine said. "Let's see what assistance they can give us. To my knowledge, we don't work with China, but maybe there's a way we can get unofficial help."

"I'll take whatever help I can get, so long as this stays my case."

"It's yours as far as I'm concerned." Madeleine gave a cursory glance around the room. "Anyone else? No? All right then, let's go get some convictions."

David poured himself another cup of coffee and headed for his office, where Jack Campbell and Noel Gardner were already waiting for him. Their haggard faces and rumpled clothes showed that neither of them had slept much.

As David sat down, Campbell cocked an eye and said, "Man, you really blew us away last night."

David shook his head. "I was scared like everyone else."

"No, you rose to the occasion, and it was one hell of an occasion."

"I only did what I thought was right," David said sheepishly. He rearranged a few papers on his desk, then asked, "So, what's happening with the immigrants?"

Campbell explained that of the 523 immigrants on board the *Peony*, 378 had already been deported thanks to the Chinese government providing an empty freighter for the return voyage. This was primarily due to the efficiency of INS officials, who had made sure that the immigrants were isolated as much as possible when they first landed. "That way they didn't have an opportunity to communicate with one another, concoct stories, even rebound enough from their ordeal to think clearly."

"No one wants a repeat of the *Golden Venture* disaster," Noel Gardner added. "It's been close to three years since that ship ran aground in New York, and we're still housing over fifty of those Chinese. At fifty-five dollars a day, that's cost us well over ten million. The INS wants to get the *Peony*'s immigrants processed and out of the country before the human-rights groups can get mobilized."

During the late afternoon and through the night, Campbell recounted, the ill, the infirm, and the weak had been separated from those who were healthy and showing high spirits. By midnight, even before David had checked out of the hospital, dozens of immigrants had showered and eaten a simple meal of beef stew. They were hastily advised of their rights to counsel and a hearing, but INS officials had stressed the benefits of accepting clean clothes, food, and passage home rather than a protracted jail stay with no guarantees of freedom. Then the immigrants were taken to courtrooms at the Terminal Island detention facility, where judges—cranky themselves for having been roused out of bed—repeated this advice. At this point, most of the immigrants chose to waive their rights and were processed with alacrity. Most of these had left the port two hours ago.

David switched gears. "Any word on the crew?"

"The Coast Guard has been watching the beaches," said

Campbell. "No bodies have washed up, but they really don't expect to see any. The storm was severe, and when the crew abandoned the *Peony,* it was still far out to sea."

"I think you'll have better luck looking in San Pedro, Long Beach, or Chinatown."

"Those are great ideas, Stark, but let's be realistic. There's Gardner and there's me. This case doesn't have high priority. The Bureau isn't going to give us the manpower we need to check out every bar and fleabag hotel. Noel and I are trying to do what you want, but we still have to prioritize. You wanted me down at Terminal Island talking to those immigrants, and I went. You wanted Noel to stick with the body, and he did."

"Jesus, the body!" David turned his attention to Gardner. "How's my body? Better yet, *who's* my body? Hey! And weren't you supposed to stay with him?"

"Don't worry," Gardner soothed. "He's locked up in the morgue down in Long Beach. He isn't going anywhere."

"Gardner gave him the full FBI treatment," Campbell boasted.

Gardner beamed. "I only told the M.E. that this was a federal matter of life and death. He agreed to do the autopsy right away, but I can't take any credit for that. Our John Doe has been dead for some time. It behooved the M.E. to get the body into cold storage as quickly as possible."

"And?"

Gardner flipped open his notebook and began to read with mathematical exactness. "The victim is a male, early twenties, weighing a hundred and twenty pounds. The hair tells us that he's Chinese." Gardner and the coroner agreed with David's assumption that the victim wasn't one of the immigrants or one of the crewmen. "Our guy's had some pretty expensive dental work done, although the coroner couldn't explain the present condition of the teeth, which were . . . "

"Black, I remember."

"And then there's the Rolex," Gardner went on. "It was real."

"What killed him?"

"That's where it gets interesting. You know that thing with the hands and feet? The skin comes off like gloves and socks if a body's been submerged in water for a long time. I can also tell you that our John Doe was tortured before death."

"Tortured?"

"Even with the decomposition, the coroner found deep burns on the victim's arms and neck. Either he was tortured or he had a very strange way of putting out cigarettes."

"Did he drown?"

"The fluid in his lungs is purely postmortem."

"Where did he die?" David queried.

"I think a better question might be, *when* did he die?" Gardner rejoined.

"Okay, then, when?"

"Let me jump in here for a minute," said Campbell. "The captain left the *Peony* so fast that he forgot his log. We found out that the ship left the port of Tianjin on January third. We faxed authorities in Tianjin, and they sent us back copies of the *Peony*'s bills of lading. I'm sure it will come as no surprise that immigrants were not listed on the manifest. What *is* a surprise is that a ship of this sort would leave Tianjin at all. Usually these ships leave from Fujian, Zhejiang, or Guangdong Province."

"Where is Tianjin?"

"I didn't know either, but it's in the north near Beijing. It's China's third-largest city."

"And what was on the manifest?"

"The *Peony* was supposed to carry needlepoint and Aubusson-style rugs, electronic gadgets, and ceramics from the interior."

"So why have an immigrant ship leave Tianjin?"

"We don't know. What we do know is that the victim has probably been dead since January third," Campbell said.

"So back to my question. If it's not death by drowning, what killed him?"

"You told me to stay with the body and I did," said Gardner. "I'm telling you, Stark, you owe me big time. The pathologist cut that guy open from stem to stern. I don't know what I was looking at. I don't want to know. But the whole time the pathologist is talking, narrating. Our guy's liver had gone to mush. His kidneys . . ." The FBI agent cringed at the memory. "His large and small intestines were eaten up with sores. His mucous membranes—I'm talking about inside his mouth and down his throat—were covered in blisters. Whatever killed him entered his body through his mouth and lungs, then systemically destroyed every single organ."

David and Campbell looked at each other, then waited as Gardner took a sip from his coffee.

"The pathologist ran a toxicology scan. But let's face it, Long Beach doesn't have the most sophisticated equipment. A city pathologist isn't going to be able to sort this out. This thing is weird."

"What do you mean?"

"How did the pathologist put it? 'We've got an organic toxic critter thing going here.'"

"So whatever it is—this poison—came from an animal?"

"An animal, an insect, a snake, a spider—the pathologist wasn't sure. I had him draw tissue samples. They're on their way to Washington to the FBI crime lab with everything else."

"What 'else'?"

"Dental impressions, the contents of his wallet, the gloves. Unfortunately, when a body's been submerged, we lose fibers that we could tie to a crime scene."

"Hang on! Hang on! What's all this?"

"I forget you aren't used to dealing with murder victims."

"You're damn right."

So Noel Gardner explained how the FBI would work in this situation. Given time, the local M.E. might be able to identify the compound of the poison and still not know what it came from. He would have the expertise to take dental impressions and fingerprints from the gloves, but he wouldn't have the resources to make any matches.

"As for the wallet," Gardner continued, "it was in the water a long time. But it's amazing what our guys in Washington can do. They may be able to pick up traces of ink or an official stamp."

"Good work, Gardner," said Campbell.

"Great work," added David, "but how long will all this take?"

"Who knows? Days? Weeks? Months?"

"I keep coming back to his identity," David reflected. "If he wasn't one of the immigrants, who was he? A crewman? A gang member?"

"Poison isn't a typical modus operandi for Asian organized crime," said Campbell. "If the victim is one of their own—say, some-one who betrayed them—you'd expect to see his arms and legs cut off—"

David's phone rang. Lynn Patchett, an INS lawyer, was on the line.

They met in a small conference room at Terminal Island. Lynn Patchett, who'd postponed her day's calendar of hearings for *Peony* immigrants, paced along the length of one wall. She was dressed in a square-cut navy-blue suit, a white blouse buttoned to her neck, and blue flats. Jack Campbell paced against the adjacent wall. In the cor-ner where they should have met in their nervous wandering sat a court reporter, who waited patiently for someone to speak so she might do her job. At David's side, Noel Gardner scratched geometric designs on a yellow pad.

Mabel Leung, a court interpreter who spoke Mandarin, Cantonese, and several other Chinese dialects, had pulled her chair a foot away from the table and industriously knitted on what looked to be a sleeve. So far no one had needed her linguistic skills. Milton Bird, a court-appointed immigration attorney, checked his notes. Next to him sat Zhao, his arms hanging limply at his sides. He wore a red jumpsuit with black numbers stenciled on the back and bright white tennis shoes—the official uniform of those incarcerated at Terminal Island.

It was now late afternoon. They hadn't broken for lunch, although Mabel had ducked out for a few minutes and come back with her arms full of diet Cokes and bags of potato chips bought from a vending machine. This strange repast combined with the stress had left them all jittery.

So far the meeting had been an exercise in perseverance. Zhao wanted to buy his freedom; David desperately wanted information. Zhao reminded David that he had promised to help; David struggled with the definition of "help." They had talked over terms: identification of the body in exchange for Zhao's freedom. If the case ever came to trial, David expected Zhao to appear as a witness. The government wouldn't pay Zhao any money, but the INS would agree to give him a green card. David could see that Zhao wanted to take the deal. At the same time, David could see that the immigrant was even more frightened now than he had been aboard the *Peony*.

As the day wore on, David read through Zhao's file a couple of times. According to his INS interview, Zhao Lingyuan—who, according to Chinese custom, placed his surname first—had once been a student at Beijing University, which explained his fluency in English. In 1967, during the Cultural Revolution, he'd been sent to the countryside. A decade later, when other students went home, Zhao stayed behind. All these years later, with the market economy sweeping China, Zhao had decided to come to the United States to start over.

Campbell suddenly stopped his pacing and burst out, "Look, Zhao, we're going to have to fish or cut bait. You know what that means? It means either you talk or forget it!"

When Zhao didn't move, Campbell growled in frustration, hit the wall with his fist, and resumed his metronomic gait. David flicked his pen open and shut. Then Zhao said in a flat voice, "I don't know how to say these words."

Mabel set down her knitting, and the two of them spoke for five minutes in Chinese. Occasionally, Mabel would say a word in English—*dragon, bear, phoenix, rat, mole*—and Zhao would repeat it. As their chattering came to an end, it seemed as though the two of them had reached some sort of agreement. David looked questioningly from Mabel to Zhao, then back again. Mabel wordlessly picked up her knitting and Zhao hunched back down in his chair, his eyes focused on the bare table in front of him. Milton Bird pulled out his handkerchief and wiped his brow. Gardner stretched his neck from side to side, then flexed his arm muscles.

"We have a saying in China." Zhao's voice was heavy with resignation. "Dragons bear dragons, phoenixes bear phoenixes, and moles bear sons good at digging holes."

David waited.

"This man, he is a dragon's son," Zhao continued. "I am a mole's son. Do you understand?"

"No, no, I don't."

Now that Zhao had broken his silence, he couldn't stop. "On the ship, we know the man is in the water. That water was for drinking. By the time the crew tells us to get our water from that place, that man is stinking inside there. We open the water crank at the top of the tank and that smell comes out. Most of us are peasants. A farmer, he floods his fields to grow rice. There is no way to warn the animals that the water is coming. Animals sometimes get trapped in there. Sometimes they swim away. You see rats swimming with their noses just above the water. Sometimes a rat gets caught in the plants. Days later, weeks later, I would smell it. This happens sometimes, so on the boat we know something dead is in that place."

"What did you do?"

Zhao slowly lifted his eyes to meet David's. "No one wants to look inside that place. Some people, they are afraid of ghosts. Some people, they are afraid of the crew."

"Did the crew know?"

"The crew is stupid. They see people getting weak. They see people getting sick. But they don't ask questions. We gather rainwater. We . . ." He turned to Mabel and asked her a question.

Mabel said, "Ration."

"We ration our good water. Then we are getting close to America. Now the crew has no water. Now they go to that place. They look inside and find the man. They get scared. They say, 'Who is that man?' They fight. Should we throw him away? What should we do? They say to us, 'You tell us who that man is. You tell us who killed him. You tell us or we won't give you food. You tell us, or we tell the gang when we get to America.' Everyone is afraid, but no one says a word."

"But you knew who he was?"

Zhao nodded. "He is from the special class, the son of a senior cadre. He is a Red Prince, a *Gaogan Zidi*." Zhao took a breath and continued. "That first day, when we went for water, everyone was afraid. But some of the men said they would look inside. If it was just a rat, they would pull it out. We would boil the water. They climb back up to the top of the tank and open it again. They find a package wrapped in plastic. Inside is the man. He has been dead and in the water already a couple of days."

"But how did you know who he was?"

"Those men, they look inside his wallet. He had papers saying he was Guang Henglai."

Jack Campbell let out a whoop of triumph.

David shot him a look, then asked, "What did they do next?"

"They put the body back."

"They didn't tell the crew?"

Zhao snorted. "No, they put Guang Henglai back. Then they come and talk to the rest of us. What can we do? We are moles on that boat. Even those men in the crew are moles. Who would take responsibility for telling the crew? What if they thought one of us killed him?"

"What are the names of the men who found the body?"

"It doesn't matter . . . "

"It matters to me."

"Those men are gone. They are on boat to China."

David, not knowing how much longer Zhao would talk now that he'd broken his silence, tried to remain focused. "Let's go back to this Guang Henglai. Who is he and why were all of you afraid of him?"

"We are not afraid of *him*," Zhao said derisively. "He is the son of a dragon."

"His father's important?"

Zhao snorted again. "His father is Guang Mingyun."

"I'm sorry, Zhao, but we don't know who that is."

"I am only a peasant. Do you understand? I am only a peasant, but even I know of Guang Mingyun. He is one of the Hundred Families. He is very powerful and very rich."

"Is he the leader of the Rising Phoenix?" David asked.

Zhao laughed bitterly. "He is not triad. He is a dragon. The triad is less than a dog to Guang Mingyun."

Gardner cleared his throat. "But if you reported his son's death, wouldn't you receive a reward?"

"I tell you something. When the crew learned that there was a body on the boat, they didn't feed us. They didn't give us any water. We are on the sea for many days. But the people who own the boat, they say, you can't come to America until you say who this body is and who put him there. This boat has many people and many ears. There are no secrets. Every night people gossip about what they see and hear. They say the captain is talking to the leader in America. The news must be very bad, because they say they will beat us until someone confesses. Let me tell you something. The Chinese people are very strong. We are used to punishment. But no one likes to lose face. Two men tell what they know. Those two men lost too much face. They cannot go forward to America, because everyone on the boat knows how they screamed and begged. They cannot go home, because if they return to their home village how can they face their families? How can they pay back their trip money? Those two men were hungry and thirsty and tired. They tell what they know and then they jump overboard. The captain calls to shore. He is yelling. Everyone can hear it."

"Who was he talking to?"

"The leader in America."

"Do you know his name?"

"I am not there!" Zhao spat out. "I am not listening! I do not want to die!"

"Take it easy, Mr. Zhao," Milton Bird said. "Maybe this is enough for today . . . "

"No, I want to finish! I want to leave this place! You tell me I can leave after I tell you."

"That's right," David agreed. "We promised you could leave as soon as you told us what you knew. Please finish. What did the leader say?"

"I do not know. But the storm comes. The other boat comes and the crew leaves. We think that the crew knows you are on the way. That is all I know." Zhao lowered his eyes back to the table.

"What more can you tell us about Guang Henglai? Do you know who might have killed him and why?"

Zhao, reverting to Chinese, spoke to Mabel. When he came to the end of his speech, she said, "There are many phrases in Chinese that are similar to what you have in English. One of these is—look the other way. Mr. Zhao says that he looked the other way and you should, too."

"You ask questions and you get in trouble," Zhao added. "You want to know about the crew, I tell you. They ask questions. They get the answer and they are dead."

David started. "You told me they left the *Peony* on lifeboats for a rescue ship."

"You don't hear me," Zhao said. "I don't see them die, but I think they are dead. It is true, I tell you that I see some of them wash off their little boat when they try to get away. But I tell you, those men are dead. The leader in America will kill them."

"They didn't do anything wrong." Even as the words came out of his mouth, David wondered what he meant.

"Guang Henglai is a Red Prince," Zhao warned. "His father is powerful. Don't be a fool. You look the other way, too. If you don't, you will die."

4

January 23
Beijing

The suspect, a Mr. Su, had already confessed, been handcuffed, and taken away. The body of his victim, however, was still sprawled under a stained blanket in the communal bathroom. Blood congealed in a wide smear across the floor. The odors of human habitation—garlic, ginger, sweat—combined to create the fetid smell that was so much a part of Liu Hulan's daily life. Murders in China rarely happened far away from humanity, and so Hulan was here today in an apartment building where dozens of multigenerational families—literally hundreds of people—lived and had become witnesses to the crime.

Hulan sat on a stool at a small table tucked into the corner of Mr. Su's tiny apartment. A few neighbors crowded against the wall. They listened as Hulan conducted her interviews, and they noisily passed whatever information they could out to those who had pressed into the corridor to see what was happening. Across from Hulan sat Widow Xie, the deputy head of the Neighborhood Committee in charge of this apartment complex. It was her duty to keep an eye on people's comings and goings and to report anything untoward—from political misstatements to acts of corruption to monopolizing the communal bathrooms.

"Mr. Su was nothing more than a country bumpkin," Widow Xie remarked. Hulan winced at this insult. *Country bumpkin* had become one of the vilest and commonest epithets in China; now the government was trying to bar it from speech. But the woman seemed unaware or unconcerned about this new rule. "He came here and stayed. I asked him many times for his residency permit. I hope you will forgive me for being lax in my duties, for I didn't report him earlier."

"Did Mr. Su and Mr. Shih argue frequently?"

"Those troublemakers put rat shit in the porridge pot for everyone," the woman answered, staring at the gun that hung from Hulan's shoulder holster. "They are both bumpkins. They come in here. They don't wash. They don't change clothes. They don't work. They stay in this room. They always disagree. They fight in their vulgar dialect. I tell you, it is ugly to the ears. Everyone—not just me—has to listen."

"Why were they arguing?"

"One man, he says, 'It belongs to me.' The other says, 'No, it is mine.' All day, all night, we are listening."

"But *why* were they arguing? What was it they wanted?"

Widow Xie's eyes narrowed. "I don't know. Do you think I know everything?"

A police officer pushed into the room and handed Hulan several manila folders. The effect on the residents of the apartment complex was immediate. Their chatter and jostling dwindled and was replaced by the soft footfall of people trying to leave as unobtrusively as possible. Without looking their way, Hulan spoke. "Stay right where you are. I will call on each of you when I am ready."

The silence deepened. Liu Hulan began to sort through the folders, finally coming across the one belonging to the murderer. Inside was Mr. Su's *dangan*, his personal file, which had been forwarded to Beijing three years ago. Hulan quickly perused its contents. Mr. Su had been a diligent worker at the Bamboo Village commune until 1994, when he disappeared, leaving behind a wife and a child. Family members said that they believed him to be dead; his file, however, noted that the Su family had lived better since his absence. Local officials suspected that Mr. Su had gone to Beijing to seek better wages, but officials were too overwhelmed to look for one man when thousands of peasants were flooding into the capital every day.

Hulan looked up to see Widow Xie's face lined with worry. "This is Mr. Su's personal file," Hulan said. "Before I look at yours, is there anything more you want to tell me?"

"I didn't report him," the woman said in a quavering voice. "He was a bumpkin, but he paid his rent promptly."

"In other words, you followed a one-eye-open, one-eye-closed policy," Hulan said.

"I did no such thing!"

"Well, then, is it your habit to allow people without the proper permits to stay in this building?" Hulan gestured toward the hallway. "Will I find others in this place who do not have a *hukou*, a residency permit?"

The deputy head of the Neighborhood Committee stared intently at her hands folded tightly in her lap.

"Just tell me," Hulan pressed, "was Mr. Su a legitimate resident here in Beijing? Was this argument over a true possession or over something that belonged to neither man?"

This time the woman's voice came out in a hoarse whisper. "Inspector . . . "

"You must speak up!"

The woman looked defiantly at Hulan. "The Supreme Leader tells us that to be rich is glorious."

"Deng Xiaoping didn't tell us to get rich by taking bribes, by harboring the criminal element, or by lying to the Ministry of Public Security." Hulan looked past the woman's shoulder to a uniformed man. "Take her down to the office. Have her make a full confession."

Hulan followed Widow Xie as she shuffled through the crowd of neighbors. At the door, Hulan raised her voice. "If some of you are here in Beijing illegally, I can assure you that I will be more forgiving to those who volunteer that information. Downstairs, you will find several police officers waiting for you to approach them if you have anything to discuss. If anyone has something to add specifically about this crime, I would like you to stay here and tell me immediately. If you have no business with either the officers downstairs or with me, go to your rooms. I will allow you just ten minutes to pass the word to the other residents and to make your decisions."

Hulan regarded the stony faces. She had already offered more options to these people than any of her colleagues would have dared. But she wasn't finished.

"I'm sure I don't need to tell anyone the consequences if you are found to be lying," she called out down the hallway. "You know the saying—leniency to those who confess; severity to those who hide. Already Widow Xie has been detained. Her case is compounded by her dishonesty. I would not like to see this happen to any of you."

A moment later, the room emptied. As she expected, no one chose to speak with her. Still, she hoped that at least some of them would come forward, because the stack of personal files on her desk was much smaller than the number of residents living in this building.

Hulan sat still waiting for calm to settle over her, but she was angry. How could the deputy head be so stupid? Out of greed, the widow had forgotten her duty. Many times in her career, Hulan had elected to look the other way—to follow her own version of the one-eye-open, one-eye-closed policy—thinking that there was no harm in people seeking a flyspeck of freedom. But today there was little Hulan could do except watch as China's "iron triangle" closed over not just the suspect in the murder, but also over Widow Xie and who knew how many others? It was this latter group—all innocents, really—who had had the pure misfortune to have traveled here illegally, to have found someone who was willing to twist the rules and rent them a room, and to have ended up in a place where a murder would bring the triangle's ineluctable force down on them.

The three sides of the iron triangle controlled a quarter of the world's population. At one corner of the triangle was the *dangan*, the secret personal file, which was kept by local police stations and work units. If someone was unwise enough to make a political mistake (offering even mild criticism against the government) or make an error in behavior (getting caught having sex with an unmarried member of the opposite sex or showing a selfish attitude at work), a note would be placed in the file. This information would then follow a person throughout his lifetime, keeping him from getting a job, from being promoted, or from moving from province to province even for private matters. (Here, Hulan was letting a Western attitude invade her mind, for there were no words in Chinese for *private* or *privacy*.)

At another corner of the triangle stood the *danwei* or work unit, which provided employment, housing, and medical care. The work unit decided if you could get married and issued pregnancy permits. It determined whether or not you were eligible for a one- or two-bedroom apartment and if you would live close to your factory or miles away.

At the apex of the triangle was the *hukou* or residency permit. It looked like a passport of sorts, and that's exactly what it was. It stated your name, listed your relatives, and said where you were from. Even though in the last ten years the government had loosened just slightly its stranglehold on the population by allowing its citizens to travel on vacation within China without getting permission, it was still nearly impossible to change the status of a *hukou*. So, if you were from Fooshan and were accepted into Beijing University, you would be allowed to go, but at the completion of your education you would *have* to return to Fooshan. If you were from Chengdu and fell in love with someone from Shanghai, you would have to abandon the romance. If you were a simple peasant, eking out a meager existence in the countryside, there you would remain just as your parents, grandparents, and great-grandparents had.

Today, the iron triangle had trapped at least two people—Mr. Su and Widow Xie.

The allotted ten minutes had passed. Hulan stood, gathered the files, and went downstairs. In the courtyard, one of the officers reported that two residents had confessed to being in Beijing illegally. A few had added what they could to the story of Shih and Su. But most of the people had come to make reports on Widow Xie's corruption. Hulan had anticipated this last wrinkle. Making public criticisms of people who were falling out of favor was as old as the regime.

Fatigued and depressed, she got into the backseat of a white Saab. Her driver, a compact young man who liked to be called Peter, asked, "Where to now, Inspector?"

"Just take me back to the office," she said, laying her head back on the soft seat cushions.

Peter pulled away from the curb and began making his way toward Tiananmen Square and MPS headquarters. Hulan had no illusions about Peter Sun. He was an investigator third grade, and his main job was to inform on her. She did her best to circumvent this by relegating him to the position of driver rather than partner. He seemed shy and unprepossessing until he got behind the wheel.

Now here he was as usual, honking the horn at bicyclists, yelling out the window—"mother of a fart" and "mating worm"—frantically cutting in front of other cars even if it earned him only a few feet, and ignoring the invective that was hurled back at him. Hulan preferred this to the alternative: Peter turning on the siren, paying no attention to anything or anyone in his way or whether he was going the wrong way down a one-way street. "We have the right to do this," he used to say, and she would answer, "But the people will see it as an abuse of power, and I'm not in a hurry." After several months of working together, he had grown used to her ways and she had accepted his.

Twenty minutes later, they turned into the gray stone low-rise multibuilding compound of the Ministry of Public Security. Two smartly dressed guards carrying submachine guns waved the car inside once Peter flashed his identification. Despite the cold weather, a group of MPS agents were playing half-court basketball near the parking area. Hulan got out of the Saab, walked through an archway, into an inner courtyard, and through a set of massive double doors. Her shoes clattered along the stone floor as she avoided the main stairs and crossed the lobby to the rear of the building. She turned left and made her way up a back set of dimly lit stairs. Up here the stonework gave way to worn linoleum. Just as there was every day, a woman was on her hands and knees washing the floor. Hulan skirted the wet areas, passed several closed doors, and entered her office.

Eleven years ago, a year after her return from the United States, Hulan had been hired by the ministry as a tea girl. With her American law degree, she had been overqualified for the job, which required that she look pretty, smile, and pour tea. Eventually she had gone to her superior and asked to be assigned to a case, then another. By the time *his* superior found out, she had already solved enough crimes that to demote her back to tea girl would have caused several people to lose face.

Since that time she had received standard promotions based on seniority rather than the accelerated promotions based on political integrity or "staying in touch with the people." As a result, for the last decade, she had been tucked away in what was perceived to be an unimportant part of the building, which was fine with her.

Gray winter light filtered into the drab room. It was sparsely out-fitted with a proletarian metal desk, two swivel chairs, a telephone, a bookcase lined with notebooks, and a single file drawer, which she kept locked. The only decorations on the walls were a calendar left over from last year and a hook on which to hang her jacket. The room was chilly—most government buildings in the capital were—so she kept her coat on and her muffler draped around her shoulders as she sat down at her desk to write her report.

Five hours later, as frigid darkness settled on the city, Liu Hulan still worked at her desk. The phone rang. "*Wei*?" she said into the receiver.

A voice said, "You're wanted in the vice minister's office. Please come immediately." The caller didn't wait for a response.

Hulan sat in the anteroom of the vice minister's office for a half-hour before being summoned inside. She stepped into the room and, not for the first time, marveled at its richness. The crimson carpet felt plush and thick under her feet. A Ming dynasty altar table served as a credenza. On it were gaily painted ceramic cups each with its own ceramic top to keep tea warm, an oversized flowered thermos, which Hulan assumed was filled with tea, and a tin of Danish sugar cookies. Several straight-backed chairs lined the walls. The windows were cov-ered with red velvet drapes edged with thick gold trim.

At the center of the room was a desk. On her side, two overstuffed chairs, upholstered in a deep blue velvet, angled toward each other. On the backs and arms were tatted antimacassars. In one chair sat her immediate supervisor and the head of her work unit, Section Chief Zai. Behind the desk, Vice Minister Liu leveled his enigmatic gaze on his daughter.

"You may sit down," he said.

Hulan did as she was told, then waited. She knew that silence was one of her father's favorite ways of making people ill at ease. Although she had known both men her entire life and saw both weekly and sometimes daily, it had been many months since she was last in their company at the same time. Her father looked prosperous, as usual. His suit was natty—probably custom-made in Hong Kong. The appearance he presented gave no hint of the hardships of his life. His hair was still black, his face unlined, and his back rigid. He was lean, sinewy, and still strong. Like many in his generation, he wore severe black-framed glasses. Other than this last concession to his age, he looked to Hulan every inch the smooth politician as he feigned disinterest in their presence and impatiently tapped a stack of papers with the sharp tip of a pencil. Section Chief Zai—her father's old friend—brooded in his chair. His suit bagged at all the wrong places, his cuffs were frayed, his hair was mostly gray. He looked more beaten down than usual, and Hulan wondered if his pallor was due to illness.

Finally Vice Minister Liu looked up. "I have been wondering about your progress with the case of the death of the son of the American ambassador. No one has been arrested."

"This is correct, Vice Minister Liu," Hulan said.

Section Chief Zai cleared his throat. "We understood that the ministry did not want our department to pursue this matter."

The vice minister waved his hand, as if dispersing a bad smell. "I am waiting for Inspector Liu to explain herself."

Zai sank deeper into his chair.

"What we know is this," Hulan began, "Billy Watson was found in Bei Hai Lake. Pathologist Fong and I did not believe that it was an accident. I requested that he perform a full autopsy. The boy's parents did not want us to go ahead with this."

"And yet," Vice Minister Liu observed, "I see from the file that you disregarded their wish in this instance."

"Yes, I did," Hulan admitted. "I took it upon myself to authorize the autopsy. I did not plan to attend, but after Pathologist Fong opened the body, he asked me to come to his laboratory. The boy showed no outward signs of physical deterioration. Pathologist Fong expected this, as the body had been frozen and therefore preserved. However, what he found *inside* the boy gave us considerable cause for concern. The postmortem showed damage to all of his major organs. They had begun to liquefy. Clusters of capillaries had burst in several of his organs. The worst damage was in his lungs, which showed hemorrhaging and a buildup of other fluids in addition to general deterioration. Pathologist Fong concluded that the immediate cause of death was that the boy had drowned in his own blood."

"What would cause that?"

"We have no idea. Pathologist Fong found a strange residue on the lung and esophageal linings. As the vice minister knows, Pathologist Fong was unable to complete his investigation."

"But what does he suspect?"

"He doesn't like to speculate, but it must have been a very strong poison. There's no doubt that the boy's death was not an accident, but the American ambassador was not interested in these facts." Hulan hesitated, then added, "But you know all of this, Vice Minister. You spoke with Ambassador Watson yourself. The order to release the body to the Americans came from you."

Vice Minister Liu changed the subject. "A delicate situation has arisen. I'm sure that you have heard about the death of the son of Guang Mingyun. Officially, the boy's body was found in U.S. territory, but those foreign devils, they believe that the boy died here, in China. None of this would be our concern, except that there are some similarities between the two deaths."

Hulan sneaked a glance at Mr. Zai, who remained silent. Again Hulan spoke. "What similarities?"

"Apparently the foreign devils have also discovered—what did you call it?—a strange residue in the boy's lungs." Vice Minister Liu held up a hand to keep Hulan and Zai from interrupting him. "I won't explain the rest now. What matters is that Guang Mingyun is as important a man to us as Ambassador Watson is to the Americans. Because of who these boys were, our two governments have agreed to ally themselves to each other so we might look for the person who committed these crimes. The ministry has decided that Inspector Liu—because of her experience with foreigners and her facility with their language—should work with them."

Hulan and Zai took this news in stunned silence. Neither could remember a single instance when law enforcement agencies from the two countries had worked together successfully. The only previous joint effort—the infamous "Goldfish" case—had ended in disaster. The Chinese had arrested, convicted, and sentenced a man, Ding Yao, for his involvement in the drug trade. The DEA had asked that he be sent to the United States to testify against the people implicated on that side of the Pacific. The Americans promised that nothing could go wrong. But as soon as Ding Yao took the stand, he asked for political asylum. The American judge ignored the facts and took the view that China was inhumane. Not only was the case against the American smugglers thrown out of court, but Ding Yao was now living in Las Vegas. In the end, the Goldfish case had proven two things. One, it was politically dangerous to become involved with Americans. (The Chinese agents who had worked on the case had lost face and their positions.) And two, Americans did not operate fairly or honestly. Now Vice Minister Liu was assigning his daughter to work with them.

As if reading Hulan's thoughts, Liu said, "This is not my decision. It comes from much higher up. It is not my job to argue with my superiors. Besides, you have the most experience with foreigners. You lived in the United States. You speak their language. You are familiar with their decadent ways."

Once again, Liu looked down at his notes. "So," he said after a few tense moments, "the best news I can give you is that this time the United States is sending a representative here. Let me see . . . I have his name here somewhere. Donald, Daniel, Darren?" The American names rolled smoothly off his tongue. "No. His name is David Stark, an assistant U.S. attorney."

Vice Minister Liu looked up and smiled expectantly at Hulan.

Next to her, Zai shifted uncomfortably in his chair. Hulan said nothing.

"We must give this American a helping hand," Vice Minister Liu continued, still smiling. "In doing this, we will also be helping our countryman Guang Mingyun. But I must stress to you both how important it is that the foreigner not see anything unpleasant."

"That's rather difficult in a murder investigation, wouldn't you say?"

The man opposite her laughed heartily. "Inspector Liu, do I need to remind you that China has customs and rituals for dealing with guests? Use your *shigu*—your worldly wisdom. Remember that all foreigners—whether strangers to a family or foreign devils like these visitors—are potentially dangerous. Don't be tempted to say what you think. Don't show anger or irritation. Be humble and careful and gracious." Vice Minister Liu stood and walked around the desk. He put his hand awkwardly on Hulan's shoulder. "Draw them in. Let them think they have a connection to you, that they owe you, that they should never cause you any embarrassment. This is how we have treated outsiders for centuries. This is how you will treat this foreigner as long as he is our guest."

Hulan left the office deep in thought. She jumped when she felt a hand on her arm, then looked up to see Zai. He motioned for her to follow him. He didn't stop until they had reached the back stairs. He looked around to see if anyone was nearby.

"Your father has always been clever at getting facts," he said.

Hulan laughed. "I was thinking just the opposite."

Section Chief Zai spoke sharply. "Think, Hulan, think! He must be very familiar with your *dangan* to have made the connection between you and the U.S. attorney."

Hulan nodded pensively. "Yes, I was in America. Yes, Attorney Stark and I worked at the same law firm. But my situation was curious in those days. I don't think it's a secret, uncle." She deliberately used the honorific to show that she understood and respected Zai's concerns.

"Don't you wonder who agreed to this cooperation? It has to be someone very powerful. Maybe it's come from the Ministry of Foreign Affairs, maybe the Ministry of State Security, maybe—I don't know . . . "

Hulan looked into her mentor's worried face. "Uncle, if the order comes from Deng himself, what do I care? This is my assignment. I have no choice."

5

JANUARY 27–29
Madeleine Prentice's Office

Thanks for coming, David," Madeleine Prentice said, motioning him into her office. Jack Campbell stood near Madeleine's desk with his arms crossed. A pale, redheaded man sat in a standard-issue executive-office armchair. "David, this is Patrick O'Kelly from the State Department. Patrick, David Stark." After everyone shook hands, Madeleine said in her no-nonsense way, "Patrick, why don't you get right to it?"

When O'Kelly opened his mouth, David was surprised to see the shine of braces. "I am here because of the murder of Guang Henglai."

"What do you know about him?"

"His father is Guang Mingyun, the sixth-richest man in China. His company, the China Land and Economics Corporation, serves as an umbrella for a variety of businesses with assets of more than one and a half billion U.S. dollars. His personal wealth is in the neighborhood of four to five hundred million dollars."

Campbell whistled.

O'Kelly spent the next few minutes summarizing the State Department's dossier on Guang Mingyun. He was destined by birth to become a worker in a provincial glass factory like his parents before him, but his secondary-school achievements had attracted the attention of people in Beijing, who brought him to the capital to attend Beijing University, where he excelled in engineering and math.

"By the early 1980s, Guang had started several privately owned factories," O'Kelly explained. "But his biggest break came in 1991, when he traded five hundred railroad cars of Chinese goods for five Russian-made airplanes. This one transaction catapulted Guang from relative obscurity into the first rank of wheeler-dealers. Since then, he's expanded into real estate, the stock market, and telecommunications. His profits allowed him to launch the Chinese Overseas Bank, an investment bank based in Monterey Park with several branches in California."

"I'm familiar with it," David said. "How does owning a bank here help him?"

"It gives him a way to funnel U.S. funds—specifically those of overseas Chinese—into China, and for Chinese nationals to send money to the U.S., where the political situation offers banking stability and security," O'Kelly answered. "Now, what makes Guang truly different from other entrepreneurs is that he recognizes that change in China must happen across the country, not just along the coast."

"Excuse me?"

O'Kelly nodded agreeably. "Here's what we're looking at. The Chinese economy is booming all along the coast—in Shanghai, Guangzhou, Shenzhen, and Fujian Province."

"And Tianjin?" Jack Campbell asked.

"And in the city of Tianjin," O'Kelly confirmed. "There are some villages in those areas where the average income is better than in the U.S. But if you were to go inland a thousand, five hundred, or even a hundred miles, you would see a very different picture."

"Isn't that all rice farming?"

"Farming of every sort. But the peasants make only about three hundred and fifty dollars a year. In China, capitalism has created an economic chasm unlike any seen before in history. The problems for the Chinese over the long term are: How can they bring prosperity to the entire country? If they can't, what will they do when those peasants—nine hundred million strong, one in six people on the entire planet—get pissed off? In other words, how will the government control the have-nots, when the government's mandate came originally from the peasants?"

"And Guang has an answer?"

"Perhaps. He's not only privatizing industries—and I'm talking here about everyday essentials like salt, pharmaceuticals, and coal—but he's taking them inland to the poorest provinces. He's bringing modern technology to the countryside and rewarding people who work hard."

"For profit."

"Absolutely. He can pay peasants far less money than workers along the coast. Simultaneously, he's building their loyalty and trust."

"How does this connect to the case?" David queried. "Are you suggesting that Guang Mingyun was trying to cut in on the triads' businesses in the interior? That his son was kidnapped as a warning or for ransom? That the whole thing was botched and they dumped the body?"

"We don't know yet. We've already been in contact with Beijing..."

"You what?" David asked sharply.

"Let me say at the outset that we at the State Department were well aware of Guang Henglai's disappearance." O'Kelly paused to let this revelation sink in, then went on. "The boy has been missing for almost a month. Those of us at the State Department—even recent tourists to China—are familiar with the case. China is well known for being able to find anyone at anytime anywhere. During these last few weeks China has mounted its largest manhunt ever. Needless to say, they found neither Guang Henglai nor anyone who could give them any information as to his whereabouts."

"So there's been no evidence of foul play on Chinese soil?" David asked.

"I'm not saying that. But with the current political tensions—the ballyhoo in the Taiwan Strait last year and Hong Kong this summer—the State Department felt it was important to notify the Chinese government and thus Guang Mingyun as soon as possible. We don't want it to appear as though the U.S. could be involved in any way."

"How could we be involved?" David asked. "The body was found rotting on a Chinese freighter, for Christ's sake!"

"David," Madeleine cautioned. "Let's hear him out."

"We know the body was found on the *Peony*," O'Kelly continued. "We know that Guang Henglai has been dead a long time. But how do we prove that to the Chinese? How can we prove that he didn't die at the hands of an immigration officer—either on the boat or at Terminal Island? With things the way they are right now, the Chinese have every reason not to believe us."

David shook his head skeptically. "I have to assume that his parents will want the body for burial. Their own experts could tell them how long he's been dead, and that he certainly wasn't the victim of a beating or gunshot wound or whatever else they might imagine."

"Let me throw something else into the mix," O'Kelly went on. "If the coroner is right that the boy died before he left China, the timing would coincide with the death of the son of Ambassador Watson."

Jack Campbell's lips formed for another low whistle.

"You just lost me," David said.

"Watson's the ambassador to China," O'Kelly explained. "His son was found dead in Beijing at the beginning of the year. It was written off as an accident."

"But it wasn't?"

O'Kelly shook his head. "As you might expect, relations with China are rather chilly right now. Nevertheless, when we contacted the Ministry of Foreign Affairs—our Chinese counterpart—we were informed of several things. First, the Chinese themselves don't believe the accident theory."

"And there's evidence to support that?"

"I must stress that what we're talking about here is extremely confidential."

"Go on."

"Despite what you may read in the paper, we do have friends in China. A copy of Billy Watson's autopsy was wired to us. I think you'll be interested to note several similarities. Both Watson and Guang were the same age. Both Watson and Guang were found in water. And"—O'Kelly paused to get their full attention—"both boys had a mysterious substance in their lungs."

"What are we talking about here?" Madeleine asked. "A Chinese serial killer?" She looked around the room. "Is there such a thing?"

"It's too early to draw any conclusions. We need more investigation, and we need to get our own man in that investigation. This is where you come in, Stark. The Chinese have apparently heard what happened on the *Peony* and they are willing to work with *you*, whether out of respect, gratitude, or because they want to look you in the eye when you relate the details of finding Guang Henglai's body. We think . . . "

"Before we go any further," David broke in, "I have a couple of questions."

"Shoot."

"How did you get access to my case files?"

"I don't think you need to worry about that."

"I think I do." David turned to the FBI agent. "Jack?"

"You asked me to make some phone calls and I did," Campbell reminded him.

"So did I," Madeleine also admitted.

"We're all on the same side here," O'Kelly said. "We want the same thing."

"Really? What's that?"

"To find a killer," said O'Kelly. "I would think you'd be interested not only in finding the murderer but also in getting a conviction for once against the triads."

Stung, David retorted, "You've done your homework."

Jack Campbell averted his gaze. Patrick O'Kelly shrugged.

David eyed the man from the State Department suspiciously. "What do you want me to do?"

"Go to China . . . "

"You can stop right there," David said. "They'll never let me in. I've applied for visas before and—"

O'Kelly cut in. "The Chinese have already issued you an official invitation to come and work with their investigators. You have a plane ticket and a multiple-entry visa—which, since you'll only be making this single trip, you really don't need, but what the hell. You'll be leaving tomorrow."

"Wait a minute—" snapped Madeleine.

"No," O'Kelly said. "We can't wait."

"I don't think you know who you're talking to," she said tartly.

O'Kelly sat back in his chair and said, "I know exactly who I'm talking to. I hope the U.S. attorney will remember that yours is an appointed position. Everyone in this room works for the government and has pledged that they will support the government. Now it's time for Stark here to get out from behind his desk and do his country a favor."

"And what if I say no?" David asked.

O'Kelly considered David with something akin to pity. "You won't say no. Your sense of justice demands that you find whoever killed those men."

Two days later—after crossing the international date line and losing a day—David Stark was above Beijing in an airplane packed with businessmen and -women, a group of Tennessee two-step dancers who would perform in the capital, and a museum tour group set on seeing the ancient capitals of Asia. The pilot had just made another of his periodic announcements. If the fog cleared, they would be able to stop circling and land. "If not," the pilot said, "well, we only have so much fuel. If we don't see an increase in visibility in the next twenty minutes, we're going to have to turn around and go back to Tokyo. You'll spend the night there, and we'll get you out as soon as we can." These words were met by tired groans. Another five hours back to Tokyo! That would make this a ten-hour trip to nowhere.

"It happens all the time," the woman next to David said. These were the first words she'd spoken. She'd spent the last five hours hooked into her computer looking at spreadsheets. "You fly to Tokyo, wait around for an hour or so, get on a new plane, fly up here, and half the time you have to turn around."

"Why can't we fly to—I don't know—Shanghai or someplace?"

"The Chinese won't let foreign airlines fly domestically. If we went to Shanghai, we'd have to take CAAC or one of the other smaller airlines. Believe me, you don't want to do that. The only other choice is to take the train. But United won't do a thing for you, except set you down. You're on your own to find a seat, and they're hard to get. And even if you do get a seat, you're going to spend about twenty-four hours riding with chickens and God knows what else. You're welcome to it."

"It shouldn't be too hard to get out tomorrow. Can't we just take this plane first thing in the morning?"

The woman laughed. "Hardly! You'd better be ready to fight your way off the plane if we go back to Tokyo. Seats will be on a first-come first-serve basis. We might not get out of there for days."

"But I've got to get to Beijing."

"So does everyone else." The woman peered at him through the corner of her eyes. "Your first trip to China?"

David smiled. "It's that obvious?"

"Well, let's see. You've checked your passport about ten times. You've double-checked your immigration and customs forms about as many. You keep looking through your briefcase. I have to guess you're double-checking things there too."

"You'd make a good detective."

"Actually, I'm the vice president of a refrigeration company. We have a factory outside Beijing. I make this trip once a month now—two weeks here, two weeks in L.A.—but when I first started I was like you. Did I have my money in a safe place? Did I dot my *i*'s and cross my *t*'s? I didn't want to have any trouble with the *authorities*, if you know what I mean."

"I guess I do."

"Don't worry. The Chinese are very modern. They aren't the big bad Communists we were raised to think they were."

"And you make this trip by yourself?"

"Of course."

"Is it safe for a woman to travel alone?"

"About a million times safer than going to Italy," she responded. "But I take the usual precautions. I have my own driver, whom I've used for three years now. I think I've bought his loyalty. I carry a lot of cash, but I don't throw it around. When I'm nervous, which is hardly ever, I use the side entrance to the hotel. I read *that* tip in a guidebook my first trip out. But I'll tell you, if a Chinese were foolish enough to assault a foreigner, within about five minutes the police would take him out and put a bullet in his head."

The woman closed her file, snapped her laptop shut, and turned her full attention on David. By the time the pilot announced that he'd received clearance to land, Beth Madsen had told David what to see, where to go, what to eat. When the flight attendants came through, picking up headsets and encouraging people to stow their belongings, Beth slipped over David's lap and went to the bathroom. As she edged past him, she regarded him with undisguised interest. He felt a throb begin in his groin. What was he thinking?

When she was gone, he closed his eyes. There had been a time when he yearned to go to Beijing. Now that he was actually on his way, his mind was filled with advice—from Jack Campbell and Noel Gardner, from Rob Butler and Madeleine Prentice, from that asshole Patrick O'Kelly at the State Department, and now from this woman. It ranged from the sublime to the ridiculous to the downright scary. If he had a chance, he should go to the Friendship Store. (Madeleine had picked up some great souvenirs when she was there.) But he could certainly pass on the restaurant that specialized in snake. Rob Butler's advice had been simple—"Keep your nose clean." Beth Madsen had told him where he might find good deals on silk and jade. Of course he'd be busy, Beth said, but he shouldn't miss the Great Wall. She'd be happy to take him there.

Jack Campbell and Noel Gardner had taken him out for hamburgers at the Carl's Jr. across the street from the courthouse. With his usual earnestness, Gardner had latched onto Madeleine's idea that the two murders might be the work of a serial killer. "We don't know where Watson and Guang were killed," he'd remarked, "but if you find that place, you need to determine what elements make the scene stand out. Think about what the killer's motive could be."

Serial killers, David learned, were driven by three main motives—domination, manipulation, and control. The serial killer seldom directed his anger toward the focus of his resentment. He—and serial killers were universally men—could be counted on to be charming, highly articulate, even glib. "If this is a serial killer, we don't know if these are his first and second murders or his tenth and eleventh," Gardner had gone on. "But I can guarantee you that if he goes on with his crimes, he will become more flagrant with the bodies. He'll take great pleasure in taunting law enforcement."

"But are there serial killers in China?" David had asked, echoing Madeleine's question.

"I don't know," Gardner had replied. "But if you find anything that points in that direction, go to the embassy, send us a fax, and Jack and I will talk to our behavioral science department."

This whole conversation—with Gardner taking the serial angle seriously and Campbell's ominous silence—had been unnerving. But David's last-minute "advice" from Campbell and O'Kelly had a strange cloak-and-dagger feel to it. O'Kelly began with a lecture on protocol: "Always address the Chinese with their full titles. For one thing, women keep their maiden names; for another, the Chinese are very formal. So say, 'Pleased to meet you, Vice Minister Ding or Subhead Dong.'" O'Kelly had laughed heartily at his tasteless joke, then once again settled into his forbidding tone. "Remember, in China everyone has a title. Butcher Fong, Dentist Wong, Worker Hong. But if you don't know someone's title, use mister or madame."

O'Kelly had quickly moved to more serious admonishments: "Watch what you say in your hotel room." (All hotels for foreigners were supposedly bugged.) "Don't say anything significant on an unsecured phone." (If hotel rooms were in fact bugged, this made sense to David, but no one had really explained to him either *why* he would need a secured phone or *how* he would find one.) "Don't eat too much." (They didn't want him to seem like a glutton.) "Don't drink too much." (Or an alcoholic.) "Don't get into any card games. Don't play mah-jongg or bet on anything." (In other words, don't look like a gambler.) "Don't be too friendly. You're not anyone's friend." When questioned on this, Campbell finally had to spell it out. "Keep your dick dry." David supposed this fell somewhere under the heading of "Keep your nose clean," and he said so.

"Mr. Stark, this isn't a joke," O'Kelly had said. "You're going to be under constant surveillance. Do you know why?" When David hadn't answered, O'Kelly had explained. "You're a potential mark for them. They may try to compromise you—through drinking or fooling around with a woman—so that they can blackmail you into spying for them."

At this David had laughed, but again neither Campbell nor O'Kelly had joined in. What was most disconcerting, now that David thought about it, was the lack of humor in any of these discussions combined with the sense that O'Kelly—and, he hated to admit it, but Madeleine, Campbell, and Gardner—seemed to know a lot more than he did. But whenever David tried to ask a question or get some semblance of reassurance, his colleagues had avoided the subject by going back to their recommendations, reminders, and warnings.

"You have been issued an official invitation from the Ministry of Public Security—China's leading intelligence service," O'Kelly had reminded David. "They may want to turn you for themselves or even hand you over to the Ministry of State Security, which also handles espionage and counterintelligence overseas."

"I think I want to stay home," David quipped.

"We don't think so," O'Kelly said tersely.

"Who's this 'we'?" David asked.

O'Kelly ignored the question. "This is the first time we've been invited to cooperate with the Chinese in an investigation on their turf."

"What do you mean, the first time on *their* turf?"

"We've had some dealings with China in the past. Let's just say that things didn't work out. We've got a tough political situation going on right now with the threat of trade sanctions. This case—this invitation—is the only thing that's going right between our two countries. We just don't want it—or you—to go south on us."

"Are you questioning my loyalty?"

"You wouldn't be here if we were. We know your record. We know your family and associates from your FBI check before coming to the U.S. Attorney's Office. We aren't worried."

"Can't Jack come with me?"

"I wasn't invited," Campbell said, breaking his silence.

"And we don't think it's appropriate to send the legate from Hong Kong either," O'Kelly added.

"I don't like this."

"Mr. Stark, no one asked you to like it," the man from State had said. "You found a body. China—for whatever reason—has an interest in that body. And we have an interest in stabilizing our diplomatic relationship with China by whatever means possible. You seem to be that means."

Now, as Beth Madsen sidled back across David, this time grazing her breasts against his left cheek, he wondered if she was on his list of don'ts. Could the Chinese really bug each hotel room? That seemed both daunting and dull. What could they learn from a gaggle of Tennessee two-step dancers?

The terminal was hardly an advertisement for the newly affluent society he'd been led to expect by Patrick O'Kelly. Instead, as he followed Beth down a bleak hallway and into a cavernous room, he saw numerous soldiers in drab uniforms, old women with kerchiefs on their heads sitting together and gossiping, and exhausted travelers nervously clutching bags and passports. A layer of dirt coated everything, and the smell of cigarettes and simmering noodles hung in the air. But what struck David most was the cold; he could see his breath even inside.

He stood behind Beth at passport control. The surly uniformed officer didn't say a word or even look at David as he handed over his passport to be stamped. He waited with Beth as the luggage came through on the carousel and walked with her to the Customs check, where they were waved through without opening their bags.

"I have a driver if you need a lift," Beth offered.

David gazed out past the temporary wooden barricades that separated the secured area of the terminal and the exit, which was jammed with Chinese—civilians and more soldiers in green greatcoats. He wasn't sure if it was an acoustical anomaly or if the people were really shouting. He watched as another passenger pushed into the cacophonous swarm and was instantly assaulted by people asking him if he needed a ride.

"I'm supposed to be picked up," David said a little nervously. "Where do you think I'd go to meet someone?"

"Follow me," Beth said.

He hitched up his suitcase in one hand and his briefcase in the other and stepped into the throbbing crowd. He felt the crush of warm bodies against him but pressed on. "Taxi?" "Driver, cheap." "I take you to hotel." David finally broke through and into the open.

The air was thick with coal smoke, exhaust, and the freezing fog's lingering dampness. Along the curb, pristine luxury cars were sandwiched between dented heaps that looked like oversized tin toys. Reunited families gathered here and boisterously crammed belongings and relatives into the cramped confines of the Chinese-made cars. A couple of generals—dressed austerely in long olive-green coats—silently stepped into their Mercedeses, while a bevy of American tourists fretted over a mountain of suitcases being passed into the underbelly of a tour bus.

"Here's my car," Beth said, pointing to a Cadillac Town Car. "I'll be at the Sheraton Great Wall if you want to get together for dinner or anything."

"I'm staying there too."

She eyed him again in her hungry way. "Sure you don't want to come with me now?"

"No, I'd better wait here."

As Beth slid into the backseat, David started as a voice asked, "Mr. Stark?" He turned to see a Chinese man in his twenties dressed in a gray suit with a knit vest. His hair hung lankly over his collar and his eyes shone a deep black. The man took David's silence as affirmation.

"I am Peter Sun, an investigator for the ministry and your driver," the man said in lightly accented English. "Please follow me."

David tried to take a seat in front, but Peter shook his head. "It wouldn't be right for a guest to sit up here. Please sit in the back. You've had a long journey. Rest and enjoy the ride."

Peter announced that he would take David on the scenic old road instead of the new toll road. The old road was lined with poplars. Their bare trunks created bony silhouettes against the gray sky. Beyond the trees, bare fields melted into fog banks.

Speeding along the road, they passed peasants bringing their wares into town. David saw a bicycle loaded down with a pig carcass—one half strapped to each side of the bike. Seemingly oblivious to her bloody cargo, a young girl pedaled with quiet dignity. A half mile later, they passed a load of used tires that bounced and swayed precariously on the back of a flatbed bicycle truck pulled by a man with a deeply lined face. Sitting on the handlebars in front of him was a small child bundled in a hot-pink padded jacket. Peter honked at this slow-moving obstacle, swerved wide around it, and aimed a few angry words out the window. Neither the little girl nor her father acknowledged the epithet.

By the time they got into the city, darkness had fallen. Still, the streets were choked with people, bicycles, and cars. As Peter jerked the Saab through the crowds, yelling when people didn't move out of his way fast enough, David was amazed to see just how Western things seemed. Neon lights advertised Kentucky Fried Chicken, McDonald's, Pizza Hut, and Waffle King. Garish signs proclaimed FRENCH BREAD COOKED ON PREMISES and BEIJING IS WAITING FOR YOU. Below a second-story window a draped banner advertised the HEAVENLY BODIES STUDIO. Inside, a group of women bounced to music David could not hear. When he commented on how busy things seemed, Peter said, "We're still far from the center of Beijing. Tomorrow, when we go to MPS headquarters, you'll see the Forbidden City and Tiananmen Square."

Peter pulled into the porte cochere of the Sheraton Great Wall Hotel, opened the car door for David, announced he would return at twelve the next morning, then sped off into the night. A bellman took David's bag, and together they pushed through the revolving doors and into the hotel. The lobby—an atrium rising six stories—bustled with activity. Walking to the check-in desk, David heard English, German, Spanish, Japanese, and, of course, Chinese. He saw signs pointing the way to separate restaurants that served food from four different Chinese provinces.

In the elevator, the bellman rattled off the hotel's amenities—tennis courts, gym, indoor swimming pool, coffee shop, and cocktail lounge with nightly entertainment. At the end of his monologue, the bellman asked, "What kind of business are you in?"

"I'm a lawyer."

"You need help? Do you want to *xiahai*, plunge into the sea?"

"I don't think so."

"I have good *guanxi*, good connections. I can get you anything you want."

David thought the bellman was trying to set him up with a prostitute. "I don't need anything like that."

The bellman looked at him quizzically. "I know people. You want find good building for factory, my uncle can help you. You want help getting contracts, I have cousin who can help you. If I help you, you help me. We can be partners. We can plunge into the sea together."

"No, no, nothing," David said as the elevator slowed to a stop.

"Umbrellas." The bellman jabbered on as they walked down the corridor. "What do you think about umbrellas? It rains all over the world. We can have a business. Something like Imperial Umbrellas of China or Royal China Umbrellas."

David pressed some bills into the budding capitalist's hand and shut the door after him. The room was stultifyingly hot. David turned off the heat and tried unsuccessfully to crack open the window. He flipped on the air-conditioning and stripped down to his underwear.

It was still early, but David stretched out on the bed. He was bone tired but wide awake. Jet lag. David thought about calling Beth's room but immediately dismissed the idea. He wasn't hungry, he didn't want a drink, and he definitely wasn't up to considering the alternatives. His mind raced. The events of the last week had certainly gotten him out of his regular life.

And yet he had tried so hard to hang on to that life. He had kept the house he'd lived in with Jean, when all it did was remind him of how alone he was. He had refused to be set up on dates, thinking that he wasn't ready to handle them. Instead, he had immersed himself in work, knowing that even as it kept him from thinking of his ex-wife, it was the one thing that had driven her from him. Mostly he had held on to an idea of Jean that had little to do with who she was or even who he was.

Just before he'd left for China—God, when was that? Two days ago now?—he had called her. Jean had sighed when she heard his voice, then her resignation quickly turned to impatience. "We're divorced, David, I don't know why you feel you need to let me know everything you're doing."

"I thought . . ."

"David, you *think* too much and you *work* too hard. Why don't you try *living* for a change?"

This was an old complaint. Their arguments, it seemed to David, had always revolved around work, responsibility, principles. Of course, Jean had had a very different perspective on their disagreements. "Our lives together can't just be about your career, about which bad guy you're going to nail or which good guy you're going to save," she used to say. "What about *me*, David?"

A few years back, when he was still at Phillips, MacKenzie, he had tracked down the hidden assets of a deposed dictator. He'd flown to Manila, Hong Kong, London, Cannes, and Frankfurt. He'd been passionate about the case, giving interviews, talking to anyone who could help, even once going to Washington to meet with a group of senators to discuss foreign aid. It was exhilarating to feel that he was making a difference in the lives of thousands of people he had never met.

After one two-week trip he had come home flush with the excitement of success. He was a fool, he knew now, but he'd chosen that moment to ask Jean if they should start a family. "A family? Children?" she'd scoffed. "You've got to be kidding. You don't even have time for me."

He'd been surprised at her reaction. "You can't begrudge my work. It's so important. What I'm doing—"

"Is applying your excess of principles to me and our marriage," she'd finished for him.

"But I'm helping an entire country."

"Yes, you are, at the expense of our relationship."

"But I have to do the right thing."

Jean had sighed. "David, your moral code is awfully hard to live with day after day. I can't snuggle next to it in bed. It doesn't comfort me at the end of a hard day."

"Are you doubting my feelings for you?"

She had looked at him squarely as she said, "I don't come first for you. Can't you see that? How could I bring children into the world who wouldn't come first for you either?"

That was the turning point in their marriage. Later, he'd tried to argue his position as he might in a courtroom, but he hadn't gotten very far. Jean was stubborn, smart, fearless, and she deserved a husband who would love her wholly.

During this last phone call he'd wanted to talk about the things that had been happening to him. But where could he start? And how many of them really were state secrets? This was another thing that had driven Jean crazy during their marriage. "Who do you think I'm going to tell? *The New York Times*? The *National Enquirer*?" But many of his cases were "sensitive," and he wasn't supposed to discuss them. So another wall had built up between them.

When David had pushed past her chariness and told Jean that he was going to China, a long silence had followed. Finally Jean had spoken again. "I hope you find what you're looking for," she'd said softly, then the phone had gone dead.

Outside this building was a whole new world. Maybe he would find what—who—he was looking for.

6

JANUARY 30

The Ministry of Public Security

David woke abruptly at 3:00 A.M. He tossed and turned for a while, trying to go back to sleep. At four he got up, searched around for a brochure outlining the hotel's facilities, and discovered that breakfast wouldn't be available until seven. Too tired to read a book or do any work, he turned on the television to International CNN. How strange the news was on this side of the world. He watched sports reports on cricket in England and soccer in India. He saw a documentary on the sultan of Brunei. He listened with vague interest to a report on the rupture in U.S.-China relations caused by the arrest of several Chinese nationals caught smuggling nuclear trigger components into Northern California.

At six, he pulled open the heavy drapes and looked out at a cold sepulchral dawn. Just below him, the Liangma River crept past. Across the river, which seemed little more than a canal, the German-owned Kempinski Hotel and Department Store rose up. To his left, across a large thoroughfare and a raised highway, he could make out the Kunlun Hotel.

David knew that only exercise would clear his head. He pulled on a warm-up suit and went down to the front desk to ask directions to a jogging path. When the clerk suggested David use the hotel's tread-mill, he decided to take his chances outside.

Before leaving Los Angeles, he'd looked up the weather for Beijing in the newspaper, but nothing could have prepared him for the freez-ing air that hit him as soon as he swung through the hotel's revolving doors. Two doormen stared at David in wonder as he nodded and set out, jogging over to the path that bordered the river. The cold stabbed his lungs and hurt his eyes, but as his muscles warmed with activity and his body reached an easy rhythm he began to take in the sights around him. Where the hotel's grounds ended, low buildings spread as far as David could see. This residential neighborhood seemed ancient, gray from age, closed off from the modern world. Looking down the few alleyways that cut between the buildings, he saw laundry frozen on bamboo sticks, piles of refuse, a bicycle leaning up against an earthenware jar. Once he caught the eyes of a woman as she threw the contents of a slop bucket out her door. He saw an old man loading large baskets onto a low-slung boat. Some of these he hefted easily onto his back, while others made him bend over until his face nearly touched his knees.

The longer David ran, the more people he saw. Early risers, bun-dled in bulky padded jackets, bicycled or trudged resolutely to work or school. He saw faces wizened by age and hard times. He saw sweet-featured children who looked like they could be in storybooks, walking, skipping, giggling along the path with backpacks and book bags. The few teenagers he passed looked as if they might freeze to death. They had dressed in what David realized must be the Chinese version of trendy. The girls wore leggings and bright scarves; the boys wore jeans and black scarves; both sexes completed their outfits with leather jackets and army boots.

In the days to come as David made this run a part of his routine, his presence would become more familiar, but for now most of the people ignored him pointedly. Others looked at him in bewilder-ment. He could imagine what they thought: Only a foreigner would be so incurably strange as to run for exercise in weather like this. A few people even called out to him in Chinese. He didn't speak the language, but he was sophisticated enough to hear the difference between the Cantonese that was so prevalent in Los Angeles and the Mandarin of Beijing with its abundance of *shi, zhi, xi,* and *ji* sounds.

Back at the hotel, he showered, then went downstairs for breakfast. He perused the buffet, passing on the steamed dumplings and rice gruel with salted fish in favor of bacon and scrambled eggs. He spent the rest of the morning at loose ends—reading the *International Herald Tribune* and watching CNN in his room. He hated waiting, but he didn't know what else to do.

Looking at a map, he saw he was far from any of the tourist attractions, and he felt nervous about venturing into the neighborhood that he had run past this morning. With its walls and exclusively Chinese residents—who looked like they were living just above the poverty line—that area had seemed as if it wasn't for tourists. He didn't want to risk getting in trouble by going someplace he wasn't wanted or wasn't supposed to go. But even as he waited in his room for twelve o'clock to roll around, another part of him wanted to say, Fuck it. I'm on the other side of the world. I'm on an adventure. I can do what I want.

Visitors to Beijing cannot ignore its imperial quality. David too would see this as soon as Peter drove him from the Chaoyang District, where he was staying, to the Ministry of Public Security, where the Eastern City and the Western City Districts meet. The Forbidden City—home to the twenty-four emperors of the Ming and Qing dynasties who carried the Mandate of Heaven throughout their reigns—stands at the very heart of the city. Everything else blossoms out from it on a pure north-south axis and an east-west axis. The wide Chang An Boulevard, Avenue of Perpetual Peace, runs east and west before the Forbidden City, dividing Beijing into northern and southern sectors. Just across the street from the Forbidden City lies the broad expanse of Tiananmen Square. Just below this Qianmen Street goes south, while above the Forbidden City Hataman Street heads north. These two streets split the city on its east-west axis.

Beijing's layout recalls the traditional concepts of yin and yang. Yin represents the north—night, danger, evil, death. The first barbarians—the Mongols—came from the north. Emperors—usually invaders—also lived to the "north" in the Forbidden City. Residents were warned never to insult the emperor by spitting, urinating, or weeping while facing north. Homes and businesses in Beijing, as in most of China, open to the south, allowing the sun to pour in with the attributes of yang: daylight, refuge, goodness, life.

To control this pattern over the centuries, the Chinese built walls. The old empire itself was protected by the Great Wall to the far north. Massive walls with gates at the four compass points defended the ancient city. The emperor fortified himself behind the Forbidden City's high walls. Even his subjects—meek as they were—screened themselves from bandits and nosy neighbors by living behind walls in courtyards. Since Chinese law decreed that no building could ever be higher than the emperor's throne, these houses—like those David had seen on his morning run—were built close to the ground. Between them lie the *hutongs*, an ancient labyrinth of little alleys and lanes. It is the tangle of *hutongs* that gives Beijing its human character.

Until the last decade of the twentieth century, a Beijinger could cross the city without ever leaving a *hutong* neighborhood. But in the year that David Stark traveled to Beijing, land in the city commanded as much as $560 a square foot; the *hutongs* suddenly seemed obsolete. Hundreds, thousands of old courtyard homes were marked in stark white paint with the Chinese character denoting "to be demolished." At least two-thirds of the old neighborhoods were to be razed to make room for high-rise apartment buildings. Families—who, of course, don't have titles to their land—were packed up, issued new residency permits, and sent to live in high-rises on the outskirts of the burgeoning city. Far from being unhappy at losing their homes, most residents were delighted to leave the crowded neighborhoods, the dilapidated conditions, the primitive facilities.

By the turn of the century, according to Beijing's aggressive urban planners, only three *hutong* neighborhoods will have escaped demolition. Two of these lie to the east of the imperial lakes of Shisha and Bei Hai. The other is just west of the Forbidden City and the Zhongnanhai compound, where Communist leaders live. Liu Hulan lived in her mother's ancestral home—a traditional courtyard compound nestled securely in the *hutong* near Shisha Lake.

The compound had been in Hulan's mother's family for many centuries. The Jiang family had been blessed with generation upon generation of royal performers—acrobats, puppeteers, singers of Peking Opera. But after the Manchus' fall, the family found itself in reduced circumstances. Hulan's mother, Jiang Jinli—young, beautiful, talented—eventually ran away to join the revolution. In the countryside, she learned peasant songs and dances; in exchange, she taught the peasants songs of the revolution.

By the time she returned to Beijing with Mao and his troops in 1949, her family had either escaped from the country, disappeared into an outlying province, or been killed. But Jinli had no regrets. She was well on her way to making a new family with a good revolutionary background. Her husband, who was handsome, young, and brave in battle, had also turned his back on his family. The Party forgave the two their pasts but didn't forget them. Therefore, they assigned Hulan's father to the Ministry of Culture. The Party decided that the best place for the newly married couple would be in the old Jiang family compound, since that of the Lius had been destroyed. Here, Jiang Jinli would serve as a living lesson to her neighbors. Even with the most bourgeois background, a person in the new China could be rehabilitated through hard work and devotion to the revolution.

Hulan was the only one who lived here now. After the travails of the Cultural Revolution, her mother and father moved into an apartment. "Too many bad memories," her father had said when Hulan returned from California. She tried to live with her parents, but within weeks she went back to her true home. Her arrival caused the Neighborhood Committee director to call a meeting to discuss the Lius' history. Soon after, several families who had squatted in the house during the Lius' protracted absence hastened for more politically correct quarters.

What was now called the Liu compound had been built according to old Chinese ideals. The exterior was humble, giving no hint of the wealth or prominence of those who lived behind its gray walls. The roof was composed of a gentle slate-colored tile that curved up delicately at the edges. Inside the exterior walls were several buildings—originally intended for different family groupings—each connected by small courtyards, colonnades, and pavilions. At this time of year the gardens languished; withered and stark from frost, snow, and bitter wind. But in spring and summer, the wisteria and pots of flowers would bloom in the dappled shade created by a canopy of jujube, willow, and poplar. In the corner near the old outdoor kitchen, the fleshy fruit of a persimmon would ripen.

The only thing that differentiated this compound from others in the neighborhood was the decoration over the front gate. Most homes had carved stonework—some centuries old—with symbols designating class and trade. Many had traditional sayings over the front gates: "Hail jewel in the lotus," "Happiness coming in the gate," "Ten thousand blessings," "A tree has its roots." In the old days, the saying above the Jiang compound had been a Confucian couplet about the harmony of family relationships and prosperity. (The memory of the night that piece of stonework was smashed to jagged bits was never far from Hulan's consciousness.) In the Liu family's absence, the squatters had chipped in for a new tablet— "Long Live Chairman Mao." Hulan had never bothered to take it down.

So much had changed in the compound since Hulan left it for the first time in 1970 to go with others her age to the countryside to "learn from the peasants." Two years later she returned to the city for two days. She had been in her old home just long enough to do her duty, pack a few mementos, and watch as many of her family's treasures were destroyed or confiscated. When Hulan returned to China in 1985, she found that the rest of her family's belongings had been ruined or sold. All that had survived inside to remind her of the house's former beauty were two intricately carved Ming dynasty screens that created the pattern of two Foo dogs over the windows.

Upon her arrival, one of her first errands was to go to the government and ask that the confiscated goods be returned. After months of repeated visits, she'd finally been handed a few crates. Opening them, she found her mother's clothes—her costumes, her day dresses, her exquisite evening wear—a few photographs, some miniature portraits of relations painted centuries ago on glass, and two ancestor scrolls. Since then, Hulan had combed the city's antiques and junk shops looking to replace what had been lost. Now the simple, clean lines of Ming furniture and the delicate beauty of porcelains decorated the house.

This morning, as Hulan threw some coal into the kitchen and living room stoves, prepared a pot of chrysanthemum tea, and set out a little plate of salted plums, she could hear the *hutong* coming to life. Just over the back wall of the compound the muted voices of the Qin family could be heard as they went about their morning routine. Hulan could imagine Mrs. Qin, with her baby thrown carelessly over her shoulder, stirring the pot of *congee*, rice gruel, while Mr. Qin chopped slivers of pickled turnip for flavoring.

Hulan could practically tell the time and day of the week by the routine of the peddlers who passed through the *hutong*. The first voice she heard each morning was the bean-curd peddler's as he made his early rounds. By the time she was ready for work, the prune-juice seller would have gone home with his jugs empty and his pockets jangling with coins. On certain days, the needle and thread salesman would visit, singing the praises of his wares in his nasal twang. Once a month, the knife and scissors sharpener would set up a temporary shop—really no more than a blanket, a satchel, and several honing blades.

Just as Hulan could mark time by the movements of these peddlers, she could also predict the arrival of the local busybody, Neighborhood Committee Director Zhang Junying, whose business it was to watch everyone in this honeycomb of compounds. Hulan heard the gate creak open just as the tea reached its full fragrant strength.

Zhang Junying's hair was thinning and dyed an almost purple black. She kept it in a tidy bun held in place by a black hair net at the nape of her neck. She was short, plump, and waddled when she walked. Zhang Junying settled her ample grandmotherly form into a chair and reached for a salted plum. She popped the sour morsel in her mouth, then got to the purpose of her visit. "Inspector Liu, I have noticed your absence more than usual."

"Don't worry, auntie. I have been working."

"You're always working! What else is new? But this new case . . ."

"Don't let them scare you, auntie."

The old woman frowned. "They say, 'You watch out for Inspector Liu. She will be working with a foreign devil. You watch for any changes.'"

"You shouldn't tell me this."

"Your family, my family, we have been neighbors for many generations," Zhang Junying cackled. "You think I care what those people tell me?"

"You're the one who needs to be careful," Hulan teased.

"*I'll* never get caught in a changing tide," she countered, and Hulan, who had known this woman all her life, knew she was right.

"Thank you for warning me," Hulan said lightly.

The old woman turned serious again. She took a noisy sip of tea to show her appreciation and approval of the drink. She set the cup down, then clapped her hands to her widespread knees. "You do not have to work so many long hours," she stated, and Hulan knew that while Madame Zhang appeared to be staying on the same subject, the conversation had taken a subtle, inevitable turn.

"I do what my superiors tell me to do," Hulan replied.

Zhang Junying's wizened face crinkled. "What do old men know about young women? Pretty soon, you are too old to have children. No one will marry you then."

"Maybe I don't want to marry . . . "

"*Aiya!* You always were a stupid girl!"

"Too stupid to be a good wife. This is true."

"This is a problem," the old woman agreed, then brightened. "I know what! You know the Kwok family? They are an old family. They have a son. Forty-five years old."

"He's the one too old to marry!"

"No, no, he is a good son."

"What does he do?"

"See? You are thinking like a bride." Zhang slapped her hands on her knees. "That's good."

"Not like a bride," Hulan corrected, "like a fat pig before Spring Festival."

Zhang Junying croaked a phlegmy laugh. "You are a funny girl. You should be married. Make your husband laugh. Better yet, you make your mother-in-law laugh."

As the two women bantered, Liu Hulan mentally ticked off a list: Am I dressed right? Should I carry my gun or keep it in my desk? Does my hair still shine? Can I keep my voice steady? Over the years, Liu Hulan had perfected the art of keeping her emotions in check, of hiding her thoughts, of presenting a placid facade to the world. It was how she survived.

After an early lunch, David was picked up by Peter and whisked away in the Saab. "Your appointment is at one," Peter announced as he honked at a caravan of camels loaded with goods as they loped through the traffic. After a few turns, the boulevard widened and Peter's pace quickened. Suddenly everything opened up and David saw the vast emptiness of Tiananmen Square on the left and the deep-red fortress of the Forbidden City on the right. On the square, a group of Western tourists stood in a dejected cluster with their cameras and tote bags, men in dull green army uniforms carried machine guns, and a few old women swept the expanse with homemade bamboo brooms.

Peter turned right, down an alley that ran alongside the Forbidden City, then made three consecutive lefts, so that they circled the old imperial palace. Stark dismissed this as a quick tour until Peter went around the block again. Noticing his look in the rearview mirror, Peter gave David his first inkling of how Chinese officials would deal with him on this trip. "You're not expected for another ten minutes," Peter explained. Everything David did would be controlled to the minute.

Peter escorted David through the Ministry of Public Security's damp halls and into Vice Minister Liu's office promptly at one. Amid handshakes and hearty welcomes, David quickly took in his surroundings—the plushness of the office, the obsequiousness of the vice minister, and the cautious manner of Section Chief Zai.

"We are honored to meet you," Liu said with a slight bow after introductions were made, "and honored that the United States has sent to us one of its finest lawyers to help in solving this horrible crime against one of our most respected citizens."

"It is an honor for me as well," David responded with a similar tip of his head.

"Surely we are two great nations united in the pursuit of a common goal."

As they stood exchanging stilted pleasantries, David felt like a gangly teenage boy—not knowing the right words and feeling very uncomfortable in his suddenly very large body.

But from her vantage point in the doorway, Hulan saw a very different figure. David Stark stood with his side to her so he couldn't see her as she observed him. How little he had changed in twelve years. He still had what she'd always thought of as a runner's body, lean and long. Only his brown hair seemed to have changed—now showing a little gray at the temples. He was tall compared to her father and mentor but of average American height. Like the two older men, he wore a Western-style suit, but how dissimilar he looked from them.

David had the comfortable physical looseness that came with political freedom and regular exercise. Under his strained, formulaic words, the warmth of his voice cut across the time of their separation. She took a final moment to calm her breathing, smooth her hands along the slim lines of her skirt, and compose a look of serenity on her face.

As she stepped forward, her father and Zai regarded her with enough interest that David turned in her direction. When Zai introduced her as the inspector in charge of the Chinese investigation, David's face paled, then flushed.

"Hulan," he breathed.

"David Stark," she said, taking his hand firmly. "It's been many years. How wonderful to see you again." She hoped her businesslike demeanor would give him the time he needed to realize that he shouldn't act on impulse. (She didn't know what that would be exactly. Would he take her in his arms? Would he be as stiff as she? Or would he walk out and disappear from her life as she had from his?)

"This is a surprise," he said.

"Yes, how fortuitous," Vice Minister Liu said. "We are old friends here, are we not?"

Without taking his eyes off Hulan, David spoke with chilly formality. "Old friends, new friends. It makes no difference. As you said, Vice Minister, we are here to work together as two nations united by a common goal. I'm sure we'd all like to see the Rising Phoenix come to justice. Perhaps you can tell me about your progress."

An awkward silence followed. David had unknowingly made his first mistake, Hulan thought. He had openly spoken about a touchy subject, which, in turn, elicited an immediate loss of face for her two superiors.

"Unfortunately, we have been unlucky in prosecuting the Rising Phoenix," Section Chief Zai said finally.

"But we hope that through this new affiliation we will reach a satisfactory conclusion," Vice Minister Liu added smoothly. "Please be assured that we at the Ministry of Public Security will be watching the two of you in your pursuit. If there's anything you need from us, please inform Section Chief Zai and he will provide it." When no one spoke, he unceremoniously closed the meeting. "There's nothing more to say at this time. Inspector Liu, I suggest that the two of you begin."

Hulan was conscious of David's nearness as they walked down the deserted hallway. She began muttering more to herself than to him. "No courtesy. No manners. They didn't give you tea. They didn't suggest a meal. They didn't even offer you a seat."

David's mind was far away from the slights that she'd perceived. "Hulan, I can't believe it's you." He spoke softly. She never hesitated in her step, never turned to look at him, but kept her eyes focused on the worn linoleum before her. She surreptitiously shook her head. David followed her down one flight and then halfway down a second. Convinced that they were really alone, Hulan stopped and turned to face him. She pulled gently on his upper arm, bringing his face close enough that she could feel his breath.

"This isn't a safe place for us to talk." The syllables came out low and raspy. "I know it's hard, but we have to be careful, okay?"

She let go of his arm, turned, and continued on to her office. She put on her coat and suggested he do the same. Then she sat down, motioned for him to take the chair opposite her desk, pulled out a file, and opened it. "We should get to work," she said, then slowly moved her gaze from the manila folder, across the desk, and up into the depth of his eyes.

As he clinically recounted his investigation of the *China Peony*, his gruesome discovery of the body, and the eventual identification of Guang Henglai, he watched as her face shifted from interest to disgust to concern. As she spoke with dispassion about the discovery of Billy Watson and his parents' differing yet strange reaction to his death, David's face mirrored her own confusion. (She didn't mention that she'd been pulled off the case—that would only raise questions whose answers would not show the Chinese government in a positive light.) Through it all, they sounded politely professional, so that anyone listening would glean nothing of their past relationship other than cool civility. Anyone in the room, however, would have felt the tension of restrained emotions.

"I understand from the vice minister that your pathologist found a residue in Henglai's lungs similar to what we found," Hulan ventured. She was careful not to use her father's full name. David hadn't made the connection and she didn't want to tell him. She'd have enough trouble working with him without her odd family history coming into it. "Was he able to determine what it was?"

"Not exactly. He thinks it's from some type of insect and that it's extremely toxic. But other than that, nothing. How about your guy?"

A frown crossed Hulan's features, but her voice was businesslike as she replied, "Pathologist Fong noted that the teeth and fingernails had turned a dark color unlike anything he had seen before. Did your pathologist find something similar?"

David vividly remembered the color of Guang Henglai's teeth grinning out at him as he lay in the hold of the *China Peony*. "Our coroner dismissed that as some sort of degradation consistent with the extended period of decomposition."

David expected Hulan to add to her report, but she only made a slight humming sound followed by "We were unable to perform forensic tests."

David waited for more, but Hulan kept her silence.

"Tell me what you know about the Rising Phoenix," David said after a moment.

Hulan sighed. This was another subject she would have to be careful with. "Section Chief Zai has ordered various investigations of the Rising Phoenix. I haven't worked on them, but I do know that they have not been successful."

"It's hard to get anyone to talk," David said. "No one wants to betray the gang."

"Actually," she said cautiously, "we've come quite close several times, but the Rising Phoenix always seems to know we're coming."

"You think they're getting inside information?"

"Could be. Everything's for sale in China."

"What kind of evidence have you gathered?"

"I don't know," she answered. "Like I said, I haven't worked on those cases."

"But with what I know maybe we can put something together," he offered.

"Perhaps," she said. "It doesn't take much evidence to get a conviction in China, but whatever facts we've gotten have never been enough for the vice minister."

"Then we'll have to find them," David concluded.

Their eyes met again. Hulan fought the impulse to talk about more personal matters.

David cleared his throat, looked away, and said, "Inspector Liu, this is your turf and your investigation. What do you suggest we do next?"

"What would you do if you were me?"

"I think we should start with the parents."

"Ambassador Watson is a difficult man."

David shrugged. "He's a politician, too, and we have to assume that he's not stupid. This is a highly unusual situation. I suspect that he'll recognize that and see us. What about the boy's mother?"

"I think we'll do better if we interview Mrs. Watson alone, but I'm not sure how to arrange that. Her husband seems very much in control."

"Friends?"

"I know of none, but I haven't looked."

"That doesn't sound like you." The words were out of his mouth before he could think.

Another awkward silence filled the room. Finally, Hulan spoke. "The grass points where the wind blows. In China, I do what I'm told. I obey my superiors, especially in political matters. Do you understand?" She paused, then continued. "I have waited for your arrival to speak with Guang Henglai's family."

"What can you tell me about Guang Mingyun?"

"He is an important businessman in our country. You would not be here if not for him."

"And his son was considered a Red Prince?"

"That is not a term I like to use."

"Nevertheless . . . "

"Nevertheless," Hulan acceded.

The afternoon wore on. The room became darker and colder as whatever sunlight there had been disappeared behind the thickening cloud cover. Hulan turned on her desk lamp and tried to come up with another subject. But they had said all there was to say about the case, and this wasn't the place to talk about the past.

"What do you want me to do now?" he asked.

"I think it will be best if Peter takes you back to the hotel." David shook his head, but Hulan continued, "You are in China. I will make our appointments." She stood and extended her hand. "Tomorrow then?"

"Hulan . . . "

"Good," she said, reluctantly loosening her hand from his. She crossed to the door and held it open. "I will leave a message for you at your hotel telling you the time."

Peter, who waited just outside the door, jumped to his feet, spoke in rapid Chinese to Hulan, then led Stark back through the maze of corridors and stairwells to the courtyard. In her office, Hulan stood with her back against the closed door, trying to catch her breath.

*   *   *

By the time Hulan left her office it was already dark. She buttoned her coat against the cold and draped a scarf over her head. Others in the building hurried to their bicycles. She was aware of how they kept their distance, how they ignored her as she walked with them along the length of the bicycle park.

She hitched up her skirt, swung her leg over her silver-blue Flying Pigeon, pedaled out of the compound, and melted into the anonymity of hundreds of her countrymen commuting home. How peaceful this was compared to the fits and starts of Peter's driving. The smooth, quiet rhythm of her own bicycle among hundreds of others all around her became a soothing meditation.

She relished those moments when she stopped at a traffic light and was able to witness the city's domestic life. On a street corner stood a cart laden with candied crab apples on bamboo skewers. On another, a man grilled fragrant strips of marinated pork. On yet another, a small crowd of people clustered around a kiosk to slurp redolent noodles from enameled tin bowls before handing the empties back to the proprietor.

Hulan parked in front of one of the city's new high-rise apartment buildings. She rode the elevator to the fifteenth floor and knocked on a door at the end of the hallway. A maid escorted Hulan into the living room. There was little in this room to suggest the personalities of the people who lived here. The couch was covered in a polyester floral print. Several straight-backed chairs were grouped around a low coffee table. Plastic plants collected dust in wicker baskets. Oil paintings of decidedly Western landscapes hung on the walls.

A woman sat in a wheelchair staring out the window.

"How is she today?" Hulan asked the maid, taking off her coat. She much preferred the cold of old buildings like her *hutong* home and public facilities to the overheated rooms of the new apartments and Western-style hotels that had sprung up in recent years.

"Quiet. No change."

Hulan crossed the room, knelt next to the wheelchair, and gazed up into her mother's face. Jiang Jinli stared into the middle distance. Hulan gently reached for her mother's hand. The skin was translucent and Hulan traced the delicate veins with a finger.

"Hello, Mama."

There was no response.

Hulan pulled a porcelain garden stool to her mother's side and began talking about her day. "I had an interesting visitor, Mama. I think you remember me talking about him before."

Hulan carried on as if her mother were fully engaged in the conversation, because sometimes—after hours or even days of total silence—Jinli would become quite talkative. At those times, few as they were, Hulan realized how much of her monologues had seeped into her mother's consciousness.

As a girl, Hulan had been in awe—and sometimes a little jealous—of her mother's beauty. After all these years and after all that her mother had been through, Jinli still looked much the same as when she was the young wife of a rising cadre assigned to the prestigious Ministry of Culture. Hulan could remember how her mother had loved to dress in vivid colors—fuchsia, emerald, and royal blue—made all the brighter next to the proletarian gray of the people who used to gather in the Liu family home for an evening of folk songs and Peking Opera, dumplings, and shots of mao-tai. She could remember how her father used to invite friends like Mr. Zai, who could play the old instruments so that they might accompany Jinli as she sang of unrequited love. Hulan remembered how still her father sat while he listened to Jinli as her voice lilted and her eyes sparkled with love for him.

Hulan treasured the memories of her parents' friends taking her into their laps and laughingly whispering in her ear, "Your mama and baba are like a pair of chopsticks, always together, always in harmony," or "Your mama is like a gold leaf in a jade branch"—meaning Jinli was the ideal woman. All these years later, it seemed as if her mother had frozen in that time like jade buried beneath so much rock. She had not aged. Her beauty was untouched by the physical and mental hardships she had endured. It was as though time only passed in those infrequent periods when Jinli was lucid.

For almost twenty-five years, Jinli had been immobilized in her wheelchair. Hulan's father had been single-minded in his care for his wife. He paid back-door bribes so that Jinli would have access to the best Western doctors. He paid exorbitant fees for special traditional Chinese herbal concoctions designed to improve and strengthen Jinli's physical health. Whether due to Western medicine or Chinese medicine, Jinli was not prone to the usual opportunistic infections that plagued paraplegics. However, nothing had improved the ailment that dwelled in Jinli's mind. In fact, her mental condition had slowly deteriorated since the "accident."

When Jinli's head was clear, she and her daughter spoke of light things. How the cherry blossoms looked lovely along the hillside at the Summer Palace. How Old Man Chou was selling the first snow-pea greens of the season. How the silk that Hulan had chosen for a dress shimmered. They never spoke of Jinli's illness. They never spoke of Hulan's father—how he had been posted to the Ministry of Public Security twenty years ago, how he had worked his way up through the ranks, how he had been promoted into his current position after the events in Tiananmen Square in 1989. Naturally, they never spoke of Hulan's work, as her mother had no idea of what her daughter did for a living. So on this evening, as the lights of Beijing glittered below them, Hulan didn't talk about the case or even how David had come to be in Beijing, but only how he looked and sounded.

When Hulan's father arrived, she stood hastily, kissed her mother, and began to gather her things.

"*Ni hao*," he called out, "hello." He came into the room rubbing the cold from his fingers. His posture was correct, his gait brisk. A warm smile spread across his features.

"Good evening, Vice Minister."

He gave no sign of surprise at her decorous form of address.

"Have you eaten yet?"

"Yes, I have, and I'm just on my way."

"Surely you will drink tea."

"Thank you for your graciousness. But truly, I must return home."

They had had this precise conversation for many years now on those rare occasions when he had come home early or she had stayed too late. Hulan knew what would come next.

"Your mother would be honored if you stayed."

No matter how long she might protest that she had eaten or had her tea or had a place to go, he would not rest until she had given in. Rather than fight, she shucked off her coat.

"Good," he said. "You can help me with dinner."

In the kitchen, counters gleamed under the glare of harsh overhead lights. Hulan's father rolled up his sleeves and set to work peeling and chopping ginger and garlic. Hulan washed the rice until the water ran clear, then set it in a steamer decorated with pink peonies. Then she ran several heads of baby bok choy under water to rinse away dirt and any remnants of night soil. Later, Hulan watched silently as her father seared slivers of pork in a smoking wok. His hands moved quickly. The muscles of his forearms were taut as he effortlessly lifted the wok with its aromatic contents and poured them into a low serving dish.

In the dining room—so Western-contemporary with its chandelier, oval dinette set, and breakfront filled with Melmac dishes—Vice Minister Liu selected the most delectable morsels out of the main dish and put them into his wife's bowl. As he raised his chopsticks to Jinli's lips, he cleared his throat. Outside the pure stilted etiquette of their professional relationship, conversations between Hulan and her father always revolved around obedience and responsibility. For a modern man, a cadre with a fine revolutionary background, he betrayed a distinct adherence to Confucian beliefs.

"Hulan," he began, "so many times I have asked you to come home and live with us."

"Vice Minister, I do not consider this our home. I live in our real home."

"That place is old. We are in a new era. Your true home is with your parents." He jutted his chin out. "But you know this is not what I mean. I am talking about duty to your family."

"Filial piety is one of the olds."

"That is true. Mao did not believe in old ways. He had many mistresses and wives. When they had children, he did not hesitate to leave them with peasants in villages by the roadside. But Mao is dead. I do not need to tell you this."

"No, you don't, Vice Minister."

"Family is a sanctuary. In China, there is no ambiguity about where we belong. Your mother and I are held together by our ancestors, as you are held to us as well as to your ancestors."

"Baba."

This break from the normal pattern caused her father to look her way.

Hulan took a breath and tried again. "Baba, I owe you and Mama a great debt for raising me. I know I can never repay you." The meaning of her words was as clear to the vice minister as if she'd spoken them aloud. *You taught me. You fed me and clothed me. In your lifetime, even if I were a son, I might not be able to repay that debt of obligation, of duty. But in your death, I would see to a proper burial. If I were a son, I would see that paper clothes and paper money were burned so that you might be rich in the afterlife. And each year, at Spring Festival, I would have my wife and daughters prepare you a whole chicken, a whole duck, a whole fish to symbolize unity and prosperity for the family. We would light incense for you. As your son I would* chu xi, *pay you back with interest for the gift of life. But I am only a daughter.*

"A daughter is not such a bad thing," her father said, slipping the wrinkled form of a tree ear mushroom into Jinli's open mouth. "For centuries our family has named its daughters."

"I see Mama every day."

"This is not the same thing. You are unmarried." And what he meant was: *When a girl, obey your father. When married, obey your husband. When widowed, obey your son.*

"I also work, Vice Minister."

He snorted dismissively. "You do not need to do this work."

"You hired me."

"No one expected you to do more than pour tea. To do the investigations?" His face contorted. "It is not proper. You should do something cleaner. I can arrange this."

"Have I not done my job?"

"You disregard the point. You are a Red Princess. You do not have to work at all."

"I'm good at what I do."

"Yes, you are," he assented. "But your mother needs you. Come home to us. Take care of her."

She neither agreed nor argued. But as she sat there, picking at the last few grains of rice in her bowl, she knew that everything he said was true.

7

JANUARY 31
The Fathers

The American embassy was made up of several large dirty-beige buildings with gray tile roofs. Most of the windows were covered with iron grates. On the corners of each eave, video cameras swept methodically back and forth. The compound itself was enclosed by a high wrought-iron fence broken at regular intervals by gray pillars. Just inside this fence, sparse hedges grew and dormant trees sent ragged branches into the gloomy sky. Along one side of the compound, hundreds of bicycles stood in neat rows.

The front entrance to the embassy was flanked by guardhouses. The one on the left served as the first of many stops for those Chinese wishing to obtain visas to the United States. Several churlish guards dressed in green uniforms and black fur hats kept their countrymen at bay. Just across from the embassy, people waited either to be allowed into the preliminary visa line or to be called for their interviews. Just to their right, the street turned into Silk Road, where splashes of purple, red, and yellow enlivened open-air stalls.

Hulan and David passed through the gate, several other human and physical barricades, and into a reception room, where they were introduced to Phil Firestone, the ambassador's secretary and right-hand man. Despite his blue pinstripe suit and red polka-dot tie, Phil's sandy hair and the baby fat that still clung to his face gave him a decidedly boyish look. His smile was open and all-American.

As they waited for the ambassador to finish with his previous appointment, Phil chatted about home and how he ended up in China. "My family's also from Montana, so we're long acquainted with the ambassador and his family. My mother worked on Bill Watson's senatorial campaign, and I was lucky enough to become part of his staff in Washington. When the president appointed Senator Watson to the ambassadorship, I leaped at the chance to come to Beijing."

"Are you married?" David asked idly.

"No, I guess that's why I don't mind being uprooted. I can follow the ambassador without worrying about the impact on a wife or children. I see how hard this life can be for some families." Realizing that this might not have been the most diplomatic thing to say in front of Hulan, Phil tried to cover his mistake. "Not that Beijing isn't wonderful. Personally, I love the people."

"Don't worry, Mr. Firestone," she said. "I, too, have been abroad. I know how difficult it is to be away from home. I think I missed the food most of all."

"Boy, what I wouldn't do for a hamburger sometimes."

"We have McDonald's."

Phil Firestone laughed good-naturedly, then checked his watch. "The ambassador should be able to see you now."

Phil shepherded them into an adjoining office. "If you'll just wait here, the ambassador will be with you shortly," he said, then left them alone.

David felt an itch of irritation, but Hulan seemed unperturbed. Her body remained still and contained, but her eyes roamed the room, from the American flag that hung behind the desk to the official seals and plaques on the walls to the Frederic Remington bronze cowboy on the desk. Inside, however, Hulan was boiling. The ambassador was savvy enough to know that the Chinese valued promptness. He was being intentionally rude.

"Sorry to keep you waiting." The ambassador's voice came to

them even before he had stepped fully into the room. "I've been tied up all day, what with these difficulties we're having." He extended his hand. "David Stark, I presume. I've heard good things about you."

"It's a pleasure to meet you."

"And, of course, I remember the inspector here." The ambassador's blue eyes settled on Hulan. "I must say, I didn't expect to see you again."

"Things don't always work out as we wish," Hulan allowed.

The ambassador seemed temporarily mystified, then let out a reverberating laugh. "You are a funny one. Here," he said, motioning to a red leather couch, "please make yourselves comfortable. Phil?" he called out. "Where's Phil? Phil?"

His adjutant poked his head into the office. "Sir?"

"I think coffee—or would you prefer tea?—is in order."

"Coffee's fine, thank you," Hulan murmured.

"Coffee it is then, Phil." The ambassador sat down in a matching red leather wing chair opposite them. He smiled, then addressed the American attorney. "What can I do for you?"

"First," David began, "let me say that I'm sorry to hear about the loss of your son. I realize that it can't be easy for you to talk about." The ambassador got a faraway look in his eyes but didn't respond. David went on. "Inspector Liu has told me many of the details of your son's death. As I think you may now know, they are remarkably similar to what we found with the body of Guang Mingyun's son."

"I couldn't help the inspector before. I doubt I can be of assistance today."

"If you could just answer a few questions . . . "

The ambassador sighed. "Go ahead."

"Were you acquainted with Guang Henglai?"

"I never met the boy."

Hulan interrupted. "I see from the photographs, however, that you have met his father."

"How could I do my job in Beijing and not meet the esteemed Mr. Guang?"

"But you're sure you never met his son?"

"Inspector, I don't think I need to remind you that you and I had trouble before. When I answer a question, you must expect nothing but the truth from me as a man and as my country's ambassador. I told you I never met this Guang Henglai and that remains my answer."

"Perhaps you can tell us a little about your son," David suggested into the awkward silence.

The older man shrugged. "How does a father describe his only son? Billy was a good boy. Of course, he got into the usual scrapes in high school. But, Mr. Stark, I'm sure you and I got into the same sorts of trouble."

"I understand he was going to college."

"I got my appointment just as Billy graduated from high school. He decided—and Elizabeth and I agreed—that he should take a year off and come here. What better education could there be for a young man than a year abroad? But after that first year I thought it would be best if Billy started his college education. I didn't want him falling too far behind his peers. He was accepted at the University of Southern California."

"What was he studying?" Hulan queried.

"You must not have much contact with young Americans. They study whatever they want."

"You don't know what he was studying?" Hulan insisted.

"I just answered that! If you plan on asking me everything twice, we'll be here a very long time!"

This time the embarrassing lull in the conversation was broken by the entrance of Phil Firestone. He registered the situation with diplomatic deftness. "Here you are," he said brightly, setting down a silver tray. "Coffee, sugar, and cream. Mr. Stark, you probably don't know how hard it is for us to get real cream here in Beijing. It's a veritable treat."

"That'll be all, Phil. Thanks."

Phil's manner shifted immediately. "Yes, sir. Just call if you need anything else." And he was gone.

"Ambassador, I'll be blunt," David said. "I'm confused by your hostility. Surely you now accept that your son was murdered. We are simply trying to discover why and how and, most important, by whom."

"Yes, I know."

"Please try to answer the inspector's question."

"I don't know what my son was studying. He was an undergraduate at USC. He lived in a dorm. He only came home for vacations. I guess Elizabeth and I thought it was more important that Billy seemed happy than what classes he was taking."

"Fair enough. So how often did you see your son?"

"He came for winter break and part of the summer." The ambassador nodded toward Hulan. "As you know, it can be pretty damned miserable in Beijing in the summer."

"Did he bring friends home?"

"You mean from California during vacation? No, never."

"Were there people he liked to hang out with when he was here?" David asked.

"I don't know. I don't think so."

"What did he like to do in Beijing?"

"I hate to admit it, but again I don't know. I'm an awfully busy man. When Billy was here, he slept late. By the time he woke up, I was probably into my third meeting of the day. When I got back to the residence, he was usually already gone for the evening."

"Where did he go? Who was he with?"

"Mr. Stark, I simply don't know. He was a college boy. I didn't think it was appropriate to question his activities."

"Perhaps Mrs. Watson knows something," David suggested.

"Mrs. Watson?" The name lingered in the air. "Yes, my wife. Yes, she may be able to help you."

"Can we see her?"

"She's at the residence," he said hesitantly.

"But?"

"Believe me, I want to see Billy's killer found more than anyone. But Elizabeth is . . . How can I say this? Billy's death has been very hard on her. I don't want to put her through any more pain. Surely you can appreciate that. Can you give me a day or two? Let me talk to her first?"

David turned to Hulan, who had been noticeably quiet since Bill Watson's earlier outburst. David had not seen Hulan in many years, but he could still recognize the look of anger lurking just under her placid facade.

"Inspector Liu?" He hoped she would keep her feelings in check.

She agreed with a curt nod.

Ambassador Watson's look of concern melted into a toothy grin. "Good," he said, bobbing his head in hearty agreement. He stood and extended his hand to David. "I'll have Phil give you a call in a day or two."

As soon as they slipped into the backseat of the Saab, Hulan's passion overrode her prudence. She knew Peter would be listening, but her emotions still got the better of her. "I don't need you to protect me."

"Protect you? I wasn't protecting you."

"You were and you know it."

In the front seat, Peter was all ears. Hulan snapped, "Drive!"

"Where to?"

"The offices of the China Land and Economics Corporation."

Wordlessly, Peter backed out of the space and pulled out of the compound.

Hulan refused to look at David. Her voice when it came was low and bitter. "You have always tried to shield me."

"I didn't do anything."

"You interrupted my questioning!"

"Maybe I did. But consider this. He doesn't like you. He wasn't going to answer your questions. Why do you suppose that is?"

She turned to face him. He could see the tension around her mouth as she spoke. "This is my country and my case."

"Yes, well, I don't mean to spoil your day or anything, but you haven't gotten very far with it. In fact, you wouldn't have been in there at all if it weren't for me."

"Do you know why I hate you, David Stark? It's because you argue like a lawyer."

"I am a lawyer, and you are too."

She turned away again.

"I guess we're having our first fight," David mused. When she didn't respond, he said, "Although I guess it isn't really our first . . . "

She whipped around again, but this time instead of anger he saw the same caution he had seen the day before at the Ministry of Public Security. Her eyes motioned to the back of Peter's head.

David continued blithely. "Of course, in my country, colleagues always disagree. That is part of an investigation, part of a trial. We are here under unusual circumstances. I think it would be best if we try to be aware of our different methods and work together."

"Quite."

"Tell me, Inspector Liu, has the ambassador changed at all since you last met him?"

"He's still an arrogant American."

"So that's why you provoked him?"

Hulan finally smiled. She glanced toward Peter, who had eschewed his colorful epithets in favor of eavesdropping. "In the MPS, we have a lot of leeway in how we interview witnesses."

"So I've heard," David said dryly.

"But I try to let witnesses speak for themselves. We are a reticent people, Mr. Stark. Everyone in this country understands the power of the MPS, but sometimes no pressure delivers better than domination. I think of it as the power of silence."

"I do that too. A witness feels compelled to fill the void. I get some of my best stuff that way."

"Yes, there's that, but I'm talking about something more. In China, to be allowed your own thoughts, to be allowed the freedom to speak when you want, creates a situation where your guard is down, where your thoughts begin to flow."

"You think that wouldn't work with the ambassador?"

"Americans have all the freedom they want, perhaps even too much. I think the ambassador would use that kind of silence to come up with a good story."

"But why?"

"I don't know."

"I look at that man and see a politician. Nothing more, nothing less. I think you just don't like him."

"That's true. There's something about that man that—what's the American phrase?—rubs me the wrong way."

"I'd say it's the other way around," David said.

"Perhaps."

"Going back to my original question, is he different?"

"He acts the same—the same bluster certainly."

"He doesn't strike me as a man in mourning."

"People deal with grief in many ways," Hulan said thoughtfully.

She turned to stare out at the traffic. Peter sent an eloquent string of curses out his window.

The headquarters of the China Land and Economics Corporation was a shimmering tower of glass and white granite. The lobby contained a photographic exhibit of the conglomerate's many ventures: dams holding back treacherous rivers, satellites hurtling through space, munitions coming off an assembly line, thousands of workers manufacturing tennis shoes, wholesome peasants using modern equipment to increase farm productivity, doctors prescribing medicines to smiling mothers and their children. In the center of the lobby, glass and chrome cases highlighted different divisions and subsidiaries of the China Land and Economics Corporation. The Ten Thousand Clouds Company manufactured parkas, rain hats, and galoshes; the Time Today Company created Chinese-red clocks that showed the minute and hour hands as the arms of prominent politicians; the Panda Brand Pharmaceutical Company packaged ginseng, herbal powders, dried flowers, and shredded deer antlers.

David and Hulan were shown directly into Guang Mingyun's elegant office. Streamlined rosewood furniture glowed warmly. Several large bouquets of tuberoses and rubellum lilies filled the room with their fragrance. The art on the walls—crimson canvases with ideograms rendered in stark black—provided a dramatic and thoroughly modern counterpoint to the view, which looked out over the bloodred walls of the Forbidden City.

"*Huanying, huanying,*" Guang Mingyun said as he stood to greet them. "Welcome, welcome." He easily switched to flawless English.

"How do you do, Mr. Guang?" Hulan said. "Let me present to you Assistant United States Attorney David Stark."

"I am indebted to you for coming so far. But please, please sit down. Have you eaten yet? Do you drink tea?"

"Mr. Guang, we have eaten. Yes, we drink tea, but we had some just before we came," Hulan said.

As Guang Mingyun continued his banter with Hulan over whether or not she "drank tea," David could see why the businessman had been so successful. Patrick O'Kelly had told him that Guang was seventy-two, but he presented himself as a man in the prime of life—dynamic, physically fit, astute. His handshake was strong. He was the first Chinese whom David had met—and admittedly he hadn't met that many—who didn't seem to worry that someone might be listening in on him. The sadness in his brown eyes gave the only indication of mourning.

"You will drink tea," Guang Mingyun decided, and his secretary discreetly backed out of the room.

Hulan, her hands poised delicately on her lap, said softly, "Mr. Guang, we are so sorry to come at this time . . . "

"I want to offer you and Attorney Stark as much information as I can."

"Do you have any idea how your son came to be on the *China Peony*?"

"I have never heard of this boat and I'm sure my son hadn't either. I am most confused by this and cannot explain it."

"Are you aware, Mr. Guang, that your son's death may be connected to that of the American ambassador's son?"

"I am, but I am confused by this as well. How could this terrible thing have happened to both Billy and my son?"

"You knew Billy Watson?" David asked, incredulous.

"Of course I knew Billy Watson. He was my son's best friend. They were always together."

Without missing a beat, Hulan asked, "Tell me about them. How did they know each other? What did they do together?"

Guang Mingyun's voice dropped as he described the relationship between the boys. The two had met the summer after Ambassador Watson was appointed. Guang Mingyun had hosted a party at his compound and the entire Watson family had attended. The two boys had quickly become friends. And soon Billy was a frequent visitor to the Guangs' compound in Beijing and their vacation villa at the shore in Beidaihe.

The conversation paused when Guang Mingyun's secretary entered. She poured the tea into Cantonware cups exquisitely decorated with hand-painted scenes of women and pagodas. She set out dishes of watermelon seeds, peanuts, and salted plums. As soon as she left, Guang Mingyun resumed his story. When Henglai graduated from Middle School Number 4—the academy that catered to the sons of important Beijing families—he applied to and was accepted by the University of Southern California. Guang Mingyun had allowed his son to travel to Los Angeles only because Billy Watson would be attending the college as well. When Henglai decided that he no longer wanted to pursue his studies but return to Beijing, Guang Mingyun couldn't have been more delighted. "My son was precious to my wife and me. We never liked to have him away from home."

"When he came home, what did he do? Did he work for you?"

"My son is not interested in business, but he is young," Guang Mingyun answered, slipping into the present tense. "He has his own apartment. He has his own friends. He is still a boy—young, not like when you were growing up, Inspector, or I was growing up. Times are different today. These children, they don't understand the struggle. They don't understand hard work. So I think, if he wants to have fun with his friends, especially with Billy, what harm can come of it? These days relationships between the two countries should be encouraged. We can all profit from those friendships, and, in the meantime, my son will grow up."

"Is there any possibility that your son was trying to escape to America?" Hulan asked. "Did he want to emigrate?"

"No, he had everything he could want here."

"Some young people want to leave China."

"Inspector Liu, if you are trying to get me to say something against our country, that will not happen. My son had every chance in China. And besides, he could travel back and forth to America whenever he wanted."

"You mean he still traveled to America?"

"Oh, yes." Guang Mingyun stood, went to his desk, and opened it. "I have my son's passport here. You can see, he had no trouble getting visas. That's because he always came home."

Hulan took the passport but didn't open it. "May I keep this?"

"Of course."

Hulan slipped the passport into her purse, then asked, "Tell me about his friends."

"What can I tell *you*? You know who they are. You know where to find them."

"Mr. Guang, I thank you for your help." Hulan rose to leave.

"Excuse me," David said. "But I have a few questions. What are your business ties in the United States?"

Immediately, David felt the atmosphere in the room change. Hulan sat back down, resumed her pose, but looked away, as though she weren't part of the conversation. Guang Mingyun's full lips tightened to a slit.

"I have business ventures in the United States, but I don't know how they could have anything to do with your investigation."

"I think it's important to explore all the possibilities," David said. "Your son was found on a boat allegedly owned by the Rising Phoenix. Are you familiar with that gang?"

"No."

"You have never heard of the Rising Phoenix?"

"I have heard of them, of course, but I am not familiar with them."

"Tell me, who runs your business ventures in the United States?"

Guang Mingyun sighed. "The China Land and Economics Corporation is a very large company, what you would call a worldwide conglomerate. I don't know all of my associates by name. If you wish, I can have my secretary compile a list for you."

"And your personal connections in the United States?"

Guang Mingyun switched to Chinese and spoke to Hulan. She answered, then looked away again. "I have relatives in Los Angeles who left China before Liberation," Guang Mingyun answered coolly. "I have never met them, but they offered hospitality to my son during his visits."

"And their names?"

"They have nothing to do with this."

"Please answer the question."

"My secretary will provide you with that list as well."

"I understand you're quite involved in the import/export trade."

"I am," Guang Mingyun agreed with false modesty. "I bring in a little of this and send out a little of that."

"Such as . . ."

"We have brought in luxury cars. Mercedes, Cadillacs, Peugeots, Saabs. We send out shoes, T-shirts, furs, toys, Christmas ornaments. Much of this work is done in the interior."

"Which province?" Hulan asked.

"Sichuan," Guang Mingyun answered.

"It is good that you are bringing prosperity—"

David was not about to be sidetracked by more of Hulan's pleasantries. "How about immigrants? Are they one of your exports?"

"I don't know what you're talking about."

"Are you aware, Mr. Guang, that the Rising Phoenix is reputed to have deposits in the Chinese Overseas Bank in California?"

"I would not have knowledge of that."

"But you are aware that you own the bank."

"It is one of my businesses."

Hulan shifted in her seat. "Mr. Guang, you must forgive our American friend's ways. I feel I must assure you that the Ministry of Public Security is not *aware*"—her emphasis of the word underscored her seeming distaste for the American's methods—"of any wrongdoing on the part of your son or yourself. The ministry has only the highest respect for Guang Mingyun and his family. This is as it should be. But I am thinking about your son. I know you want to know what happened. I know you want to bring the hooligans responsible for his death to justice."

"This is true, Inspector."

"And I know, too, that you want to help the ministry in its work."

"Of course. What can I do?"

"May we visit Henglai's home? We may find something that will help us to know him. It may help us to find his killer."

"Have your driver take you to the Capital Mansion on Xinyuan Road in Chaoyang District."

As David and Hulan pulled on their overcoats, Guang Mingyun's jovial manner returned. "Next time, we will have a banquet."

"Your hospitality is too generous, Mr. Guang," Hulan said.

"Please give my best regards to your father," he replied, gazing into her eyes.

"I will, and I hope you will express to Madame Guang our family's deepest sentiments."

In the elevator, David said, "One of those men is lying." Hulan focused on the electronic numbers as the elevator continued its rapid descent.

8

LATER THAT AFTERNOON
Bei Hai Park

When they reached the car, Hulan abruptly announced that she wanted to show David the place where Billy Watson's body had been found. Peter asked to stop on the way so that he might buy cigarettes, but Hulan refused him outright. When Peter pulled into a parking place at the south gate to Bei Hai Park, she told him to wait in the car. He opened his mouth to speak, but she hushed him with a brittle torrent of Chinese. Peter feigned submission, folded his arms, and sank down in his seat.

David followed Hulan along the path that rimmed the lake. The park was relatively deserted. The kiosks, a Kentucky Fried Chicken franchise and a kiddie arcade with its colorfully painted rides, were all closed. With the season nearly over, only a few skaters were on the ice.

Hulan stopped at a bench and motioned for David to sit. "This is where I talked to the Watsons," she said. Next to her, David listened and followed the direction of her finger as she pointed out across the lake to where Billy Watson was found. But David knew she had not brought him there just to see the crime scene. As she spoke she kept her eyes focused on something in the distance—the sky? the opposite shore?

"Hulan." David couldn't help his pleading tone. "Can we talk? Please?"

Hulan ignored his questions. "We need to concentrate on this case, then you can go home to . . . "

"You disappeared all those years ago," he said. He took her hand and held it in both of his. "I never expected to see you again, but I hoped that somehow I would find you here. And I did. Doesn't that mean anything to you?"

"Please listen," she said neutrally, gently pulling her hand away. "We don't have much time. Peter is probably calling the office now. He'll have help here soon, so we must be quick." She looked around. Satisfied that no one was nearby, she said, "We need to be careful."

"Any time I try to talk to you, you tell me to be careful," he said. "Why don't you listen to what I have to say for once?" She didn't respond, so he repeated himself. "When I came to China, I had no idea I would find you. Do you know what it means to me to see you?"

"I don't know if you can understand this." Her breath steamed in the air. "Everywhere we go we are watched. I have counted up to four cars following us today. Everything we say is listened to, analyzed. Everyone we talk to will undoubtedly be talked to again."

"I can't believe that," David said.

"Why not, David? You think you are some tourist simply visiting a foreign country?"

"Everyone has been welcoming . . . "

"You don't know what you're seeing," she said. She tried to explain that Beijing was a large city but that nearly one million of its habitants were engaged in watching—from the Neighborhood Committee at the domestic level to the behind-the-scenes intrigue at the highest tiers of government. It was the level between those extremes that concerned Hulan most of all.

"Along the roadways, the government employs agents on foot who watch as cars go by. At major intersections, video cameras are mounted to follow cars from place to place. Even if you weren't who you are, even if I weren't who I am, we would be watched. They see us, they listen to us, they tape us, they photograph us. Didn't your government explain that?"

When he said nothing, she continued. "I brought you here without informing anyone of our plan. I wanted to talk without Peter eavesdropping on us."

"I want to talk to you alone too."

"Don't you hear what I'm saying? Peter spies on me. By tonight the car will be bugged and I won't be able to get us away from the listeners and watchers so easily." She took a breath. "I know you think we're getting nowhere, but we've learned a lot. But you have to understand, we're dealing with—"

"The triads," he said, deciding to go along with her for now. "I know that."

"This isn't about the triads."

"I disagree. Everything points to them. The immigrants. The body found on the *China Peony.*"

"But the triads are sophisticated. If they wanted someone to disappear, he would. Why was it so easy to find the bodies of Watson and Guang?"

"I wouldn't say it was easy. I'd say it was an accident, and accidents are how murderers get caught."

Hulan shook her head. "Try looking at this through my eyes. Ask yourself some simple questions. Why was *I* given this case? Why were *you* asked to come here?"

"You already had the case—"

"No! I was assigned to look into Billy Watson's death. I had hardly begun my investigation when I was pulled off of it, and I wasn't involved at all with the disappearance of Guang Henglai. All I knew about that case was what I had read in the newspaper or heard on television."

"But it still makes sense. These murders are connected. As for me, who else would they ask?"

"You don't understand. You don't know what you're seeing."

"All right then. What am I missing?"

Hulan sighed. "Guang Mingyun is a powerful man—"

"I know that," he said impatiently.

"I'm not talking just about money."

"That's what I've been trying to say. Guang Mingyun also has ties to the U.S. You must find it suspicious that he owns the bank where the Rising Phoenix keeps its money."

"Suspicious, perhaps. Conclusive, absolutely not. And besides, that's not what I'm talking about." She wondered how blunt she should be, then decided on: "His kind of power can be dangerous in this country."

"Power corrupts."

"It's more than that, David. He can make things happen. He has strong affiliations with the army, which makes him a very influential man in our government."

"Your point?"

"I'll say it again. You don't know what you're seeing."

David leaned back against the bench. "Then explain it."

"In China, we hide behind etiquette and formality. Even given these extraordinary circumstances, I would have expected to pass through many layers of bureaucracy before meeting Guang in person. Did you notice how he immediately asked if we drank tea? Guang wasn't content with my polite refusal. He continued to press the tea on us. Remember?"

David nodded. It had seemed unimportant at the time.

"The longer this ritual is protracted, the greater the honor bestowed on the guest, which, in turn, reflects on the host. Conversely, when the vice minister offered you nothing, he insulted you."

"I didn't notice."

Hulan smiled. "I know, and I'm sure he didn't like that at all."

"So this whole tea thing tells you what?"

"It tells me that Guang isn't blocking us. He *wants* us asking questions. We wouldn't be here if it weren't for him."

"I guess I botched it," he said after a few seconds.

"It's not your fault, David."

He thought for a moment. "So when you switched to Chinese, what did you say to him?"

"I apologized on your behalf."

"So something else happened that I didn't understand."

She nodded slowly. "Just as we were leaving he asked about my father."

"And?"

"I also asked in which province he bases his enterprises."

"Sichuan, right?"

"My father was imprisoned at a labor camp in Sichuan Province during the Cultural Revolution. Guang was also imprisoned during the Cultural Revolution. It's part of his mystique. I think he was at the Pitao Reform Camp with my father. They must have known each other then."

"I still don't see the problem."

"I didn't know my father and Guang Mingyun knew each other."

"Then why would he tell you that?"

"It was like the tea, a kind of code. It was as though he had stated, 'We have a deeper relationship here.' But what's so strange is that I've never heard of it."

"So he's still hiding something."

"Everyone in this country is hiding something"—Hulan shrugged— "even Ambassador Watson."

"You're changing the subject," he said. He eyed her levelly and waited.

Finally she laughed. "Okay, so *I* botched that one, but there's something about that man I don't like, don't trust."

"He didn't tell us the truth, as *we* know it. But so what? He said himself he's a busy man. He all but told us he wasn't a good father. Listen, I'm sure my own father wouldn't have known the names of my friends in college." But David had had enough of this conversation. "Can't you forget Billy Watson and Guang Henglai for a minute?" She turned slowly to him. Wisps of black hair had escaped her scarf and blew gently across her face. God, she was beautiful, he thought. "What about us?"

Her voice was flat as she said, "You have to forget about that."

"I can't."

"You're married."

"How would you know?" he asked in surprise.

"They put together a file on you. I read it."

"Well, let me tell you something," he said hotly. "They—whoever *they* are—have their facts wrong. I'm divorced."

She looked back across the lake. "It doesn't matter."

"I never stopped loving you." He gently touched her cheek. Her skin colored under his touch.

"All that was a long time ago. I've forgotten about it," she lied. "Soon you will return to the United States. You will go back to your life and I will go back to mine. Those who watch us are mistaken to think otherwise. Come. We must get back before Peter finds us."

But instead of going back the way they'd come, she led him deeper into the park.

He waited for her to speak, then dove in himself. "I don't know why you left me like you did."

"You know why I left." Her words burst forth in a rush. "My father wrote to me and said my mother needed me urgently. We talked about it, David. Don't you remember?"

"We talked about our *both* going to China," he corrected her.

"That was out of the question."

"Why?"

"You thought it would be a vacation, but I knew I'd be acting as a nurse. I saw no reason for you to come here."

"I understood that. Then we agreed you'd be gone for a week or two."

"That's right."

"But that's not how it turned out," he said calmly. He wanted the truth from her, but he was afraid of scaring her into silence. Hulan had always been secretive; he had always questioned her, trying to break through her reserve, to get her to finally reveal herself to him.

"My mother was sicker than I thought."

"You never called." He continued to press her.

"I wrote. I told you."

"That's true. After a month, I got that letter saying you loved me and that your family needed you. How was I to understand from those few words that you weren't coming back?" He hesitated, recalling the arguments he'd had over the years with Jean about his shortcomings. He had come to believe that Hulan had left him for the same reasons. Finally he said, "For years I thought about why you left me. I was so ambitious. I'd made partner and was working eighteen-hour days, out of town on cases for weeks at a time. You used to say I wasn't being true to my goals. Now I can see my failings, but back then I thought I was a walking advertisement for moral rectitude."

"It had nothing to do with that. My mother was sick. That's all."

As the memories came back, he found he wasn't ready to listen to her. "I started to believe that you weren't in China at all. Sure, you'd left on that pretense, but were you really here? After all, you'd rarely talked about your family. You never talked about Beijing. Do you remember the trip we took to Greece?"

He saw her nod and tried to read the thoughts behind her eyes.

"Do you remember that day at the Parthenon?" he asked. "I was reading from the guidebook about Athena and how she had sprung full-grown from the head of Zeus. I said you were like that. You didn't speak to me for the rest of the day. That's what it was like whenever I made a reference to your past or your family. You didn't like to talk about them or China. So when you said you'd gone back to your family, I didn't believe it. I thought you'd simply run off with another man."

She stopped, impulsively grabbed his hand, then just as quickly dropped it. "How could you think that?"

"Because I kept trying to blame someone other than myself, because I was tormenting myself with my belief that I'd done some-thing to drive you away. I held myself responsible. All those times I had tried to talk to you about your past . . . 'Tell me about your father,' I'd say. You'd answer, 'He's in a labor camp.' I'd say, 'Tell me about your mother.' You'd always accuse me of interrogating you. 'I'm not on trial here, David. I'm not guilty of anything. Don't treat me like a witness.' And then you were gone. How many letters did I write to you? You never answered. That was wrong, Hulan."

"I'm sorry. I regret that."

"I thought, I'll fly over there and I'll bring her home. I don't know how many times I applied for a visa. They always turned me down."

"I wish you had come," she said.

He started to reach for her when he heard Peter's voice. "Inspector Liu! Inspector Liu!" David turned to see Peter hustling along the walkway in the company of three other men, one of whom held a walkie-talkie. "I was worried about you, Attorney Stark," the investigator said as he neared them. "We have already had one murder here. We don't want another. You and Inspector Liu should come along back to the car. I know you still want to see Guang Henglai's apartment."

Later, as the Saab sat in midafternoon traffic, David put his gloved hand over Hulan's. She did not pull away.

When the door swung open to Guang Henglai's apartment in the Capital Mansion, Hulan heard David's swift intake of breath. She knew, without even stepping a foot inside, that with its $6,000-U.S.-a-month rental price, it would be vulgar in the extreme. She had already anticipated its excesses, and now as she stood in the doorway, waiting and observing as she always did at a scene, she watched as David moved quickly into the foyer with its glossy black marble floor and smoky glass walls, then disappeared into what she presumed was the living room.

What a shock all of this must be to him, she thought. She could bet that he hadn't expected the elegance of her father's office, the opulence of the China Land and Economics Corporation tower, or the extravagance of this apartment. But these things were nothing compared to the jolt of being thrown together again. She, at least, had prepared herself, but he clearly hadn't known he'd be working with her. But her advance knowledge hadn't stopped her from wanting to say she still loved him, because she did. At the park, she was ready to put her arms around him and press her lips to his. He seemed only too ready to pick up where they'd left off, but how could they? She knew there could never be any hope for them.

What David valued above all else was justice and truth. He left no room for hedging or extenuating circumstances. But just as his strong beliefs were what she loved most about him, they were also what she most feared, because there were so many things she couldn't tell him.

Her truth and his rigid sense of justice would destroy all that had been between them.

Hulan walked to the middle of the living room and slowly turned, taking in everything around her. Guang Henglai had chosen a place that was new, expensive, and cheaply built. Everything inside these walls conveyed extraordinarily bad taste. She was not being critical. This excessive display of wealth was expected of a Red Prince.

Hand-woven rugs of elaborate design were spread beneath her feet. Soft black suede upholstered the furniture. Flashy modern Chinese landscapes hung on the walls.

David stepped into the room. "Look what I found," he said, holding up a set of bankbooks. "I think you'll be surprised at where they're located and how much cash he had stashed away."

She doubted that but didn't say so. Instead, she took the bankbooks from him and fanned them out. Bank of China. Hong Kong National Bank. Sanwa Bank. Sumitomo Bank. East West Bank. Cathay Bank. Chinese Overseas Bank. Citibank. Bank of America. Glendale Federal Savings and Loan.

"All of those banks have branches in the U.S.," he said. "Several of them—East West, Cathay, Glendale Federal—are based in Los Angeles, and the Chinese Overseas Bank, as you know, is owned by the Guang family."

Hulan opened one of the bankbooks. She flipped through the pages, noting deposits and withdrawals of $10,000 here, $20,000 there. She opened another. The same thing. She slipped the books into her bag. "We'll need to take a closer look at these. Compare his deposits with his trips."

"My God, Hulan, Henglai was loaded," he said, amazed at her nonchalance.

"Yes, he was, but remember who his father is. I would expect to see these. If we *didn't* find them, I'd be concerned."

"But they were just lying around . . . "

"This is China. Stealing from a Red Prince would likely be grounds for execution."

David shook his head. She thought, Different culture, different values, different punishments.

"Let's look around," she said.

The kitchen was a spotless panorama of chrome, granite, and modern appliances. She opened the refrigerator, but it had been emptied. She guessed that the Guang family had sent someone over to remove perishables after Henglai's disappearance. The bedroom was another story. His clothes—expensive Zegna suits, Gap jeans, and a nice collection of leather jackets—were stuffed into the closet. The den—again, more leather furniture, this time in sumptuous beige— was messy. Henglai had probably employed a maid, but his personal belongings had been off limits. A few bills, a personal letter or two, and some notes scattered across a mahogany desk.

Above the desk were pinned several photographs. Hulan leaned in to take a closer look. She saw Henglai—painfully young to her eyes— seated at a banquet. His straight black hair flew out rakishly from his head; his arm looped casually over the shoulder of a friend. In another photograph, Henglai posed with Mickey Mouse along Main Street in one of the Disneylands. Several other photos had been taken at a nightclub. Some showed people dancing. In others, Henglai held a microphone and appeared to be singing.

She pulled these photos off the wall and shuffled through them again. Guang Mingyun had been right. She did know Henglai's friends and she knew exactly where to find them.

When they left the apartment, Hulan insisted that Peter drive them back to David's hotel. "You must be tired," she said. "You need to rest for tonight." David objected strenuously. He wanted to go back to interview the ambassador. "We've got to clear up the differences in their stories."

Hulan disagreed. "Ambassador Watson and Guang Mingyun aren't going anywhere. We can see them another time. We need to understand those two boys—who they were, what they did, who they associated with—before we can begin to know their killer."

At ten that evening, Peter picked David up and drove him to the Palace Hotel near the Forbidden City. Unlike most modern edifices in the capital, the hotel's architecture was rich, even excessive, in its use of Chinese motifs. The eaves of the red-tiled roof swept upward.

Bright green, gold, and red paint, gilt, and enamel decorated the ceremonial gate before the circular driveway. The owners of this establishment, the general staff of the People's Army, had spared no expense.

When David pushed through the revolving doors and into the lobby, Hulan was waiting for him. He was dressed in the same suit he'd put on that morning. She, however, had gone home to change. She wore a dress of fuchsia silk cut in the traditional Chinese style. The cheongsam had a high mandarin collar. Frog buttons above Hulan's right breast and under her right armpit held the fabric tight against her body. Her lavender coat draped over her arm.

He followed her as she swayed through the lobby, down a corridor, and into Rumours Disco. They passed several closed doors as they walked down another hallway and into the disco itself. A mirrored ball slowly rotated in the center of the ceiling, casting specks of light on dancing couples. The music was loud, the lyrics in English. Hulan took David's hand and pulled him onto the dance floor. She kept her distance and began to rock slowly from foot to foot. She showed a clumsiness very much at odds with his memories of her. But as David looked around, he noticed that all the dancers had this same awkwardness. The women, he saw, were dressed in miniskirts or tight jeans. The men wore collarless shirts, jeans, and leather jackets. Everyone kept a safe distance from their partners. Their movements were jerky and not necessarily in time to the music.

The song came to an end. In the bored applause that followed, Hulan inclined her head to David and spoke just loudly enough for him to hear. "These are the *taizi*—princelings. You see that man over there?" David followed her gaze. "He was in one of the pictures in Henglai's apartment. See that girl over there?" David looked across the room to a young woman sitting at a table with a tall, icy glass filled with a green drink. "We have her photograph as well."

"Do you know who they are?"

She nodded as a new song blared through the speakers. Strobe lights pulsed to the beat. She began to dance again. An Australian disc jockey began shouting over the loudspeaker as a fog machine sent cool white mist billowing across the floor. They danced for another minute or so with Hulan moving slowly back the way they'd come. David was relieved when they stepped off the dance floor and back onto carpet. He was even more relieved when Hulan sat down at one of the small tables that bordered the dance floor. Just as the thought that Hulan looked stunning tonight floated through his brain, he realized that they were here to be seen. She had dressed not for him but to call attention to her arrival. She had chosen this table because it was prominent.

Hulan's strategy had the desired effect. A hostess came to the table and asked them to follow her. They retraced their steps back down the corridor toward the entrance, stopping at one of the closed doors. The hostess hesitated. Hulan didn't speak. Finally the girl opened the door and the three of them stepped into the room. Cigarette smoke clogged the air, but the smell of American tobacco was clouded by the pungent aromas of perfume and hard liquor. Someone who had been singing stopped abruptly, and the conversation died.

The hostess backed out of the room, closing the door behind her. Even in the tenebrous light, David could see that everyone was looking at them. Still, Hulan waited, saying nothing. Finally, a man dressed from head to toe in leather stood, crossed the room, and said in English, "Inspector Liu, I see you brought with you the American lawyer. We wondered how long it would be before you came to see us."

"There are no secrets in Beijing," she said. "We have no such thing as a windproof wall."

The young man laughed and the others joined in.

"I am Bo Yun," the young man boomed out, bringing a fist to his chest.

"Yes, you are," Hulan said.

Bo Yun and his friends laughed appreciatively. "No secrets, right, Inspector? You know us. We know you. We are all friends."

"We are here to talk . . . "

"Good, good. Come, join us. Sit down. Here, here." Bo Yun took David's arm and led him to the red banquette that ran along the room's perimeter. "What would you like to drink? We have orange juice. We have Rémy Martin. A hundred and fifty dollars U.S. a bottle."

Now that Hulan's eyes had adjusted to the light, she could see perhaps two dozen people in their early twenties lounging on the banquettes. Ashtrays overflowed with cigarette butts. Numerous bottles of brandy and cognac, pitchers of freshly squeezed orange juice, and glasses filled with these drinks littered low lacquer tables.

The *taizi* smiled a lot. They laughed boisterously when their leader made a joke. They wore Rolexes, carried beepers, and at least two were talking on cellular phones. These were the youngest of the Red Princes and Princesses. They were corrupt yet forward thinking. Surveying the room, Hulan began to recall who they were and what they did. Some, of course, didn't work at all. Others had been handed cushy jobs—chairman of a factory, manager of an international hotel, deputy governor of a bank, director of an arts organization.

Once again, Hulan wondered if David understood what he was looking at. He probably saw innocent faces, harmless kids out on the town spending their allowance. He couldn't possibly know the power they wielded or the money they received just through the luck of their birth. The young man who was associated with the hotel was known to charge American businessmen up to $100,000 U.S. for audiences with his father. The young woman seated to David's right was wearing a bracelet worth more than what an entire peasant village might earn in a lifetime.

Between David and Bo Yun sat Li Nan, whose grandfather served on the Central Committee. The Chinese press had not been kind to Li Nan. She was allegedly worth $20 million. She was reputed to have a large collection of American pornographic videotapes with which she stimulated innocent young men. She liked to bathe in champagne. She owned a fleet of classic automobiles but preferred to be driven around the city in a white limousine.

Hulan had recently heard a story about how Li Nan had ordered a hundred-dish "emperor's banquet," featuring such delicacies as camel hump, moose nose, and bear paw. Hulan's co-worker had lavished particular attention on the bear paw. It was one of the eight most precious ingredients in Chinese cuisine; the left front paw was recognized as the most tender and sweet because it was the one that the bear used to extract honey from bees' nests. The meal cost $100,000 U.S., the investigator had told Hulan, and was totally illegal, since the bear meat and several other ingredients were protected by Chinese environmental laws.

This kind of story could circulate only because Li Nan's grandfather had been accused of corruption. Hulan suspected Li Nan, like Henglai and everyone else in their circle, had bank accounts, stocks, and real estate in the United States, Switzerland, and Australia. If Li Nan had any brains, she would understand the old saying—as soon as the guest leaves, the tea becomes cold—and abandon China for her penthouse in New York before her grandfather lost all of his power or his life.

Hulan knew too well that Li Nan and her friends were powerful only in the sense that they had protection. If their father or grandfather died in disgrace, they could lose everything. Even the secure ones would have to wait for the older generation—men in their sixties, seventies, eighties, and nineties—to die before they themselves could assume real power, political power.

"Ning Ning, Di Di, sing us a song," Bo Yun called out. A lovely woman, the daughter of China's most famous opera singer, and a raffish fellow, the youngest son of a general, stood and went to the center of the room. The soft strains of a romantic melody filled the room as a giant video screen lit up with the image of a beach at sunset. A Chinese girl walked in the surf; a Chinese boy sat on a rock nearby. Ning Ning and Di Di each took microphones, then sang of love as the Chinese ideograms appeared at the bottom of the screen.

Bo Yun took a gulp of brown liquid from his snifter. He sank back into the banquette and beamed contentedly. "So, you want to talk about Guang Henglai. What can we tell you?"

"What do you know?" Hulan asked.

"He was rich," Bo Yun said.

"Don't try to be clever," Hulan said. "His father was Guang Mingyun."

"No, I mean *Guang Henglai* was rich."

"Maybe his father spoiled him. He was an only son."

"Henglai made his own money. Don't you know that?"

"How?" David asked.

"He didn't tell us these things."

"Did he have a girlfriend?"

Bo Yun lit a Marlboro. Ning Ning and Di Di were holding hands now, mimicking the lovers on the screen.

"I used to see him," Li Nan said. "But that was over a year ago."

"Anyone else?"

Bo Yun exhaled a great gust of smoke and put a possessive arm around Li Nan's shoulder. "Actually, we didn't see him much anymore. He kind of disappeared after he broke up with Li Nan."

"You mean he wasn't welcome here?"

"No, nothing like that," Li Nan said.

"She's right, you know," Bo Yun agreed. "We all liked Henglai."

"And Billy too," Li Nan added.

"Billy Watson?" David clarified.

"You bet," Bo Yun said enthusiastically. "He was part of our crowd. It's good for us to be friendly with the American ambassador's son."

"For *guanxi*," David said.

"You have learned the ways of our country very quickly," Bo Yun said.

"Guang Mingyun also told us that his son and Billy were friends," David said.

Bo Yun shook his head. "No, no, more than friends. They were business partners. Pretty soon, they are too busy making deals to spend time with us. Between you and me"—Bo Yun leaned forward confidentially—"none of us like to work too hard." He fell back on the cushions and laughed. His friends, once again, joined in.

"What kind of deals? What were they into?" Hulan queried.

"You think they're going to tell us? We might steal their ideas!" Bo Yun chortled. "You know something, Inspector Liu. We are honored by your visit, but you are talking to the wrong people."

"You were their friends . . . "

"*Were*, Inspector Liu. We *were* their friends." Bo Yun addressed the group. "Pour another round. Come on, David—can we call you David in the American way? Come on, David, have a drink with us, maybe sing us a song, and we will tell you who to talk to."

As Ning Ning and Di Di's serenade came to a sorrowful close, Hulan gently laid a hand on Bo Yun's knee. The young man didn't wince or allow his eyes to be drawn to its delicate presence. Instead, he turned to face Hulan, looked her directly in the eyes, dropped his carefree manner, and spoke in an even voice. "I said you are talking to the wrong people. You need to talk to the *Gaogan Zidi* of your generation, Inspector Liu. They know Billy and Henglai. You know how to find those people just as you knew how to find us."

"The Black Earth Inn?"

Bo Yun looked over at David and said, "That is why she is an inspector." Then he brightened again and called out, "Ning Ning, Di Di, another one. Sing us an American song. What's that one? 'Tie a Yellow Ribbon 'Round the Old Oak Tree'?"

A few minutes later, David and Hulan said their good-byes and headed for the lobby. "What kind of business could those two boys have been involved in?" David asked.

"I don't know. It could be anything."

"Smuggling the immigrants?"

"I don't see it, David, but whatever it was probably got them killed."

David thought for a moment, then asked, "What's the Black Earth Inn and how does it fit in?"

"It's a Cultural Revolution–nostalgia restaurant, but all kinds of people go there—Japanese tourists, corporate pirates, even triad leaders. It's a place for people in trouble, people who want to get in trouble, and people who just want to do business. We'll go there tomorrow."

They whisked through the revolving doors and out into the brisk night air. Peter jumped to attention, stubbed out his cigarette, and opened the rear door to the Saab. Hulan extended her hand to David, which he shook without thinking. "I think we accomplished a lot today, Attorney Stark," she said, once again adopting her formal tone. "Investigator Sun will drive you back to your hotel."

"Can't we be alone?" he asked, keeping his voice low so Peter wouldn't hear him. "I want to be with you."

Hulan ignored the desire in his voice. "Investigator Sun will call you tomorrow morning to say what time he'll pick you up." She pulled her lavender coat tight around her, nodded good night, gave a slight wave to Peter, and turned away. David watched the lavender apparition step onto the sidewalk and slowly disappear into the ever-present sea of people.

9

FEBRUARY 1
The Black Earth Inn

A t eleven-thirty the next morning, a Saturday, Peter pulled up
to the three-story Black Earth Inn. At the entrance, the owner
had put up a display of Mao buttons and T-shirts silk-screened with
the Black Earth slogan. That slogan was also rendered as a Cultural
Revolution–style big-character poster on one of the walls: IN THOSE
YEARS OUR SWEAT WAS SPRINKLED ON THE GREAT NORTHERN WILDER-
NESS; TODAY WE MEET AGAIN IN THE BLACK EARTH INN. Unlike the
usual Chinese restaurant, where a single hall might accommodate a
wedding banquet for four hundred, the inn's dining rooms were
small and decorated to resemble rustic log cabins.

The inn catered primarily to the former Red Guard of the Cultural
Revolution—those who had been sent as youths to the countryside for
reeducation in the late sixties and early seventies. The patina of time
and age had tinged their memories with longing for a past where
everyone knew their place and the young felt they were part of something exciting.

David sensed people watching them as he and Hulan followed a
hostess to a table for two. Even he could see just how different the
people in this restaurant were from the *taizi* of the night before.

These patrons were rounder, softer, older—mostly in their forties and early fifties. Their clothes were not showy. The men wore hand-tailored suits, while the women dressed conservatively but expensively. Even on a Saturday, everyone here seemed to be networking, meeting with clients, or making deals.

David suspected that, as she had the previous night, Hulan wanted the two of them to be noticed, and just as they sat down, a man called out, "David Stark! Hello there! Too many years!" The voice sounded vaguely familiar, but David didn't recognize the chubby man who hurried to their table. "David! It *is* you! And here you are with Liu Hulan! Ah, just like old times, no?"

"David, you remember Nixon Chen," Hulan said.

David looked at the man again. He remembered Nixon Chen as a skinny, earnest young lawyer who worried a lot. Here he was, ten years later, plump, happy, obviously well-to-do.

"You're not going to sit here! Come! Come to my table! You'll see some of the old gang!"

Nixon Chen grabbed both of their arms and guided them through the restaurant to a private dining room. The whole time he kept talking. "I hear you are in Beijing! I am thinking the inspector wants to keep you to herself! I am thinking, Hulan forgets that David Stark has other friends in China, that she should arrange a banquet for old times' sake! I am thinking, Hulan always keeps her head in the clouds! She's too busy to think about friends! But no! Here you are! I see you walk past and I think, Ah, that Liu Hulan, she is bringing me our old friend David Stark! Here, you sit next to me. Liu Hulan, you sit there. Everyone, move over, make room for our guests!"

The round table had been set for ten, and now twelve squeezed together. Looking around at the faces, David didn't think he recognized anyone, but he wasn't sure. Nixon Chen wasn't giving him any hints, except that he wasn't switching from English to Chinese. All the while, the other guests were chattering so fast that David could barely catch what they were saying.

"Liu Hulan, too many years!"

"Liu Hulan, we don't see you enough."

"Liu Hulan, come and eat memories."

"So many old friends here," Nixon Chen allowed. "Right, Hulan?"

Hulan nodded.

Nixon turned to David. "We know Hulan since we are all of us children. Did you know that when we were at Phillips, MacKenzie? No?" Nixon laughed good-naturedly. "Well, you know it now!"

The first dishes began to arrive. David had been to plenty of Chinese restaurants, but he'd never seen a meal like this. On the table were placed primitively made ceramic bowls filled with pungent sauerkraut, steaming whole yams, beef tendon stew, and sorghum. Instead of rice, the waiter brought out corn bread and flat peasant loaves. The lazy Susan in the middle of the table spun as the group dipped their chopsticks family-style into the communal dishes.

"You want Peking duck, you go to Sick Duck, Big Duck, or Super Duck Restaurants! You want a meal like what we ate in the countryside during the Cultural Revolution, you come to the Black Earth Inn. They give you all the food of those days. Do you remember, Hulan? How we used to talk all day, all night in the countryside about the special meals we would eat if we ever got home?"

"I remember you always talked about food."

"And look at me today!" Nixon Chen laughed, patting his stomach. "Ten years ago, you never see someone fat like me in China. Today, I am a fat cat, no?" He beamed, pleased that his comment had different yet similar meanings in English and Chinese. "Today we eat our simple meal to bring back old memories. Tomorrow, we go to Laosanjie and order the Educated Youths Reunion Platter. You'll like it, Hulan! It has all those delicacies we craved—shrimp, sea slug, squid, pineapple, bitter melon."

"I'm sorry, Nixon, we are too busy," Hulan said.

"On Sunday?" Nixon shook his head. "You should be taking David to the Great Wall or the Summer Palace, not making him work!" Nixon addressed David. "Liu Hulan never changes, no? I remember when she is a girl. She was always serious. Then we are sent to the countryside. Well, we didn't all go. Some of us here were too young," Nixon said, motioning to some of the others at the table. "But those who were old enough went to the countryside. Not to the same place! Some of us are sent to different provinces, some of us together. Some of us"—he gestured around the table—"we are crying. We are missing our families. We are missing school. We are even missing our teachers!"

"And we are thinking about all the bad things we said in those dark days," interjected one woman. "The things we said against our own parents . . . "

David saw a shadow cross Hulan's face.

Another man positioned his mouth over his plate, spit out a piece of gristle, then asked the group, "Remember when we denounced our teachers as old farts?" He turned to Hulan. "Do you remember that day?" When she didn't respond, he went on. "Mr. Stark, Hulan was only ten years old, but she was the bravest and most eloquent among us. She called Teacher Zho a pig ass. She said that his family was not red. She said he had come from the landlord class and that he lived in a honey jar. She said that to listen to him lecture was to betray our great Chairman. Her words were so strong."

"I remember," said another, "when we went to the commune. Was that two years later?"

"How can you forget?" asked Nixon. "It was 1970. We are sent to the Red Soil Farm. We thought the peasants were making a political statement with that name, but no. The earth was red and dry. For centuries they tried to make that earth yield a crop with no luck. Then they sent a bunch of city kids to 'learn from the peasants.'"

The first woman shook her head at the memory. "We were only twelve years old then. We had struggle meetings every day. Always Liu Hulan stands tall. Always she is firm. She did not allow leniency. She did not forgive even the most minor transgression. You remember that?" the woman asked the table at large. A couple of people nodded appreciatively.

"Our Hulan is named for a famous revolutionary martyr," said Nixon Chen. "But she never speaks of that Liu Hulan. No, she is the one who studies Lei Feng, a bigger hero. She memorizes all of his slogans and can quote his sayings to suit any situation."

"*Eeee*, remember that time? We are all still together at the farm. In the last struggle meeting against our group leader, Liu Hulan stands

up and speaks the words of Lei Feng. She holds up her arm just so."
The speaker raised his arm as if declaiming and continued in a voice
filled with conviction. "'Treat individualism as the cold autumn wind
sweeps the fallen leaves.' That put an end to our group leader's
capitalist-roader activities!"

Everyone except Hulan and David laughed at the recollection.
Nixon Chen wiped tears from his eyes and said, "We also remember
the day Mr. Zai comes to the collective. It is 1972 and your President
Nixon has come to China, but we didn't hear about things like that
on the farm. We are fourteen years old and we have been away from
our families for two years already. We have been working so hard—
up before dawn, working in the fields all day, struggle meetings at
night. We are brown from too much sun. We are dirty and tired and
homesick. One day we are digging up stones from a field and we see a
cloud of red dust coming toward us. Finally a big black car comes
bumping across the dirt. It is Mr. Zai. We know him. He is from one
of the old families. He takes Liu Hulan away. He says she is going to
America to study. We are thinking . . . "

"We are thinking, Hulan, the reddest of us all, is going to
America?" said a woman, whose hair, streaked with gray, was pinned
into a severe knot at the back of her head. "We are thinking—and
remember we are so lonely for home—Liu Hulan has the best *guanxi*
of us all. Then we think, The Chairman must have some great plan.
Hey, Mr. Chen, did you think we too would go to America a few
years later?" The woman picked up a toothpick, then, in the traditional Chinese style, covered her mouth with one hand and went at
her teeth with the other.

"No, Madame Yee, I think we are going to die in those fields . . . "

"Madame Yee?" David asked.

The woman in question laughed, pulling the toothpick from her
mouth and wiped a morsel of food on the edge of her plate. "I didn't
think you recognized me. It's been a long time."

Nixon Chen looked at David with feigned surprise. "You don't
know who we are? Everyone here was an associate at Phillips,
MacKenzie & Stout."

David searched the faces and suddenly began to recognize old friends, but many of them were still strangers—people who must have come to the law firm after he left.

"There are more of us in Beijing, you know," said Nixon. "Whoever can come for lunch comes. Some Saturdays we have as many as thirty attorneys."

"You were in the countryside together *and* at the law firm?" David asked incredulously.

"China, despite our millions, is a small world. It is an even smaller world for the privileged, right, Hulan?"

She didn't answer.

"Madame Yee, Song Wenhui, Hulan, and I were at the Red Soil Farm," Nixon continued. "The others, as I said, were either too young or somewhere else. But yes, we are all from the law firm. Chou Bingan over there only came back from Los Angeles last year. We like to meet and make connections. But"—Nixon's face crinkled in mock disappointment—"we never see our Liu Hulan."

"I never imagined . . ." David said.

"That those scared students Phillips, MacKenzie took a chance on would amount to anything?"

"No, that there were so many of you."

"Today, in Beijing, we look back and think with great fondness on Phillips, MacKenzie. Every year since 1973 they've taken one or two law students as summer associates or full associates. When did you start, Hulan?"

"I started working as a summer clerk my first year in law school."

"In 1980," David said.

"Yes, that's right, because when I came three years later, Hulan was already working full-time as an associate," Nixon said. "She had already been in America for eleven years. She was absolutely fluent in English. She had no accent. She was no longer Liu Hulan, model revolutionary. She was Liu Hulan, almost American! She looked at us like we were fresh off the boat—and we were! Madame Yee came the year after me. Oh, do you remember how she missed her children? It was terrible!"

"Your children," David said, remembering. "How are they?"

"They're all married and working. I'm a grandmother already. One grandson."

"I tell you this"—Nixon reflected—"Phillips, MacKenzie was very smart. The partners thought ahead to changing times and changing business. We came home, and some of us kept our American names and our American ways. Whenever we can, we send work back to them."

"And what do you all do now?" David asked.

Madame Yee was general counsel for a beer company that sold its products worldwide. Mr. Ing worked for Armani's Beijing branch. Two other attorneys were employed by American law firms with branches in Beijing. But none was as successful as Nixon Chen.

"I have sixty lawyers in my office," he announced. "You know what we charge? Three hundred and fifty dollars U.S. an hour. But enough about us. How can we help our old friend?"

"We are looking into the murders of two boys," Hulan said.

"Yes, yes, yes. We know that. They come in here all the time, isn't that so?" he asked the table. His friends nodded. "We are always thinking—no, everyone in this restaurant is thinking—these are young boys. What do they want with a lot of old farts like us? But do we care? Billy has good connections to America. Guang Henglai . . ." Nixon shrugged. "We all need to keep up our fee schedules. We all need to pay salaries. So we are all friendly."

"Did any of you actually do business with them?" When no one answered, Hulan asked, "Do you know what they were into?"

"No," Madame Yee responded.

"Hulan tells me that people from the triads often come here," David said. "Did the boys meet with them?"

"Everyone comes here sometime. The president, Deng's daughter, the American ambassador, your boss," Nixon said, pointing to Hulan, "even the great Guang Mingyun. But the triads? Who knows? We are all honest people here. How do we know what goes on behind closed doors?"

"Everything Nixon says is true," Madame Yee added. "But I saw Billy and Henglai with Cao Hua many times."

The others murmured their agreement.

"I don't know him," Hulan said.

"He's not one of us," Madame Yee continued. "He's our age, but two years ago he owned a stall on Silk Road. Today he has millions."

"How did he make his money?"

"I know your business. You know my business," said Nixon Chen. "This is how China has always been. But today things are different, and Cao Hua was very good at keeping secrets."

"You must know something," Hulan said.

"Is this a friend asking or the ministry?"

"A friend."

"Cao Hua is doing business with the Guang family," Madame Yee said at last. "What it is I truly don't know, but he is traveling a lot. To the United States, to Korea, to Japan. He is very arrogant, very rich. You know the type."

"Is he here today?"

"Cao Hua? He is probably away—"

"In Switzerland, spending his money!" someone finished.

Everyone laughed.

"Where is his office?"

Hulan's old friends laughed again. "Cao Hua has no office!" Nixon Chen explained between breaths. "He is here, he is there. No one pins him to the ground."

"He must live somewhere," Hulan persisted. "I can look it up or you can tell me."

"The Capital Mansion—same floor as Guang Henglai."

10

LATER

Cao Hua's Apartment

I n the car, David brought up a subject that he felt sure was safe to talk about in front of Peter. "Liu Hulan, revolutionary martyr?" he asked. "Why didn't you ever tell me you were named after her?"

"That was just a romantic thing my parents did," Hulan said with the same indifference she'd shown in the restaurant. "It doesn't have much to do with who I am."

She seemed content to leave it at that, but Peter jumped into the conversation. "Inspector Liu is being modest," he said. "We all know the story of the real Liu Hulan and many people try to emulate her. I, like many of us, have memorized her slogans."

"Who was she?"

"She was just a girl who had the misfortune to die at a young age," Hulan said.

"Inspector, she was far more than that! You should tell Attorney Stark about her brave deeds."

When Hulan didn't, David asked, "So? What did she do?"

Again Peter answered. "She was born more than sixty years ago in the village of Yunchouhsi in Shansi Province. Liu Hulan's family was very poor. They poured their blood, sweat, tears, and sorrows into the soil. Hulan worked in the fields under a sun as scorching as a bonfire. When her little sister got tired, Hulan sent her home away from the heat, then continued the work herself." Peter paused, then said, "My parents used to tell that story to my older sister, but she was still mean to me."

Peter then described how Hulan spun cotton to make her own clothes and how she helped her mother with household chores when others went to sleep in the hot afternoons. "Once," he recounted, "when Hulan was picking wild herbs with other village children, the landlord's son tried to scare them away. She stood up to that bully. She said, 'Landlords are fed on rice, flour, fish, and meat, yet we are not allowed to gather wild herbs for food. Well,' she told the boy, 'we are going to!' She was just a girl, but she was not afraid."

An old-fashioned bridal procession of several pushcarts and bicycles loaded with the bride's dowry crossed in front of the car. As Peter waited for it to pass, he caught David's eye in the rearview mirror. "When the Japanese came, Liu Hulan spied on traitors in the village. She learned that it was 'better to die than to become a slave.' When the Kuomintang came, that same slogan was used."

Once the procession was out of the way, Peter turned left into a large parking area. As he pulled up to the entrance of the Capital Mansion, he rushed to finish his story. "One day a Communist soldier came to the village to recover from his wounds. Hulan helped to hide him. She told the other children, 'He has fought and bled for the sake of the people. Now we must take good care of him and feed him as many eggs as we can so he can go back to the front.' One thing led to another, and the two fell in love. It was 1945 and she was thirteen years old."

Hulan told Peter to wait in the car, then she and David headed into the high-rise. At first, the elevator was crowded, but after the fifth floor, David and Hulan were alone. David moved to her, placed his hands on the wall on either side of her head, and leaned into her. She had nowhere to escape, but she wouldn't have tried even if she could. Her black eyes met his.

"So," she said casually, "it seems Billy Watson and Guang Henglai kept secrets from their fathers."

"Ummm" was David's response. He took a strand of Hulan's hair that had fallen across her forehead and moved it delicately from her face. "I don't want to talk about them," he said. "Tell me more about Liu Hulan."

Knowing she could avoid the subject no longer, she said, "There is a saying: 'The revolutionary marches toward the storm.' This is what Hulan did. She went to a training class for female cadres, then she went back to her village and taught the women how to economize in their daily lives. She organized them to make shoes and collect string for the People's Army. Although Hulan was very young, she already knew that these things were not enough. It was important to deal a fatal blow to the enemy, preserve the revolution at all costs, struggle to the bitter end."

Hulan's voice fell to a whisper as David traced a finger along her cheekbone. "The Kuomintang army—growing up we called them the Kuomintang bandits—came closer and closer to the village. At last, they invaded Yunchouhsi. The soldiers demanded that all of the villagers meet in the square. Hulan wanted to hide with a woman who was giving birth, then realized that if they were caught, they'd all be killed. Hulan said, 'If I must die, I'll bear the brunt alone,' and stepped out onto the square."

The elevator slowed to a stop and the doors opened. For a moment, David didn't move, then he pulled away and said with a smile, "After you." They stepped into the stuffy corridor and the elevator closed behind them. Hulan started down the hall, but David held her back. "Finish the story."

"I told you it doesn't matter," she said impatiently.

"Humor me," he said. "Tell me who you are."

She took a deep breath, then continued reciting from memory. "The Kuomintang officer told the crowd that if the person sympathetic to the Communists did not come forward, then many villagers would die. Hulan gave her mother her ring, a handkerchief, and an ointment tin, then, with her head raised, her eyes clear, and her spirit unbroken, she approached the guards. A soldier asked her, 'Don't you regret having to die when you're only fifteen years old?' She responded, 'Why should I be afraid? I won't yield before death. I'll never surrender my mind. I have lived for fifteen years. If you kill me, in another fifteen years I will have been reborn and I'll be as old as I am now.' She strode bravely to the chaff cutter and they cut off her head. Less than a month later, the Eighth Route Army regained control of Wenshui County. Four years later the murderers were caught and punished. Mao Zedong praised Liu Hulan: 'A great life! A glorious death!' Posthumously she was given full membership in the Communist Party."

"Why would your parents name you after someone who came to such a sad end?"

"They didn't see it that way," she answered. "They named me for her because she was resolute in the most difficult and dangerous situations. She was stalwart and empathetic. When I was born, my parents saw a great future for themselves and me in the New China. They hoped I'd have Liu Hulan's zeal and her iron will. I'm afraid that, if anything, I've exceeded their hopes in ways that still shame me."

Before David could ask what she meant, she had turned away and headed down the hall. She stopped in front of Cao Hua's apartment. The door stood ajar. Hulan called out, *"Ni hao, Cao Xiansheng. Ni zai ma?"* She received no response. Hulan gently pressed the muzzle of her gun against the door and it slowly swung open. Before David could react to the weapon, she raised her voice again, inquiring if Mr. Cao was at home. Again only silence. From where Hulan and David stood, they could see only a marble and glass foyer identical to the one in Guang Henglai's apartment. An incongruous odor of skunk, wet dirt, and rust wafted out to them. She stepped through the threshold, and David asked, "Don't we need a search warrant or something?"

"Stay here, David," she responded, ignoring his question. Of course he followed her. Their steps seemed inordinately loud as they crossed the foyer to the living room. Hulan saw it first and instinctively recoiled, backing into David. She turned and buried her head in his chest. For a brief moment, David mistook her action for affection, but when she looked up into his face, he saw that the color had drained from her cheeks and lips.

"Please, David," she quavered. "Go down and get Peter. Don't come any farther." She took a breath to steel herself before stepping into the room. Again, David followed right behind her.

Unlike the excesses of Guang Henglai's apartment, Cao Hua's living room was furnished in Spartan style—a couch, a coffee table, a couple of pictures on the walls. These meager decorations highlighted the morbid display before Hulan and David. Blood splattered in an arc against a wall. The body—she surmised it had to be Cao—sat on the carpet beneath the red arterial spray in a pool of still-wet blood. His head was grotesquely deformed. He had been hit by something hard enough to crack his skull open like a ripe melon. But the killer hadn't stopped at this. He had propped up Cao against the wall with his pulpy head tilted at an improbable angle. His legs were splayed out and his hands decorously laid, palms up, at his sides. Then the killer had slit Cao open from sternum to pubic bone. His intestines had been pulled out and artfully arranged on the floor in the very center of the room.

All of this Hulan absorbed in a fraction of a second. Then her attention was drawn back to David, who was bent over, head down, hands on knees, gasping for air and mumbling to himself. "David, I told you not to come in here."

"What have they done?"

"David, come on. We'll go outside."

"No! I'm all right." He slowly straightened up. As he once again took in the scene, he exhaled, and it came out as something between a sigh and a groan. Hulan watched his jaw muscles tighten and his throat constrict as he fought the impulse to vomit.

"David," she said, putting a hand on his arm. "Look at me." He turned his face to hers, but his eyes remained on the monstrous spectacle. "David," she said sharply. "Look at me!" She could see the horror in his eyes. "You have to get Peter. Tell him we need help. Go."

He staggered away. Hulan knew she had only minutes alone with the body. Slowly she skirted the blood and the intestines. She edged close to the wall and examined the bloody splash. It, too, was wet. She fought a wave of fear as she realized that the killer might still be in the apartment. She remained immobile, stretching her senses. The apartment was dead quiet. Either the killer was here—waiting, watch-ing—or he had just left.

Carefully but quickly, she retraced her steps, hoping to get to the hallway and begin a search of the building but guessing that it was too late. By the time she reached the door, David and Peter were there. Peter had his gun out. When he saw the intestines on the floor, the air wheezed out of him. "*Aiya!*" His voice was filled with wonder.

David watched as Peter and Hulan spoke in Chinese. They seemed to be arguing about something. Peter kept gesturing at the intestines while Hulan nodded and spoke softly, smoothly. David forced himself to look at the grotesque mess again as the two Chinese talked. Finally Peter jutted out his chin in disgust and left. As soon as he was gone, David said, "Hulan, I think the intestines have been made into some kind of a design."

"Not a design, David. It's a character."

"A character? What does it mean?"

"Let's not talk about it now. We don't have much time before the others get here."

"No! I want to know now!" Her tranquillity infuriated him. "Don't keep me in the dark. Tell me."

"The Chinese language . . . "

"I don't want a lecture!"

"The Chinese language," she began again, "is very complex, and the Chinese people like wordplay. For example, the word for *fish*—*yu*—sounds like the word for *prosperity*, so we eat it as one of the cele-bration dishes at Chinese New Year. In paintings, you often see a vase or a bottle because that word—*ping*—sounds the same as *peace* or *safety*. Similarly, Deng Xiaoping's name means 'little peace,' but it sounds the same as 'little bottle.' When Deng was coming back to power, the people sent a message of support to the government by placing little bottles around the city."

As David stood there listening to her, he remembered how much Hulan loved the complexity of Chinese. He also recalled she often used pedantry as a way of deflecting his probing questions.

Hulan put a hand on his arm. Her face twisted with worry. "David, are you listening? Are you all right?"

Feeling the warmth of her hand, hearing the concern in her voice, David smiled wanly. "I'm fine. Go on."

"The killer," she said, "has used a double meaning here. The word for intestines is *chang*, which has the same sound as the word for *flavor* or *taste*. The killer has written the character for *flavor* with the intestines. This is a message, a warning, to us. I believe the murderer is giving us a 'taste' of what is to come."

Side by side, their shoulders touching, they stared down at the bloody calligraphy.

Soon the local police arrived, as did Pathologist Fong. They did their jobs—securing the scene, examining the body, taking photographs, interviewing neighbors—amid much animated oohing and aahing over the intestinal message. While these men worked, David and Hulan searched the apartment.

Hulan assumed that the killer had known that they were coming, that he had gotten so involved with the creation of his artwork that he hadn't had time to remove evidence. She opened drawers and found bankbooks and a passport. She peeked in the refrigerator and found only a few Giant Panda Brand herbal remedies; she checked the closet and found a box of tourist T-shirts made by the Glorious Cotton Company. David tried to look at the scene as his FBI agent friends had told him to. The MO was certainly different from the other murders, but a stage had clearly been set. As Noel Gardner had predicted, the murderer was flaunting not only his own work but also his knowledge of David and Hulan's movements.

They met in the kitchen. "Take a look at these, David," she said, handing him the passport and bankbooks she'd found. As he opened the passport, she said, "He was traveling to L.A. about once a month."

"Just like Henglai."

"That's right," she said. "And look at those bankbooks. I don't have Henglai's with me, but aren't these deposits in the same amounts as his?"

David leafed through the pages and thought she was right. "Why is all this money in L.A.?"

She looked around. The others were in the living room with the body. "There's so much uncertainty in the government," she said in a low voice. "People like to keep their money safe."

"But how do we know this money is coming *from* China? This could all be U.S. money."

"If that's the case, where's *that* money coming from?"

"That's the question," he said. He took her elbow. "Come and look at this." He led her to the door of the living room. A couple of investigators dusted for fingerprints. Pathologist Fong was hunched over the body. "What makes this murder different from the others?"

She looked at the guts on the floor and the arterial arc against the wall. "It's bloody?" she ventured.

"It's more than bloody," he said. "It's flamboyant."

"We still don't know what killed Billy and Henglai," she cautioned. "For all we know, their murders were flamboyant, too."

David considered that possibility. "Yes, the blackened teeth, the dissolved innards. Neither of our pathologists could determine what killed those boys, though. Is there some poison your people haven't thought of? I'm talking about something esoteric, something uniquely Chinese, something *flamboyant*."

"There's Chinese herbal medicine," she said doubtfully. "But it *is* medicine."

"Medicine can be toxic if used incorrectly."

"David, you could be right!" She grabbed his arm. "Come on. There's someone we should see."

She left orders with the other investigators, said a few last words to Pathologist Fong, rounded up Peter, then took one last look at the scene to commit the details to memory. In the elevator, she told Peter they'd be going to the Beijing Chinese Herbal Medicine Institute. "My parents are great believers in traditional Chinese medicine," she explained to David. "My father says that Dr. Du is the seventh-best Chinese herbal medicine practitioner in the whole country."

Like most older buildings in China, the six-story institute had no heat. The floors were swept but hadn't been washed perhaps ever. The walls had been painted a long time ago and were marred by fin-

gerprints, gashes, liquid stains, and who knew what else. The building itself was made from cast concrete, and David, being from
Southern California, hoped that there wouldn't be an earthquake.
This was just the kind of structure that would sandwich in on itself at
about six on the Richter scale.

There were no directories or signs. David and Hulan walked
down one corridor and saw no one. They turned down another corridor and all of the doors were shut. Finally Hulan poked her head into
a couple of patients' rooms to ask for Dr. Du. In these moments,
David saw the differences between Chinese and American concepts of
convalescence. At the institute, the rooms were outfitted with simple
steel-frame beds. The sheets looked clean but old and soft from
repeated use. The down quilts—with their faded colors and patched
areas—looked like they'd been used for decades. In room after room,
relatives gathered around the sickbeds, talking, laughing, and eating
from steaming bowls filled with noodles or rice and vegetables.
Guests and patients wore sweaters or padded jackets to guard against
the brisk temperature of the hospital.

At last David and Hulan found a nurse who told them that the
doctor was in his office on the top floor. The elevator didn't work, so
they walked up the six flights. Up there were the consultation offices,
and in each of these a doctor sat behind a desk. Some appeared to be
taking the pulse of a patient, others just sat with their hands folded in
front of them, waiting for customers. Hulan and David reached the
office of Dr. Du, where diagrams of the human body outlining its
acupuncture meridians covered the walls. The curtains on the windows were torn and faded.

Dr. Du, a round little man, stood to greet them. His full cheeks
were made more so by sideburns that came down almost to his jaw-
line. Circles under his eyes hung on his face like half moons. When
Hulan introduced herself, Dr. Du smiled warmly and asked after her
mother. Then, for David's sake, Dr. Du switched to English. "I have
been to the United States many times," he said, "to visit Chinese medicine colleges and to speak at your universities. I have also been to
Disneyland and Mount Rushmore. Have you been to those places?"

When David said he hadn't been to Mount Rushmore, Dr. Du

pulled out a few snapshots. While David looked at them, Hulan explained why they were there. When she was done, Dr. Du addressed David. "You are right. Many of our herbs and minerals are very dangerous if used in excess. You take something like cinnabar. You know it sedates the heart and calms the spirit. You think, I will take extra. The next thing, you are very sick, maybe dead, because cinnabar contains mercury. You know ginseng? You can buy this anywhere—even an American drugstore, no? You think, This will help my longevity. This will make me more of a man. You take it home, cook it in a little water, and drink a lot. Next thing, you have a bloody nose. The life is coming *out* of you, not going *into* you."

"If you wanted to kill someone very quickly," Hulan asked, "what would you use?"

The old doctor clapped his hands together as he realized they'd come to him on MPS business. "You want me to help you! I like this! We must have tea, and I will think." He called out to the hallway and a young woman came in, poured tea into stubby waterglasses, and backed out of the room. Dr. Du asked about the victims' general physical makeup.

"They were both men in their early twenties."

Dr. Du shook his head sadly. "So young for death, no?" Then he asked, "Did your labs check for realgar? Do you know this word? We call it Male Yellow. The active ingredient is arsenic."

"I'm sure they checked for that," Hulan said.

"Can you tell me the condition of the bodies?" Dr. Du asked.

As Hulan gave a clinical synopsis, the doctor stood and paced. Suddenly he stopped. "I know! I have it! We have a beetle in China that's very poisonous. Our beetle is black with yellow stripes. You have it in the West, too. We call it *ban mao*. You call it by three different names—myalbris, cantharides, or, the most common name, Spanish fly."

"The aphrodisiac?" David asked.

"Could be that, could be for skin fungus, muscle pain, or maybe a tiny bit fried with rice for cancer treatment. But you take only thirty milligrams"—Dr. Du pinched the end of his pinkie to show just how small a dose that would be—"and you are dead."

"Symptoms?"

"Just what you have told me. Stomach hemorrhage, kidneys and liver melt away. Very painful. You hope you die! And who knows *ban mao*? The body comes in and it is in ugly chaos. Only a very fine doctor, maybe only ten doctors in all the world, would understand what they were looking at."

"And you'd know from the damage to the organs?"

"No, no, no." Dr. Du wagged his finger back and forth as a small smile appeared at the corners of his mouth. "I would know because the teeth and nails would turn black."

"Just like Billy's and Henglai's," David said.

Dr. Du's full face broke into a broad smile and he once again clapped his hands in delight.

Hulan and David's next stop was the Ministry of Public Security and a visit to Section Chief Zai. Despite his title, Zai's office was as simple and unprepossessing as Hulan's. He listened gravely as Hulan described finding Cao's body, the subsequent discovery of his monetary records and passport, and the recent visit to Dr. Du. Occasionally, Zai shifted his attention to David, observing his reactions. Hulan had been warned not to let the big nose see anything unpleasant. A body with its guts spread across the room clearly violated this mandate.

"We have followed the information given to us," Hulan explained. She related their interviews with Ambassador Watson and Guang Mingyun. When she mentioned that Guang Mingyun and her father may have been in the same prison camp in Sichuan Province, Zai didn't seem particularly impressed. "Yes, your father and Guang Mingyun were at Pitao together. I was sent there, too, you know. Of course by then they had already left."

To David's eyes, Hulan appeared embarrassed by this last detail. "We now know that the boys' lives were definitely intertwined," she hurried on. "Cao Hua was my last hope for a free word. If we want more information, we will have to use alternate methods."

"But the princes are not used to those," Zai observed.

"I know, that's why we came to you. Does the ministry want us to go back to the *Gaogan Zidi*? Do you want us to go back to the American ambassador?"

"Let's think about the money," Zai suggested. He turned to David. "Financial crimes are a new phenomenon in China, so we are not always prompt in spotting them. We can contact the Bank of China, which is the main commercial bank of our country. I am sure that officials there will cooperate and give us details on these two accounts."

For the second time today, David asked, "Don't you need a warrant?"

"The bank is state owned," Zai said matter-of-factly. "We are entitled to that information."

"Besides, we don't have search warrants," Hulan added.

"But I am less concerned with what we will find in the domestic accounts," Zai continued, "than with where the money was going when it left our country. Could they have been playing with exchange rates?"

"They would need connections at the bank to do that," Hulan said skeptically.

"You're right. I don't think that would happen. Too many people watching, too many official seals to obtain. They couldn't move quickly enough."

"And that kind of corruption brings a death sentence," Hulan reminded him.

"I do not think the hooligan is afraid of the consequences. This is what worries me."

"Why is that?"

"Why?" His tone showed surprise. "Too much profit is being made. By whom we don't know. But we have already had three murders, Inspector. The question is not who do you interview next, but should you continue at all? These murders are terrible, but you have done your best. As for Attorney Stark—he is a lawyer. He is not an investigator. He came to China to help us, and he has. But perhaps we must accept the fact that the killer is too smart for us. He is probably triad—too clever, too slippery to be caught."

"I didn't come all this way to look the other way," David interrupted.

"The killer has done you the courtesy of giving you and Inspector Liu a warning. I don't think you will get a warning the next time."

"You're right. I'm just an attorney, not a professional investigator. I'm not immune to the horror of death. But I can tell you that you're wrong to walk away from this."

Zai considered, then asked, "What would you do, Mr. Stark?"

"From their passports we know Cao and Guang were going to L.A. regularly. We also know they kept large sums of money there. I want to know why, and I want to know how Billy was involved. I think that if we follow the money, the lives—and deaths—of those three will become clear."

"Follow the money," Zai mused, then considered. "Yes, yes, you are correct. This is exactly what you must do."

"But that means going to California," Hulan said.

"This is true, but you will be out of the way. I think you will both be safe there. Come," he said, standing up. "We must talk to your father."

David was surprised at who that turned out to be. But even now that the connection had been made, there still was no proper introduction or anything in the conversation—either in words or emotion—that would convey that Vice Minister Liu was Hulan's father. Instead, as Hulan and Zai ran through the details of the case, the wiry man simply listened, puffed on his cigarette, and jotted down a few notes. When they finished, silence filled the room. Smoke from the vice minister's Marlboro curled up around his face. He tapped his note pad with his pencil. Finally he said tersely, "You may go."

"We ask the vice minister to please take this information under consideration," Zai said, and for the first time David heard the supplication in the man's manner.

"I am saying she may go. To America," Liu amended. "I am relying on you, Section Chief Zai, to make the arrangements quickly. The sooner this case is over, the better for our two countries."

That evening when Liu Hulan got back to the *hutong*, she immediately went to the home of Neighborhood Committee Director Zhang Junying. Hulan informed her old friend and observer that she would be gone for a few days, but Zhang Junying had already been made aware of this and offered to go back to the Liu compound to take away any perishables. "To waste food," the old woman cackled later as Hulan handed her a bag of fruit and vegetables, "is to mock the blood and sweat of peasants." As Hulan escorted Zhang Junying to the outer gate of the Liu compound, the old woman took her arm and squeezed it tightly. Madame Zhang's eyes filled with tears. "We have always been close to your family. Things happened in the past—this I won't deny—but I always had respect for the Liu clan."

"Don't worry," Hulan said. "I will come back."

"In time for Spring Festival?" Madame Zhang asked querulously.

"I promise."

Hulan watched as the old woman, bundled in a padded pea-green Mao suit, hobbled down the alleyway and out of sight. Hulan went back inside. The early rituals of Spring Festival—the celebration of the lunar new year—were just days away. Hulan spent a few minutes putting together an altar to commemorate her ancestors. She arranged a few oranges on a plate, placed sticks of incense in a bronze pot filled with sand, then set out a few framed photographs and painted minia-tures of long-dead relatives. This done, she made a pot of tea and began packing. For the first time in many years, she allowed herself to feel deep regret, sorrow even. If only there were a way to turn back time, to go back and repair the damage, to set events on a different trajectory.

These thoughts were interrupted by a knock at the door. She had been expecting it and opened the door without a second thought. Without waiting for an invitation, he entered in his usual way. He eased himself onto one of the stools that ringed the kitchen table. His hand felt the side of the teapot. It was hot. By the smell, he knew she had selected his favorite tea. She pulled out two ceramic cups. As he poured, she sat down opposite him. Here, under the bright overhead light, she saw the coldness in his eyes. His voice—so familiar to her—was harsh and unforgiving.

"Tomorrow you leave," Section Chief Zai said. "Of course, you have been away in America before. You came back when you were asked. This time, we won't ask you to come home. We expect you to return. Do you understand?"

"Yes."

"It is my responsibility to caution you. Our country has come a long way since you first left us. Today we have eyes and ears in many places, not just China. We will know if you do or say anything to embarrass our country. We will know if you try to contact dissidents, reporters, or other groups that do not give China the proper respect. We will know if you try to defect. We most certainly will know if you try to give away any state secrets."

"I would do nothing to harm China," she said.

"Liu Hulan, you have many people that you love. Your mother, your father, this David Stark." He held up a hand. "Do not try to deny it. This is your weakness. You know it. I know it."

"I have never been able to argue with you," she admitted.

Zai ignored her comment.

"You have been very lucky. You have had many opportunities. You have always had connections. You have had friends who looked out for your safety. But this is a different situation. A wrong move and *you* could lose your residency permit. You could have a note put in *your* personal file. *You* could be sent to the countryside. You could be lost to the world and spend the rest of your days as a peasant. You could die a stooped old woman at the age of fifty—without a husband, without children, without any family at all."

Zai took a last sip of tea and stood. He put a hand on her shoulder. "As you travel, I hope you will remember this conversation. Good-bye, Hulan."

11

February 2
Los Angeles

Four days after he arrived in China, David was back at Beijing
International Airport. Four days, and David's senses still had
not adjusted to the strangeness that the terminal presented. The light-
ing remained portentously dim. The rooms—painted a dull green—
were characteristically cold, and the smell of wet diapers and noodles
filled the air. In the area for outgoing travelers, little kiosks offered
magazines, candy, cigarettes, and last-minute curios—stuffed panda
bears, cheap jade chopsticks, silk scarves. Everywhere he looked, as it
seemed everywhere he'd looked throughout Beijing, he could see soldiers—some on leave, others serving as guards.

Typically, David was not allowed to explore the airport. He
waited instead with his delegation in one of the lounges. The group
was led by Section Chief Zai, who spoke about the duty of his comrades as they traveled to the United States. "Today we are proud of
you, Investigator Sun, for accompanying Inspector Liu Hulan to a
faraway land. We are confident that you will find triumph there.
Your families anticipate your victorious return." Then for two hours
they waited—Zai and Peter chain-smoking Red Pagoda cigarettes—
for the fog to clear.

On the plane, David and Hulan sat together. Peter sat across the aisle. He was exuberant, smiling, chattering happily to his seat companion.

MPS agents never went abroad alone, Hulan explained. They usually traveled in threes and fours. But since she had returned from the United States before, the MPS had assigned only Peter to watch her. So it seemed that once again David and Hulan were to have no privacy.

For the first five hours, as they flew to Tokyo, David and Hulan spoke in hushed voices of casual matters, always aware of Peter just across the aisle. In Tokyo, Peter wanted to go to the duty-free shop and left David and Hulan to watch the coats and carry-on bags. As soon as he disappeared into the crowd, David took Hulan's hand. They sat with their eyes focused on the door to the duty-free shop.

During the second leg of the flight, David bought Peter a beer. The young investigator picked at his meal, then settled back to watch the first movie. By the time Peter dozed off, Hulan's head had tipped onto David's shoulder. He could smell her hair. He could feel the warmth of her arm and thigh radiating through her clothes, then his clothes, onto his skin. He felt the swell and release of her body against his as she breathed. It was exquisite, forbidden, and completely comfortable. He, too, closed his eyes and drifted off. In this way, they crossed the Pacific Ocean and the international date line.

Several hours later, David woke up, sensing that someone was staring at him. He looked across the aisle and met Peter's grim eyes. David pushed gently with his shoulder and Hulan shifted away from him, her head falling to the other side. Peter nodded expressionlessly, then turned back to the screen at the front of the cabin.

The familiarity of his surroundings began to have an effect on David. Now, flying above the ocean, with the credits for the second American movie rolling, the American flight attendants quietly passing down the aisle inquiring if anyone needed anything, and the fatigued American passengers stretched out or nestled together in their seats, David was suddenly able to see things much more clearly. He knew that finding Hulan again after so many years had impaired his judgment. As a result, he hadn't paid enough attention. When he'd walked down the streets in Beijing, distracted by the smells and bustle, it was as though he had forgotten how to observe, how to analyze, how to zero in on deceit.

"What are you thinking?" Hulan asked.

"I thought you were asleep."

"I was." Her groggy look melted into pleasant surprise. "I think I felt you wake up." He took her hand again under the blanket. "So what were you thinking?"

"How much I feel like I've—we've—not been in control of this case."

"What do you mean?"

"You're assigned to the murder of Billy," he began. "Two weeks later, I find the body of Henglai. A coincidence, right?"

"Right."

"But after that everything seems so planned. This guy, Patrick O'Kelly from the State Department, comes to the office and tells me that the Chinese have requested my presence. He gives me a diplomatic invitation signed by Section Chief Zai. But once in China, as you pointed out, there was no official reception, no sense that anyone actually wanted my help."

"No one wanted my help either," Hulan reminded him.

"But you can see that our governments are saying one thing, but their intent is very different."

"I think that's a stretch."

"I have more. I didn't react well to discovering Guang Henglai. Well, who would? But I think that knowledge—like so much other information—was passed on, so that the murderer or murderers knew to go out of their way to create the gruesome spectacle of Cao Hua. Someone somewhere wanted to throw me, and it worked." He paused, thinking how to broach his next concern. Finally he said, "How do you explain the fact that we were assigned to work together?"

"It was a coincidence. You found Henglai . . . "

"I'm sorry, but I can't shake the feeling that our meeting was strategized as meticulously as a move in a chess game. Someone reckoned on my brain being fogged by the sight of you, by your physical proximity, by the feel of your head on my shoulder as you sleep on this plane."

"I'm sure people know about us. We both work for government entities. It's their job to know our private lives."

He watched her face as he asked, "Why didn't you tell me that Vice Minister Liu was your father?" He was not surprised to see a hooded look come over her features.

"I thought you knew," she said evenly. "We share the same last name after all."

"Hulan . . . "

"I think you're right about being watched," she continued, ignoring him. "Of course I told you that"—she lowered her voice—"Peter was watching us. I hope you believe that now. But do you think you were being observed in L.A.?"

David deliberated. He could push her or let her have her way for now. He decided on the latter course.

"I think I've been watched since I boarded the helicopter to fly out to the *Peony*. How? Zhao, one of the immigrants on the ship, implied that the crew knew that the Coast Guard and the FBI were coming. But consider this. It's not just Peter watching us. The killer knew we were going to visit Cao Hua."

"Do you think we've met the killer during our interviews?"

"Maybe. Or maybe he has an informant."

"We've spoken to a lot of people." Hulan weighed the possibilities. "It could be anyone from Rumours or the Black Earth Inn."

"Or Peter."

Hulan glanced over David's shoulder to her subordinate. Peter? Could he be that corrupt?

"What was it you said?" David asked. "That there are no secrets in China? All I'm saying is that everyone we talked to seemed to know we were coming. So of course the killer—or killers—would know we'd show up at Cao's apartment when we did." He sighed. "All this leads back to the ultimate question: Who? Everywhere we look seems to take us further away from the triads, but I still think that everything that's happened has been orchestrated by the Rising Phoenix."

When Hulan shook her head, David said, "I know you have a lot of resistance to their involvement, but only they would have enough eyes and ears to get so much information and to be in so many places at once."

"Anyone could pay for those things. All it takes is money."

"It keeps coming back to that, doesn't it?"

Hulan nodded. He squeezed her hand and smiled. For the first time in days, David felt he was regaining his equilibrium, and it felt good.

Given the time change, they arrived in Los Angeles on the same morning they had left China. Jack Campbell and Noel Gardner waited for David and the Chinese delegation at the top of the ramp leading from the Customs area to the public terminal. Introductions were made all around, then the FBI agents hustled them through the terminal to the curb, where they piled into a van.

When they left Beijing that morning, the day's high was expected to be eighteen degrees. Now, as they prepared to live February second over again, the weather promised to be a perfect seventy-five degrees. A mild Santa Ana had blown away the winter storms. The sun shone. The sky was cloudless, the air clear. Technically it was still winter, but this far south spring was in full bloom. Bright shocks of magenta, pink, red, and orange bougainvillea covered trellises on houses and office buildings. The wild purple of morning glory spread across the occasional garage or vacant lot.

As the van sped north on the San Diego Freeway, Peter gawked at the variety and quantity of cars sweeping—without honking or abrupt swerves—along the wide, clean stretch of asphalt. The young investigator pointed out billboards that flanked the freeway. David himself looked at these as though he were seeing them for the first time and was struck by the voluptuousness of the female models, the tanned brawn of the men, the perfect smiles of both sexes.

Jack Campbell seemed in fine spirits, instantly establishing a rapport with Peter. "Well, Investigator Sun, this is what we call a freeway. You know those car chases in the movies? This is where they film them. See those trees over there? Palm trees. You have those in your country?"

Without waiting for an answer, Campbell continued. "The FBI doesn't often get visits from Chinese law enforcement officers, so, in addition to our work, we've planned some activities. Disneyland. Universal Studios. That sort of thing."

"We don't think you'll want to put in a full day today," added Gardner. "It's Sunday after all, and you must have jet lag."

"Right," Campbell concurred. "I figure—if it's okay with you, Stark—we'll go down to your office. Madeleine Prentice and Rob Butler have arranged to be there to meet our Chinese friends. Then we'll take some time to talk. We have a lot of catching up to do. Hey!" he asked suddenly, looking in the rearview mirror to Peter. "You following me? Federal courthouse. Meet the boss. Talk about the case. Got it? Good! Then tonight Special Agent Gardner and I have made reservations for dinner. Not the kind of place we would usually go, but it will give you a feel for local color. Then we'll take you back to your hotel. Tomorrow, what do you say we go kick some ass?"

After parking in the underground garage across the street from the U.S. Attorney's Office, Campbell continued to play the host with enthusiasm. As they rode up the escalator to the plaza, he asked Peter if he'd ever seen an underground garage before (he hadn't), if he'd ever been on an escalator (he had), if he liked fast food (he enjoyed McDonald's).

In the elevator, Campbell asked if the Chinese cops had a lot of security in their headquarters, but at this Peter clammed up. He wasn't supposed to answer questions that might be construed as giving away state secrets to the FBI, which was exactly what Campbell had been trying to ascertain through his good-natured chatter. Instead, Peter spoke softly to Hulan. Campbell gamely asked Hulan what they were talking about. She gave him a cryptic look. "Investigator Sun says you talk a lot for a black ghost."

As they got off the elevator and David unlocked the security door, he reflected that Campbell's interrogation technique—be friendly, ask lots of innocuous questions, then slip in a lulu every once in a while—was exactly by the book. Peter, in turn, was doing what David had learned in the last few days the Chinese did best—never answer a direct question unless the answer was meaningless.

Jack led them down the hall to Madeleine's office. Here again David saw the hallway, the few attorneys getting ready for tomorrow's court appearances, even Madeleine's office, through fresh eyes. How different this was from the Ministry of Public Security with its drafty corridors, its usually dark and austere furnishings, and the sense among its denizens that others were watching and listening all the time. What had always seemed to David utilitarian and bland now appeared light and fresh. Open doorways suggested a convivial atmosphere; there were no secrets between these colleagues.

Madeleine and Rob greeted them. Handshakes all around, more platitudes about the two countries working together, then an exchange of gifts. David was surprised at how well prepared Madeleine, Rob, and the Chinese were for this visit. Here were Rob and Madeleine giving Department of Justice T-shirts, Jack and Noel handing out FBI lapel pins and baseball caps, and the Chinese presenting red and gold plaques for all. More handshakes. More nodding. More smiles and pats on the back. Then they were swept away to a conference room.

The FBI agents had done a miraculous job getting things ready. David's charts balanced on easels. New pieces of chalk lay in the blackboard's well. Two computer terminals sat at opposite ends of the long table. A tray of sandwiches, soft drinks, and a basket filled with assorted chips occupied the top of a credenza. "I hope you don't mind, Stark, but I took the liberty of setting things up in here," Campbell explained sheepishly. "We'll have more room to spread out and we can eat lunch while we work."

There was nothing to do but plunge in. For Campbell and Gardner, David gave a brief recap of his trip to China, ending with the visit to Dr. Du. As soon as he finished, Campbell said, "We've got every high-tech forensics computer in the world back in Washington. If those kids were killed with Spanish fly, our boys will find it."

David then moved to the easels. He looked at Hulan and Peter.

"We've talked to a lot of people, but I'm still convinced this is all going to tie back to the triads. I don't know how much you know about them—"

"We know a lot," Hulan immediately interrupted. "The history of the secret societies, as we call them, began two thousand years ago with a group called the Red Eyebrows. In the mid-1300s, the White Lotus helped to position the rulers of the Ming dynasty. But what we consider the first modern triads date to 1644, when the Mongols invaded China, overthrew the Mings, and established the Manchu dynasty."

"In the south, where I am from, the people did not want to kowtow to the Manchu rulers," Peter said in his lightly accented English. As he spoke, David understood that both Peter and Hulan would not be passive observers on this trip. They had information and they wanted to share it. "Imperial warriors went to a monastery to kill the last of the monks, who were brave in martial arts and fierce in battle. They were loyal members of what seemed to be the last remaining secret society and were dedicated to overthrowing the corrupt Manchus. After the attack, only five monks were left alive. These men went on to establish the Heaven and Earth Society. Today all triads—hundreds of them around the world—trace their beginnings to those five monks."

"We know you want to speak to us about the evil ways of the secret societies," Hulan said, "but I hope you will understand that these groups have been important to the history of China, Hong Kong, even Taiwan."

"People had a hard time living under the Manchus," Peter continued. "The people looked to the triads for justice against criminals, to settle disputes, to loan money."

"And in the United States," Hulan picked it up again, "if you know your history, the triads—*tongs*, as they were called here—helped the Chinese immigrants who came to work on your railroad. I'm sure you've heard them called hatchet men, and yes, they used hatchets as weapons when they fought over territory and possessions. But the triads also fed immigrants when they were too poor to buy food. They helped men when they got in trouble with the law. When a sojourner died, they sent his bones home to China for a proper burial."

But Peter was impatient to tell his part of the story. "Once the Manchus fell, Dr. Sun Yat-sen—you have heard of him?—fled to the United States. He was a member of different secret societies from the time he was a teenager. By the time he returned to China to become the president of the Republic, he was a senior in the Chung Wo Tong Society and the Kwok On Wui Society of Honolulu and Chicago."

"But we have no affection for the triads," Hulan clarified. "Sun Yat-sen and his successor, Chiang Kai-shek, allowed the triads to do as they wished. They extorted money from the poor, put women into prostitution, and sold drugs to the people. They were gangsters who did their best to kill Communist leaders. Eventually, as you know, Chiang and his criminal friends fled to Taiwan."

Though they did indeed know much of this history, the three Americans kept quiet; Campbell and Gardner because they were still sizing up the Chinese, and David because he was intrigued by the mixture of awe and disdain these Chinese agents had for the triads. Did Hulan really consider the Kuomintang and Taiwanese to be criminals, or was she saying that for Peter's benefit?

But there was something else as well. These people were changing before David's eyes. Peter was having a good time sharing his expertise, and the reserve that had appeared to shroud Hulan permanently was now falling away from her shoulders and face. She no longer averted her eyes from his in front of others; she no longer held back.

David refocused on Hulan as she said, "Even today the triads pose a threat to China. At the MPS, we have determined that the greatest threats to domestic tranquillity are terrorism, narcotics, corruption, and illegal emigration. The triads are involved in all of these activities. But this is not all."

Hulan chose her next words carefully. "We are at a cusp in China. Deng Xiaoping, our paramount leader, is old. No one knows what will happen when he dies. Our government believes that the country will go on as before. After all, Deng has already picked his successor. But we must be prepared for other eventualities."

"Such as?"

"Some say his death could bring back the warlords. Some say China could disintegrate in much the same way that Russia has. Others predict that a new leader will come from the provinces. But there is yet another possibility. As I have already pointed out, the triads have found their greatest strength in times of political unrest. We understand that you are worried about the influx of triad members to Los Angeles after Hong Kong rejoins China. But we are worried that upon Deng's death, the triads will grab that opportunity to solidify their positions in China. They are rich, they are many, and their *guanxi* are undeniable."

"Now that we're finally being frank, Inspector, why haven't you discussed these issues with me before?" David asked.

"Because, unlike you, I don't believe that the triads are involved in these murders. Look at the facts. All three murders took place in China. We have nothing to connect those deaths to triad activity in the U.S. except that Guang Henglai was found on board the *Peony*."

"And the money."

"Perhaps the money. Can you tie the money back to the Rising Phoenix?"

David looked at his charts, then surveyed the faces in the room. "That's what we're going to try to do, because I think that even if the killer isn't in the States, the *reason* is." He considered, then said, "You have told us a lot about the history of the triads, but maybe we should take a minute or two to look at their activities in the U.S. today."

He went to the chart that outlined the family tree of the Rising Phoenix. At the top where the "dragon head" should be was an empty space. From the dragon head, a line led down, then split into three others leading to boxes representing the top lieutenants. Of these, only the names for Spencer Lee and Yingyee Lee were known. From here, the lines branched again and again, with about half of the names filled in. There were no photographs in the top half of the pyramid. Those at the base were mug shots taken of the few gang members who'd been arrested over the years. The next chart outlined the triad's legitimate and illegitimate businesses, which ranged from tea shops and bean-curd factories to floating gambling clubs and prostitution rings.

"You know all this?" Peter asked. When David said yes, the young agent asked, "And you don't arrest them?"

Jack Campbell grunted. "We can't get authorization for wiretaps on Spencer Lee or the others unless we can provide the court with hard evidence that these men are involved in criminal activities, and we can't get that evidence unless we get the wiretaps."

Peter looked at Campbell in disbelief. "You know what they're doing is illegal but you can't do anything about it?"

"It's the American way," Campbell said and heaved a shrug.

Peter leaned over and asked Hulan a question in Chinese, which she answered. The Caucasians in the room looked to her for an explanation. "He's wondering why you Americans keep moving your shoulders like that," she said. "In China, we don't shrug. I was just explaining what you were doing and what it meant."

Campbell shrugged theatrically. Peter nodded and laughed. He liked this man.

"So, does anyone have any suggestions for what we should do next?" David asked the group.

After a moment of silence, Hulan said, "In China what I would do is cast a flower net." She looked to Peter for agreement before continuing. "This method of fishing goes back many centuries. The flower net is a round, hand-woven net with weights on the edges. The fisherman throws it out into the air, where it opens like a flower, settles on the surface of the water, sinks to the dark depths, and traps everything within its circumference." She turned to David. "We'll do as you say. We'll follow the money, but we'll also look at everything that comes in contact with our net."

They spent the next couple of hours brainstorming. Peter suggested that they go back and interview everyone that David and the FBI had ever suspected of being involved with the Rising Phoenix. Hulan wanted to go to Chinatown to restaurants, herbal shops, grocery stores, sweatshops. "Let's talk to real people—common people," she said. "It's a small community. Maybe someone will have heard something. I think they will talk to one of their countrymen before they would ever talk to you."

David preferred a more direct approach. He wanted to go to the handful of banks where the financial transactions had taken place and to investigate other businesses that fell under the auspices of the China Land and Economics Corporation. "It can't be a coincidence that Guang Mingyun owns the Chinese Overseas Bank, that his son laundered—for want of a better word—money in that bank, and that he was found dead on a boat used by the Rising Phoenix to transport illegal immigrants."

They would also have to find time to interview Guang Mingyun's relatives and business associates, especially those who had come in contact with Henglai. "I don't want to forget Billy Watson," Hulan added to the growing to-do list. "Let's go to the university and see what we can find out."

Noel Gardner, with his accounting background and Peter Sun's assistance, worked at one of the computer terminals, inputting data from the bankbooks found in Guang Henglai's apartment with those found in Cao Hua's, then comparing the financial transactions with the exit and entry stamps in their respective passports. Sometimes the two men had traveled on the same day, often separately. Either way, deposits and withdrawals had been made either just before or just after a trip. Beyond this, Gardner and Peter determined that certain deposits had leaped from bank to bank, probably as a way of hiding the trail.

By the end of Gardner and Sun's session, they had pieced together a pattern. Guang and Cao had traveled to Los Angeles on the first and third Tuesdays of every month. Cao Hua had continued with this itinerary even after Henglai's death. The first Tuesday of February was two days away. Would someone take Cao's place? And for what purpose? Campbell called an old friend who worked for U.S. Customs at LAX and arranged for the group to be down there when the earliest flight from China came in.

For the first time since he got on the helicopter to fly out to the *Peony*, David felt that the investigation was going forward in a way he could understand. Peter was surprisingly receptive to Campbell's and Gardner's ideas. In fact, these three men from two very different cultures had found common ground in law enforcement. As they laughed and kidded one another about the relative superiority of weapons and techniques, David regretted that Campbell and Gardner hadn't been able to come with him to China. It might have broken the ice sooner.

But then he thought that maybe it just came down to home-court advantage. David was in his own country. He was surrounded by his charts and support staff. He understood how things worked in Los Angeles. From here on out, he would act, not react. He would pursue, not be pursued. He would push, not be pushed. He would watch, not be watched. He would apply the pressure that his title provided him, bringing all the power of the U.S. Attorney's Office to bear on those who lied to him. To use Hulan's words, he would cast a flower net and trap anyone or anything that lay within its reach.

At two in the afternoon, dizzy with excitement and fatigue, everyone piled back into the van and drove the few blocks to the Biltmore Hotel. David walked the Chinese agents up to the front desk. While Hulan filled out registration forms, Peter gaped at the lobby's elegance—the huge bouquets of fresh-cut flowers, the lush carpets that lay resplendent beneath their feet, the sweeping double staircase, the ceilings with their hand-stenciled designs. David reminded everyone to be ready in two hours. They would just have time to take a quick nap and clean up before they met again for the first of Campbell's excursions.

Campbell then drove David, who felt focused and very much awake, up Beachwood Canyon to his home. He changed into his running clothes and jogged around the Lake Hollywood Reservoir. Then he showered, slipped on khakis, a clean shirt, and a cashmere sweater, and drove down to the Biltmore to join the others.

As Campbell navigated the van out west to the beach, Peter fiddled with his camera and talked animatedly to Gardner. David and Hulan sat in the last seat. She, too, had changed clothes. She wore a peach silk skirt cut on the bias and an embroidered blouse of creamy silk. Just as on the plane, David felt breathless being so close to her.

In Venice, Campbell turned down a side street and pulled to a stop in front of 72 Market Street, a restaurant one block from the ocean. He handed the keys to the parking attendant, saying, "We're going for a walk before the sun goes down. We'll be back for dinner."

As they stood together on the sidewalk, David saw just how "foreign" Peter looked in his polyester plaid business suit and knit sweater vest. David suddenly worried that they would lose Peter, but Campbell was already on top of it. "Investigator Sun, this is very important. You stick with us. Okay? If you get lost, remember where we left the car. Come back here. You understand?"

"*Dong, dong.*" Peter nodded enthusiastically, reverting to Mandarin.

"Don't wander off," Campbell repeated. "Very important."

"*Dong, dong.*"

"He understands, Mr. Campbell," Hulan said.

"Okay, then, let's do it."

They got to the strand and turned left. The air felt balmy after the wintry cold of China. They had come to the beach at the perfect time of day. Most of the weekend crowds had gone home, but the walkway was still alive with rappers, bums, girls in thong bikinis on roller skates, teenage boys hotdogging on their bikes. Open-air stands offered T-shirts, sunglasses, shoes, suitcases, and gauzy dresses for sale.

As they walked—the FBI agents pressing ahead with Peter—Hulan reached out and took David's hand. He couldn't believe it; they were in public. He looked at her and wondered again how in just a few hours she could have transformed so much. She was still beautiful and her hair still hung in tendrils around her face, but she looked so relaxed, so different from the cautious Hulan of Beijing.

At the old Venice Pavilion, the landscape widened and the pedestrian traffic increased. David led them out past the crowds so they could watch the sun set behind the shimmering horizon. As they headed back to the restaurant, Peter ducked into a kiosk that sold shoes and came back out with two pairs. "Genuine leather," he said, incredulous. "Cheaper than Beijing!" Then he picked up a pair of sunglasses and Hulan bought a flowing floral dress. After that, they stopped at every stall to check the prices and variety of T-shirts. Hulan bought a set of three for $10, but Peter surprised them all by bargaining with a woman who spoke mostly Spanish and coming away with three T-shirts for $7.50.

They got back to the restaurant in time for their reservation. "We have a protocol department," Campbell said, "and they've been doing research on your customs." Peter became serious but instantly changed as Campbell addressed the waiter. "We need liquor for toasts. Bring us a bottle of scotch, a bucket of ice, and some glasses. I'll take it from there."

With considerable panache, Campbell filled the glasses, passed them out, then held up his own. "I believe the word is *ganbei.*"

"*Ganbei!*"

"*Ganbei!*"

"Bottoms up!"

For the second round, Campbell added ice, but with their jet lag and their empty stomachs, the liquor did much to loosen whatever inhibitions were left in the group.

Hulan translated the difficult words on the menu and tried to decipher for her compatriot the ingredients in ahi with papaya and chili salsa and in fresh ravioli filled with mascarpone. Peter prudently ordered the duck "done in the Cantonese style," which turned out to be a quarter of the bird still in one piece. He looked at it in confusion, then grunted happily as a platter draped with a huge steak—thick, aromatic, and also in one very large piece—was set before Jack Campbell. Peter waited until Hulan picked up her knife and fork and began sawing her meal into bite-size pieces before attempting to attack his with the barbaric utensils.

By the time they returned to the hotel—David thought it was a miracle that Campbell hadn't been pulled over for driving under the influence—everyone was sated with food and drink. At the Biltmore, David, Hulan, and Peter got out. Peter yawned, waved, and disappeared through the Biltmore's double doors with his purchases in hand. Hulan followed right behind him.

David waited in the cool night air. When his car came around, he gave the valet a ten, put the ticket stub back in his pocket, and entered the hotel. At Hulan's door, he knocked gently. She opened it and drew him in. Feverishly they fumbled at buttons and zippers, stripping each other of silk and cotton, gabardine and cashmere. Hulan's flesh was hot beneath his fingers. Her lips sought his. The smell of her came back to him as from a distant dream. They had not been together this way for twelve years, yet David's hands and lips seemed to remember just how to increase Hulan's ecstasy. Gradually their frantic gropings dissolved into a languorous rhythm. The rest of the night was sweeter and wilder than he ever could have imagined. But as keenly as David felt the primitive pain of passion and the exquisite thrill of release, there was a part of him that held back. He loved Hulan, but he knew he needed to be wary of her.

12

FEBRUARY 3
Chinatown

"Did you sleep well, Inspector Liu?" Peter Sun asked Hulan as she slid into a chair beside him in the coffee shop the next morning.

"Yes, very well, thank you," she said, keeping her voice steady.

"All night I am wondering if your sleep is gentle or if you are dreaming of traveling to Kaifeng," Peter continued soberly. "But I think, Liu Hulan is a sensible person. She is not porcelain with scars."

Hulan couldn't help but blush at his innuendoes. The city of Kaifeng sounded like *kai feng*, which meant "unseal," and was often used as a way to describe the wedding night. His porcelain metaphor was a time-honored way of describing loose women.

Peter puffed out his cheeks like a blowfish, then let his air out in a whoosh, laughing heartily.

"You!" Hulan warned, finally catching his teasing tone.

"We are away, Inspector." Peter shrugged, imitating his new American friends. "I am here to watch you and I will. But you have done nothing that I wouldn't do if *I* had the chance. Only one problem. No chance for me, hey? You see them bringing their females around me? No, just that woman attorney with the big smiling teeth.

She is as appetizing as a wooden chicken! I would rather die than do the house thing with her!"

"True, but the only way to catch a tiger is by visiting the cave," Hulan advised, laughing. "Investigator Sun, I did not know you were so . . ."

"What? We are away. If we return home, we have no problems. If you forget who you are and where you belong, that is a different matter." Peter took a sip of tea. "Inspector Liu, here is what I think. We are in America. We have some fun, then we go home. But I think the old philosophers said it best. It is difficult for a snake to go back to hell once it has tasted heaven. I say, while we're in heaven, we should gorge ourselves."

"You are a corrupt man, Investigator."

"I guess I am," he said, and giggled.

They met in the lobby at nine sharp, then split into three groups. David and Hulan would go to Chinatown in the morning, USC after lunch, and call on the Guangs' relatives in the late afternoon. Gardner and Peter would also go to Chinatown to visit the banks, hoping to glean as much information as possible from an industry that was at least partially in the business of secrecy. Campbell would head east to Monterey Park with the list of alleged members of the Rising Phoenix. Maybe he'd get lucky.

Before setting out, the Chinese agents asked if they could be provided with weapons. "Absolutely not" was Jack Campbell's prompt response.

"We don't know what or who we're dealing with," said Hulan. "You can't leave us exposed without any recourse."

"You won't be alone for a minute. *That* I can promise you," said Campbell. "If you need protection, the FBI will provide it. But you're not getting any weapons!" So that was that. The teams left the hotel not on the best of terms and went their separate ways.

David had been to Chinatown many times, but he'd never had the kind of access that being with Hulan brought. They walked along Broadway, then looped over to Hill Street. The old buildings with their upturned eaves, neon lights, and gaudily painted gates hadn't changed since the 1930s. The old-timers still had their curio and antique shops. But in the last decade, Hong Kong money had made an impact on the enclave in the form of shopping centers and strip malls that were occupied by bustling restaurants, electronics stores, and import/export enterprises. The biggest change, from Hulan's point of view, was demographic. There were far fewer Cantonese in Chinatown than she remembered. Today she saw Cambodians, Vietnamese, Burmese, and Thais. She also recognized a variety of Chinese dialects—Fujianese and Shanghainese mostly—sprinkled in with the Cantonese and Mandarin.

David and Hulan focused on Chinese-run shops, many of which were festooned in red and gold New Year's decorations. They wandered in and out of grocery stores redolent of ginger and fermented bean curd, butcher shops with roast ducks hanging in the windows, herbal emporiums filled with strange remedies. At some of these, Hulan would buy a tin of Danish sugar cookies, a pack of cigarettes, a box of candy. Occasionally, they would detour up a set of stairs, where Hulan would talk to the residents of a crowded apartment or boldly enter a sweatshop to converse with the workers. They stopped in small cafés and talked with busboys and waiters. Hulan even led the way back into cramped kitchens to chat with dishwashers and chefs. Sometimes, to get people to talk more freely, Hulan would give away one of her purchases.

She insisted on walking down the alleys that divided the main thoroughfares. Here the *hutong* life was conducted on a small scale. Laundry hung from lines strung overhead from building to building. Preschool-age children played tag and hide-and-seek. Large baskets filled with tubers and leafy vegetables sat outside restaurants. On the sidewalk before a fish market, they came upon a tub of live eels. Here and there, a few scrawny cats picked at leftovers in overturned trash cans.

Off one of these alleyways they ran into Zhao, the immigrant who had helped David on board the *China Peony*. Hulan, as she had throughout the day, had simply walked through a doorway that opened onto the alley. Inside, perhaps thirty women sat at sewing machines doing piecework. A dozen men were spread around the room doing a variety of jobs—carrying bolts of fabric, steaming finished pieces, and shrink-wrapping them for shipping. The radio blasting Chinese pop music, the unending clickity-clack of the machines, and the gossiping voices combined in a clamorous din. Although it was still early February, the workers were sweating from their exertions. David hated to think of what it would be like in here on a suffocating hundred-degree August day, with no air stirring and smog choking the lungs and burning the eyes.

In her usual ingratiating way, Hulan bent over one of the women and began talking. Although David couldn't hear the conversation, he saw the woman's shy smile as she answered Hulan's questions. Then suddenly David saw Hulan's action in a whole new light. Her way of bending down, of making eye contact, of speaking in a low, confidential voice, was less a show of empathy than it was a means of intimidation.

Before he could begin to puzzle this out, he felt a tug on his arm. He turned and there was Zhao.

After an exchange of greetings, David said, "I see you got out of Terminal Island all right."

Zhao quickly looked around to see if anyone was listening. "Yes, I did, thank you."

"You found work, too, I see."

"My friends found me."

"I didn't know you had friends here," David said, then realized his mistake. Zhao's "friends" were the Rising Phoenix.

David needed to think like Hulan—interrogate through "kindness" and indirection. "You look healthy, much better than on the *Peony*. You must be getting good meals."

"They feed me."

David tried to keep his words simple. "This is hard work, and yet you don't look too tired."

"I have a bed to sleep."

"Are there others with you?" David asked softly.

Zhao nodded. "Many."

"You are living close by?"

Zhao shook his head.

David smiled and clapped Zhao on the back. "So you have done well enough you already own a car. Good for you."

No answer.

"Have you seen much of the city?"

Zhao held up his fingers and began counting. "Terminal Island. The street outside Terminal Island. The room where I sleep. This room. Three times a day, I carry boxes two blocks to a warehouse. That's it." He stared at David.

Through these terse answers David determined that Zhao had been rounded up by the gang right outside Terminal Island's gates. This meant that either Zhao had called the Rising Phoenix, which David doubted, or the gang had inside information that Zhao would be released. Either way, Zhao had been put right to work earning back his passage to the United States. The fact that he was living with several other people led David to believe that he was being housed with other immigrants—probably those right in this room. All meals were supplied by the gang. All entertainment—probably just this radio—was also provided by the gang.

From his knowledge of triad business practices, David deduced that the triad was keeping the immigrants in one place—not in Chinatown proper, maybe Monterey Park—where they were picked up in the morning. From there, they were driven to work, transported back to the apartment or warehouse in the evening, and locked up for the night. These immigrants were, in effect, prisoners.

"You are a hero, Mr. Zhao." David then clarified this for those who were listening: "With your help, we saved many lives on the boat. What I say is, once a hero, always a hero. I hope you will remember that."

Zhao looked away. David couldn't tell if Zhao was embarrassed or frightened. Their conversation came to an abrupt end when Hulan walked up. Zhao slunk away, and David and Hulan left to rendezvous with Noel Gardner and Peter Sun, who they were scheduled to meet at the corner of Broadway and College.

For lunch Hulan said she wanted to go to the Princess Garden, a Hong Kong–style dim sum restaurant in a mall on Hill Street. The restaurant seated about five hundred people, so the atmosphere was lively as parties prattled and called out orders to the waitresses, who walked through the aisles pushing carts laden with different kinds of tea cakes. Soon the table was covered with plates of rice noodles, Chinese broccoli, which a waitress deftly cut with pinking shears, little bamboo steamers stuffed with barbecued pork buns, dumplings filled with shrimp and water chestnuts, and tiny custard tarts. Investigator Sun declared that the dumplings were a hundred times better than any you could get in Beijing and almost as good as those made in Guangzhou, where his family was from.

Over lunch they talked about what they'd seen and learned so far. They'd found out that the Rising Phoenix, the strongest of the local gangs, had a forceful presence in Chinatown. "But whenever I mention the names of Spencer Lee and Yingyee Lee," Hulan remarked, "the people suddenly can't remember a thing. So I think your information is right. Those two, if not at the very top of the organization, are very high up." Hulan plucked up some of the broccoli and put it on David's plate. "Aren't you wondering why I chose this place?"

David patted her thigh under the table. "I wasn't going to press you. I knew you'd tell me when you were ready."

"Spencer Lee eats at VIP Harbor Seafood in Monterey Park on Tuesdays and Thursdays. He comes here on Mondays, Wednesdays, and Fridays."

"And today is Monday."

"I'm sure at this very minute our Mr. Lee is awaiting our arrival in one of the private dining rooms." Hulan tilted her head and smiled demurely.

David marveled at how easily Hulan had been able to get that information. "Most of the people we talked to today were new immigrants," she explained. "I'm sure they recognized me as someone from the MPS."

"They sure saw *us* coming," added Gardner, to which Peter bobbed his head in vigorous agreement.

"Exactly," Hulan said, then popped a dumpling in her mouth. After a few seconds, she said, "That man you were talking with knew what I was."

"Zhao? How could you tell?"

"Didn't you see how he reacted when I walked up? They left China to get away from people like us, hey, Investigator Sun?"

Peter nodded and kept chewing.

"Are you talking about the same Zhao who helped us at Terminal Island?" Gardner asked.

"The very one," David answered, then described Zhao's situation. "I feel sorry for him. It's hardly the dream of America that he envisioned."

"That's a problem for people who come here," Hulan said, her tone suddenly severe. When everyone turned their attention to her, she amended, "What I mean is, people build up an idea of the United States, how their problems will be solved, how they will strike it rich. But they really can't leave the past behind, and the future for an immigrant like your Zhao is very bleak, no?"

David absentmindedly stirred the tips of his chopsticks in the little porcelain dish that contained his portion of hot mustard and chili paste. "Noel, could you drop what you're doing with the banks? I'd like you and Peter to stake out the place where Zhao is working. Could you do that?"

"Sure, but why?"

"I want to know Zhao's daily routine. I want to know where the immigrants are kept at night. I want to be able to pick up Zhao on a moment's notice."

"Why?"

"Because he wants to help me."

"You have a lot of faith in this Zhao," Hulan observed.

"I don't know why, but I do."

"It's only going to cause him trouble," she said. "You realize that, don't you? 'Sweep the snow in front of your own doorstep, and do not bother about the frost on your neighbor's roof.' He should mind his own business."

As soon as they finished their meal, Gardner and Peter left to begin their surveillance. A few minutes later, Hulan led the way back toward the front of the restaurant, turned down a hallway, and, without knocking, entered a private dining room where a group of businessmen were eating. Hulan asked a few questions in Chinese. One of the men answered and Hulan went on to the next room, where another dozen men dressed in suits sat at a large round table. The lazy Susan in the middle was filled with a variety of steamed and fried dumplings, as well as noodles, roast duck, and slivers of jellyfish.

"To say we are expecting you would not do this occasion justice," said a young man wearing small dark glasses.

"You are Spencer Lee?" Hulan asked.

The man nodded, then gestured for them to come forward. "We meet at last, Mr. Stark," Lee said cordially. "And you, Inspector Liu, are not unknown to us. We are very pleased to make your acquaintance."

David had spent months staring at the name of Spencer Lee on his office chart, but he had never seen a photograph or even interviewed anyone who had met Lee face-to-face. Nothing had prepared David for either Spencer Lee's congenial greeting or the youth that he exuded. He looked to be in his early twenties. His hair was cropped so close that his scalp showed through. His cream-colored linen suit was fashionably wrinkled. David was amazed that someone so young, and so obviously fresh off the boat, could have risen so high in the triad hierarchy.

"We are investigating two murders," Hulan began.

"I don't know what that could have to do with me or anyone else in this room." Lee's attitude was self-assured, even cocky.

"These murders took place in China . . . "

"Well, if they took place in China, then they *truly* are no concern of ours. I don't have to answer your questions."

"I wouldn't be so sure about that," David said.

"We aren't in China, Mr. Stark. The MPS has no power here."

"I'm saying I wouldn't be so worried about Ms. Liu." With David's thinly veiled threat, the atmosphere in the room changed. "I have a few questions and I expect you to answer them without any bullshit. Understood?"

"Do I need my lawyer?"

"I don't know," David said. "Do you?"

Lee threw his head back and laughed. When no one joined in, he lounged back in his chair.

"What can you tell us about the *China Peony*?" David asked.

"I don't know. What is it?"

"I thought I made myself clear. We aren't playing games here. I've spent the morning looking at your gang's handiwork and I don't like it. In fact, I'm pretty pissed off. So either we can do this right here, right now, or you can come down to my office."

Spencer Lee brushed nonexistent lint from his linen pants.

David took a breath. "The *China Peony* was a freighter that the Rising Phoenix hired to bring about five hundred immigrants to U.S. soil illegally. On that ship was a dead body."

"You can't prove any connection between the *Peony* and the Rising Phoenix, and you need evidence in this country. You know, innocent until proven guilty."

"Suppose I tell you that I have witnesses."

"I would respond that there is no one who could point a finger at me and say, 'Ah, there is Spencer Lee. I have seen him on this boat. I have paid him money.'"

"In point of fact, I have witnesses, available through the Ministry of Public Security, who say that members of your gang hired the *Peony*," David bluffed. "I also have some officials in the port of Tianjin who are already incarcerated for taking bribes from the Rising Phoenix."

"They have made full confessions, and as I'm sure you remember, Mr. Lee, our legal system works quickly and efficiently," Hulan said solemnly, following David's lead. "We only await a confession on this side of the Pacific, then those men will receive their final sentences. Meanwhile, they are in a labor camp."

Spencer Lee glared at Hulan. He attempted a light tone but the menace came through. "I'd like to meet the inspector in China one day."

"As I would you," she retorted.

"I am in Beijing every other month. Perhaps we can meet for a drink sometime," he shot back.

"Or at *my* office."

Again Lee's manner turned harsh. "Don't threaten me, Inspector Liu. I have friends in Beijing. You can't touch me, because my friends don't want you to."

"Forget about China," David interrupted. "Instead you should tell me about triad activities in Los Angeles."

"I can only think that you are mistaken about us. Our organization is a benevolent society. We do good in the community. We provide jobs. We help feed people when they are new to your country."

"And prostitution, extortion, drugs?"

Lee grimaced. "We have gotten—how do you call it?—a bad rap. These things are not Rising Phoenix. You look at the other gangs. You look at those Fujian gangs! Yeah, the Fuk Ching, they're the ones bringing in illegals, not us. You talk about prostitution, drugs, you look at the Hong Kong gangs. The Sun Yee On—now there's a bunch of low-life thugs! I'll tell you something. If someone was trying to horn in on our territory, and I'm talking now about honest businesses, we wouldn't sit back and take it. You understand me?"

"Enough with the Chamber of Commerce speech," David countered. "What about the murder of Guang Henglai?"

"That has nothing to do with us."

"So you admit you know about this death—"

"Whatever you say, I will have to take the Fifth." His cronies laughed, but Lee's bluster seemed hollow. After this, any question David asked was met by the same flippant answer.

Walking back out to the lobby, Hulan said, "You did well."

"I got nothing!" David was exasperated.

"He practically admitted everything," she corrected. "You can't prove it in court, but you still know that you're right about the Rising Phoenix. Most important, he lost face in front of the people under him. That news will travel, and *that* will help us."

13

LATER THAT AFTERNOON
Silverlake

Still aggravated from his interview with Spencer Lee, David zigzagged his way on surface streets to the University of Southern California. Hulan took his silence for frustration, so when they pulled into the parking lot she refrained from commenting on how strange it was to be back at her alma mater, nor did she ask if they might take a stroll to her old dorm room or peek in on her favorite professors. Instead, they walked directly to the Administration Building.

Hulan remembered the woman who stood behind the counter. In twenty years, since Hulan was first an undergraduate at USC, Mrs. Feltzer hadn't physically changed. Her hair was still a preposterous red, her waistline was still on the far side of forty inches, and her dress with the little belt that cinched in at that ample waist was still decidedly 1950s. Supposedly it was Mrs. Feltzer's job to help people, but she truly excelled at asking students to fill out incomprehensible forms or sending them on fanciful campaigns to get unobtainable signatures from professors. Hulan thought Mrs. Feltzer would have fit in perfectly in Beijing's bureaucracy.

"May I help you?"

"I'm from the U.S. Attorney's Office," David said. "We're doing an investigation on the deaths of two boys who were students here."

Mrs. Feltzer was not impressed.

"It would help us a great deal if we could look at their records."

"I don't think I could let you do that," Mrs. Feltzer responded firmly.

David put his elbows on the counter, adopted a slight smile—nothing too blatant, just friendly, *entre nous*—and captured Mrs. Feltzer's gaze in his own. She became the center of his attention, and Hulan knew that was a nice place to be. "Now come on, Mrs. Feltzer, I'll bet you could do anything in here you wanted," he cajoled. "I bet you know where every last slip of paper is in this office."

This was how Hulan had first experienced David. During her first week at Phillips, MacKenzie, she was in the photocopying room trying to get the woman in charge to finish copying and binding the closing documents for a merger. The materials were a half hour late, and the lead partner had screamed at Hulan that she was about to have the shortest career in the history of law if she didn't get those documents on his desk within the hour. The woman in photocopying took a different view. "That asshole is just going to have to wait! I've got five other orders before his and I'm taking my lunch break at noon. He can just cool his ugly little heels." Hulan pleaded, begged, even began to cry, but the woman would not be moved. If anything, she seemed to enjoy tormenting the powerless woman.

Then David, already an associate, came into the room to get a couple of cases copied for the partner he worked for. Within three minutes, the woman dropped everything and was working on Hulan's job. David and Hulan stayed to help. Twenty minutes later the task was done and David had asked Hulan out on a date, which she refused. It took a full year—her next summer at Phillips, MacKenzie—before she agreed to have dinner with him, and that was only because she'd decided it was the only way she'd get him to leave her alone. Things hadn't turned out that way. He'd used the same charm and persistence on Hulan that he'd used on the woman in photocopying and now on Mrs. Feltzer.

"The boys are dead, Esther," David was saying. "The best way we can help them is to learn what happened. For all we know, there could be something of vital importance in those records. I'm sure you wouldn't want to stand in the way of a government investigation."

Guang Henglai's record was easy to find, since it was in the file for students who'd left the school. During his one year at USC, he'd taken basic courses typical for a freshman; his grades were predictably low. He'd stayed in a dorm for the first semester, then moved off campus for the second.

While they scanned this unenlightening file, Esther Feltzer continued to look for the active file of one William Watson Jr. She ran a tight ship and was unused to not having things at her fingertips. "Someone has misplaced the file," she said sternly. "Either that or your information is wrong."

It was hard to imagine that Mrs. Feltzer would allow a clerical error in her office, so David considered her alternative. "Could you try the files for departed students?"

"I thought you said he was enrolled here." Mrs. Feltzer's grumpy tone was returning.

"I'm just responding to your fine suggestion," David said. "I can't tell you how much we appreciate everything you're doing for the victim and his family."

But David's charms were wearing thin. With a "Humph," Mrs. Feltzer walked away. A few minutes later she came back, dropped the file on the counter, and said in disgust, "Just as I suspected, he is no longer a student."

Billy Watson's academic career was as short and lackluster as his friend's. They had taken almost the same schedule of classes and gotten almost the same grades. They'd been assigned to the same dorm but had not been roommates. At the end of the first semester, though Guang Henglai had moved out, Billy Watson had kept his residency in the dorm. Unlike Henglai's file, the rest of Billy's was filled with formal grievances outlining the young American's troubled career at the school.

During his first week, Billy Watson had been caught throwing full beer cans at people attending a frat party. The dean of students wrote sympathetically that this episode showed bad judgment but that Billy had promised that nothing like it would happen again. Two letters from female teachers reported that Billy interrupted their lectures, made inappropriate comments in class, and had not turned in a single assignment. By the end of the first semester, Billy had racked up close to $500 in unpaid parking tickets. These were duly paid by his father before the second semester started. Apparently Billy didn't learn his lesson, for in the second semester the total for tickets reached $625.

Private schools like USC accepted vast sums of money in the form of tuition and endowments from wealthy, influential families like the Watsons. Allowances might be made. Nevertheless, Billy Watson had taken it upon himself to voluntarily leave the school. In a letter dated August 14, he wrote that he would not, after all, be returning in September. He asked that his tuition be refunded promptly and that the check be made out to him. That was two years ago.

"So what was he doing?" David asked as they walked back to the car. "Where was he living?"

"I'm wondering why his parents didn't know what was happening. Ambassador Watson said he sent a tuition check each year. But how can that be? How could he not know that his son wasn't in school?"

"I don't know, Hulan. There was a case a year or so ago that was in all the papers here. For four years, parents from Fort Lauderdale sent tuition and living expenses to their son at the University of Michigan. He wrote them letters each month, talking about the courses he was taking, reporting on his grades, detailing his plans for graduate school. Then came time for graduation. The parents flew up to Michigan for the ceremony. Their son's name wasn't in the program. Afterward, they looked through the crowd but didn't find him. They went to the administration office and discovered that their son hadn't been a student for three years. He wasn't living where he said he was either. In fact, he was nowhere to be found. I don't remember what happened after that—whether it was foul play or the kid had just come up with a scheme to dupe his parents."

"You think that's what happened with Billy Watson?" Hulan asked doubtfully.

"I'm beginning to think anything's possible."

David drove while Hulan learned how to use the car phone. She got information for Butte, Montana, asked for the number of the sheriff's office, dialed again, and hit the button for the speakerphone. Of course Sheriff Waters knew the Watson family. Why, he'd known Big Bill since high school and had worked on all of his campaigns. When Hulan asked about Billy, there was a reluctant pause on the other end of the line. "Naturally we all knew Billy, too," the sheriff said cautiously.

"You know he's dead?"

"Yes, and it's a tragedy. Must be hard on Bill and Elizabeth."

"Listen, Sheriff," David said, as he guided the car onto the Hollywood Freeway, "we're trying to find out what we can about Billy. We think if we can understand him, then maybe we can learn about his killer—"

"Yeah, yeah, yeah, even an out-of-the-way law enforcement officer like myself has been back to the FBI behavioral science lab at Quantico."

"So can you help us?"

For a moment David thought they'd lost the connection, then Sheriff Waters's voice came back wearily on the phone. "You have to understand, the Watsons are good people. They didn't deserve to have a kid like Billy. He was born to trouble and he died that way, too, I guess."

"Tell us about him."

"How can a guy like me pick on an innocent little kid? That's what I used to think when the Watsons would bring Billy to the ice cream social and he'd do some crazy-ass thing like tip over the ice cream table or push little Amy Scott into the fountain. People around here used to say Billy was just spoiled; I used to say he'd grow out of it. But, man, that kid hit high school and it was nonstop pandemonium. Nothing life-threatening, nothing I could ever haul his ass in here on, just stupid pranks, just always pushing the boundaries to see how far he could go."

"What kind of pranks?"

"Aw, hell, getting caught speeding with a six-pack on the front seat on prom night. Shooting an elk the day before hunting season started. One time—and you got to hand it to the kid for ingenuity— he filled the back of his pickup with old tires, drove to the center of town in the middle of the night, and somehow got those things on the flagpole. It took us days to figure out how to get those cussed tires off of there. See, he was just driving his mom and dad, and me, too, if you don't mind my saying so, nuts with this crap."

"When was the last time you saw him?" Hulan asked on a hunch.

"Fall, I suppose. He liked to come up here with that slant-eyed friend of his. They'd hang out at the ranch doing whatever the god-damn hell kids nowadays like to do. Seems to me it was one party after another."

"Who were they partying with up there?" David asked.

"Aw, I don't know. Pretty girls and cowboys. Hell, they couldn't get enough of those cowboys. You'd have thought Billy was paying them to come over."

Silverlake is one of L.A.'s oldest neighborhoods. The lake itself is a reservoir nestled in low hills between Echo Park and Burbank, close to downtown. Narrow streets snake up hillsides on which classic Spanish-style and newer overbuilt, high-tech houses cling. Most of the residents are older, original buyers who raised their families here. Many of them are Chinese, since Silverlake was one of the first neigh-borhoods in Southern California outside of Chinatown to bend its residency requirements after World War II. This enclave appealed to the Chinese sensibilities of *feng shui*—wind and water; the wind rus-tled through the bamboo, bodhi, and persimmon trees they had planted to remind them of home, and the water of the lake glistened outside their picture windows.

After David parked, Hulan went through her morning's purchases and pulled out a tin of Danish sugar cookies, saying, "It wouldn't be polite if we didn't bring a gift." They walked down a short flight of stairs and banged the heavy wrought-iron knocker on the dark-stained paneled door. They waited, hearing nothing. David used the knocker again. They waited some more.

Finally the door opened. A tiny, ancient man stood before them.

He was Sammy Guang, Guang Mingyun's eldest brother. David and
Hulan introduced themselves and gave him the box of cookies. He
shuffled very slowly to the living room and motioned for them to sit
on the loveseat. He asked if they wanted tea, and when they said yes,
he snarled an order in Chinese to someone in the kitchen. His movements were painful to watch as he creaked to a sitting position on a
straight-backed wooden chair.

As Sammy Guang did this, David and Hulan had time to take in
their surroundings. The modest house had not been kept up. The living room had probably been decorated for the first and only time
when the Guangs moved in. The low loveseat was covered in a practical but ugly fabric that had just barely held up for fifty years. The
fireplace was composed of tiles in the muted colors so prevalent in the
1920s, but this was the only interior concession to the house's original
architecture. A few Chinese "antiques"—not good, just old—spotted
the room. On the floor before the picture window sat several baskets
of azaleas in full bloom and a potted kumquat tree draped with a red
ribbon—the beginnings of the Guang family's Chinese New Year celebration. On the mantel, in the place of honor, were graduation photographs of what Hulan presumed were Sammy Guang's nine—if she
was counting correctly—sons.

The old man squinted at them. "You want know about Number
Four?" His accent was one of the densest David had ever heard.

"Is Guang Mingyun your fourth brother?" Hulan asked.

"Number Four is in China. I am Number One. Two brothers
dead many years—one in America, one in China. One more brother,
Number Five, he live over there." Sammy raised a hand gnarled by
arthritis and pointed across the lake. "You want to talk to Number
Five, too?"

"Yes, your brother in China also gave us his name."

"You want me call him, say come over here?"

"If it's not too much trouble."

Sammy pulled himself slowly out of his chair and shuffled over to
an old rotary telephone. Sammy peered at the numbers, trying to
make them out. It took three tries before the call went through. He
hung up and looked around. "Old woman," he called out in Chinese,

"bring that tea. You take too many years!" Then he again shuffled across the room as a woman with a face like a wrinkled walnut emerged from the kitchen balancing a tray laden with a teapot, cups, and a saucer of watermelon seeds. Her back was folded into a hump as she tottered wordlessly from the kitchen to where David and Hulan sat.

"Mrs. Guang?" Hulan ventured.

Sammy cleared his throat gruffly and said, "She no speak English. She come here sixty years ago. I bring her here and she never learn English. You imagine that?"

Hulan switched to Mandarin, introducing herself and thanking the woman for tea.

When they heard the knocker, David jumped up to prevent Sammy from having to cross the room again. He opened the door to a sprightly man of about sixty-five. Harry Guang, Number Five, proved to be quite talkative. He was retired, just like his brother. He explained that One and Two had left China in 1926 when they were twenty and eighteen years of age. "That was a hard time to come here. You know the Exclusion Law? No Chinese were supposed to be let into the U.S., but my two older brothers came as paper sons. Lucky for them they bought papers to say their last name was Guang. Otherwise, we could be Lews or Kwoks. My brothers worked very hard, very hard. They thought they were coming here to become rich men. But they worked in the fields. They worked in a factory. The Depression came and it was very bad. They lived in a house for single men. Number Two got pneumonia and died—no money for a doctor in those days. Number One didn't have enough money to go home."

"I stay here by myself," Sammy said. "You think it easy for a man alone—no family, no wife, no children? I go to letter writer in Chinatown. I mail this letter to China. *Send Number Three!* Four months later a letter come back. I take the envelope to that same letter writer to have him read it. I pay my money and he tells me, Number Three is dead. Baba dead, too. I can't believe it! I find out Mama has two more children. I don't know these boys."

Harry picked up the story. "The Japanese came to our village, burned the house, killed our mother. By then, Number Four was twelve years old. I was six. It was 1938. Number Four borrowed money from the neighbors. Not much. One day we started to walk. We walked and walked and walked until we came to the sea. I was crying, but Number Four looked at me with a cold heart. He said, 'You go to Number One.' He put me on the boat by myself. I tell you, I was crying the whole time. I was at Angel Island by myself. Only six years old! When I came out, Number One was there. He brought me to Los Angeles. My brother put me in an American elementary school and he continued to work. That's why my English is pretty good and his is . . ." Harry shrugged. "The rest, as they say, is history."

"What happened to Mingyun?" Hulan asked, "Number Four?"

"We think he dead," Sammy said. "China is fighting the Japanese. We are here, working with others in Chinatown trying to raise money. Then America goes to war. I am too old to fight, but I am not too old to work in factory for war effort. My first real American job." Sammy gave them a gummy smile. "After war, I get my citizenship, Number Five, too. I buy this house, Number Five go to college. He an engineer."

"When the Bamboo Curtain fell," Harry said, "we wrote letters to our old village, but no answer. We thought, if Number Four was alive, he would write us."

"So when did you see him again?"

"Ha!" Sammy grunted. "I never see Number Four in my life. He is not born when I leave."

"But he's traveled to California. He has businesses here." David had difficulty keeping the surprise out of his voice.

"Too many years," the old man said, shaking his head. "What he want with know-nothings like us?"

"But you knew his son."

Sammy nodded. "My nephew, yes. He come here maybe three years ago. He go to college like Harry. The Old Woman makes dinner. We visit. He a good boy, tells us all about Number Four. You know something? Number Four a rich man now. First millionaire in our family. Can you imagine?"

"And that was the only time you saw Guang Henglai?"

Sammy waved his hand. "We see him many times! Always he says, 'Father rich. You come work for Father.' I am laughing, because you know how old I am?" When David and Hulan shook their heads, he answered, "Ninety. What I need job for?"

"But the nephew got my granddaughter a summer job at the bank," Harry Guang said. "And Number One's third grandson works in the China Land office in Century City."

But Sammy was still back in his own conversation. "Always that nephew comes here and says, 'You want job? You want job?' He says, 'You know old-timers here. You know people who like the old ways. Not hard work. Easy work. Good money.' I'm thinking, This boy need have his head examined!" Sammy laughed at his witticism.

"What kind of work?" David and Hulan asked simultaneously.

"He wants me to sell something. 'You make good money,' he tells me."

"What was the product?" David asked.

Sammy shook his head. "What I care? I am old man. What I need to sell merchandise for? I tell that boy, 'I'm retired. Leave me alone.'"

"And Guang Mingyun?"

The two brothers exchanged a look. "We don't know him. He doesn't know us. He's a big man now. We are"—Harry searched for the appropriate word and settled on—"insignificant."

"But family—"

Harry cut Hulan off. "My older brother took care of me when my mother died. He sent me to California to make sure I'd be safe. I will always be indebted to him for that. But what happened later, who can say? You are from China, Miss Liu, maybe you can tell us what changed him."

But David knew the harsh but honest answer, and it had come out of the mouth of another Chinese immigrant. Guang Mingyun had become a phoenix. His two brothers were moles.

Driving back down the narrow road, David pulled the car over and turned off the ignition. "What were those kids selling? Drugs?"

"It would fit with the triad angle," Hulan said.

"Yeah, but I don't see Sammy selling heroin to the old-timers in Chinatown."

"But maybe they were selling drugs up in Montana," Hulan suggested.

"Then how do you explain Sammy? Why would Henglai want to use him anyway?"

"The Chinese not only trust their relatives but they try to help them. It's our duty to take care of the older generation."

"But I don't think Henglai was much of an altruist, do you? No, I think it has something to do with the product. Not drugs. Jade? Gold? What's something an old person in Chinatown would want?"

Hulan shook her head.

David tapped the steering wheel as he thought. "And what's with the cowboys up in Montana? Henglai was a Red Prince. That kid was used to Beijing's nightlife—Rumours Disco, the karaoke bar, Rémy Martin, and the rest of it. Why go up to that ranch? Why have those parties?"

"That's easy. You think we haven't heard about cowboys and the romance of the American West? He probably just wanted to tell his friends back in Beijing that he'd experienced the real thing."

David went back to his tapping as he ran through the facts again. "Billy Watson lied to his parents about being enrolled in school. Instead, he's hanging around up in Montana throwing parties, showing his friend your romance of the West." When Hulan nodded, he continued, "You've got two rich kids in their twenties, right? I see the pretty girls. In fact I see *lots* of corn-fed cowgirls."

"Billy and Henglai were young men. It makes sense."

"So why do they keep inviting back the cowboys? Wouldn't one party have been enough? Wouldn't they have wanted to keep all those girls to themselves?"

"You tell me. You're the man."

"That's just it, Hulan. I can't explain it because I can't get those cowboys out of my mind." He threw out another possibility. "Do you think Billy and Henglai were gay?"

"No, I would have seen it in Henglai's personal file. Believe me, my government wouldn't miss something like that."

"But what if it did?"

"Then we would have heard about it from Bo Yun or Li Nan, even Nixon Chen."

"Okay, all right," he agreed, "but I still don't think Billy and Henglai were interested in the girls. Those boys were liars and connivers. They wanted something from those cowboys just like they wanted something from Henglai's uncle. The connection—and don't ask me what it is because I don't know—has to be the product."

"If we're lucky, we'll find it at the airport tomorrow." She put a hand on his knee, then slowly let it glide up to his crotch. "Come on, there's nothing more we can do today. Let's go back to the hotel."

It was the most brilliant suggestion he'd ever heard.

14

FEBRUARY 4
Los Angeles International Airport

The next morning, an hour before the United flight from Beijing via Tokyo was scheduled to arrive, the whole group—minus Noel Gardner, who was orchestrating the surveillance on Zhao—met Melba Mitchell at the U.S. Customs Service desk on the passenger departure floor of the Bradley Terminal at Los Angeles International Airport. Melba, a middle-aged black woman, was a liaison for Customs.

As the group made their way across the terminal floor, Melba briefed them on the role of Customs in the airport. "We enforce six hundred laws for sixty different agencies. This means we're looking for *everything*—gems, narcotics, cash, child pornography, computer chips. I'd say that seventy-five, maybe eighty-five percent of the people who come through are honest. But the rest—either knowingly or unknowingly—are trying to bring in illegal goods."

As they rode the elevator to the lower level, David asked, "How do you know what to look for? Do you have a profile of the typical smuggler?"

Melba opened a door marked SECURITY. "If you mean, do we look at every bag belonging to a person of Mexican descent, the answer is no." She frowned. "We don't search people on ethnic, gender, or age grounds."

"Then what are you looking for?"

"Let me show you," Melba said. By this time they were in the Customs area. The liaison pulled back a couple of ribboned barriers, and the group walked to one of the carousels, where travelers waited for their luggage from a Paris flight. "As I was saying, we don't have a specific profile for smugglers because we know that they're trying to blend in. So we look at where travelers originated. Did someone start out in Bogotá and switch planes in Guadalajara? We consider the time of year, especially for narcotics. Obviously, we're more vigilant during the periods after the harvest seasons for marijuana and opium poppies. We look at trends in other ports around the world. Handbags. Pharmaceuticals. Diamonds. And we're always looking for products manufactured in embargoed countries. In other words, we're looking for anything made in Iran, Iraq, or Cuba."

"You just do random inspections?"

Melba Mitchell laughed. "Hardly." She pointed to a man and woman wearing uniforms and carrying walkie-talkies. "Those two inspectors wait with the passengers. They're looking for people who look nervous or fidgety, if they're sweating, if they just got off an Air France flight like this one and have a whole new set of Louis Vuitton luggage, if they're wearing clothes that are inappropriate."

"Like?"

"Like an overcoat on a flight from Cabo San Lucas." Melba watched the passengers silently for a moment. "We also look for people who don't look like international travelers. I'm talking poor people. We often catch folks who earn maybe two hundred dollars a year but have been asked to carry something for seven hundred. But what you see right now is only part of it. We also have agents out there in plainclothes who appear to be waiting for bags. They mingle, look around, and usually find things for us before the passenger even gets up to the inspection area."

"Are you getting many Chinese immigrants in here with forged passports?" David asked, changing the subject.

"Actually that's an INS function, but we're all together down here and do a lot of our work jointly." Melba looked nervously at the Chinese delegation.

To put Melba at ease, Hulan said, "We know that a lot of Chinese are caught at Kennedy airport in New York."

"We made several arrests out here a few years ago. But again, it's a trend. The immigrants—rather the snake heads who run them—realized it wouldn't work in Los Angeles. But I will say that we're preparing for a big rush later this year. You know, people wanting to get out of Hong Kong."

Peter looked grim. "How will you catch them?"

"Immigration has a great computer system," Melba explained. "They keep track of names, entry, and exit dates, how much money people are traveling with, how long they'll be here."

"We have dates of entry and exit for Guang and Cao," Hulan said. "Could you do a search checking those dates for other people following the same pattern?"

"That information would be protected by the Freedom of Information Act," Melba said.

"Don't you work with the Department of Justice and FBI?" David asked.

"Yes," the woman from Customs answered. "But . . . "

"You're worried about our visitors," David acknowledged. "Let me assure you, they are here on business that affects our country and they are here as our guests."

When the liaison still seemed reluctant, Jack Campbell said, "I'll vouch for them, and if you don't want to take my word for it, I've got a couple of names you can call to get clearance."

Melba passed on the phone calls and took them over to the immigration area along the back wall. She stopped at one of the booths, where an INS officer was just about to take a break. She explained the situation and they began their search. The officer typed in the dates, then waited for the information to come up on the screen.

"Look at that!" David put his finger on the screen where the name William Watson appeared sandwiched between Wang and Wong. "Can it be our Billy Watson? Do you have more information?"

The officer typed in the name and a new screen popped up, showing the data collected on William Watson, twenty-one; born Butte, Montana; permanent address, Beijing, China.

"How many times did he travel back and forth to China?" Hulan asked, her voice echoing David's excitement. Together they counted. Billy Watson had made the trans-Pacific journey once a month for eighteen months before his death.

"Can we go back to the previous screen?"

The officer hit a couple of keys and the earlier screen appeared. The list contained fourteen names, including those of Watson, Guang, and Cao. Of these, some had made the trip only once, others had made it as many as ten. None of them had stayed in Los Angeles—assuming that was the final destination—for longer than seventy-two hours. None had been detained for further questioning when they passed through Immigration or Customs.

"Your flight's arrived," Melba announced. "The passengers should be down here in about five minutes."

"Is there a way you can highlight these names and let the other Immigration people know we're looking for these individuals?"

"You bet. I'll put it through on everyone's computer right now. As soon as an officer types in the name from the passport, the data will come up."

"Do it. And thanks!"

"Do you want us to make an arrest?" Melba asked.

David looked at Hulan. "What do you think?"

"We don't even know if any of these people will be coming through today. If one or more does, then let's keep an eye on them. See what they do."

Campbell cut in. "And there's nothing to say that it will be someone from this list. It looks like they—whoever *they* are—were relying on variety, on new faces."

"I'll alert our plainclothes officers," Melba said, "but maybe you'll want to circulate with the passengers as well."

Their five minutes were up, and the first- and business-class passengers were already scrambling to be first in line for passport control. David, Hulan, Campbell, and Peter drifted apart and into the center of the room. Peter, trying to look inconspicuous, wandered off to see what carousel the Beijing baggage would come in on.

Gradually the travelers passed through the passport line and into the baggage area. The first-class passengers looked remarkably refreshed after their full night's sleep. The rest looked as if they hadn't slept in a year. Melba came by once, whispering that Hu Qichen, one of the people who had appeared three times on the list, had indeed arrived. She discreetly pointed him out to David, then went to notify the others. David kept a safe distance from the man. Hu Qichen wore a gray polyester suit and a navy knit vest. His face was full and his hair was a thick black mop. Like many of the other travelers, Hu Qichen was loaded down with a carry-on bag, a coat, and a plastic shopping bag filled with gifts.

David surveyed the crowd, looking for Hulan. He spotted her on the other side of the carousel standing next to a Chinese man who had two plastic bags wedged between his feet. Hulan walked by the man, circled back to him, leaned in and said something.

Then everything seemed to happen at once. The Chinese man quickly looked from side to side. When he saw one of the uniformed officers take a few steps toward him, he suddenly bolted, almost tripping over his bags, and shoved through the other passengers. "Stop him!" Hulan called out. Some of the passengers ducked instinctively, others pushed out of the way. David saw two officers grab Hu Qichen. As the other man ran back toward the passport-control area, David took off after him.

The Chinese man knocked over a woman in a yellow pantsuit standing at one of the Immigration booths. David leaped over her sprawled body and shouted, "Get help, for Christ's sake!" But everyone seemed too dazed to move. The fugitive ran down a corridor and up a flight of stairs. Just as David seemed to be closing in on the man, he pushed through a set of double doors and disappeared from view. David pushed through after him and suddenly found himself on the tarmac beneath the belly of a 747. The engine noise was deafening.

He stopped for a moment to get his bearings, desperately looking for the runaway or security guards. David saw a fuel truck pulling away and several baggage handlers throwing luggage onto a conveyor belt leading into the giant plane. With his hands clapped over his ears, he took a few tentative steps forward. One of the handlers saw him and started shouting, but David couldn't hear a word. He jogged to just past the plane where he could see several gates at once. The Chinese man was running down the pavement between two of the terminal's wings. David broke into a run. Finally he was just able to reach the man's shoulder, and as he did so, they both lost their balance. They tumbled to the tarmac. For a moment they both lay still, panting, trying to catch their breath. Then the man began struggling. David had never hit another person and didn't want to start now, so he tried to pin the man's arms down.

David heard a voice say, "Hold it right there!" Then another yelled in Mandarin. The man beneath David went limp. David slowly released his grip, edged back, and stood on unsteady legs.

"Not bad, Stark," Campbell said. The FBI agent had his gun aimed at the Chinese passenger, as did three uniformed men. "Inspector Liu," Campbell said, "can you please tell this fellow to stand up real slow, put his hands on his head, and not try any more funny stuff?"

Hulan barked out these commands. As soon as the man stood, one of the other officers grabbed his hands and handcuffed him.

The two Chinese passengers were put in separate holding rooms. Inspectors were brought out to find their bags and carry-ons and bring them to their owners. Melba bustled about with computer printouts of the information that both men had given as they passed through Immigration. Both said they lived in Beijing. Hu Qichen reported that he had $2,000 in his possession, while Wang Yujen, the man who had attempted the foolhardy escape, carried just $50. Both said they were in Los Angeles for pleasure and would return to their native country in three days. Both said they would be staying with relatives and not in a hotel.

In one room, Jack Campbell, Peter, and a couple of other officials did their best to question Hu Qichen. His responses were circumspect. He was in town for a family visit. (But he wouldn't give an address or a name to go with that family.) He had brought in a few gifts, all under the acceptable allowance. (But he wouldn't say who they were for.) When asked about his frequent short trips to Los Angeles, he jutted his chin noncommittally. (So that's how the Chinese shrug, Campbell thought.)

What Hu Qichen lacked in answers he more than made up for in arrogance. "Go ahead," he said. "Search my bags. You will find nothing. But if you detain me, I promise I will make a full complaint to our embassy." Two Customs agents did search his bags and found only clothes, a few tourist curios, a rice cooker, and a tea thermos. This activity prompted more vociferous complaints from Hu Qichen. Investigator Sun shut him up with a powerful punch to the jaw, which caused all manner of consternation among the American law enforcement officials.

In the other room, a first-aid kit had been brought in. David's hands had been scraped on the asphalt and Hulan dabbed at the raw spots with Mercurochrome. She then bandaged the knees and elbows of Wang Yujen, who seemed dazed and disoriented.

"Maybe he's in shock," David said.

"I don't care what he is," Hulan said unsympathetically. "He needs to answer some questions." She turned her attention back to the man and spoke to him in Mandarin. She was breaking every personal code she valued, but like David in China, she felt off kilter, not herself. "Who do you work for?" she demanded. "Do you know Guang Henglai? Do you know Billy Watson? Are you a member of the Rising Phoenix? How were you going to stay in Los Angeles for three days with only fifty dollars? Who were you going to meet? If you really have family here, as you reported to the inspector, who are they? Where do they live?" When Wang Yujen didn't respond, Hulan shouted at him, "Answer my questions!"

Wang Yujen shivered uncontrollably.

"Hulan, I can't let you do this," David said.

"Then step out of the room!"

"You know I can't and won't do that."

Jack Campbell poked his head in the door. "Is everything all right in here?" Hulan glared at him, but Campbell went on. "We've gotten all we can from next door. Can we come in and search Wang's bags?"

Campbell and the other inspectors entered the room. They

opened the suitcase and found a couple of folded white shirts, an extra suit, some underwear, and toiletries. Then the inspectors started on the plastic shopping bags that Wang had abandoned when he ran away. They found a bottle of whiskey and a carton of Marlboros bought in the duty-free shop in Tokyo, half a dozen sandalwood fans, a rice steamer, and a thermos. At these last two, Campbell said, "Wait a minute. The other guy also had these."

"We get those all the time through here," Melba said. "They like to bring them as gifts to their families here in the U.S."

"This man has no family here," Hulan said.

Melba glanced at her computer printout. "He says he does."

"He lied."

"Look, ladies, let's not argue. Let's think instead about these two items." Campbell picked up the box that held the rice steamer, weighing it in his hands, giving it a gentle shake. He pulled the appliance out of the box. It looked like any other rice steamer—a metal cylinder inside, a clear lid, a plastic exterior decorated in a floral motif. "I don't see anything strange about this. Let's see that thermos." It looked normal as well.

As Campbell did the inspection, David watched Wang Yujen. The man's shaking increased and beads of sweat formed on his upper lip. When Campbell shook the steamer, a low whimper escaped from Wang.

Keeping his eyes on the Chinese man, David reached over and picked up the steamer again. He lifted the lid, pulled out the plug, shook the steamer. He looked closely at how it was put together, then asked, "Does anyone have a Phillips head screwdriver?" A couple of minutes later, David unscrewed the appliance. The inner cylinder came loose, and David lifted it out. Taped to the sides in the empty space between the outer shell and the cylinder were small glass vials.

"What the fuck?" Campbell said.

As David peeled off the tape, Campbell picked up the thermos and worked at it until it too came apart. At the bottom of the thermos's cavity was a Baggie filled with a brown crystalline powder.

"Does anyone know what we're looking at here?"

Peter picked up a vial. It looked like an amber-colored test tube topped with a cork stopper covered in red wax. Inside appeared to be more of the brown powder. A narrow sticker of gold and red was glued to the glass. The design showed a panda and several Chinese characters. "*Xiong dan*," Peter said, and Hulan nodded.

Melba Mitchell said, "We know what it is. We just haven't seen it brought in this way before. We've seen this stuff brought in coated in chocolate, floating in jars of honey, hidden in boxes of cookies, but this is a new one." When she saw the Americans' looks of incomprehension, she said, "It's dried bear bile."

David glanced over at Campbell. The FBI agent looked as confused as David felt. Melba repeated the words, then Campbell asked her to spell them out. "That's what I thought you said."

"So what's bear bile?" David asked.

Melba gestured with her head at the Chinese. "They use it as medicine. You know, Chinese herbal medicine?"

"Like ginseng?"

"Ginseng is common, but they also use all sorts of exotic ingredients like Siberian tiger penis, rhinoceros horn, and bear bile."

"So?"

"So, it's illegal to import or export that stuff in any form—pills, powders, shampoos, teas, creams, plasters, tonics, whole organs. These animals are endangered species and are protected by international treaty—the Convention on International Trade in Endangered Species of Wild Fauna and Flora, or CITES for short. And I have to tell you something: This bear bile you're looking at has a street value higher than heroin."

"You've got to be joking."

Melba shook her head. "I'm absolutely serious. Dried bear bile salts sell for anywhere between two hundred and fifty to seven hundred dollars a gram compared to three hundred dollars for heroin. Like any other contraband, price is determined by authenticity, availability, faith in the seller, and relative need." She turned to one of the Customs inspectors. "What do you think we have here, Fred?"

"Depends on the weight," the inspector answered, pulling out a pocket calculator. "But if we go conservative at five hundred dollars a gram for pure bile salts, you could maybe get about two thousand for each vial once it's cut and adulterated. So, if you figure we've got about two dozen vials, that comes to forty-eight thousand dollars. Then thirty or forty grams in the Baggie—and that's just a guess— puts us at between fifteen and twenty thousand dollars, if it's pure. That translates to between sixty to eighty thousand dollars once it's adulterated. Altogether, you're looking at about a hundred twenty thousand dollars. Not bad for one trip."

"Holy shit," breathed Jack Campbell.

"I think we'd better take another look at Mr. Hu's belongings," David said.

A few minutes later, they had uncovered another cache of the dried bear bile in the rice steamer and thermos Hu Qichen had brought for his "relatives." Customs inspectors then performed a more thorough search through both sets of baggage, tearing apart linings, opening up every bottle and container. In a jar that looked as if it might hold pomade, the inspectors found a dried piece of flesh about the size of a small pear. It was a whole dried gallbladder. Altogether, Customs had confiscated a minimum of $250,000 in bear products from the two Chinese men.

In all the excitement, Hu Qichen and Wang Yujen were temporarily forgotten. But once the evidence was taken away to be weighed and cataloged, attention turned back to the two men. Against all reason, Hu Qichen maintained his arrogance. Wang Yujen, however, seemed to sense how much trouble he was in. He hadn't stopped shaking and mumbling to himself. Both men were arrested and taken to the Terminal Island detention facility.

Now David and Hulan sat in one of the holding rooms drinking coffee from paper cups. The case had just taken a 180-degree turn, and none of them seemed to know what to do next. "Well," David said finally, "we've found our product and why the boys wanted Sammy Guang's help. He easily could have unloaded the bile to his friends in Chinatown."

"But a quarter of a million dollars' worth?" Hulan said. She shook her head. "No, this was a lot bigger than that. The boys and whoever their other partners were must have brought in millions of dollars of the stuff. "

"Yeah, this is fucking big," Campbell commented to no one in particular.

"Come on, everyone," David said. "We're going back to the U.S. Attorney's Office. I want you to meet Laurie Martin."

When the whole group trooped into Laurie's office an hour later, she was bent over massaging her swollen ankles. As David—with Campbell and Hulan interrupting every chance they got—explained what they had just found, she regarded them sardonically. "The office has always laughed at these cases. Now you're coming in here for help?"

"I never laughed."

Laurie gave David a look that said otherwise, but let it go at that. "And this has something to do with the body you found on the immigrant ship?" she asked. This question launched the group into another long explanation of the *Peony*, the body in Beijing, the triads, and now this discovery. "It doesn't sound weird to me," she said, her hands folded over her pregnant belly. "It sounds like exactly the move the triads should be making."

As her statement sank in, they all began talking at once. Finally, Laurie held up her hands for silence, then said, "According to Interpol, human beings do about ten billion dollars a year in the international wildlife trade. About five billion of that is illegal. In California, the illegal trade in bear parts alone is valued at about a hundred million dollars. Do you know where that puts this stuff?"

When everyone shook their heads, Laurie said, "It generates more profit than illegal arms sales and comes in second only to the narcotics trade. But you're ten times more likely to find someone walking down the street with wildlife on their person in the form of wallets, shoe, or belts, than drugs. Think about it."

"If that's so, then why do we all have it?"

"Because," Laurie answered, "it's not illegal to *possess* wildlife. You could enter a parade with a panda bear—one of the most endangered species in the world—and nothing would happen to you. Try that with a machine gun or heroin and you're looking at serious jail time. But as you know, David, we prosecute when we can."

"The snails?"

"Right, but other cases, too. We had a case a couple of years ago involving bear bile. I don't know if you were here then. Customs opens some guy's bag at LAX and they find pills, vials, things that look like little turds. Turns out the perp has about eleven pounds of bear bile, worth about one million dollars in those days. The rest was various compounds, mostly harmless, but it was enough to get a conviction. Twenty-one months."

"Go back to what you said earlier about the triads," David urged Laurie. "Where do they fit in?"

"Haven't you been listening?" she responded irritably. "This stuff is profitable. There's practically no competition. The market is growing. And the risk is negligible. You don't have a DEA agent hiding behind every corner, informants in every shadow, no competitors trying to take you out. And, if you're caught, instead of twenty years in the federal penitentiary, you get a slap on the wrist. But it's not just the triads. We're seeing lots of different organized crime groups getting involved."

"Like?"

"The white supremacists, the Freemen, the Vipers—all those nuts up in Montana and Idaho. Poaching American black bears and selling their gallbladders and paws is one of the primary fund-raisers for the militia groups. A dealer then sells the stuff in Koreatowns and Chinatowns around the country, as well as exporting it to Asia."

"Billy and Henglai must have been buying fresh gallbladders from the cowboys," Hulan said.

But David wasn't so sure. "What if you *aren't* a white supremacist?" he asked Laurie. "Might regular people still shoot bears to earn money?"

"Where have you been?" Laurie retorted. "We kill about forty thousand bears in this country each year, and most of them are killed legally—with permits and all. Even a weekend hunter can be tempted to earn back his license fees and gas money."

"What kind of money are we talking about?"

"For a fresh gallbladder? I've heard a low of two thousand dollars to as high as eighty thousand," Laurie answered.

"That's a lot of money in Montana," David said.

"That's a lot of money anywhere," Hulan amended.

"That's why we're finding bear carcasses around the world with nothing taken but their gallbladders," Laurie continued. "In China, bag a bear, sell its gallbladder—or sell it live to a bear farm—for about five hundred dollars U.S.; that's more than a year's salary. A damn good incentive, if you ask me, except for one thing. China has the stiffest penalties in the world because its bears are under a greater threat of extinction than anywhere else. The sun bear, the Asiatic black bear, the panda—all of them are on the CITES I list, meaning they're threatened by extinction. Kill a panda bear—which, by the way, doesn't secrete the right kind of bile because it isn't a true bear—you get the death sentence. Kill a moon bear, you're looking at making sneakers in some prison factory for the next hundred years or so. Farming and selling bear bile? *Totally* illegal, but it's happening in China."

"What are bear farms?" Hulan asked.

"You don't know? Scientists in your country have figured out some way to extract the bile without killing the bear. But other than that, we don't know that much about them either," Laurie confessed.

Laurie stood and walked over to the window. Turning to the group, she held her arms out wide. "The world market for medicinal herbs—I'm talking the whole shebang now, the herbs, the animal derivatives, the roots, the patents, the raw drugs—is huge. In the U.S., between the people interested in holistic medicine and the Asian population, we're spending like crazy. This stuff is cheap compared to Western medicine, and it seems to work in a lot of cases. But see, that's what's hard for us. We can go out and educate people not to wear fur coats or jewelry made from ivory, but how do you tell parents whose kid is dying from a strange form of liver cancer that they shouldn't take a chance on bear bile? How do you ask a doctor—sworn to protect human life—not to prescribe rhino horn if he thinks it will save his patient?"

A hush fell over the conversation as David, Hulan, Jack Campbell, and Peter Sun tried to absorb all they'd heard.

"Our government has other concerns as well," Laurie went on.

"The Chinese manufacture thousands of different patent medicines. This stuff comes over here and shows up in Chinese herb shops, in acupuncturists' offices, in health-food stores, in the Save-on down the street. Basically, they're sold everywhere over the counter and they're supposed to cure everything—headache, flu, the common cold, back-ache, cancer."

"So what's the problem?" David asked.

"Say a mother in Brentwood buys some Chinese cough syrup for her kid. The directions say one teaspoon twice a day. She thinks, Why not four times a day? Better yet, I'll make it every four hours like Robitussin. She gives it to the kid and he goes into convulsions and almost dies. We send the syrup to the forensics lab and we get a call back that it has whatever herbs and minerals are advertised on the package, as well as arsenic or mercury. We're talking about products with serious poisons in them that you can just buy over the counter."

"David, this is starting to make sense," Hulan said slowly.

He looked doubtful.

"We've got the cowboys and the bears up in Montana, right?"

He nodded.

"And now the patent medicines," she said. "We've seen them before."

"We have?"

"Oh, yes. We saw Panda Brand medicines in Cao Hua's refrigerator."

"Was it bear bile?"

"I don't remember. It didn't seem important at the time." She ran her finger over her bottom lip, thinking. "We also saw Panda Brand one more place."

David regarded her curiously as she ran back over it in her mind. "I know!" she said. "We saw it in the lobby of the China Land and Economics Building. Panda Brand is one of Guang Mingyun's companies."

"*Aiya*," Peter groaned. This wasn't going to be good for his career.

They should have stopped to play out this new information, but they were so caught up in the moment that David simply turned back to Laurie and asked, "Has Guang Mingyun's name ever come up in any of your smuggling cases?" When Laurie shook her head, David sighed and said, "As much as I'd like to connect him to the Rising Phoenix we still don't have a single piece of real evidence."

"We've got the couriers," Hulan reminded him.

"But you'll never nail the triads with two uncooperative accomplices," Laurie said.

"What we need is someone who can make the final link for us," Hulan said. "We need someone to slip in, deliver the contraband, and ask some questions."

"What about Investigator Sun?" Jack Campbell suggested. "Could he pose as Wang?"

All eyes turned to Peter, as they considered. He seemed perplexed at the idea. "If something happened to him . . ." David said.

"*That's* not the problem." Then realizing how that sounded, Hulan bowed her head in apology. "Forgive me, Investigator Sun." She turned back to David. "The problem is he looks like he's MPS. *I* look like MPS. Why do you think Wang Yujen ran away at the airport? He recognized me for what I am. No, we need someone different. You look at Hu Qichen, he's arrogant. He tries to act like a big man, but he's not. And Wang . . ." She snorted lightly. "He's just a courier. Not smart, not educated."

David brought his hands to his face and rubbed his forehead. Suddenly he felt very tired. When he looked up, they were all waiting for him. "I know who we can use. "

"Your Mr. Zhao," Hulan said.

"Yes, my Mr. Zhao." David's voice was hoarse as he said, "Jack, you'd better call Noel. Have him grab Zhao during his next trip to the warehouse."

15

FEBRUARY 5
The Green Jade Café

At eleven the next morning, Zhao stood in the middle of the electronics room at the FBI stripped to the waist as a technician taped a wire to the immigrant's gaunt, hairless chest.

This time David had little to bargain with. The Rising Phoenix had picked Zhao up as soon as he left Terminal Island. They had provided him with a job and a place to sleep. He was little more than a slave, but his life was not in jeopardy. Now David was asking him to do something that was at best risky, and with nothing in return. David couldn't promise Zhao a job, a place to sleep, food, or clothes. And yet Zhao had not hesitated. David correctly understood that Zhao's cooperation was directly tied to the presence of the two Ministry of Public Security agents. He didn't ask who they were because, as Hulan kept repeating, they were recognizable. Nor did Zhao question why the MPS was in the United States. Perhaps he simply didn't know any better. Perhaps this was just one more example of his American dream shot to hell: You risk your life trying to go to the United States, hoping for a better future, and when you get there, all you find is more hard work and the MPS to boot. No matter, Zhao was between the proverbial rock and a hard place. From his position, he could live out his indentured servitude to the triad or face the wrath of the MPS. Neither was a choice David would have wanted to make.

Which was not to say that David's conscience didn't bother him. He was keenly aware of just how suspect his actions and those of the two U.S. government agencies were by not giving full disclosure to Zhao. He suspected that the FBI agents, like himself, were justifying the means with the ends they anticipated—the murders would be solved, the smugglers caught, and the triad exposed. Still, David worried that the Rising Phoenix would recognize that Zhao was not a courier but merely a man who owed them his passage to America. Noel Gardner, who'd been watching the sweatshop, reassured David that the gang leaders wouldn't recognize a single face out of all their workers. In fact, as far as Gardner could tell, no one important from the Rising Phoenix had ever come by the shop. Zhao agreed with this assessment.

They tried to work calmly, quietly with the immigrant, but spirits were running high and everyone had an idea of what Zhao should or should not say, questions he should or should not ask, and how he should respond to those asked of him.

"Tell them we arrested Hu Qichen," David said. "You were questioned, but we didn't open your rice cooker or your thermos. When you were finally released, there was no one there to meet you. You didn't know what to do. You waited in the terminal."

"Finally you saw another of your countrymen." Hulan picked it up. "You went up to him and said you were lost. This man was very kind. He told you to . . . "

"Take a bus, which you did." David seemed momentarily stumped. "The money. How does he get money?"

"Wang Yujen had about fifty dollars on him. He had it exchanged at the airport, then got on the bus."

"I'll call RTD and find out about buses from LAX to Chinatown," Gardner volunteered.

"No, wait," David said. "Maybe he should go to Monterey Park. We know the Rising Phoenix has business in both cities. But where will Zhao end up? At someone's house? At headquarters? We don't know where any of those places are, but I'll bet those guys aren't living in Chinatown. They're probably up on some hill above Monterey Park taking advantage of the *feng shui*."

As Gardner disappeared to make his call, David returned to his scenario. "You get to Monterey Park and you start asking questions . . ." David seemed at a loss again. "And then . . . and then . . . And then you're on your own."

"Say you've got a package for Spencer Lee or Yingyee Lee," Hulan said. "Play dumb."

"And when you get there, try to tell us where you are if you can," Jack Campbell said. "We're going to be listening. You won't be able to hear us, but I promise you won't be alone. If you need us, just shout. We'll be right there."

"And one more thing," said Hulan. "Ask him about Guang Mingyun."

For the first time, a shiver rippled through the immigrant's body. Wordlessly, he shook his head. But Hulan was firm. "You ask how Guang Mingyun is involved, how much money he makes from this trade, and who he uses in China to send the products out of the country."

By now her MPS colleague had caught on to what she was suggesting. Peter argued with her in Chinese, but she cut him off in English with fierce finality. "I will take full responsibility." Then she put a gentle hand on Zhao's bony shoulder. "You ask about Guang Mingyun if you think you can."

They drove together in a surveillance van supplied by the FBI. During the long trek across the city, the seriousness of his position began to register with the immigrant. By the time they dropped Zhao off at an intersection two bus stops away from downtown Monterey Park, he looked pale and drained of all energy. He walked a few steps, then turned and grinned bravely. Noel Gardner called out one more time, "We'll be with you the whole time. Don't worry." Then Gardner pulled the sliding door shut and the van pulled away.

The plan moved ahead with amazing accuracy and precision. Zhao had been a perfect choice, since he didn't have to feign ignorance of the city in which he found himself. He walked along the streets of Monterey Park, which were quite different from the two blocks of Chinatown that he'd been allowed to see in the course of his deliveries. He recognized the Chinese characters on the shop signs, but the rest—the vast restaurants, the luxury cars, the bejeweled women—was foreign to him.

He was lost and he looked it. Several times women approached him, mistaking him for a homeless man and offering him small change. When he asked for Spencer Lee or Yingyee Lee, they shook their heads and said they had never heard of those men. One matron asked Zhao his name. When he told her he was Wang Yujen, she suggested he go to the Wang family association house. She gave directions, pressed a dollar bill in his hand, then briskly continued on her way, calling out a final few words of reassurance. "They will help you."

Zhao did not go to the family association house, where an immigrant might find help and where American-born Chinese of the Wang clan could find companionship and common interests years after their family's arrival in the United States. Instead, he wandered into a video arcade, where the wire transmission was lost in the noise of simulated battles, drag races, and the players' squeals and shouts of delight, outrage, encouragement, and triumph. But once back on the street, Zhao seemed to know exactly where to go.

He entered a 7-Eleven and again asked for Spencer Lee or Yingyee Lee. At first the clerk denied knowledge of either man. When Zhao insisted, his voice rising in frustration, explaining that he had a delivery for one of the Lees, that he'd been detained at the airport, that he'd come all the way to Monterey Park by himself—as a foreigner and totally new to the city—the clerk relented. "You wait here," he said. "I will make a phone call." When the clerk came back, he told Zhao to wait outside. Someone would be by to pick him up shortly.

From their vantage point in the van, David and Hulan could see Zhao anxiously standing on the street corner. He shifted from foot to foot, paced a few steps in one direction and back again. Then, in an apparent effort to calm himself, he squatted on his haunches, setting his small suitcase and his packages beside him. He could have been on a street corner in any Chinese city.

A black Mercedes with smoked-glass windows pulled up to the curb. The driver rolled down the window and called out, "You are Wang Yujen?"

Zhao nodded enthusiastically.

Inside the van, David groaned. "He's got to talk. The tape won't pick up nods."

Zhao opened the door to the backseat, put his belongings inside, and, without a glance toward the van, got into the front seat of the car.

The driver said in disgust, "You smell like you haven't taken a shower in ten thousand years."

"Sorry, so sorry."

Keeping a safe distance, Jack Campbell followed the Mercedes through the business district, then into a residential area. The Mercedes began to snake its way up a winding road. The houses got bigger, changing from 1950s tract homes into ostentatious mansions too large for their lots.

"Chinese people live in these villas?" Peter asked. When he found that they did, he shook his head in disbelief. What was called a villa in Beijing was nothing compared to the size of these Spanish-style monstrosities.

The Mercedes slowed, waited for a pair of electronic gates—each with the character for happiness rendered in wrought iron—to slide open, then pulled inside. The driver didn't bother to close the gate behind him. Gardner parked the van across the street. When Spencer Lee got out of the car, David immediately recognized him. Tonight he was nattily dressed in a silk shirt, creamy white slacks, and tennis shoes.

"Hurry up, hurry up," he ordered.

Zhao got his possessions out of the car and followed Spencer Lee up the marble steps and into the house. Over the transmission, they could hear Zhao exclaiming over the foyer and the living room. "Be quiet," Lee snapped. "Too much noise. You sit down and tell me why you are here."

The next few minutes proved to be the toughest for the team in the van as they listened to Zhao—through Hulan's translation—recount his misadventures at the hands of the law. To David, Zhao sounded like a groveling fuck-up. Zhao was just a poor peasant. He didn't understand anything of what happened. He was afraid when the foreign devil came up and took him away. He thought he was going to be executed. In other words, David thought Zhao sounded believable, but Spencer Lee was not so easily satisfied.

"They take Hu Qichen. They put you in another room. Okay. I see that. But why are you here? Why do I not see Hu Qichen?"

Zhao's reaction surprised David. "Fuck my mother! Fuck your mother! Someone says, You go to America, you come home, you make some *yuan*. I think, Maybe I earn enough to buy an automobile. Maybe I can be a driver for foreigners. But I tell you what happens. I come to America. The policeman looks in my mouth. He puts his fingers up my asshole. I'm thinking, Next thing this man is going to put a bullet in my head. My children will have no father. My wife will go and marry Noodle-man Zhou. He has his eyes on her for many years. I'm thinking, Maybe I don't want to buy a car. Maybe I want to stay alive. Better to be a poor man in China than dead in this ugly place. Fuck your mother!"

The tirade—shrill and loud—ended as abruptly as it began. Dead silence followed, then Spencer Lee began to laugh.

"Sit down, Mr. Wang. Have a cup of tea."

"*Eaaah*," Zhao grunted, still annoyed.

During the next few minutes, tea was brought in and Spencer Lee checked his contraband. When Zhao saw what the merchandise was, he once again feigned curiosity.

"What do you have there?"

"Bear bile."

"I bring that into the country for you and you don't tell me?"

"Yes, but you will be paid, remember?"

As Spencer Lee measured the loose crystals, Zhao asked, "Where do you get that?"

"It is no concern of yours."

"You tell me things, I will understand. Next time I make this trip for you I do an even better job."

There was silence on the transmission as Lee considered. "Yeah. Okay. You did a good job. You got here, right?" Zhao didn't respond. "Up in Jilin Province, too many Koreans. They're not trustworthy and the price is too high. Heilongjiang Province is too remote—close to Beijing if you can fly but dangerous, and it's too hard to get merchandise to Beijing overland. So, we get our bear products from Sichuan Province."

In the van, Hulan said, "That's where Guang Mingyun was in the labor camp."

David thought, Right, and so were your father and Section Chief Zai.

The transmission resumed with Spencer Lee. "Hundreds of bear farms around Chengdu and the police don't care who buys, who sells. You know what I mean? We go to the airport. We tell the officials that our bear bile comes from a farm with a license. Everything is legal. No problem."

"Why is some in a bottle, some loose like that?"

"Different products, different farms, same price."

"But that one in the bottle is Panda Brand. That company is Guang Mingyun company."

"So?"

"Guang Mingyun works for you?"

In the van, as Hulan translated this exchange, David marveled at how deftly Zhao was playing to Lee's ego.

"Guang Mingyun has many businesses," Lee replied enigmatically.

"I see," Zhao said, as though deep in thought. "Guang Mingyun is Rising Phoenix, too."

"A curious man can become a dead man," Lee remarked. "Guang Mingyun likes money. I like money. You like money. That's enough to know."

Zhao nervously fell back into the sycophant role. "You use me again next time, right? I bring more in for you, maybe work for you. Maybe come to America?"

"We'll see," Spencer Lee said.

"What do you want me to do now? You have another job for me?"

"You go back to China, like the original plan. Next time I need someone, I will have Cao Hua contact you." In the van, the team heard the sounds of teacups being set down, a chair scraping on the floor, and Spencer Lee opening his wallet. "Here's your money. I'll have someone take you to a motel. You stay there. Don't get into trouble. Tomorrow we'll take you to the airport. You did a good job for us. I will remember you next time."

As Zhao offered profuse thanks, Hulan said, "That's our cue. Let's go."

The group walked up to the front door and rang the doorbell. When Spencer Lee answered, Jack Campbell said, "You are under arrest. You have the right to remain silent . . . "

Even sitting in a federal jail interrogation room, Spencer Lee's impertinence showed no signs of diminishing. If anything, he became even more haughty. So far he had refused his right to an attorney or to a phone call. He seemed convinced that he could rely on his wits. Only his chain-smoking betrayed any tension.

At David's insistence, Hulan and Peter were barred from the room. From where they now stood on the other side of a two-way mirror, they could see Spencer Lee in profile sitting on one side of the table with David sitting directly opposite. Their faces were just inches apart and the intensity with which each man spoke was perceptible even through the glass.

"Isn't it a fact that you are a lieutenant in the Rising Phoenix gang?"

"Rising Phoenix? I have told you before, we are a fraternal organization."

"You and your cohorts chartered a boat called the *China Peony* in December of last year. At the beginning of January, you picked up Chinese immigrants and brought them to America. Your crew deserted the ship."

No answer.

"Who do you purchase bear bile from in China?"

Again David received no answer.

"How did Billy Watson and Guang Henglai fit into your scheme?"

"I'm unfamiliar with those names."

"They weren't couriers in your business?"

"I don't know what business that could be," Lee said evenly.

"Tell me about your connection to Guang Mingyun."

"Guang Mingyun?" Spencer Lee let the name linger on his lips contemplatively.

"You spoke with Mr. Zhao about Guang Mingyun this evening."

"You must be mistaken." Lee lit another cigarette.

"I'm going to ask you again," David said calmly, deliberately. "Would you care to elaborate on Guang Mingyun's involvement in the smuggling of medicinal products made from endangered animals?"

"I'm getting tired of these questions," Lee said.

"I see from your passport that you travel back and forth from China with some regularity," David continued.

"A month here, a month there. No difference."

"Not every Chinese gets a visa so easily," David tossed out.

"The American embassy . . ." Lee hesitated.

"Yes?"

"I have a good record with the American embassy." Cigarette smoke curled about Lee's face.

"Are you implying that you pay bribes for your visas?"

Spencer leaned forward, putting his face close to David's. "Mr. Stark, you have no proof of anything. Why don't you let me go home?"

David stared Lee straight in the eye. "I do have one more question concerning your passport."

"Go ahead."

"A passport, as you know, records the dates of exit and entry."

"So?"

"I see you were in Beijing for a little more than a month from December tenth to January eleventh."

"So?" Lee repeated.

"So, the *China Peony* was chartered on December eleventh. It was a large ship, so its cargo took a couple of days to load. This took place on January first and second. On January third, it set sail. But of course you know all this."

"I have already told you I know nothing about that ship."

"During this time there were two other occurrences in Beijing that are of interest to me," David said in a conversational tone. "On December thirty-first, Billy Watson, the son of the American ambassador, disappeared. On or about the same date, Guang Henglai, the son of Guang Mingyun, also disappeared. As I'm *sure* you know, the body of Henglai was found aboard the *Peony*. Perhaps even more intriguing from where I sit is that the body of Billy Watson was found on January tenth. And why is that interesting? Because the very next day you flew to Los Angeles."

The eyes of the two men remained locked. The muscles of Spencer Lee's jaw clenched. David's look was stony. The Chinese man broke the silence with a toss of his head and a light laugh. "I guess I will make that phone call now."

Twenty minutes later a triad lawyer sat at Spencer Lee's side vehemently arguing that his client hadn't been advised of his full rights, claiming unlawful entry, and generally making a loud fuss over the lack of sufficient evidence. Spencer Lee was booked and put in the lockup. His lawyer was told that there would be a bail hearing before a federal magistrate in the morning.

The arrest, even without the satisfaction of all the questions being answered, was cause for celebration. Instead of going together as a group, the different factions came to a tacit agreement. Jack Campbell outlined an evening of American debauchery for himself, Gardner, Peter, and Zhao: a visit to Universal Studios for a tour and rides, followed by bar hopping and putting away as much liquor as their bodies could handle, followed perhaps by a couple of lapdancing clubs. Zhao declined the invitation, saying he was exhausted. David and Hulan would have a quiet dinner.

But first a certain amount of paperwork and other odds and ends needed to be handled. Hulan wanted Spencer Lee sent to China, where he would be tried for the murders of Watson and Guang, rather than have him stay in the United States, where he would face only the relatively minor smuggling counts.

But China didn't have an extradition treaty with the United States. Phone calls were made to the State Department and to China's Ministry of Foreign Affairs to see if an exception could be made, but David and Hulan were basically told by their respective governments that they were out of their minds. "We just caught those bastards trying to sell nuclear trigger components in our country," Patrick O'Kelly responded. "If the Chinese want to discuss the proliferation of nuclear arms, then we will be happy to listen." When David argued that the man from the State Department had gotten him into this, that he was the one who wanted the murders solved, O'Kelly answered, "The situation has changed. National security is far more important than the deaths of two people half a world away." When David said that Ambassador Watson might not feel that way, O'Kelly hung up on him.

O'Kelly's counterpart in Beijing was no less adamant. "The United States government is nothing but an aggressive regime. The president is weak-minded, fat, and a braggart! The Americans are trying to use the face-washing basin to cook fish! But we will not stand for their nonsense or their insults. There are no triads, and we certainly aren't selling our nuclear technology abroad. These fantasies are insulting to the people of China. Tell the Americans to get their warships out of the strait, then maybe we can talk."

After the calls, Hulan asked, "Isn't there something we can do? Can't you deport Lee?"

"We need to have grounds for deportation—that he entered the country illegally or that he was here illegally," David answered. "As far as I can tell, his papers are in order. We can deport him *after* he's tried, convicted, and served his sentence for smuggling, but . . . "

"But what?"

"But that doesn't necessarily mean he'll end up in China. He'll get to choose which country he wants to go to. We can't be assured that he'll pick China."

"Especially if he knows I'll be waiting for him."

"In the meantime, everything Laurie's told us about the light penalties for smuggling convinces me that Lee will be released on bail tomorrow." David could only hope that the magistrate would listen to his pleas that Lee presented a threat to the community, that the U.S. Attorney's Office believed he was tied to the smuggling of human beings as well as the murders in China, and would decide to hold him. Either way, Hulan and David would continue looking for evidence to tie Lee to those crimes.

Before the two groups went their separate ways, something needed to be done about Zhao. He had spent the last couple of hours sitting in an orange plastic chair in the jail's lobby. In those two hours, he had seen a side of America that made him long for the familiar hardships of his home village. David had in the back of his mind that they would put Zhao in the witness protection program, but this took time to set up. David pulled out his wallet, gave $100 to the immigrant and a credit card number to Noel Gardner, and said, "Take Mr. Zhao to a hotel—a good one. We're all tired. We'll figure everything out tomorrow."

With smiles, bows of the head, and a final round of shaking hands, Zhao was led away by Gardner, who would drive him to a nearby hotel, then hook up with Campbell and Peter later. As Zhao walked down the grungy hallway, David saw a man who still looked confused by the world around him but was no longer resigned to his fate. Zhao bobbed his head once more and gave a thumbs-up, which meant the same thing in China and America.

At last, David and Hulan left the station and headed out to Patina Restaurant on Melrose. David ordered champagne. The waiter popped the cork, poured the liquid into fluted glasses, then quietly backed away. David and Hulan sat in companionable silence. They were both tired but feeling a deep sense of accomplishment.

Finally David said, "I've been thinking about Guang Mingyun."

He didn't notice Hulan's grimace.

"He has all the money in the world. Why would he risk getting caught for smuggling?"

"Sometimes people get addicted to making money," Hulan said.

"But why would a guy like that deal with the Rising Phoenix?" David persisted.

"We don't know for sure that Guang is involved with them. Remember, Zhao asked the question, but Lee didn't answer it."

"Okay, but just suppose he is."

"The triad has a method of transporting the merchandise and the connections here to sell it."

"I see that," he agreed. "But then why would they kill Henglai? Or Billy, for that matter?"

"I don't know. Maybe Guang was trying to cheat the triads and they retaliated. Maybe the boys were trying to cheat Guang."

David shook his head. "Neither of those can be right."

"Why?"

"As you said yourself, neither of us would be working on this case if it weren't for Guang."

Hulan reached across the table and took his hand. "Let's not talk about the case anymore. Please?"

He looked at her then, relishing the delicious irony of her request. Only a few days ago, he was pleading with her to talk about something besides the case. Besides, she was right. They had done a lot in the last two days. What harm could there be in having some time just for the two of them?

After dinner, they returned to Hulan's hotel room. They stood facing each other. He put his hand on her cheek, then slowly let it glide along her neck, over her collarbone, down to her breast. They took their time unbuttoning each other's clothes. His mouth lingered on Hulan's nipples. She moaned in response to the caress. Soon her lips sought the tender nook under his left ear, then went to the hollow place at the base of his neck before continuing their downward journey. Tonight David and Hulan would make their passion last.

Several hours later, they were awakened by the ringing phone. It was a sign of how much Hulan had let down her guard that she didn't hesitate to answer.

"Hello," she said sleepily.

She and David had been nestled together on their left sides like two spoons. His hand had draped over her waist and held her left breast. Now she felt that hand begin to travel as the voice on the phone said in educated Mandarin, "We have something to discuss. Please meet me at the Green Jade Café on Broadway. You may of course bring Mr. Stark."

Hulan put the receiver down and pushed David's hand away. In a low voice, she reported what she had just heard. He sat up, looking worried. "We'd better call the FBI. They can get ahold of Gardner and Campbell. Let them take care of this."

She shook her head. "No. The caller asked us to come. He wants to tell us something. If we want to hear it, we'd better go alone."

"It's dangerous," he insisted, but her look told him she was not afraid.

After David and Hulan left the room, they stopped and knocked quietly at the door of Peter Sun's room. When they received no answer, Hulan glanced at her watch. It was after midnight.

"He should be back by now," she said.

"He's just with Campbell. Don't worry about it."

David drove down to Chinatown. Pink, yellow, and green neon lights from the closed shops and restaurants glowed on the deserted streets. David pulled into the open-air parking lot of one of the strip malls that lined Broadway. For the first time since being in California, Hulan felt chilly, and David put an arm around her as they walked to the Green Jade Café. Neither of them carried a weapon.

Once David and Hulan reached the windows of this modest establishment, they could see that it was closed for business. Hulan suddenly flashed on the image of Cao Hua's body. Believing now that another gruesome spectacle awaited them inside the restaurant, Hulan wished that they'd followed David's advice and called the FBI or the police. The Green Jade's door stood wide open, and they entered. The smell was enough to tell them why they had been summoned there.

"Maybe you should wait here," Hulan whispered.

"I was going to say the same thing to you."

"I'm accustomed to death," she said.

He took her hand. "We'll do this together."

Cautiously they walked into the restaurant. They listened but heard nothing. David gestured toward the kitchen and Hulan nod-ded. They edged around the cash register and pushed through the swinging doors.

Zhao lay in five pieces. His arms and legs had been cut off in the traditional punishment for betrayal against the triads and tossed care-lessly aside. His head and torso lay discarded in the middle of the floor. Behind him, on the stove, a huge triple-layer dumpling steamer sent out putrid fumes. Hulan was the first to move, crossing the blood-smeared floor gingerly and turning off the burner. David bent over Zhao, looked into the man's eyes, and relived the moment on the *Peony* when he had felt that tug on his pants leg. Gently David closed Zhao's eyes, stood, and went to Hulan's side. She seemed para-lyzed, staring at the huge steamer.

"I don't think I can do it," she said.

David carefully lifted the large bamboo lid and set it on the counter. Inside lay a mass of steamed flesh. This was all that remained of Noel Gardner.

16

FEBRUARY 6–7
The Federal Courthouse

They phoned the police and the FBI. They called the hotel and woke up Peter, who'd returned from his night on the town. An FBI agent brought him down to the restaurant an hour later still half-drunk. When Jack Campbell didn't answer his phone or page, a couple of FBI agents went out to his house and found the phone off the hook, the pager on an end table in the living room, and the agent sprawled across his bed in a deep sleep—his reward for an evening of boozing and rabble-rousing. Campbell arrived at the Green Jade, claiming he wanted to see with his own eyes what had happened to his partner. Afterward, he sat down in one of the dining room chairs, put his head in his hands, and cried.

It was close to four in the morning when David and Hulan left the restaurant. As they stepped through the doors that led to the street, they were immediately assaulted by minicam lights, microphones thrust in their faces, and a barrage of questions from local news teams that had picked up the reports on their police scanners. David took Hulan by the arm and they pushed through the crowd to his car. As he drove toward Hollywood, he kept one hand on the steering wheel, while the other held tightly onto Hulan's cool palm.

Once off the freeway, David let go of Hulan to focus on the curves that wended from the bottom of Beachwood Canyon up the narrow road to just below the HOLLYWOOD sign. He pulled into the garage, opened the door to the house, punched in the security code for the alarm system, and led Hulan through the kitchen and into the living room. She was drawn to the arched picture window and stood before it, gazing at the lights of the city below. How many times over how many years had he longed for this moment? But looking at her profile silhouetted in the dim light, he felt only desperate sadness.

"Do you want a drink? Brandy? Water? A cup of tea?"

She turned to him and said mournfully, "I feel responsible."

"So do I, Hulan, but we're not. We couldn't know it would turn out this way."

"Did they have families?"

"Noel was single. God, he was just a kid, you know? He hadn't really started his life. And Zhao? I read his file, but I can't remember what it said."

Hulan rubbed her eyes. There was nothing to say.

He took her by the arm. "Let's go to bed."

David held Hulan to him, and suddenly he wanted to tell her everything that he'd held back since first seeing her again at the Ministry of Public Security.

"You haven't asked about my wife," he said.

"It doesn't matter."

She sounded sincere, but he said, "I don't want any more secrets. If tonight has shown us anything . . . Life is short. The future is uncertain. They're clichés, Hulan, but there's truth in them." He squeezed her closer to him. "I just don't want the past to stand between us. Not now, not ever again."

He could feel her breath against his chest. Finally she said, "Tell me about her."

"We met on a blind date. Jean was a lawyer, too, and Marjorie—remember her? at the firm?—set us up. It was Jean who first suggested that I was looking at what had happened with you all wrong. *You* left me in the worst possible way. You didn't give me an opportunity to try to change your mind. You didn't give me a chance to argue. You must have had a plan in place all along and it specifically involved hurting me. And I have to tell you, when I realized that, I hated you. Because I'd loved you when we were together. Because you'd lied to me. Because I couldn't stop loving you even though you'd treated me so badly."

"I'm sorry . . ."

"No, let me finish. We got married very quickly. You could say I was on the rebound, or that I wanted to trap her before she could get away, or that I needed to prove to myself that I could keep a woman. In retrospect, all of those things were true up to a point. I gave the marriage as much as I could. We bought this house. Our careers were going well. We had friends and went on vacations. I wanted to have children. But here's the truth of it: I didn't love her."

"You don't have to say that."

"But it's true," he admitted. "Throughout our marriage I was still acting in reaction to you. What would you think if you saw this house? What would you think if you saw the necklace I bought Jean for her birthday? What would you think if you saw us with two children, a dog, and—Christ, I don't know—a Volvo?"

"So you divorced her."

David laughed bitterly. "She left me. She often threw you up to me. She called you the phantom who haunted our happiness. But when it came down to the end, she didn't leave because of you. She left because I went to the U.S. Attorney's Office. 'Why leave private practice when things are going so well?' she asked. What she meant was, Why leave a cushy, high-paying job for a hard, low-paying one? What could I say? That I remembered how you used to talk about doing good in the world? That I remembered how we had talked about how we could make things better through the law? That even five, seven, ten years after you disappeared I still thought about you, that I still cared about what you would think of me if we ever met again?"

Hulan waited, sensing that he wasn't finished.

"I got to a place where I couldn't bear the thought that I would run into you and the best I could say for myself was that I'd filed another lawsuit, written another brief, or billed two thousand hours," he continued. "In this country, people talk a lot about being true to oneself, about midlife crisis, about living for the moment. I made the move to the U.S. Attorney's Office knowing it would drive Jean away and knowing at the same time that it was my only hope to regain my sense of who I was. No one in the office really cared about Asian organized crime, so I asked Rob to let me have those cases. I bugged him and Madeleine, too. The whole time—whether I won or lost—I was thinking, hoping, that maybe I would run into you."

"And you did." Hulan pushed herself up on her elbows and stared at him. "You had no idea what I was doing. You were going on blind faith. And still you found me."

"I love you," David said simply.

Hulan ducked her head. When she raised it, he saw that her eyes were bright with tears. "I love you, too," she whispered.

"Now that we're together again, I want us to stay that way."

"I don't know . . ."

"You don't have to go back to China. You can stay here. I'll get you asylum. Everything will work out."

"I want that as much as you," she said.

She put her head back down on his chest and closed her eyes. Outside a pink and lavender sky pushed away the night. Birds greeted the dawn tumultuously. David lay awake for a few more minutes, wondering.

An hour and a half of fitful sleep and David and Hulan were up again. David had never gotten used to the time change going to China and had woken up there every morning at three. Since coming back to Los Angeles, he and Hulan experienced the reverse, partly due to jet lag and partly to desire. But this last night was different. They were running on adrenaline now, but still thoroughly exhausted.

David showered, shaved, and dressed in a suit. They left early so that Hulan could stop by her hotel to change. From the Biltmore, David drove to the parking lot used by assistant U.S. attorneys. David put an arm around her shoulders as they walked up to the federal courthouse. On the twelfth floor, Lorraine buzzed them through. Outside David's office they found Jack Campbell, Peter Sun, and dozens of other special agents from the FBI already waiting for them. Campbell looked terrible. His clothes were rumpled. He needed a shave. His eyes were red from tears and a raging hangover. He smelled as though he'd been sweating everything he'd drunk the night before—a corrosive combination of scotch, beer, and black coffee.

David and Hulan were introduced to the other agents—white, black, old, young, but basically interchangeable in their suits, ties, starched shirts, holstered guns, and outrage. They were all expressing that anger in frustrated, intense voices. Finally David shouted, "Shut up!" At his outburst they did just that and David said, "We've got a preliminary hearing to set bail for Spencer Lee in a half hour. And I'm telling you right now, he's going to walk out of here unless you can give me something—some real piece of evidence to tie him to Noel's death."

"And the death of Mr. Zhao," Hulan added, but the immigrant was far from the minds of the assembled agents.

They went over their scant and circumstantial evidence. At the end, David said, "I think we have to face facts. Lee's going to be on the streets in about two hours, which means you've got that much time to do whatever you need to do to get your surveillance in place. He may not have committed these murders, but he's the key to them, and I don't want to lose sight of him for a minute."

At this point Madeleine Prentice summoned David, Hulan, and Peter to her office. Rob Butler was there, as were two men from the Chinese consulate in Los Angeles. Madeleine made the necessary introductions, then said, "Okay, I want everyone to see this." She flicked on the television and with the remote control zapped from channel to channel, stopping at local morning news shows.

On one station, the honorary mayor of Chinatown reassured the populace that the enclave was still a safe place to visit. On another, the Chinese consul general in Los Angeles viciously attacked local law enforcement, the city, the state, the nation, and the president for the death of a Chinese national and for placing in jeopardy two Ministry of Public Security agents who had come here at the invitation of the United States. On one of the networks, Patrick O'Kelly unctuously opined that these murders were not connected to the arrest of the Chinese involved in the sale of nuclear trigger components of a week ago. And, of course, there were late-night clips from the crime scene. Body bags. Agents dressed in windbreakers with "FBI" printed in electric yellow on the back. Hulan and David leaving the restaurant, saying "No comment," slipping into his car, and driving away. Jack Campbell—his face blotchy, his eyes puffy—ferociously putting his hand up over a camera lens.

Madeleine flipped off the television, then said, "We've got several problems going at once. David, I understand you're going to be in court in a few minutes. We'll get back to that one in a minute. I'm dealing with Washington as best I can. I've got to tell you, you've put me in a tough position. And someone's going to have to talk to the press. We need to get our voice in there and do a little damage control if we can. David?"

"Can't we put the press off?"

"Are you crazy? Forgive me, but an FBI agent doesn't get chopped up and cooked every day, and there's the little matter of the illegal. What was his name?"

"Zhao."

"Right, Zhao. What *were* you thinking? How could you have used someone like that? At the very least, we needed to discuss it. Christ! Don't you watch the news? We've got an international crisis going on and you're sending an illegal Chinese undercover."

"It seemed like a good idea at the time . . . "

"Well, your good idea has turned into an international incident of its own. Washington's gone ballistic over the death of Special Agent Gardner. The mayor of Chinatown is threatening to sue. On what grounds, I don't know, but he's been a busy man these last few hours. He's either been on every morning news show, as you've already seen, *or* he's been on the phone to me, yelling and screaming about how badly this reflects on his community."

As David started to say something, she held up her hand. "I'm not done. Given all this, I've asked the consulate for help. We were the sponsoring agency for this fiasco, and I personally feel terrible about what happened. Mr. Chen and Mr. Leung very graciously agreed to come to this meeting. They are worried about the safety of Inspector Liu and Investigator Sun and believe they should return home immediately."

David wasn't going to let that happen. "We still need Inspector Liu to advise us on the case."

"I agree," Peter said. David and Hulan looked at him in surprise. "She's needed here."

"She is wanted in Beijing," said Mr. Chen.

"She will return when the case is over," Peter retorted.

"You will both return today," Mr. Chen commanded.

Hulan cleared her throat. "Excuse me, but don't I have a say in any of this?"

"We have received orders . . . "

"*You* have received orders. *I* have not. And until I hear personally from Section Chief Zai or Vice Minister Liu, Investigator Sun and I will remain to fulfill our obligations." It was a ruse, but one that might buy them some time.

The two men from the consulate argued with Hulan in Chinese, but she remained firm. Then the men stood, made curt bows to Madeleine Prentice, and left. The U.S. attorney sighed.

"What about the press?" she asked wearily.

"I've got court in a couple of minutes," David said, "then I want to stay with the FBI."

She looked at him in disappointment. "I remember a day not too long ago when you said you wanted to stick with this as long as it was *your* case. We gave you a lot of rope." Mercifully, she didn't add, *And you're hanging yourself with it.* "I'll deal with the press, all right? You get down to court and do everything you can to keep Spencer Lee in custody."

When the meeting was over, David hurried down to the courtroom. Hulan and Peter hung back. "I think I owe you an apology," she said, thinking of all the times she had cut him out of her investigations.

"There is no need, Inspector."

Hulan pushed the button for the elevator. "What you did in there . . ." She was having trouble finding the words.

"I was only doing my job."

Hulan met his eyes. "Thank you," she said, then extended her hand. After a moment he took it and they shook.

By the time Hulan and Peter got down to the magistrate's court, the FBI agents had already settled into the first two pews on the right side of the aisle. They looked formidable, and David worried that Judge Hack would be less than pleased to see such a show of force in his courtroom, but there was little to be done about it. The agents were, in fact, here to be intimidating. Nothing David could say would induce them to leave the courtroom. On the defense's side of the aisle sat four extremely beautiful Chinese women in their early twenties. Girlfriends of Spencer Lee or women simply hired to look innocent and sympathetic, David did not know.

Inside the bar on the left-hand side, Spencer Lee sat with his attorney. Lee had changed from his prison uniform into an exquisitely cut three-piece suit of the finest Zegna wool. His tie was a deep red and his breast pocket held a matching silk handkerchief. He appeared rested and happy, smiling and chatting amiably with his new attorney. Since last night, Lee had replaced the triad lackey with Broderick Phelps, one of the highest-priced attorneys in the country, having defended dozens of well-known and well-heeled miscreants in the last two decades.

Judge Hack called on David. He needed to stick with the main case—the smuggling of a quarter of a million dollars' worth of bear bile, which violated the U.S. Endangered Species Act. Knowing how foreign this crime had seemed to him when he first heard about it, David explained at some length about the importation of bear bile, that its street value was greater than cocaine or heroin, and that it was taken from endangered species protected by international treaty.

He played the tape of Spencer Lee accepting the bile from Zhao. David used the charts from his office outlining Asian organized crime in Los Angeles to explain where Spencer Lee fit into the organization and to delineate the Rising Phoenix's activities in Southern California. He gave a brief synopsis of the murders in Beijing, the hiring of the *China Peony*, and the dates of travel for Spencer Lee. He ended by saying, "I'm sure Your Honor is aware of the terrible tragedy that transpired last night in this city. The persons who were killed in the Green Jade Café were the FBI agent assigned to this case and the man who volunteered to deliver the bear bile to Mr. Lee."

Then Broderick Phelps stood to make his case, which was simply that the government had entrapped poor Spencer Lee who, as the judge could see, was an upstanding pillar of the community. To prove his point, Broderick Phelps produced several letters from other upstanding Angelenos willing to testify on Spencer Lee's good character and a copy of the deed to his $2.5 million house in Monterey Park. "Spencer Lee is neither a threat to the community nor a flight risk," Phelps opined in resonant tones.

Phelps then asked if he might respond to the government's other accusations and proceeded to do so. "I see no reason for my esteemed colleague to bring up the matter of the triads when he has been unable to prove that they even exist. Nor do the allegations about crimes in China have any bearing on this case. We do not have an extradition treaty with China, nor, I might add, should we, when we consider that country's gross violations of human rights. But I would offer one more thing. I have to question Mr. Stark's motives today. He has audacity—I'll give counsel that—but I am outraged that he is even *implying* that my client could be responsible for crimes that occurred in China. During the same dates that Spencer Lee was abroad, there were a *billion* other Chinese also in that country. How Mr. Stark can implicate my client is simply beyond me."

Broderick Phelps's voice rose in indignation as he went on. "As for what happened in our city last night, well, Your Honor, I simply don't know what to say except that my client was a guest of the federal government. In fact, I would say that the assistant U.S. attorney is using the worst sort of stereotyping to attack my client. If Mr. Lee were of Italian descent, would Mr. Stark be calling him a member of the Mafia? I'm sorry to say that I expect so. Our city has withstood a lot in the last few years stemming from just this sort of prejudice. Spencer Lee is innocent of these ludicrous charges and we ask that bail be granted in this case."

"Mr. Stark?" The judge's tone was dubious, but he was willing to hear David out.

"Your Honor, I am in no way trying to imply that all Asians are involved in crime. Today I am here on behalf of the U.S. government as we try to determine Spencer Lee's involvement in several cases—"

"Hold it right there, counselor. Allegations are not enough to jail a man in this country. If you have proof of Mr. Lee's involvement in any of these other crimes—and I'm speaking specifically about those occurring on U.S. soil—I am willing to listen. If you don't, then you'd better sit down."

When Judge Hack granted bail, Spencer Lee turned in his chair to face his coterie of women and raised two fists in triumph. Then he swiveled toward the FBI agents and smiled smugly. The agents sitting on either side of Jack Campbell had to hold him down. Finally, Lee turned his gaze to David, cocked his head, and lifted his eyebrows questioningly. Instead of feeling incensed, David felt a strange kind of sympathy for him. People in his line of work with his foolish bravado often died young.

Having signed over his house as collateral and handed in his passport, Spencer Lee was on the street by 11 A.M. and in the company of the four young women. As they drove along Alameda, turned up Ord Street, then right onto Broadway, they were not alone.

Fifty agents were assigned to Lee's round-the-clock surveillance. In the air, he was covered by two tag-teaming helicopters. On the ground, a whole fleet of cars—each with two men apiece—followed Lee wherever he went. As soon as he got out of his car, he would be followed on foot by at least five agents. When he was at home, agents would cover the iron gates, which provided the only entrance or exit to the property. To be on the safe side, additional agents would be stationed around the perimeter of the property in case Lee tried to jump the fence. The FBI believed he would make a mistake somewhere along the way, and when he did, they would be there.

His first stop was Chinatown and the Princess Garden. The FBI agents watched as Spencer Lee circulated around the huge dining room, stopping here and there to say hello, even exchanging a few business cards. With his bevy of women, he took a table near the front of the room and ordered dumplings, stewed duck feet, rice noodles, and warm tapioca soup.

Later, he took a walk with his groupies, first along Hill Street, with detours on Chungking Court, Mei-ling Way, and Bamboo Lane. He stopped in curio shops, in herb shops, in noodle emporiums, and in a couple of antique stores. Obviously the FBI agents didn't follow him inside these enterprises, nor should they have. But they were there on the streets of Chinatown, posing as tourists, loitering, like homeless men, or striding purposefully as though they had business to attend to.

By two in the afternoon, Spencer Lee was ensconced in his mansion. The FBI agents sitting in their cars pulled out thermoses of coffee and bags of doughnuts. Over the next two hours, several guests came to pay calls on Spencer Lee, presumably to celebrate his release from jail. The gates would open and a Mercedes or a Lexus would pull through. By the time the gates closed, the license plate number would have been radioed in to the FBI and the owner traced. All of these activities were relayed to David and Hulan in his office.

At four, the party—much like those in China—abruptly ended. Everything seemed quiet. David and Hulan went back to his house for the night. All any of them could do was wait.

At two in the morning, David was roused from his sleep by the ringing of the phone. Jack Campbell was on the line and he seemed half crazed. "He's gotten away, Stark!"

A few hours later, the mood in David's office was grim. The FBI agents roiled with a volatile combination of fury and chagrin. At about midnight, although they could see someone walking inside the house, they'd begun to suspect that Spencer Lee had slipped away. At 1 A.M., Jack Campbell had begun pleading with his superiors that someone had better go in there and check things out. Half an hour later, frustrated and racked with guilt, Campbell, ignoring orders, marched up to the front gate and rang the buzzer. The voice that responded over the intercom was not Lee's. In fact, he was not at home. According to Campbell, he must have left the mansion's grounds in one of his guests' cars, which gave him as much as a ten-hour head start.

Everyone considered the possibilities. Lee had left the house by car, which meant he could have done any number of things. He could still be driving. He could be in Las Vegas, hoping to wait things out. He could have gone three hours south to Mexico. He could have headed north, thinking that Canada was only a couple of days away if he drove straight through. But David discarded these ideas. From what little he knew of Spencer Lee, he was convinced that the young man didn't have the gumption to go on the lam without his cronies.

So, during the night, domestic and international airlines were checked. Again, there was no telling which way Lee might have gone. Paris? Chicago? Hong Kong? Hulan thought not. Lee was a Beijinger, she reasoned. He would travel back to that city, where he would have the protection of family and his triad connections. That the name Spencer Lee did not show up on any passenger lists came as no surprise. His passport had been turned in, as was customary, but they had hoped that he'd travel under a recognizable Rising Phoenix alias, maybe even keep the last name of Lee.

At 9 A.M., FBI agents hit the streets of Chinatown to search every business that Lee had entered during his walkabout the day before. Most of the enterprises in this part of Chinatown were run by old families, some of whom had been in the United States for a hundred years or more. They listened to the agents and offered what help they could. Yes, they remembered Spencer Lee's visit. No, they didn't know him personally, but over the years they'd met his type many times before.

But in a stationery store where calligraphy brushes, ink, and practice paper were sold, the owner insisted he had never seen Spencer Lee, knew nothing about the triads, and had never heard of the Rising Phoenix. The FBI agents noticed that Bright Peony Papers looked as if it had never served a single customer, which was strange given how busy all the other shops had been. Seeing a door at the rear of the shop, one of the agents asked what was back there. When the owner refused to answer, the agents burst through (to hell with a warrant), went down a set of stairs to the basement, and found a counterfeiting operation. After a few minutes and a little excessive force, they had an alias for Spencer Lee.

Twenty minutes later, as Hulan predicted, the name was found on a passenger manifest for a direct flight to Beijing. The flight had left from San Francisco at one this morning, which meant that Lee had been in the air for nine hours. He would be arriving in Beijing very shortly. Hulan called the Ministry of Public Security. "Find Vice Minister Liu, find Section Chief Zai! We need someone arrested at the airport."

A couple of hours later, a call was patched through to David's office for Inspector Liu Hulan. David couldn't understand the Chinese she spoke, but early on he picked up from her expression that Lee had been caught. After she hung up, there was silence. Finally she asked, "Do you think Spencer Lee is responsible for all this—the deaths in Beijing, the *Peony*'s cargo, the bear bile, and the murders of Zhao and Gardner?"

"I don't think he's smart enough or rough enough. We have a word for what he is, Hulan. Spencer Lee's a patsy."

"I think so, too, because as complicated as this has been, as *twisted* . . . " She didn't finish. She smoothed a few strands of hair from her face. She looked exhausted. "They want Peter and me to come home."

"I thought we decided you wouldn't do that."

"I know, David, but let's look at this. Five people have died. Someone is making a profit—on people, on medicines. We thought the answer was here, but we were wrong. I think we have to start over again. I have to go back. It's my duty. You see that, don't you?"

That he saw it didn't make him feel any better about it.

"Then I'll come with you."

Madeleine Prentice thought otherwise. "I've had calls from both the State Department and the Ministry of Public Security. Everyone is satisfied that the culprit is in custody. The Bureau, of course, isn't too thrilled, but I think they'll take some consolation in the fact that the Chinese have a very different judicial system than we do."

"He's not the murderer."

Madeleine shrugged. "It's political now, David. Let the Chinese handle it. Spencer Lee's the scapegoat. Take it. Be happy with it. Try to put this whole disaster behind you."

As David walked down the corridor, he thought over what Madeleine had said. In his office, Hulan waited for him. No matter how things turned out, they would be together.

"Let's go," he said.

He took her hand and they went down the hall to find Peter. The trio left the Federal Courthouse Building and walked to David's car. When they got to his house, David opened his wallet, pulled out his American Express card, and made three reservations on United to Beijing via Tokyo.

Later, after they stopped at the bank to get as much cash as he could, David and Hulan didn't speak much. They were taking a tremendous risk. David's career in the government was effectively over, a realization that gave him a strangely exhilarating sense of freedom.

He did, however, worry about Hulan. In the last week, as the story of the illegal sale of the nuclear trigger components continued to come out, the political situation between the United States and China had regressed to its worst state since the Bamboo Curtain fell. Most of the dependents from the U.S. embassy as well as from its consulates in other parts of China had been sent home; the Chinese had reciprocated by doing the same with about 50 percent of its personnel stationed in the United States. The State Department—while not yet issuing an official advisory against travel to China—had announced that visitors to that country should be "careful"; better yet they should postpone their trips indefinitely.

David and Hulan would go to China. They would see this thing through to the end. And then? The answer to that was out of reach, beyond anything David could imagine.

17

February 10

Beijing

Y ou're about to see why I don't practice law," Hulan said as
she and David took two seats in Beijing's People's Court. The
room was large and typically cold. Several observers still wore their
coats and scarves. But the air was oddly stuffy from cigarette smoke
and, he presumed, fear. For David, who watched as several cases
were tried and sentences meted out with amazing dispatch by a panel
of three judges in military uniforms, the whole scene had a surreal
quality.

The first trial of the day involved a man accused of bank robbery.
The prosecutor shouted out the facts of the case while the defendant
stood with his head bowed. There were no witnesses, and the defendant chose not to speak. His wife and two children, however, were
present at the proceedings and listened as the lead magistrate
announced the decision less than forty-five minutes later. "You are
not an honest man, Gong Yuan," the judge said. "You were trying to
leapfrog to a new level of prosperity by stealing from your countrymen. This cannot be allowed. The only justice for you is immediate
execution."

The second case involved a habitual housebreaker who had come to Beijing from Shanghai. This time, after the prosecutor had item-ized his accusations, the judge asked the defendant several questions. Had he known his victims? Had he come to Beijing legally? Did he understand that if he confessed he would be dealt with more leniently? The answers were no, no, and yes. Still, the defendant chose not to accept responsibility for his crimes. The judge said that twenty years at hard labor might make him see otherwise.

And on it went.

These trials, Hulan explained, were the result of the "Strike Hard" campaign that had begun a little over a year ago. Fueled by the rise in crimes for profit, the government began a crackdown that had pro-duced tens of thousands of arrests and well over one thousand execu-tions. "Once convicted," she said, "the criminals are paraded through the streets, marched through sports arenas, and displayed on televi-sion. They wear placards around their necks listing their crimes. They are denounced as barbarians by their jailers and heckled by crowds. Then it's off to labor camp or death."

Such harsh justice had a long pedigree in China. Twice a year in days gone by, posters would be displayed in cities across the nation—not in public places where foreigners might see them, but behind walls in the neighborhoods—listing the names of those executed and their offenses.

"Families of those who are put to death have to pay for the bul-let," Hulan continued.

"But all that must be for serious crimes," David said.

Hulan shook her head. "Even minor crimes merit tough sen-tences. Being fired from a job and having no other way to make a liv-ing, refusing to accept an employment assignment or housing trans-fer, or simply 'making trouble' can mean a four-year sentence to a labor camp."

"And many of those camps," David said, remembering articles he'd read, "provide cheap labor to American-owned factories in China."

"That's right. The U.S. profits from my countrymen's transgres-sions." Hulan motioned around the room. "And as you can see, justice proceeds quickly here. We have no pretrial hearings, no delays, no extensions, and rarely any defense witnesses to muddy the waters. The defendant is guilty until proven innocent. When that guilt is verified, punishment is determined and carried out promptly. An appeal is as rare as a solar eclipse."

A door opened and Spencer Lee was brought in. His fashionably wrinkled linen suit had been exchanged for a white shirt, black slacks, and leg irons. His head was bowed, but at one point he glanced up. Then, just as quickly, a guard bopped Lee's head with the heel of his fist and the prisoner's head dropped back down submissively.

Lee's trial, like the others before it, was perfunctory at best. A woman prosecutor stood. Her hair was short and permed. She wore severe wire-rim glasses. Her voice was loud and strident as she gestured to Spencer Lee and introduced him by his Chinese name, Li Zhongguo. ("'New China' Lee," Hulan whispered.) "Li Zhongguo has not only brought disgrace on his name but on his entire country," the prosecutor proclaimed. She then enumerated Lee's crimes against the people. He was involved with a gang that was trying to reach its tentacles into China. This gang was known to be involved in the worst of all trades—that of human life. The exit and entry dates from his passport and the fact that he fled—she didn't say where from—added to evidence that he was also involved in several murders.

The case was over in ninety minutes. The lead judge said, "You have been found guilty of various corrupt and vile acts. You have taken many lives in many forms. For this you should pay with your life. Your execution will be held tomorrow at noon." A murmur filtered through the courtroom. The judges gave the crowd a dour look and polite silence was instantly restored. "Until then," the judge continued, "you will be held at Municipal Jail Number Five." Spencer Lee was led away.

Municipal Jail Number Five was located on the far northwestern edge of Beijing near the Summer Palace, where the old imperial court used to retreat during the hottest months. Peter drove with loquacious vehemence, but in the backseat, David and Hulan seemed relaxed. They had all lost a day crossing the international date line. On their arrival in Beijing, a car had dropped David off at the Sheraton Great Wall. (For propriety's sake, Hulan said.) As a result, they had all gotten a good night's sleep. They would be grateful for it today. Hulan had arranged interviews with Dr. Du and Ambassador Watson after their visit with Spencer Lee.

This was the first time David had been away from the center of the city, and he took in these sights with much the same awe and excitement as Peter had shown in his travels across Los Angeles. With surprising speed the scene might change from a walled *hutong* neighborhood to a spate of brand-new cast-concrete high-rises of shoddy design and even shoddier construction. The balconies on the new buildings had been enclosed with glass to create extra rooms. Looking up into them, David could see laundry hanging on lines, plants growing bravely, lovers kissing. No matter where they drove, they couldn't escape the *life* of these neighborhoods. On a street corner, a man hunkered down with a tin pan of water, washing his hands and feet. Outside the Beijing Zoo, budding merchants sold balloons, miniature stuffed panda bears, and cans of Pepsi and Orange Crush. In fact, everywhere David looked he saw something for sale—kitchenwares, candles, incense to light in temples, bottled water, CDs, low-slung rattan chairs. Wherever there was a vacant stretch of sidewalk or asphalt, old women—dressed in thick padded jackets and wearing white kerchiefs over their hair—swept in long fluid motions with bamboo brooms. At some intersections, using exaggerated arm movements and high-pitched trills on their whistles, other women instructed the pedestrian traffic when to cross.

Along the periphery of one intersection—actually an old crossroads where several streets met in a large circle—a free market had been set up where peasants sold fruit, vegetables, meat, live poultry, eggs, and raw herbs and spices for cooking and medicine. A block from there Peter drove through high gates and into the jail's courtyard.

Inside the Administration Building, David and Hulan were met by the woman prosecutor. Away from the courtroom, Madame Huang was friendly and gregarious. David learned that she and Hulan had worked on many cases together over the years. "Inspector Liu finds the criminals and brings them to us," the prosecutor explained to David, then waggishly told him that Municipal Jail Number Five catered to VIPs. They passed several offices and a Nautilus gym for staff use; then she escorted them into an interrogation room. A tea girl came in with a thermos and poured cups of the steaming liquid for the visitors. To David, this didn't look like a place that Amnesty International would target, but by now he knew that his preconceptions were almost universally wrong when it came to China.

A pair of guards seated Spencer Lee across from David and Hulan. Lee wore an army coat to stave off the cold of the room.

"How are your new accommodations?" David asked.

"They seem all right."

"Are you being treated well?" Spencer Lee jutted his chin, then David said, "You're in a difficult position."

The young man looked around the interrogation room. He was a long way from his easy life in Los Angeles.

"The inspector and I don't believe you were involved with the deaths of those boys . . . "

"The judges said I was responsible. I guess I was," Lee said at last.

"You'll be executed," Hulan said.

But Spencer Lee didn't seem concerned. He said, "Do you think I came back to China to escape from you? Do you think I was so *infantile* that I would not know the MPS would be waiting for me when I landed in Beijing? You two are really very naive."

Hulan was about to say something, but David put a hand on her arm. She stood and quietly left the room.

"There is a plan," Lee continued. "There has always been a plan."

"Tell me about it."

"That would take the fun out of it. Besides, I'm guilty."

"Then let me ask you this," David said amiably. "If you are guilty, then why did you tell Zhao that Cao Hua would contact him when he returned to Beijing?"

A flash of doubt crossed Spencer Lee's flawless features, then he once again professed his guilt.

David looked at his watch, then up at Lee. "You have twenty-four hours left. We want to help you." He tried to sound reassuring as he said, "If Guang Mingyun is behind these crimes, let him be executed, not you."

"There will be no execution," Lee said, his confidence restored. "I told you before. I have protection. I have friends."

Hulan returned with a phone, which she plugged into a jack. "I am going to call the ministry," she said. "I want you to hear my conversation."

She dialed and asked for Section Chief Zai. When she had him on the line, she explained where she was and what the situation was vis-à-vis Spencer Lee. Then she said, "Let us put through a petition to postpone Lee's execution. I am sure that given time we will get to the truth." She listened, then said, "Yes, he is reluctant to help us. But please, let us not lose our only lead." She nodded a few times, said good-bye, then hung up the phone.

"Spencer," Hulan said softly, "the people you're dealing with have no further use for you." When he didn't respond, she said, "I am trying to save your life. My superior says he will file the petition, but you have to help me."

The young man was unmoved. "You are Chinese, Inspector Liu. You should understand that family is everything. I am protected. Now, may I go back to my cell?"

"If we can get the court to agree to the petition, then I'm sure we can stop the execution," Hulan said as they drove back into town. "Meanwhile, we have to try to find evidence, a witness, anything. If we can accomplish that, maybe Lee will believe us and maybe then he'll tell us who's really behind these crimes."

"Is it possible he's right? That he won't be executed anyway?"

"Who would have that kind of protection?" she shot back. "David, you said it yourself. He's the patsy."

Now David worried about the importance of keeping their appointment with Dr. Du. "Shouldn't we be going straight to Watson and Guang?"

"We will, David. But the bear bile is at the heart of this." When he grudgingly agreed, she said, "We don't know anything about that business. Dr. Du's the only person I know who can help us."

While David and Hulan went inside the Beijing Chinese Herbal Medicine Institute, Peter sped off to Cao Hua's apartment to look for the Panda Brand products that Hulan had seen in the refrigerator. The institute's elevator still wasn't working, so they walked up the six flights of stairs to Dr. Du's office. He greeted them warmly, ordered tea, and asked, "How can I help you?"

As Hulan and David quickly ran through their recent discoveries, Dr. Du shook his head in sympathy. When they were done, he said, "You want to know about bear bile, and I will tell you. But you have to understand about our medicine first."

Hulan glanced at David. They were in a hurry, but they needed this information. "Whatever you think best, Doctor."

"Good," Dr. Du said. In his grave, scholarly way, he told them that Chinese herbal medicine could be traced to 3494 B.C., making it the longest continuously used medical tradition in the world. "To this day, every person gets the same prescriptions, but the skill is in how you create the proper dose. If you can master that, then you can become the best doctor in all of China. You look at me. I have practiced for thirty years and seen thousands and thousands of patients, but never the same dose."

"Forgive me, Doctor, for not knowing more," Hulan interrupted, "but I remember something about medicines to cool or heat the body."

"Oh, yes. We think of the four essences—cold, hot, warm, and cool. But I also consider the four directions of action for a medicine—ascending, descending, floating, and sinking. I use the five flavors—pungent, sweet, sour, bitter, and salty."

"How do you know what dose to prescribe?" David asked.

"By the age of the patient. By the seasons. I have to determine if someone needs a cooling medicine or one for heating if it's summer or winter. By where someone is from. In China people eat different foods in different provinces. What I would prescribe for someone from Sichuan is different from what I would give someone from Guangdong Province. The weather is mild and hot in Sichuan. The people eat hot and spicy food. The medicine I would give a Sichuanese would have a strong fragrance and be powerful.

For a Cantonese, who has a cool diet, I would give something bland."

Suddenly Dr. Du stood. "Come, I will show you."

As they followed him down the hall, Hulan asked, "Do you use Panda Brand products?"

"Sometimes," Dr. Du said. "But you will see, we like to make our own prescriptions."

He stopped at a door, unlocked it, and they stepped into a store-room. The floor space was taken up with huge burlap bags, each opened and peeled back to reveal its contents. Hulan and David recognized the cloves, cinnamon, cardamom, nutmeg, and dried tangerine peel; they learned these were good for hiccup, wheezing, staph infections, salmonella, flu, and a variety of other symptoms. They saw chunks of raw minerals—some crystalline or chalklike; others were just jagged pieces of rock—fluorite, amber, pumice, borax, and cinnabar. Dr. Du showed them tubers, roots, and rhizomes in every size, variety, shape, and color. In one bag was something that looked like saffron, while in another, dinner plate–size patties of dried yellow flowers lay in stacks. They saw burdock root, lotus plumule, swallow-wort root, chinaberries, and lichee and ginkgo nuts.

Dr. Du did his best to explain what the herbs were used for. Even Hulan struggled with many of the Mandarin words, not knowing their English equivalents. Some of the herbs Hulan couldn't have translated even if she'd wanted, for they were grown only in remote areas and had esoteric names. When this occurred, she used a literal translation—"Commerce Continent," "Sweet Process," "Chicken Blood Wine," "Snake's Bed Seeds," or "King Who Does Not Stay But Departs."

Dr. Du took them to another room, which held the medicinals derived from the animal world. Here again were burlap sacks over-flowing with abalone, clam, and turtle shells. These and other minerals, Hulan and David were informed, anchored the spirit by reducing irritability, insomnia, palpitations, and anxiety. Sacks overflowed with dried sea horses—used for impotence and incontinence. Dried scorpions were separated by size and placed in large tin bowls. Similarly silkworms were separated by stages of development as well as by "healthy" and "sick." Yet another bowl held silkworm feces—good for rashes, spasms of the calf muscles, and diarrhea. They saw piles of snakes dried into coils and hundreds of dried centipedes tied together in bundles.

"I know this is a delicate issue," David said at last, "but I understand that many of the medicines come from endangered animals . . . "

"Bears, tigers, rhinos—I don't use those."

"You answer very quickly," Hulan said, the investigator coming out in her.

"I answer quickly because every spring the government sends me from province to province to educate other practitioners about alternatives."

"What about bear bile?" David persisted.

"Bear gallbladder was first prescribed three thousand years ago," Dr. Du answered. "Since then many scholars have written about the benefits of bear bile, meat, brain, blood, paw, and spinal cord. But the gallbladder is considered to be the most important part of the bear and very strong—like rhino horn, ginseng, or deer musk."

"I'm sorry," David said in exasperation, "but you can't really believe this stuff works."

There was a long silence. At last Dr. Du spoke. "The ingredients may sound strange, but actually your drug companies use many of these same compounds or synthetic versions in their products, because they've been proven to work. Ursodeoxycholic acid is the active ingredient in bear bile. The synthetic version the U.S. makes dissolves gallstones and is showing promise in treating a usually fatal form of cirrhosis of the liver."

Dr. Du's stern look transformed into a smile, the white ghost's impudence forgiven. "Now, I could use cow or pig gall . . . "

"But?"

"The pig and the bear have habits very much like human beings and they eat the same food. Some doctors use cow gall at a very high dose, but I'm not so sure. Who among us is like a cow?" When he received no response, Dr. Du continued, "I prefer to use gardenia, rhubarb, peony root, even Madagascar periwinkle in place of bear gall, but as I said earlier, only a good doctor will know how to prescribe them."

"Can't you use farmed bile?"

Dr. Du answered, "There are some people who believe they can farm bears for their bile. But let me tell you something. What they do to those bears is terrible."

"How do they extract the bile?" Hulan asked.

"Doctors surgically implant a tube into the gallbladder. This is held in place by a metal corset around the bear's stomach. The bile is draining all the time. Some people even pay to drink the bile straight from the bear at milking time."

"How can those places operate if they're illegal?" David asked.

"You're a foreigner, so you don't understand China," Du said sympathetically. "In our country, the government is very busy with other matters, so these hooligans can get away with it. In the remote provinces—Jilin, Yunnan, and Heilongjiang—anyone can go out, trap some bears, and start up a farm. Even if you go down to Chengdu in Sichuan, you can find maybe one hundred bear farms. We have over ten thousand bears living on illegal bear farms in China."

"How do you know all this if the extraction process is such a secret and the police are looking the other way?" Hulan asked.

"I already told you, the government sends me out to different provinces. On some trips I have gone on raids." He paused, then added, "Those places are very bad, but the masses are happy because they believe that the best medicine comes from the wild animal."

"Why?"

"Because you take on the attributes of that animal—bear, tiger, monkey. You think you will become strong, potent, or wise tricksters. So most of the people don't want farmed bear anyway. They want to see the wild bear with their own eyes."

"But something like bear gall," Hulan said, "how does it work? How do you use it?"

"Your mother and father are very knowledgeable about our medicine," Dr. Du observed. "Did they forget to teach you?"

"I was away in America for many years," she explained. "I forgot the old ways."

Dr. Du scratched at his sideburns, then shook his head in sorrow at what Hulan had lost in the far-off land. "Bear gall is bitter and cold. Bitter medicinals dispel heat, dry dampness, and purge the body. The cold attributes cool the blood and detoxify the body."

"Which means you use it for what?"

"I don't use it!"

"I understand that, but you would prescribe a bitter-cold medicine . . . "

"For jaundice, skin lesions, convulsions in babies, fever, ulcers, poor vision. For hemorrhoids, bacterial infections, cancer, burns, pain and redness in the eyes, asthma, sinus infections, tooth decay . . . "

"A little of everything," Hulan said. Now her skepticism was showing. "Isn't it just the placebo effect?"

"You come in here and say this to Dr. Du?" There was no mistaking his indignation this time. "Our medicine is many times older than Western medicine. It is not a placebo. *This* is why I am invited to speak at Harvard Medical School, and it is why our government lets me travel so freely."

He threw his hands up over his head. He'd had it with these impertinent fools. "You go away now! I am tired of this!" Then he began shooing them out. At the door, he shook his finger at Hulan. "You show no respect. Your parents would be very disappointed in you."

Downstairs, Peter was waiting for them. "How did it go?" he inquired as he pulled away from the institute.

"I think we insulted him," Hulan said.

David snorted. "That's an understatement."

"But did you get useful information?" Peter asked.

Hulan and David looked at each other thoughtfully. "I don't know," Hulan said. "Maybe."

"What I still don't understand is, if the farms are illegal, how can they operate?" David asked.

"Our government says no to many things," Hulan said. "Still, people want to make money. Some say they'll open a 'legal' bear farm. They say they have a permit, but I bet all they have is a permit to open a business, *not* a bear farm."

"Doesn't anyone check?"

"I guess not," Hulan said, sounding discouraged.

"*I* have good news," Peter announced. "You were right, Inspector. Cao Hua's refrigerator was filled with Panda Brand bear bile."

"The ambassador will be with you as soon as he can," Phil Firestone, William Watson's attaché, said brusquely. "We're in the middle of a crisis and, well, the ambassador is awfully busy."

"I'd like to think that he'd place the murder of his son above international intrigue," Hulan said, instantly striking an adversarial chord. For once, David agreed. He was tired of getting the runaround from this man.

"Naturally Ambassador Watson continues to mourn," Firestone said smoothly. "But sometimes we have to put others above our own needs."

"While we're waiting, perhaps you can answer some questions," David said.

Firestone started to roll his eyes, then caught himself. "Go ahead," he said with a sigh.

"How do you process visa applications?"

Firestone shook his head slightly. "Visa applications? What do they have to do with anything?" When David didn't respond, Firestone sighed again. "People come here. You've seen them outside. They stand in line. They get applications and fill them out. We interview the people. If someone wants to travel to the U.S. on business, we expect to see an official invitation from the sponsoring organization or business stateside. Potemkin Auto Leasing, the Audubon Society, the Baptist Church of Starkville, Mississippi, you name it, we've seen it. Nothing peculiar about it. The Chinese like to see the same types of formal invitations when they process visa applications for American citizens. I'll bet you got an official invitation from the MPS before you came here."

David nodded, then asked, "What if someone *hasn't* been invited by a corporation in the U.S.?"

"We treat those cases quite a bit differently," Firestone said. "After all, there are a lot of people in China who'd like to get out, and I'm not talking just about dissidents."

It was amazing to Hulan what a few days and a lot of news head-lines could do to a political toady like Firestone. His knee-jerk diplo-macy of just one week ago had evaporated as easily as a late-spring snow shower. He now saw China as a hair's breadth away from being a full-fledged enemy, while the MPS and its investigation were emblematic of all that was evil in the society.

David chose to ignore Firestone's rudeness. "Who actually stamps the visas?"

"What are you talking about?" The young man's patience was wearing thin. "If you're accusing someone of something, why not spit it out?"

"Just answer the question," David countered evenly.

"We've got a department full of people who do that. But, hell, I've stamped a couple of passports, even the ambassador has stamped them on occasion. It's all perfectly legal."

As on their last visit, the ambassador began speaking to them even before he entered the room. "We're going to have to make this quick," he said just before he appeared around the doorjamb. "I'm waiting for a call from the president," he continued as he crossed the room, modulated his voice to the more intimate surroundings, shook David's and Hulan's hands perfunctorily, and took a seat. He barely paused before he summarily dismissed his adjutant. "Phil, get these folks some coffee."

As soon as the young man left, the ambassador's public demeanor fell away and was replaced by declarations of personal gratitude for the arrest, trial, and conviction of his son's killer.

David and Hulan had discussed how to approach this man. Should they treat him as an adversary—a course Hulan recom-mended—or as the highest-ranking American citizen in China? This quandary was aggravated by the fact that they were here on two very different missions: one, to find out how Guang Henglai, Cao Hua, and the other couriers had gotten visas so easily; two, to break the news to Ambassador Watson that his son was, at the very least, involved with some pretty shady characters. They had decided that attacking on the visa issue was the most practical approach, since it would unquestionably provoke anger. Then they could tell Watson about his son. Somewhere along the way they hoped they'd learn something to save Spencer Lee.

But they didn't get very far with their preliminary inquiries before Phil Firestone, who'd returned with the coffee, burst out with "Why do you keep asking about this visa bullshit? It has nothing to do with anything, and is just a waste of the ambassador's time. I already told you that he's very busy at present."

"What we're talking about here is a serious threat to national security," David stated bluntly. "Illegally stamping passports is a federal crime. That translates, Firestone, into federal time in a federal penitentiary."

Phil Firestone flushed a deep crimson.

David now directed his comments to the ambassador. "If there are any irregularities in the embassy, it wouldn't be the first time. I'm sure the ambassador is aware of several cases where trusted employees overstepped their diplomatic bounds."

"If you're accusing me—" Firestone sputtered.

"Take it easy, Phil," the ambassador cut in. "Can't you see they're just trying to get your goat? Go on back to your office. I'll be fine. But when that call comes through, let me know right away, okay?"

When Firestone closed the door behind him, the ambassador said, "Come on, Stark, give the boy a break."

David held his palms up and shrugged. "It was worth a try."

The ambassador shook his head and smiled wanly. "I'll look into this problem, all right? Now how else can I help you?"

"It's about your son," David said.

"If you're going to tell me he got into trouble as a kid, believe me, there's not much I don't know. Billy had problems, no question, but things had really turned around for him the last couple of years."

"The last couple of years?"

"He was doing well in college. Elizabeth and I were really proud of him for that."

"Mr. Ambassador," David said heavily, "your son wasn't in college. He hadn't attended for two years."

"You're wrong," he retorted.

"I'm afraid not. Inspector Liu and I checked USC's records."

"But I wrote the checks . . . "

"To the school or to Billy?" Hulan asked.

Watson turned his eyes to her. "To Billy," he rasped. "Oh, my God, to Billy." The color drained from his face. For the first time since she had met him, Hulan saw a father devastated by grief.

"Your son . . ." David cleared his throat and began again. "Your son traveled to China every couple of months. Were you aware of that?"

"No! Billy only came home for Christmas vacation and a quick visit in the summer."

"I'm sorry, Mr. Ambassador, but your son spent a lot of time in China. He usually traveled with Guang Henglai."

"The other dead boy?"

"The son of Guang Mingyun. That's correct." David hesitated. "We believe he also traveled with some other people." He pulled out the list of suspected couriers and handed it to the ambassador. William Watson's hand trembled as he scanned the list. "These people all had their visas stamped here at the embassy."

"I'm at a loss to explain that."

The time had come to tell the ambassador the truth about his son. As David explained the smuggling of bear bile and his suspicion that Billy Watson was involved, the ambassador repeated, "It can't be true. None of this can be true."

"Inspector Liu and I are working against the clock," David said, then explained the situation with Spencer Lee. "I know it's short notice, but is there any way you can have a few trusted people look into the passport irregularities? We think it's crucial to the crimes and you'd be saving a man's life."

"No way, not ever," Watson spat out. "Lee has been convicted of killing my son. He's going to pay."

The more David and Hulan tried to tell Watson he was wrong, the more adamant he became. But David held his ground: "I can get an order from the State Department. Then you'll have to start an investigation of the visas."

"By that time," the ambassador grated, "my son's murderer will be dead and all this will be over."

Phil Firestone came in to say that the president was on the phone.

"We'll have to continue this later," the ambassador said.

"One more thing before we go," Hulan said, rising. "Your son was in business with Guang Henglai. Are you sure you knew nothing about that?"

William Watson's normally rugged face had crumbled into an old man's. "I don't know what to say, Inspector. I guess I didn't know my son very well."

Firestone said urgently, "Mr. Ambassador? The president?"

As David and Hulan headed for the door, Ambassador Watson—his finger poised to hit the button on the phone that would bring him the president's voice—made a last request. "Please don't tell my wife about this. Elizabeth's been through so much. It would just kill her."

18

FEBRUARY 11
The Crossroads

David and Hulan arrived at the China Land and Economics Tower at nine the next morning. A secretary promptly escorted them into Guang's overheated office. Tea and sweetmeats were served. Guang had, of course, heard about the arrest and trial of Spencer Lee.

"I am forever in your debt," he told them. "If there is anything I can ever do for either of you, I would be honored to do it. Please let me begin by hosting a banquet in celebration of your triumph."

"Before you do that, Mr. Guang, we have a few more questions," Hulan said.

"But the hooligan is arrested. He will be executed."

"Attorney Stark and I don't think that Spencer Lee was responsible for your son's death," Hulan said. A grim look came over Guang's features as she continued. "While we were in Los Angeles, Attorney Stark and I made some interesting discoveries. We hope you can help us understand them."

"Anything. Anything I can do."

"This may not be pleasant for you," she said.

"My son's death was not pleasant for me, Inspector. There is nothing you can say that will change that."

"We believe that your son was involved in smuggling . . . "

Guang Mingyun flinched at the news.

"Not narcotics," Hulan amended, "but medicines that are illegal in the United States and China."

Guang's denials echoed those of the ambassador. Finally, Hulan put a hand up to silence the entrepreneur, explained what the boys had been doing, then said, "We need you to answer some questions."

Hearing her formal tone, Guang obediently sat up in his chair. Too many years in the labor camp, Hulan thought.

"Do the names Cao Hua, Hu Qichen, or Wang Yujen mean anything to you?" she asked.

Guang look confused. She read down the list of other names they had found in the Immigration computer of people traveling on the same dates as Guang Henglai and Billy Watson.

"I have never heard of them."

Hulan moved on. "Your son attempted to get one of your brothers in California to sell the bile."

"I don't believe it."

Hulan didn't give Guang a chance to elaborate. Instead she asked, "What are your connections to the Rising Phoenix?"

"I told you before, I don't know anything about them."

"Have you been involved in the smuggling of human beings?"

"No!" Guang's polished demeanor seemed to be crumbling. Hulan had to keep pushing him.

"Have you been involved with the smuggling of this bear bile? Did you sponsor your son and Billy Watson in this business?"

"How many times can I tell you? I know nothing of this."

"You were not aware that your son was smuggling products made by Panda Brand, one of your own companies?" Hulan asked.

"I own Panda Brand," he acknowledged, "but I can't believe that my son was smuggling anything from there. What's to smuggle? Panda Brand products are perfectly legal."

"Bear bile isn't," she pointed out.

"I do not know much about each of my businesses, but I do know that our pharmaceutical company does scientific research." He appeared to regain his composure now that the subject had shifted back to business. "We are one of only five companies in all of China that has received permits for the purpose of investigating the uses and attributes of bear bile. I'm sure there are scientists in America doing similar work. China is trying to save its bears from extinction. Our bears are bred in captivity. When the bears reach maturity, we extract the bile. We do not use the primitive forms of extraction used on illegal farms.

"But don't ask me to reveal our process," Guang went on. "It is a secret. Anyway, our country's plan is working well. The gall produced annually by a single bear is equal to that obtained from killing forty-four wild bears. Over a farmed bear's five-year production period, two hundred and twenty wild bears are spared. Potentially, thousands of wild bears will be 'saved' each year. So yes, we do keep bears and other animals for research and display at Panda Brand, but that doesn't mean we have done anything wrong. This is why our facility is open to the public. Tourists come from all over to see our little zoo."

"Then can you explain how we happened to find Panda Brand bear bile being smuggled into Los Angeles?" David asked.

"You are wrong," Guang said, but there was no mistaking the uncertainty in his voice.

"I'm afraid not."

"Check my records. We have never manufactured that product for public use," Guang insisted, "let alone exported it to the U.S."

"Guang Mingyun, you know our policy," Hulan said. "Leniency to those who confess—"

"Don't use those threats on me," Guang countered angrily. "I spent eight years in prison camp listening to them, and they didn't change my answers."

"Then you well know the injustices that can happen in our country," Hulan continued. She checked her watch. "Spencer Lee is scheduled to die in two hours. I won't lie to you. He is involved in this somehow, but if he's executed his knowledge will die with him." She reached into her purse and pulled out a small box, which she handed to Guang. "Can you tell me what this is?"

"It is the packaging we use at Panda Brand."

"Can you read what is on the label?"

"It says . . ." Guang's voice was aggrieved. "It says Panda Brand Bear Bile."

"I will repeat," Hulan said. "Leniency to those who confess."

Guang's eyes were moist when he looked up. "Last year I received reports that someone was using our factory to manufacture forged packaging like this box. As we began looking into it, we also found that someone had also been pilfering our stock of bear bile. I have already told you, there is nothing illegal in what we do. We produce bear bile for scientific purposes only."

"What did you do when you learned about the missing stock?"

"We tightened security. We had no more losses."

"Did you suspect your son?"

This last was more than Guang could endure. A low moan issued from deep inside him. Then Guang Mingyun shuddered, took a deep breath, and said, "Not until he disappeared."

"You found something in his apartment, didn't you?" Hulan asked.

Guang nodded gravely.

"His refrigerator was empty," Hulan said. "I thought you had sent someone over to take away the perishables."

"I did. When my man brought everything to the house, I saw the bile. I don't know why Henglai kept it in the refrigerator."

"The boys probably just thought it was out of the way," Hulan said, but Guang wasn't listening.

"I went back to the apartment myself," he said. "I found more bile—more than we have ever manufactured."

David cleared his throat. Guang's sad eyes turned to him. "We learned yesterday that there are many illegal bear farms around Chengdu. Could your son have had connections to one of those?"

"I don't know," Guang said. "But he couldn't have done all this alone."

"He had Billy's help," David reminded him.

"No, I mean at our factory. He had to have inside help. If you want to know the truth, you should go there."

"But first we have to stop the execution," Hulan said. "To save Spencer Lee's life, will you testify in court about Henglai?"

Guang Mingyun slowly nodded.

Before leaving Guang's office, Hulan tried to call the jail, but the phone lines were down in that section of the city. She then called the MPS, hoping to reach Zai or her father, but was told they were both out of the office. There was no way of knowing if the petition for the stay of execution had been accepted. It was now eleven-fifteen. David and Hulan had to get to the jail themselves if they were to stop the execution.

Peter sped down alleyways and side streets, trying to avoid the midday traffic on the main roads. After about thirty-five minutes, they turned into the traffic circle they had to pass through to reach the jail. The daily morning free market was just coming to a close. Most of the peddlers were selling the last of their goods at bargain prices, while others were packing up to go home. Between the market and the gates to Municipal Jail Number Five, people lingered in the street, blocking traffic, gossiping, adjusting their purchases in their bicycle baskets, chasing after a runaway child or two. They were waiting for something.

Hulan jumped out of the Saab, pausing just long enough to ask Peter to stay put. Then she dashed through the crowd, urging David to catch up. They had not gone far when a flatbed truck rolled into the circle. Hulan saw Spencer Lee standing in the back of the truck with his hands shackled behind him and a wooden placard mounted on his back that declared his misdeeds in bold red characters. He was a murderer, a conspirator, a counterrevolutionary committed to corruption, a black mark on the People's Republic of China. The traditional execution "parade" had begun.

The people in the intersection reacted as though the circus had just come to town. Peddlers abandoned their stalls, knowing no one would steal from them. Mothers stopped their gossiping, picked up their children, and gathered around the truck, following its intentionally slow progress around the circle. As David and Hulan elbowed their way through the crowd, the people threw themselves wholeheartedly into their expected role.

"You corrupt so-and-so!"

"Death to the murderer!"

"To the killer the same fate!"

And Spencer Lee, who had never shied away from a performance, gave it his all. He shouted to the crowd that they were cowards. He called out to a winsome young woman that she was lovely and he would be happy to take her as his wife. Shouts of "Cow dung!" and "Hooligan!" met his proposal. Spencer Lee held his head high, smiled broadly, then burst into an aria from a Peking Opera. His audience was thrilled. He was one of the best doomed men they had ever seen.

David and Hulan reached the side of the truck. They each found a handhold and let themselves be pulled along as it continued through the crowd and off the main thoroughfare.

"Spencer!" Hulan called. "Spencer Lee!"

Hearing his American name through the cacophony, the young man looked out over the sea of faces.

"Spencer, we're down here. Look!"

"Inspector Liu, Attorney Stark!" Lee laughed crazily. "I go to my death. You are here to celebrate, correct?"

"No! Spencer, listen. We're here to stop this," Hulan said.

A voice called out, "Shut up! Let the man sing!"

Spencer stared out at the mass of people who pressed against the truck, slowing its progress, then he shifted his gaze back to Hulan. His swagger left him and he looked like what he was—a very young man going to his death. "It's too late, Inspector."

"I *can* stop them!"

Spencer smiled. "You can't. I can't. You see, I was wrong."

"Tell us in Chinese!" someone shouted. "We all want to hear."

"I am from the Ministry of Public Security," Hulan yelled. "Let me through. This man is innocent!"

"She must be his real wife," someone called out. The crowd laughed.

David didn't understand the Chinese words, but he could see that they would never get to the gate unless the people let them through. "Move!" he shouted. "Get out of the way!"

He felt someone jab an elbow into his side. David lost his hold on

the truck and fell back into the crowd. A man hissed, "Go away, foreigner. You have no place here." David shoved the man aside and
grabbed for the truck.

"Tell us the story of your guilt," a voice trilled. "Confess before
you die." The people sent up a loud roar in support of this suggestion, but Spencer Lee ignored them, looking over the front of the
truck's cab to his final destination. There wasn't much time left
before they would reach the high gates at the end of the street.

"I didn't kill anyone," he admitted at last.

"We know," David said.

"I just did what I was told. They promised I would be protected.
Do you understand?"

"Who? Tell us who!"

Spencer avoided their questions. "Everything you said about the
Peony was true. I hired the ship. I was there when the immigrants
were loaded. I made them sign their contracts. But that was all."

"The bear bile?"

"A new business for us. A mistake for me. Obviously."

"We're going to stop this," Hulan vowed.

Spencer Lee looked down at her. "You can't. It was fixed. It was
fixed from the beginning."

"How?"

"The embassy. Your ministry. What does it matter now?"

The crowd was getting impatient.

"Criminal!"

"Black heart!"

"Hooligan! Hooligan! Hooligan!"

"Country bumpkin!"

This last caught Lee's attention. His head jerked up. He looked out
at the faces and singled out the man, a vegetable peddler, who called out
the insult again. "You!" Lee shouted. "Who are you calling country
bumpkin? You can't even afford a stick to beat your drum. You have to
use your penis!" The crowd broke into cheers. Even the peddler laughed.
"Take your stinking fart words back to your own outhouse," Lee yelled.
"You're smelling up the whole village here!" People congratulated the
peddler for eliciting such entertainment from the dead man.

Lee found Hulan and David again. "I did as I was told and I was guaranteed protection. They lied to me. I was a dope."

The truck stopped. Guards pushed against the crowd, trying to clear a space so that the gates might be opened.

"There's no more time," Spencer said.

Hulan shouted to the guards. "I am from the MPS. You must let me through." But the guards couldn't hear her. There were still dozens of people between her and the front of the truck.

"Spencer . . ." Hulan's voice was filled with regret. There was nothing more she could do.

"Make this mean something," David said. "Tell us who you were working with in China."

"I can't. I don't know."

"Then the dragon head in Los Angeles," David said. "He sold you out. Tell me his name."

"Lee Dawei," the young man said. The truck lurched forward, then stalled.

"Give me something I can use to get him."

The young man shook his head wildly from side to side. "I can't."

David searched his mind, then blurted out, "The Chinese Overseas Bank! We think the organization keeps its money there. Give me names. Give me accounts. Make them pay for betraying you."

The truck rumbled back to life. As it crept forward, Spencer Lee began shouting out names and numbers obviously long memorized into a rhythmic chant. The truck pulled into the courtyard, the gates closed, and the crowd fell silent. Hulan pushed through the people and banged on the gate. No one answered.

Everyone but David knew what would be happening now inside the compound. The placard would be removed from the condemned man's back and tossed aside. He would be brutally pushed to his knees. The executioner would take his position directly behind the boy, aim his pistol at the back of his head, and fire. When the shot cut sharply through the air, several in the audience winced. Then the entertainment was over. The crowd, subdued now, began to disperse.

Suddenly the ground was rocked by a deafening explosion. The repercussion blew glass from windows, sending fragments slashing into flesh. Pandemonium broke out as people darted in all directions at once. Hulan and David found each other, then were pressed along in the current of humanity as everyone ran to where they could see smoke mushrooming up in a dense, acrid cloud. They poured into the crossroads. Merchants—whether injured or not—bolted for their stands, hoping that their wares weren't destroyed. A few people collapsed—overwhelmed with relief that they were alive. Some bled from cuts. Others wailed—in fear, in pain. A few called out frantically for loved ones.

At the edge of the circle, the Saab was a charred mass of twisted metal. The smell of burning gasoline, rubber, leather, plastic, and flesh billowed into the air. Inside the car, David and Hulan could see Peter's skin peeling away as flames licked up about him. Hulan rushed forward, trying to reach the car, but David pulled her back. "It's too late. He's dead." She buried her face in David's chest and he held her tight. He couldn't distinguish the shaking of her body from his. Then one of the tires exploded, sending the crowd into another chorus of cries. A few good Samaritans ran for hoses and began dousing the blaze.

David and Hulan stood together in the traffic circle staring at the smoldering Saab, their breath ragged, their hearts racing. They knew they were supposed to be dead.

The fire was out. Peasants packed up and began trekking back to the countryside. Workers went back inside to their factories. Mothers returned home to start preparing the midday meal. Only a few children—their pink faces streaked with soot—stood in nosy little groups in the traffic circle.

David and Hulan slowly regained their equanimity as well, so that by the time the Neighborhood Committee director, a man in his eighties, informed them that he had sent someone for the local police, they were already calm enough to begin plotting their next move. Hulan was about to search for a phone to call the MPS when she saw the Neighborhood Committee director poking at the burned-out car with a stick. When Hulan told him to step away, that he shouldn't contaminate the evidence, the old man wandered off. Then Hulan, with David in tow, walked to a gas station to try to put through a call to Beijing, but the lines were still out.

Back outside, they sat on the curb. Hulan fished through her bag, brought out a notebook and pen, and handed them to David. He wrote down the names and numbers that Spencer Lee had shouted. When he was done, Hulan asked, "Will that help?"

"Yes, if he told the truth, and I think he did. The way he chanted those names . . ." He shook his head, remembering Lee's final ride.

When they returned to the circle, they saw the old man with his head back under the hood. Hulan chased him away with a string of threats. Instead of being frightened by the inspector, he invited her to a café for lunch. He overrode her reluctance by saying that the phone lines to Beijing had been temperamental for the last six months, that the local police were corrupt and unresponsive, and that she could still watch the circle and the car from the café.

The Neighborhood Committee director guided Hulan and David to an open-air café decorated with New Year's banners and couplets. He introduced his granddaughter, this simple establishment's owner and chef. Hulan went with her into the kitchen and kept an eye on her as she made three bowls of noodles. Hulan warned the woman to make sure she used boiled water for the broth so that the foreigner wouldn't get sick. The woman seared slivers of ginger, garlic, and dried red chili peppers in the bottom of the wok, threw in shredded pork—fresh just this day, she assured Hulan—then added hot water from a thermos and some noodles. At the last moment, the woman scrambled some eggs in a bowl and poured the mixture on top of the soup, where it instantly floated apart into flowery petals. Once everything had boiled again to Hulan's satisfaction, the woman ladled the soup into bowls, dribbled in hot chili oil, and carried the meal to a table on the sidewalk, where the men sat next to a brazier.

David could have sworn that he wasn't hungry, that he'd never eat again, but the first sip of the hot and fiery broth brought instant warmth to his body. For a few minutes, no one spoke, preferring to slurp their noodles appreciatively. Then the old man began to talk, criticizing his granddaughter for being a bad cook and announcing that when he died she would probably starve to death. Hulan understood this for polite conversation.

Then the Neighborhood Committee director started to reminisce in the way of old-timers about the Civil War and his part in it. He had carried messages from camp to camp. He had met his wife while marching back to Beijing. "Only one problem," he said. "She didn't speak my dialect. My comrades tell me, 'This is good. You won't understand her complaints.' For fifty years, this is true. All we care about are the unspoken words of the bedchamber." When Hulan translated this to David, he surprised himself by laughing.

David's grin soon collapsed. How can I laugh, he thought guiltily, when death surrounds me?

Hulan reached over and put an arm around him. "We're human, David," she said. "All we can do is eat, breathe, maybe laugh a little. It shows we're still alive."

Meanwhile the committee director rambled on about his wartime exploits. Hulan had heard this sort of nonsense many times. If all of the old-timers who said they'd been on the Long March *had* made that journey, every village and city in China would have been emptied. Then the old man was chuckling about how he hadn't seen a bomb like this one for forty or more years. Hulan's attention snapped back into focus. "So simple to make," he was saying. "Any soldier, any peasant, can construct it, and it's deadly enough to accomplish Liberation. So easy, set the timer, walk away, and *bam!* That's why Mao liked it so much."

"What are you talking about?"

"Your bomb brings back many memories. Only an old-timer like me would remember how to make one. Only an old-timer like me could even savor the handiwork."

"You used bombs like this during the war?" Hulan asked.

"Yes. Mao liked it, but you can see the problem."

"No, I can't."

The old man sipped his tea, then said. "It's unreliable. It has a timer, yes. But half the time it goes off when it wants. *Bam!* Maybe you kill the right person. Maybe you kill the wrong person. Maybe you don't kill anyone at all."

*   *   *

David and Hulan hitched a ride in the back of a truck loaded with grain to downtown Beijing. With the wind, the temperature was well below freezing. David and Hulan huddled together against the filled burlap sacks, trying to keep warm. "When I get back to L.A.," David said, "I can open a real investigation. I may not get the Rising Phoenix on what's already happened, but money laundering and tax evasion ought to be easy."

"Do you really think they had anything to do with today?"

"Oh, Hulan, I don't know. I don't know anything anymore."

"The Rising Phoenix is a relatively young organization," she mused. David looked at her questioningly. She tilted her head, thinking. "It doesn't have a long history, and the members are young."

"So?"

"Remember what the old man said about that type of bomb? It was used during the Civil War." David nodded, and she went on. "Whoever built it had to be of a certain age. He had to have been in the army with Mao during the thirties or forties."

"An old guy's done all this?"

"You suspected Guang until this morning," she said. "He's certainly old enough."

"Who else do we know who's that age?" he asked.

"Zai. My father."

"Come on, Hulan." David laughed. When she didn't join in, he turned serious again. "What about this Lee Dawei? Maybe he was in the army."

"But, David, that's what I'm saying. The Rising Phoenix is a young organization. Spencer Lee was in his twenties and was the number two or number three man. If the dragon head was in his late sixties or early seventies, would he place that much trust in someone so young?"

"No. Lee Dawei is probably a kid, too."

"Exactly. So here's what's bothering me. We were the targets of the bomb."

"I know."

"The old man told us that it was easy to build but unreliable. Doesn't that suggest it had to be planted recently?"

"I suppose so. Otherwise it might have gone off when we weren't in the car."

"I think it was put there when we were in Guang's office."

"Now *you're* back to Guang?" His voice registered surprise.

"I know," she admitted. "But maybe he told us about the bear bile and Henglai because he *knew* we'd never be able to use it."

"Ah, Christ." He pounded one of the grain sacks in irritation. He was fatigued and no longer thinking clearly. "No, wait! What about Peter? No one could have planted the bomb with him waiting in the car."

She blanched at the mention of Peter's name, then composed herself and said, "Suppose he went to make a phone call or have a cigarette."

"That's possible."

"So again, why not Guang?"

"Several reasons," David said, and began itemizing them. "You said the person has to be of a certain age. Guang is that age, but he was with us. Do you really see him hiring someone else to hook up the bomb? I don't. Besides, he didn't have to say a word about the bile or Henglai. He could have kept quiet and we wouldn't have had a way to stop the execution. Don't you see, Hulan? Whoever wanted us dead wanted Spencer Lee dead even more."

The truck bumped over a pothole. David glanced around trying to determine where they were. When he couldn't, he adjusted the collar of his coat to keep the wind off his neck and ears, then looked back at Hulan. She was staring at her hands clasped together in her lap.

"You're thinking about Peter," he said.

"How can I not?"

He let the silence hang. Finally she spoke. "From the day he was assigned to me I didn't trust him. I knew he reported on me and I hated that. But when we were in L.A., I saw a different side of him. That day in Madeleine's office he stood up for me. He didn't have to do that."

"He was just doing his job. . . "

"Which I'd never given him a chance to do before," she said. "When we got back here, I thought, Things will be different and we'll be real partners. In the past I never would have sent him to Cao Hua's apartment. I never would have let him get this close to an investigation. And now?" Hulan looked at him in anguish. "If I'd just let him come with us . . . "

"Everything happened so fast," he said. "The other cars, the people, Lee coming through the intersection. I would have done the same."

She was going to say something more, but the truck pulled to a stop. They were at the back entrance to the Forbidden City. Wordlessly, Hulan grabbed her purse and jumped to the ground. From here, they caught a bus to her neighborhood. When they reached her house, they found a black sedan waiting outside, but Hulan didn't stop to speak to its occupants.

"They're from the MPS," she said. "I recognize the car."

She unlocked the front gate to her compound and they entered. Hulan stoked the embers in the living room stove, then excused her-self to take a bath. David was dirty, exhausted from jet lag and the constant push of the investigation, and emotionally drained from see-ing so much death. He wandered through the courtyards and open rooms, hoping to recover some sense of balance but realizing his senses were too jangled.

He'd had visions of how Hulan lived, but her home was far larger, far more beautiful than anything he had imagined. Her personality was everywhere—in the way a piece of embroidered cloth draped over a chair, in the way low celadon pots filled with narcissus bulbs perched on the windowsill above the kitchen sink, in the way she'd set up her New Year's altar, in the way the rich hues of the antique wood pieces softened the rooms' clean lines. He lingered by her desk, feeling the smoothness of the rosewood's grain beneath his fingers, picking up a cloisonné letter opener, caressing the fine lines of a Cantonware vase. Here was Hulan's life—a little plastic wind-up toy he'd given her more than a decade ago, a photograph of a woman David presumed to be her mother, a few bills, several bankbooks neatly stacked.

Absently he touched them with his finger, and they spilled across the table. Bank of China. Wells Fargo. Citibank. Glendale Federal. Chinese Overseas Bank. These were the same banks where Henglai and Cao Hua had kept their ill-gotten gains. If this weren't damning enough, there was the matter of the Chinese Overseas Bank. Not only did Guang Mingyun own it, but the Rising Phoenix was laundering its money there. David picked up one of the books, opened it, and was stunned by the balance—$327,000. He checked another and saw a balance of $57,000. He looked through the others. The total was close to two million U.S. dollars.

His knees buckled and he stumbled back into a chair as the realization washed over him. She had betrayed him.

She came out of her bedroom with a silk kimono wrapped around her slim frame and her hair tied up in a towel. The dirt, soot, and grime of the fiery intersection and the back of the farmer's truck had been washed away from her body.

"Should I hurry?" she asked, her voice as melodious as always. "I can have the car out front take us back to your hotel. I'm sure you'd like to take a shower and change." Then she walked to the coal stove, put her hands up to feel its heat, and smiled. "Or you could take a bath here. We could spend the rest of the day here if you'd like."

David was silent.

"Would you like something to eat? Maybe a cup of tea? David? Is something wrong? Are you all right?"

He opened his hands, let the bankbooks slip into his lap, and accused her with his simple question: "What are these?"

A pink flush began at her cleavage, then swiftly crept up her neck and into her face.

"Don't you have an explanation?" he asked contemptuously. "I didn't think so."

"It's my savings," she said after a lengthy pause. It galled him that she showed no remorse.

"That's one thing you could call it," he said.

He watched as her mouth formed his name. "David?"

"All this must have been very entertaining to you," he said bitterly. He closed his eyes, trying to wipe away her presence. When he opened them she was still there. "You are such a fucking liar. And I fell for it again."

"I don't know what you're talking about."

She knelt before him. The silk of her kimono fell open, revealing the curve of her breasts. He pushed her away, stood, and crossed the room. He swung about, strode back to where she sat on the floor, grabbed her arms, and hauled her to her feet. The towel fell from her head and her hair hung in wet strings. His face was inches from hers as his voice grated, "Did you think I was so *stupid* that I wouldn't figure it out?"

She shook her head slowly from side to side.

"Ever since I got here," he said, "I relied on you and you pointed me in the wrong direction time and time again. You guided me *away* from what was important. Even when I heard things I didn't listen. Remember that day at the Black Earth Inn? Remember how Nixon Chen and the others talked about you? How you were named for a model revolutionary, how you yourself were a model Red Guard, how, with your connections, you bought your way out of the commune and came to America? Was it all just an elaborate ploy, like what the Soviets did in the good old days—sending a kid to be raised in enemy territory so she'd grow up to make the best spy with the best cover and no accent?"

He pulled her up against his chest. He could feel her heart pounding against his. He lowered his voice to something almost sensual. "Remember how you *left* me, Hulan? Do you remember that? Did it mean *anything* to you?" Then he held her away from him again. "Remember in Los Angeles how I spilled my guts to you? I thought you would say something that would explain your past actions to me. But no! Why would you tell me the truth? Why would you tell me *anything*? And like an idiot, I didn't press you."

She struggled against him now, but he kept his grip. "So we come back to Beijing—your city. The whole time I'm depending on you for translation. Did you ever once tell me the truth of what was said? Even yesterday at the jail, did you really call Zai or was that just some performance? And every suggestion I made, every person I wanted to talk to, you steered me the other way. And your emotions!" A shiver

ran through him. "On the back of the truck when you were mourning Peter. Was it an act like everything else?" When she didn't
answer, he said, "In fact, when I look back on it, you have kept the
truth from me from the day we met. You never loved me. You always
used me. You're as corrupt, as foul, as revolting . . . "

He was cut off by her scream. She jerked away from him and fell
back against the wall. Her hands clutched mindlessly at the silk that
had fallen away from her body. Her face was lowered, but he could
see her breath coming short and shallow. Finally, she looked up and
met his eyes.

19

LATER
The Red Soil Farm

Y ou want the truth?" she asked. "Where do I begin? With your questions? Yes, that money is mine. Yes, I am rich. I'm supposed to be rich. I'm a Red Princess. I'm from the special class—like Henglai, Bo Yun, Li Nan, and the rest of them."

"You're lying."

"No, I'm not," she said in resignation. After all these years, all that was left was the truth David had wanted for so long. "How can I make you understand? You talk about that day in the Black Earth Inn. Why didn't you *listen* to Nixon and the rest of them? Why didn't you pay attention to Peter's stories of the real Liu Hulan? They *told* you so much about me that I was afraid down to my bones. But then I saw you didn't, *wouldn't,* hear it. I never told you things because the bitter truth is you never wanted to hear them. You think you hate me now? You just listen."

Her hands twisted the kimono's fabric. "As you know, I was named for Liu Hulan. But how do you emulate a model revolutionary when you are a Red Princess, when you are cushioned by wealth and privilege, when you are surrounded by love and creature comforts?"

She dropped the fabric and gestured to her New Year's altar and the photos of her ancestors. "This house belonged to my mother's family. They were imperial performers. I had great-great-aunts who were courtesans in the Forbidden City. This is common knowledge. But most people know little of my father's family. They look at him and see a dedicated, hardworking man. But for generations the Lius were wealthy landowners. My great-grandfather was a magistrate here in the capital. Even after the fall of the Manchus, the Liu family, unlike my mother's, kept their power. In fact, they got even richer."

"I don't care about them!" David exclaimed. "You're just telling more stories to lead me away from the truth."

Hulan didn't seem to hear him. "My father, like his father before him, was a student of history," she continued. "He looked at the world and ran away to join Mao. By the time Mao's troops marched into Beijing in 1949, my father was twenty-four years old and a trusted confidant of the Supreme Leader. My parents were rewarded for their hard work and sacrifice. You know that saying, 'Everybody works so everybody eats'? That was the essence of Mao's communism, but from those very first days, some people ate better than others."

Hulan's memory drifted back to 1966, when she was eight years old. Mao and his wife had just launched the Cultural Revolution to rid the country of bourgeois forces. "My father took me to Tiananmen Square on August eighteenth to see the first official assembly of the Red Guards. One million of Beijing's young people crammed together, wearing their parents' old army uniforms, shouting slogans, singing, waving copies of the *Little Red Book*, and fainting when Mao stepped out on the Forbidden City's walls to wave.

"Mao said we should oust the four olds—ideas, culture, customs, habits—and it was as though a hurricane hit the city. The whole country went crazy. People decided that red lights should mean go and green lights should mean stop. You could see accidents at almost every corner. For centuries, Chinese women had prided themselves on the length of their hair. But now the Red Guard tramped through the streets, stopped women at random, and chopped off their hair. They decided to rename everything—streets, people, schools, restaurants—to *hong* this, *hong* that, red this, red that. Old friends became

Red Army or Red Peony, streets became Red Peace Way or Red Road. I kept my name, for I was Liu Hulan."

"I want to know about the bankbooks," he demanded. "I want to know how you're connected to the Rising Phoenix."

She ignored his outburst. "Anyone who was considered feudal, old, or foreign was persecuted," she went on. "Doctors and artists were marched through the streets wearing dunce caps and placards outlining their defects. They were beaten, humiliated, thrown in jail. Managers in offices sat through struggle meetings where the workers accused them of being capitalist roaders, reactionaries, foreign spies, and renegades. Everywhere you went, people were spit on, bit, hit, lectured, humiliated, sent to work camps or jail for imagined crimes. Teachers were know-nothings. Students wrote *dazibao*, big character posters, criticizing their teachers as bourgeois, as backward, as running dogs of capitalism. Soon there were no more teachers, and by the end of the Cultural Revolution, seventy-seven million students had lost out on their educations."

She stopped speaking as she relived the memories.

"The past has nothing to do with *this*, Hulan."

"But it has everything to do with *us*. That's what you really want to know, isn't it?" She sighed deeply, then said, "I remember the night the Red Guard came to this neighborhood for the first time. I was ten years old, still too young to be in the Red Guard myself. They called all the neighbors into the street and selected Madame Zhang and her husband for criticism. I didn't know much about Mr. Zhang, except that at New Year's he always used to give me some good-luck money and a little candy and that he used to have tea with my father in the courtyard under the jujube tree. But the Red Guard knew a lot! They knew that Mr. Zhang was an intellectual, one of the very worst in the 'stinking ninth category' of people. We all stood there like sheep as the Red Guard plundered the Zhang home. They threw his books in a pile and set fire to them. They brought out the family's ancestor scrolls and tossed them on the blaze."

She wiped a hand across her eyes as if to erase the images.

"The whole time, they were screaming that Mr. Zhang was a monster, a cow, a snake demon. Pretty soon the neighbors were yelling, too. People were thinking, If I don't play along, the Red Guard will come to my house tomorrow night. Someone shouted, 'Zhang is never generous to us. He always hoards his good fortune.' Our next-door neighbor cried out, 'He reads too many books, but not anymore!' His wife joined in next. 'We condemn you and your wife forever!' I can still see the way the orange light from the flames flickered across the faces of my neighbors. I remember the intense scowls of the Red Guard. How do I explain this? Their faces were twisted in exultation. I remember, too, Madame Zhang. We, her neighbors, had betrayed her."

Hulan walked to the window and looked out on the courtyard. "I don't know who dealt the first blow, but soon the Red Guards were beating old man Zhang. I can still see him lying on the ground, the clubs and sticks hitting his limp body. I can hear the chants of encouragement from our neighbors to 'smash his dog head.' And the look on Madame Zhang's face when she realized that her husband was dead? I will take that to my grave."

"But you had nothing to do with those things," David said, still fighting his anger. "You were only a child."

She turned to face him. "No, I was yelling with the rest of them." She looked away again. "Let me tell you what happened in school. You already heard what the others told you. I called Teacher Zho a pig ass. I said so many things that soon Teacher Zho was crying. Imagine a man like that, educated, crying because of a ten-year-old! But I didn't stop there. I didn't stop until Teacher Zho went home and never came back."

David walked to her side.

"This whole time," she said, "our family was protected."

"Why?" he asked. He was becoming engrossed in her story.

"Because my father was high in the government, working at the Ministry of Culture and still within Mao's inner circle."

David stared into the courtyard with her.

"In 1970, when I was twelve, my parents finally allowed me to go to the countryside," she said. "I can't tell you how much I wanted to do that. I wanted to help reform society, exterminate the disparity between the countryside and the cities. I wanted to 'learn from the peasants.' I was only twelve. I didn't understand what I was doing, but I was swept up in the tide."

When David and Hulan had lived together, he had longed for the moment she would finally reveal herself to him. Now that that time was here, he had a bad feeling about it. "You don't have to say any more, Hulan," he said softly.

She cocked her head and looked at him out of the corner of her eye. "You wanted the truth and I'm telling it to you. I ended up at the Red Soil Farm. The idea was to turn infertile soil into rich farm-land. We all got up before dawn. We plowed, we planted soybeans, we watered each stalk by hand. When harvesttime came, day after day we bent our backs and swung our scythes. I learned how to weave baskets, how to castrate baby pigs, how to pluck and gut ducks, how to carry water two miles, how to cook for a hundred people at a time. We all ate the same poor rations—rice porridge with preserved veg-etables for breakfast, rice with a few stringy vegetables for lunch, rice and more vegetables for dinner, maybe a yam if we were lucky."

"You must have been homesick."

"We all learned how to pretend we didn't miss our families, movie theaters, parties for high officials, clean clothes, hot water, yes, even our teachers."

She paced to the stove and opened the grate. "I wasn't content with working twelve-, fourteen-, sixteen-hour days," she recalled as she dropped a few chunks of coal into the fire. "I wanted to be an inspiration like my namesake. So at night, instead of resting or read-ing my *Little Red Book* or gossiping with the others, I helped plan struggle meetings. Class struggle, even at the Red Soil Farm, was unavoidable. Oh, we attacked people for all sorts of things: wearing a white ribbon in your hair instead of a red one, having a mother or father or third aunt who had traveled to America once, being reticent about criticizing others, snoring and keeping your cabin mates awake, having sex—ah, this was the worst! And I tell you, I was steadfast in my criticisms. I never looked the other way."

"Then Zai came for you," he said, remembering what Nixon had told him.

"Yes," she said, nodding. "One day, two years later, he came to get me. He wasn't the section chief then. No, he worked at the Ministry of Culture with my father. You wouldn't know it to look at him now, but in those days Uncle Zai was very powerful, very strong. My father worked under him."

She fell silent again and walked back to David's side. By now, he knew she had to finish this. All he could do was encourage her. "How did things change?"

"In those days, it didn't matter how much money or *guanxi* you had," she answered. "When your time came, they would get you. It was the responsibility of the masses to drive out bad examples. Chairman Mao relied on people like me to pull weeds from the field. All this Uncle Zai explained to me as we drove to the station and then took the train two days back to Beijing. By the time we got home, I was prepared for what I had to do."

"And you'd been away how long?"

"Two years. I was fourteen and it was spring." Her eyes roamed the desolate garden as she said, "In a couple of months Beijing will be a wild burst of color. The cherry trees will be dripping pink blossoms. Yellow daffodils will grow in the parks. Everywhere you look is green, green, green. But I didn't notice a thing. I was blinded by duty and fortitude."

"What happened?"

"Mr. Zai drove me here. The neighbors were waiting for us. At the time I didn't stop to consider how they knew we would be coming. I just thought, Ah, they are here to help in the struggle meeting. My father was brought out of the house by two of our neighbors and escorted to the middle of a huge circle. I didn't run to him. I didn't kiss him or hug him. Do you remember in court how Spencer Lee kept his eyes to the ground? This is what my father did, and every time he tried to lift his eyes to look at me one of the guards hit him on the back of the head with a club. Blood ran down my father's head, soaking his shirt."

Hulan pulled the kimono's silk tight around her and started to weep as she recounted how Zai, her father's boss, had taken command and began addressing the neighbors.

"He said, 'Old Liu here has worked in the Ministry of Culture for many years now, but he has not performed as a good revolutionary might. He has not thought of the people. His position—to hire and supervise movie productions—is one of trust. But he has betrayed that trust by allowing degenerate and immoral films to be made. When his comrades tell him that he has erred, he does not make self-criticism or correct his ways. Instead, he sends those bourgeois films out into the countryside to corrupt the masses. At the Ministry of Culture, we know this can't be his only crime, and we call on you, his neighbors, and Liu Hulan, his daughter, to help this man see his heinous ways. Only through confession will he be able to cleanse himself. We need your help.'"

"And your neighbors gave it."

"Oh, yes," she said, then shifted to a strident tone: "'Liu keeps his background a secret, but some of us remember the decadent ways of his family!'" She changed her voice again: "'They were landowners—the worst class,' said another. 'We can all thank the Great Helmsman that they're dead now.' Then Madame Zhang stepped forward and asked, 'But what about *this* Liu?'"

"That's the woman whose husband had been killed?"

Since losing her husband two years before, Hulan explained, Madame Zhang had become the moral conscience of the *hutong*. "She put her hands on her hips and strode to the middle of the circle to stand next to my father," Hulan said through her tears. "'Are we going to let him get away with his selfish ways?' she asked. One by one she recited my father's alleged crimes. He had ordered some shirts from Hong Kong during a cultural exchange trip for the ministry. He had a car and driver, but he had never once helped the neighbors by taking anyone anywhere, not even when Old Man Bai had a toothache and needed to go to the dentist! He hosted too many parties and the noise—the horrible Western singing and the sounds of Western instruments—coming from the Liu compound insulted all of the ears in the *hutong*. She said my mother was even worse! 'Everyone in the neighborhood has had to endure this feudal woman's vanity,' Madame Zhang screeched. 'She mocks us with her makeup, her flamboyant colors, and her silk costumes.'"

"Where was your mother during all of this?"

"That's exactly what I was wondering. I searched through the crowd, but I didn't see her. I looked to Mr. Zai, but he was concentrating on the proceedings. Then our neighbors were calling for me to speak, just as Uncle Zai said they would. He had told me what to do and I did it. I walked to the middle of the circle, thanked Madame Zhang for her good words, turned, and spat on my father."

Hulan's tears turned to heavy sobs. "'Everything Madame Zhang says is true,' I told our neighbors. 'From the day my father was born, he was spoiled, selfish, and thought only of himself.' I could see my father trying to look up at me, but I put my work boot on the back of his neck to keep him down. This was something I had learned at the Red Soil Farm along with slogans like 'Place righteousness above family loyalty' and 'Love Chairman Mao more than your own parents.'"

Hulan told the people of the *hutong* that her father had named her after Liu Hulan only to curry favor from the government and to hide his own weak family background. "I said such terrible things, and I said them until my throat was hoarse and the people were frenzied. Soon the neighbors were shouting. Bomb the cow demon with cannon balls! Fry his hands in boiling oil! Then someone called out, 'What of Jiang Jinli, this brave and honest girl's mother?' Soon everyone took up the chant."

At that, Hulan said, Mr. Zai had held up his hands for silence. He told the Lius' neighbors that earlier that day he had taken Hulan to the jail where her mother was being held.

"Only I knew this was a falsehood," Hulan explained. "But Uncle Zai was not finished. He said—and I remember these words very clearly—'With great pride I can tell you that Hulan did her duty there. Jiang Jinli, her mother, will no longer trouble the people!' This news *released* my neighbors. People grabbed hammers and broke the old stone carving above our front gate. They went into the compound with sickles and chopped down my mother's flowers. They raided the house, bringing out many of our belongings and throwing them to the ground. When the pile was ready, Madame Zhang stepped forward and set fire to our things. No, not *things*, our *lives*. Our books, photographs of family trips, wall hangings passed down ten generations in my mother's family. Clothes, furniture, rugs. The fire roared, sending red and orange sparks into the sky."

"What was happening to your father?"

"In the lust for destruction," she answered, "he was forgotten by the mob. But in the light of the fire, so beautiful really, I saw him still on his hands and knees, his head lifted, staring at me. The guards came back, twisted his arms behind him, and dragged him away. The whole time my father's eyes were boring into me like hot coals."

Once Hulan's father was gone, Zai put her in the backseat of his car. She asked him questions. Where was her mother? What had happened to her? What would happen to her father? But Zai would only say that Hulan had saved her father's life. Instead of being beaten or shot to death, Liu would be sent to a labor camp. He would be safe there.

"Then Uncle Zai took me to the Beijing Hundred Products Big Store on Wangfujing," she continued, slowly regaining her composure. "He bought me clothes and toiletries. He bought me a suitcase. He took me to his house, made me take a shower and change into one of my new outfits. Then we drove to the airport. He pressed a passport in my hand. Inside was an old picture of me and a visa. He kissed me good-bye and put me on the airplane. I had never been on an airplane before. I remember looking out the window and seeing miles and miles of great green patchwork. In Hong Kong, I changed planes, then flew to New York. When I got off the plane, I followed the other passengers through Immigration and Customs. Outside, a white woman met me and drove me to a boarding school in Connecticut."

"How old were you then?"

"Fourteen."

"I vaguely remember you talking about that school," David said suddenly. "But I didn't know the circumstances of how you'd gotten there. It must have been a real culture shock after the farm and the rest of it."

"I don't know if I can convey to you how strange it was to be with so many girls, all wearing uniforms, all good friends, all privileged," she said. "Most of the students were the daughters of diplomats, so I can say they were more sophisticated than the usual American girls. But I'm sure I don't have to tell you how cruel teenage girls can be. Oh, the teasing I got for my farm ways and my pathetic Communist clothes."

"And your English," David added. "I remember you talking about that, too."

"Especially my English. Even my teachers made fun of me for what they called my 'Chinglish.' They said I spoke English like I was translating in my brain from the Chinese. 'You must learn to *think* in English,' they lectured me. I suppose they were trying to be kind, but they only made the other girls laugh."

"During that time did you hear from your father?"

"No. He was in the labor camp, just as Uncle Zai had predicted. I didn't hear from my mother either. For many months I assumed she was dead. Finally, after several letters, Uncle Zai wrote that she had been injured and was recuperating in a Russian hospital. He didn't say *that* exactly, since all of the mail leaving China was monitored at that time. But I could read between the lines, between the words that spoke of my mother's betrayal of the Revolution, of her decadent ways, of her selfish attitude."

In 1976, Hulan graduated and Chairman Mao died. Without his protection, Madame Mao and her cohorts—the Gang of Four—were arrested, tried, and convicted for masterminding the Cultural Revolution. While all that was happening, Hulan went to Los Angeles and enrolled at USC.

"Still, I didn't hear from my father. Two years later I finally received word from him. He had been 'rehabilitated' at the Pitao Reform Camp for six years and had returned to Beijing."

"After all that, how did he end up at the Ministry of Public Security?" David asked.

Hulan shrugged. "He found his old friends, traded on his *guanxi*, and was assigned to a very low-level job at the MPS."

Again she seemed reluctant to go on. David had to coax her. "And your mother?"

"He didn't mention her. He did, however, tell me to stay where I was." Her eyes misted again. "All I had to do was think of his face that last night in the *hutong* to know he despised me, that he didn't want to see me."

"And Zai?"

"In America you say, What goes around comes around," she responded. "In China we have something similar: Things always change to the opposite. New accusations floated around the city. Uncle Zai was accused of participating with too much vigor in the Cultural Revolution and was also sent to the Pitao Reform Camp. I don't know who made those accusations, but I have always thought it was my father. He had six years to think about what Zai had done to his family, and he wanted retribution. When Mr. Zai came out of the camp, he was a different man. No one came to his aid except for my father."

"But why would your father do that if he wanted retribution?"

"Because by that time, my father was 'climbing the ladder' at the ministry. The old boss became the lackey, my father became the new boss."

"Your father wanted to keep tabs on Zai."

"Yes, of course, but this was also a punishment. After all, Mr. Zai had to see my father every day. The gulf between them grew."

"But why didn't Zai explain everything to your father?"

"Because Baba would not listen and because Uncle Zai felt guilty himself."

"But the only thing Zai was guilty of was trying to rescue your father."

"You can say that now, David. But you weren't in the *hutong* that night. Yes, Uncle Zai had planned everything so that my parents might live rather than die. But he had stood in the middle of that circle and denounced my mother. He had made me shout out the words about my father to satiate our neighbors' desire for violence."

David was about to speak when Hulan held up her hand to stop him. "I'm not trying to justify my own actions," she said. "I am guilty of many things—guilty of persecuting Teacher Zho, who spent the next five years in the cow shed; guilty of cruelty to our group leader at the farm, who tried to commit suicide rather than face another struggle meeting; guilty of betraying my parents, who both had to pay such an exorbitant price for my adolescent rantings."

"Hulan, you saved your parents," he corrected. "Surely *you've* told your father what happened that night."

"I've tried, but it's not the Chinese way. In America, you talk things to death, but we don't. The past? Emotions?" She shook her head.

"You should still do it."

She shook her head again. "My father has no desire to relive those days."

"He seems . . ." David didn't know how to phrase it.

"Cold? Let me tell you something. My father has never accused me. He loves me. He always wants to see more of me."

"And that's how you ended up at the ministry."

"I'm getting ahead of my story, but yes. My father arranged for me to get a job. Not as an inspector! My father hired me to be a tea girl. Can you imagine me wearing some little dress, smiling stupidly, and pouring tea for men all day long?"

"No."

"I had no choice but to go behind my father's back to Uncle Zai. He's watched over me since I was a child. He sent me out of the country to protect me. He paid for my education out of his own pocket. He knew that I was a lawyer. He believed that I could think. When Baba found out, it was too late."

"It's still not too late to tell your father the truth," David reasoned. "He should know that what you did took real courage."

"No, I was the true criminal in all this. And do you know what my punishment was? I went to a fine private university. I got a job at a good law firm. I met you."

She ran her fingers through her hair, pulling the tendrils away from her face. "I was an empty shell back then. For so many years I had covered my emotions. I had promised myself I would never feel anything ever again, but you made me fall in love. You opened my heart again to joy, happiness, and honor. I thought, Maybe I can make up for my past. I believed one way I could do that was to bury my deeds. Now I know I was right not to tell you."

But she was wrong. He was thinking instead of the personal toll her mistakes and sacrifices had taken on her, on both of them. As she told her story, he had thought of their missed chances and the years they'd lost.

He reached for her, but she jerked away.

"Can't you see I never deserved you? I was never worthy of your love. It was all some horrible mistake."

"*I* wasn't worthy of *you*."

Weariness crept into her voice as she said, "Okay, so you want to know why I left you? There are no more secrets. You already know my worst sins."

"Hulan, please don't say that—"

But she spoke right over him. "We were living in the apartment by the beach, remember that?"

When he nodded, she said, "Of course you do. We used to walk along the beach on the weekends. We used to sit at the water's edge and plan our future. We would get married, we'd buy a house, we'd have children, we'd do some good in the world. I have to tell you that this last was a dream for me, a way to make amends for my past wrongs. But not one day went by that I didn't worry about how the universe would pay me back for what I'd done. Then one Saturday I learned how."

"Your father asked you to come home."

"He wrote that my mother was finally back from the hospital. She'd been in Russia for thirteen years! He said she needed me and that it was time to make restitution to her."

"Why didn't you tell me?" Again he was thinking of all the time they had lost.

"A million times I have asked myself that question. I suppose I was afraid that I wouldn't be able to bear your contempt. I, Liu Hulan, named for the brave revolutionary, was terrified. So like a thief I made my plans. I bought a ticket. I packed a single suitcase. I kissed you good-bye and said I would see you in a couple of weeks. I have to tell you that when I closed the door to our apartment, I closed the door to the only happiness I had experienced since I was a very young girl."

"When you came back here, did you know it was permanent?" David asked. When she didn't answer, he said, "I need to know, Hulan. Please."

"When I arrived, I didn't know what to expect. But when I saw my mother . . ." She put her hands over her eyes.

"What had happened to her?"

"No one has ever told me. I don't think my father knows, and if Uncle Zai does, he's not telling. And my mother? My mother was a beautiful dancer. Did I ever tell you that? She had such grace, such agility. And her voice! When she sang, the masses would cry. They said she sounded like an angel. But when I saw her again, she was in a wheelchair and her voice was all but gone. I had to stay, David. You see that, don't you?"

"My letters?"

"I still have them."

"And all the times I applied for visas?"

"I went to Uncle Zai for help. He pulled strings and your applications were rejected."

"You should have let me come. You should have told me the truth. Even if you couldn't tell me all of it, you could have said something instead of just disappearing like that."

"But how? What part of the story could I have told you? Think about it. Where could I have started? What part could I have left out? You would have asked me a hundred questions."

"I wouldn't have."

"You know how you are, David. The truth means everything to you. And your sense of justice . . . "

"Oh, God," David groaned in final realization. "My rigid sense of right and wrong kept you from telling me."

"No, not sanctimonious." She took his hand and held it to her breast. "Admirable. Fearless. Unwavering. Don't you know that these are the things I have loved most about you?"

"But they drove you away."

"Yes," she admitted. She slumped against the wall. This time when he reached out to her, she didn't pull away. Slowly he drew her into his arms.

"So in answer to your questions," she said, "I am not in cahoots with Guang Mingyun or the Rising Phoenix. That money comes from our family's past and from my father's connections. I haven't lied to you since I saw you again. I have translated everything. I have tried to explain what we have seen. Of those accusations at least I am innocent."

She felt limp in his arms, almost as though she weren't in her body at all.

"I love you, Hulan. Nothing you could do or say would ever change that."

"But what I did . . . "

"You saved your parents the best way you knew how. As for the other things—your teacher, the person on the farm . . . Jesus, you were just a little kid."

"That doesn't absolve me."

"No, but ever since then you've tried to set things right. You've devoted your life to public service. Do you see Nixon, Madame Yee, or any of the millions and millions of people who participated in the Cultural Revolution doing the same?"

He felt her body try to shift away from him, but he kept her within his embrace.

"The real question is," he continued, "can *you* forgive me?"

She looked up at him. Her eyes glistened with tears, which brimmed, then ran down her face. He held her as she cried.

20

February 12
The Official Residence

They spent the night at Hulan's house—secure in the knowledge that MPS agents were watching over them in the sedan parked outside her gate. In the morning, she was still shaky and David was wrung out, but they had never been as close. All the walls between them were finally gone. Gradually they began to concentrate their attention once again on their present predicament. Hulan made tea and they sat together at the little round table in her kitchen. They started with the premise that they had exhausted their leads.

"Someone wanted us dead," David said. "Who knew we were going to the jail?"

"Guang Mingyun."

"Besides him."

"Peter."

David considered this. "You said he was reporting our movements to someone. Who?"

Hulan hesitated. "I was his immediate superior. After that . . . Section Chief Zai."

"Zai? Your Zai?"

"But it can't be him," Hulan said. "He'd never do anything to harm me."

"But I think it would be a good idea to talk to him," David said. "It may be someone else in the ministry. Zai may know who."

But David's clothes were still streaked with soot and grime. Clearly the first thing they needed to do was get David back to his hotel so he could change. The obvious mode of transportation was the MPS sedan parked out front, but now that car's presence seemed ominous.

"If it is someone at the ministry, how do we know he didn't send the car?" Hulan asked. If she was right, then going into the ministry at all would be dangerous, too.

At ten, after telling the two low-level investigators in the sedan that they'd be walking, Hulan and David set out down a thoroughfare to the back entrance of the Forbidden City. From there, they caught a series of buses, which took them to the Sheraton, where David was finally able to clean up. Then they took a taxi to the Ministry of Public Security.

They couldn't sneak David past the guards or "hide" him from the people inside the building, so they walked as nonchalantly as possible up to Hulan's floor, pretended to proceed to her office, then ducked instead into Section Chief Zai's. When they saw he wasn't there, they shut the door behind them. They assumed that the room was bugged, so they moved as quietly as they could and kept their voices low. Hulan again repeated that Uncle Zai couldn't be involved.

"Okay, but since he's not here," David whispered, "let's look around."

Hulan mouthed the word *no*, but David walked to the desk and began looking through the papers. "This stuff is in Chinese, Hulan. I need your help."

Hulan reluctantly came to his side. "You won't find anything," she said.

David ignored her, held up a piece of paper, and asked, "What's this?" Hulan said it was a requisition form. She was surprised at the relief she heard in her voice. David held up another, then another. All were innocuous. One of the desk drawers was locked, but David used a letter opener to jimmy it open. He held up another piece of paper with a red seal stamped on it. Hulan's unconscious gasp told him he'd hit pay dirt. "What is it?"

"It's Spencer Lee's death sentence. The red mark is Section Chief Zai's chop."

"You phoned him from the jail after Lee was sentenced. You asked him to file the official petition. Do you see any papers here that show he did that?"

Hulan scanned the desk, then shook her head.

"Let's just look at this," David said. "Maybe Zai is making a play. Maybe he wants back what *he* lost. What was it you said earlier? Things always change to the opposite."

"Uncle Zai is an honest man."

"But suppose he isn't. You told him exactly what we were doing. If he is who I think he is, then he had to get rid of Lee. If for some reason that didn't work, he had to stop us."

"I don't believe it."

"If Peter reported to Zai," David whispered urgently, "then he would have known we were going to the Capital Mansion to see Cao Hua." He struggled to piece together what else had happened that day. "And remember what Nixon Chen said at the Black Earth Inn? You asked him if he'd ever seen Henglai at the restaurant. He said Deng's daughter went there, the ambassador, *your boss*. He must have meant Zai."

"But that doesn't mean anything. Everyone goes there sometime. Nixon told us that, too."

"What about when we came back to his office?" David pushed on. "He told us to back off. Then, remember what he said when I brought up the idea of going to L.A.?"

Hulan nodded. "He said we would be out of the way."

"Out of the way, Hulan! Out of the way!"

"But, David, it can't be. I've known him forever."

How could he convince her? "On the first day I was here in China, I said something about the Rising Phoenix in your father's office. Everyone acted strange after that. You told me why later."

"Those cases had been an embarrassment to us. They were a loss of face."

"Why?" he pressed.

"Zai had investigated the gang and . . . "

"Nothing happened," David finished for her. "He must have been working with them all along! And then there's the bomb. He's the right age, Hulan. Was he in the army?"

"Yes," she admitted, "but it's all circumstantial."

He held up Spencer Lee's death sentence. "This isn't circumstantial. It's hard evidence."

Seeing the look of torment on Hulan's face, he asked, "What aren't you telling me?" When she looked away, he took her hand, brought it to his lips for a kiss, and said, "No more secrets, Hulan. None ever again."

"The night before we left, Uncle Zai came to my house. He warned me to be careful."

"Did he warn you or threaten you?"

She pulled her hand away and groaned. "I don't know anymore. I'm confused."

"Don't you see, Hulan? We cast that flower net of yours and when you look at all the pieces we've caught, they point to one person."

"Zai."

"I think we'd better see your father."

Vice Minister Liu gestured for them to sit and asked a tea girl to fill their cups. With his elbows perched on the desk and his chin rested on his interlocked fingers, he listened to their conclusions. When they came to the end, he took a sip of tea, then lit a Marlboro. "As I recall, one of the bodies was found aboard a ship that left Tianjin on January third. Am I remembering this correctly?"

"Yes."

Liu leafed through his desk calendar, found the date, and looked up. "Obviously you haven't checked Section Chief Zai's travel records." He could barely conceal his disappointment in them.

"No, we didn't."

"Well, Inspector, if you had, you would have known that Section Chief Zai was in Tianjin that week." He paused, then added with a self-deprecating smile, "I was there that week as well."

"What were you doing?"

"We were conducting a routine survey of the local bureau. Nothing terribly important, just time-consuming. But now, as I recall, Section Chief Zai was not with me every day, nor did we have dinner together every evening."

"Where was he?"

"Inspector Liu," her father said in Chinese, glancing significantly at David, "it is not my business what my employees do in their off time."

"I beg your pardon," David said.

"I was telling the inspector that I didn't know what Section Chief Zai was doing. But I must say that I have suspected that he was corrupt for some time." He turned his attention back to his daughter. "I'm sure this comes as a shock to you, Inspector. I know you have always had a lot of . . . respect for this man. But I think if you look back over his life and career, you will see that his past is not glorious."

"Do you know where he is now?"

"In his office, I presume."

"We were just there. He's gone."

Vice Minister Liu stubbed out his cigarette and stood. "Then I propose that we waste no time. I'll make the proper notifications. He will be found and arrested." He walked them to the door, where he shook David's hand. "It seems I am forever thanking you for your help. We are, as a country, grateful for your insights and persistence in this matter." With that, the vice minister closed the door behind them.

"Now what?" David asked as they headed toward Hulan's office.

"We wait. The MPS prides itself on being able to find a criminal anywhere in China within twenty-four hours. By tomorrow, this will all be over." Even as Hulan said this she doubted it. Section Chief Zai was well liked by the people who worked beneath him. She suspected that they wouldn't look too hard for their old colleague. But Hulan could also see that something niggled at David's brain as well. "What's bothering you now?"

"Okay, I see Zai, but how does the American embassy fit in? We know that someone there was stamping the passports for the couriers. So who was that?"

"Not some pencil pusher."

David agreed. "It has to be someone in a high enough position to have met him socially or professionally. Zai would have needed to see this man in action, trusted his discretion, and"—David thought for a moment—"yes, *and* believed his innocent aw-shucks demeanor."

"Phil Firestone."

Still nervous about who else could be involved at the MPS and not wanting to spend the time filling out a car requisition form, Hulan flagged down a taxi outside the ministry. Quickly they sped across town to the diplomatic area along Jianguomenwai. The driver honked through the masses crowded outside the embassy and dropped them off at the gate. They were shown up to the ambassador's office, where they were told that he was "out of town" and that his adjutant was at the official residence planning a Valentine's Day tea with Mrs. Watson.

A few minutes later they knocked at the door of the austere building the Watsons called home. A Chinese woman greeted them and led the way to a parlor for receiving guests. The room was decorated in what could be described as American Diplomatic, a style that allowed for few concessions to the country of residence. Chairs and settees were covered in a variety of royal-blue damask and silk moiré fabrics. Small pillows of blue brocade and heavy gold fringe served as accessories. Low, early-American tables were set with bouquets in Chinese blue-and-white ceramic bowls, silver dishes filled with ribbon and peppermint candies, and a few photography books that extolled the natural beauties of states like Vermont, Colorado, Alaska, and, of course, Montana.

It had been two months since Hulan had met Elizabeth Watson sitting on an iron bench in the dead of winter waiting to see if the dead body frozen under the icy expanse of Bei Hai Lake was her son. Now, as introductions were made, Hulan was once again struck by Elizabeth Watson's reserve. Her sorrow still showed in the sadness of her eyes, in the circles that hung beneath them, and in her slightly sallow complexion. Nevertheless, her hair was done in one of those politicians' wives dos, each strand held in place by hair spray. The severity of her hair was offset by the casual elegance of her gabardine slacks, silk blouse, camel's hair jacket, and string of pearls. She had the air of someone who had been busy all day, planning meals and seating charts, catching up on her correspondence, perhaps even chatting on the phone with a girlfriend or two back in Montana. What she did not look like was a woman who, as her husband had explained, was so deep in mourning that she couldn't receive visitors or answer questions about her son.

"Actually you just missed Phil," Elizabeth said, "but I expect him back shortly. If you run back to the embassy, you'll probably miss him again. So let's have some tea and visit for a while."

She poured tea from a heavy silver pot and handed the delicate cups and saucers to her guests. The whole while she carried on a mostly one-sided conversation about the weather, about plans for the upcoming party, about her visits to factory nursery schools in Sichuan Province where business was booming for Chinese and American entrepreneurs. David and Hulan let her talk, knowing that, as with most parents who mourn the loss of a child, she would bring the conversation around to Billy.

"He was such a bright boy and we had such hopes for him," she said. "He had just one more year to go at USC, and I remember the last time I saw him we talked about what he might do next."

David and Hulan glanced at each other, realizing that Ambassador Watson hadn't told his wife that Billy had dropped out. Silently they decided to see where this conversation would go.

"I kept stressing the importance of an education," Elizabeth Watson continued. "'Go to graduate school,' I said. Political science, history, maybe even law school. But Billy had other ideas. 'Ah, Mom, I'm sick of school. I want to get out, start a business, make my own way.' You see, I think it was always hard for Billy growing up in a small community where his father was so important, such a force, if you know what I mean. Like a lot of kids, Billy rejected everything his father stood for. But I always saw that as a phase."

"It sounds like you and your son were close," David said.

"Close?" Elizabeth Watson laughed. "I'll say we were close. Being a politician's wife is a lonely business. Being a politician's child is even worse. Billy and I were left alone in Montana a lot of the time. Someone had to stay behind and deal with the ranch. That someone was me. And I wasn't about to let Billy go off to Washington with his father. But I'll tell you, you think winter is bad here? You haven't seen anything until you've lived through a Montana winter." Elizabeth caught herself. "Excuse me for rambling on," she said. "It's just, you know, Billy and I had a bond."

"Are you saying he didn't get along with his father?"

Elizabeth regarded them, calculating. "You're here to talk about Billy, aren't you? I thought all that was settled."

"It is settled," Hulan lied. "But we do have a few loose ends."

"If there's *any* way I can help you . . . "

"Tell us about Billy and his father."

"I guess you know by now that Billy got into trouble sometimes." When David and Hulan nodded, Elizabeth went on. "There are a lot of ways a parent can look at things like that. In my opinion, Billy never did anything that harmed anyone. I always thought he did that stuff just to get his father's attention. From that standpoint it worked. Big Bill would just *freak*. Whippings when Billy was little. Hour-long tirades when he got older. Big Bill threatened to disown Billy, cut him out of his will, turn his back on him forever if he didn't shape up. The irony is that my husband was always putting pressure on Billy to take over the ranch. 'In ten years it'll all be yours.' That sort of thing."

"That must have reassured you," David said.

"Hardly! The last thing I wanted was for my only child to end up on that damn ranch. Why on earth would I have wanted him to spend his life compiling breeding statistics, supervising the annual culling of the herd, agonizing over the fluctuations in the beef market? No, Billy was too smart for that life. He had his whole future ahead of him and he could have done anything he wanted."

"How did Billy feel about all that?"

"Oh, I don't know. He was in college, but I don't think he cared about it much. During vacations, he'd pop in here for a few days, then fly back to the ranch with that friend of his."

"What friend is that?"

"You know, the other boy who died, Guang Henglai." When Elizabeth Watson saw the look that passed between David and Hulan, she asked, "What?"

"Your husband told us Billy didn't know Henglai."

"I don't know why he'd say something like that. Big Bill was helping those two with their little business."

"What business, Mrs. Watson?" Hulan asked.

"Oh, I don't know. Something about hunting. I think it was some kind of guide service—take some city folk up to the ranch, give them a good time, take them out hunting."

"For bear?" Hulan asked.

"Deer would be my guess," Elizabeth corrected. "But you're right, what Billy really loved to do was track bear. He got that from his father, you know. Give Big Bill and Billy a pair of rifles, a couple of orange hunting jackets so they didn't shoot each other, and a few thousand acres of back country and they were as happy as could be." Her eyes clouded as she said, "After all the years of trouble, that hunting business had finally brought those two together."

"Where is your husband now, Mrs. Watson?"

Elizabeth's head snapped up at the tone in David's voice. "He went to Chengdu. I thought you knew that. We have so many American citizens there now that we opened a consulate a few years ago. It's a good thing, too, if you ask me. Everyone's jumpy over those nuclear triggers and nervous about what's going to happen to their business ventures if the political situation doesn't improve."

David and Hulan stood. "Thank you for your hospitality, Mrs. Watson, but we really need to go."

"But I thought you needed to see Phil."

"That's all right. We'll catch up with him later. Thanks again."

"Was it something I said?" she asked as she followed them to the door. "Is there something about Billy or the ambassador I should know?"

Hulan turned and took Elizabeth Watson's hand, feeling sorry for this woman who thought she had experienced misery but was about to find out it was only just beginning. "If you need anything, later, I mean, please call me."

Elizabeth Watson looked from Hulan to David and back again. "Tell me. I can take it."

"We're sorry, Mrs. Watson," David said.

The tears that had been threatening to arrive since the beginning of their meeting overflowed now. Elizabeth Watson covered her face with her hands, turned, and ran up the stairs.

With brisk steps, David and Hulan began crossing the courtyard. They talked excitedly.

"No wonder Ambassador Watson didn't want you to investigate his son's death," David said. "He knew exactly what had happened. And once the boys were dead, all he thought about was saving his own skin."

"Remember when we last saw him?" Hulan asked.

"Yeah, that bastard wasn't shocked that Billy wasn't in school. He was shocked because we were so close to the truth."

"And after we showed him the list of couriers . . . He must have panicked. He wanted Spencer Lee dead."

"When we said Spencer was going to be executed, Watson said something along the lines of 'Then this will all be over.' We just didn't understand what he meant."

"Is stamping those passports really so bad?" she asked. "Was it enough to let things go so far?"

"He's a former senator and an ambassador. He committed a federal crime. He might be sent to one of our country-club prisons, but his reputation would be ruined."

They turned their attention to the others involved in the scheme. "Henglai must have financed the enterprise," Hulan said. "Billy— and his father—had the Montana connections. Imagine them up there shooting bears and selling their gallbladders."

"But I also think the boys did the meat-and-potatoes work of setting up the couriers. That's why they went to the Black Earth Inn." David considered, then said, "They all met there—the Watsons, Cao Hua, the couriers, the people from the Rising Phoenix. It was the perfect meeting place."

"You left out Uncle Zai."

"He was the muscle, Hulan. You accept that now, don't you?"

Her exhilaration faded. "The entire operation was clean in the sense that each person had his own separate and clearly defined role," she said. "They all had different friends, business associates, and spheres of influence. They relied on the assumption that no one would connect them."

"But we did."

Hulan came to an abrupt stop in the middle of the courtyard. "What do we do now, David? Who can we trust?"

They needed help, but Hulan doubted that they would get it from the ministry, nor could they expect much assistance from the embassy.

"We shouldn't talk here," David said as he came to the same conclusion. "How can we get out of here without being seen?"

She looked around. The ambassador's residence was behind them. Guards stood at the gate, the only exit as far as she could tell. "I don't think we can," she said, "but I have another idea."

Outside the gate, she waited until several taxis passed by, then hailed one at random. She gave the driver instructions to her *hutong* home in Chinese. After she ascertained that he was from the remote region of Anhui and had never had a foreigner in his car before, she switched to English. "The ambassador's in Chengdu. I'll bet that Zai's gone there, too. They're probably at the farm."

"But we have no idea where it is."

"They had help from people at Panda Brand," Hulan reasoned. "We have to go there and find someone who can help us."

"It's a slim lead, but it's the only one we've got," David agreed. "We'll get down there and we'll follow whatever information we find. Then we'll follow the next slim lead and the one after that until the truth comes out."

She took his hand and said, "You're right. We have to finish this before . . . "

"Before they finish us?" David tried to keep his comment light. When Hulan nodded solemnly, David felt his stomach contract in fear. He took a deep breath, then exhaled slowly. "Okay," he said.

"We know that everywhere we go we can be tracked. What did you tell me that day in Bei Hai Park? There's a camera at every traffic light? But listen, Hulan. People *do* escape from Beijing. Many of the students at Tiananmen got out. I saw them interviewed on TV. How'd they do it?"

"They had friends to hide them. They had connections in Hong Kong." Hulan understood what David was getting at, but they had a problem the students didn't have. The dissidents who disappeared into China to reemerge in Hong Kong or the West were Chinese. David was a *fan gway*, a foreign devil. All of this David was thinking through as well.

"I need a phone," he announced.

Hulan had the driver drop them at a café. Hulan dialed, asked in Chinese for the room of Beth Madsen, and handed the phone to David. He didn't give his name. Instead he said, "Remember me? We sat next to each other on the plane from L.A.?" There was a pause as Beth spoke, then David said, "No, I have a better idea. Can you meet me in two hours? No, not at the bar. You know the canal outside the hotel? Leave the hotel and turn right along the footpath. In about a quarter of a mile you'll see a little store that sells kitchen goods. Meet me there." He laughed with false heartiness. "I know it sounds mysterious. Just come, okay?"

21

LATER
Escape

They caught another taxi and drove back to Hulan's home, where she hurriedly packed a few belongings and whatever cash she had in an overnight bag. Then she walked down the alley—keeping a look of indifference on her face as she passed the sedan that was still parked outside her home—to the house of Zhang Junying, the old grandmother and Neighborhood Committee director. Hulan knew that she didn't have much time, but she could not hurry her neighbor. They had tea. Hulan ate a few peanuts. They exchanged small talk. Finally, Hulan said, "Yesterday I am riding my bike home from work. A country bumpkin pushed his cart of turnips right in front of me and I crashed into him. The chain on my bicycle broke and I fell to the ground and tore my only coat. I was wondering, auntie, if you would let me borrow your grandson's bicycle so that I might go to the store to buy a new chain."

Neighborhood Committee Head Zhang agreed wholeheartedly but warned that the bike might be difficult for Hulan to ride, since it was so large and built for a man. "I promise to be careful," Hulan swore. After a few more sips of tea, Hulan said, "I do have another favor to ask of you, but I am embarrassed to take advantage of your kindness again."

"We are from two old clans in the neighborhood. Our families have known each other for many generations. I think of you as I might a daughter."

"As I told you, my coat was torn and it is very cold. Your grandson has been out of the army for many years now. Perhaps I could borrow his coat just until I can buy a new one."

The old woman slapped her hands on her widespread knees. "You wear my grandson's coat? My grandson is very tall. That coat will come down so long you will have to tie it up with rope. You will look like a pilgrim to the sacred mountain of E'Mei."

"Only for a day, auntie."

The old woman went into a back room and returned with the greatcoat folded into a neat square and tied together with a nylon stocking. Hulan thanked Zhang Junying profusely, put the coat in the wire basket on the handlebars of the bike, then retraced her steps, pushing the bike up the hill, past the sedan, and into her courtyard, where David was waiting for her.

"Are you ready?" he asked.

She looked around the garden, so barren in winter, and nodded.

"Are you afraid?"

She nodded again. He enclosed her in his arms, immersed himself in her essence, then whispered in her ear, "So am I, Hulan, so am I."

Then he pulled away. For their plan to work, they needed to move quickly and with absolute assurance. David put his coat in a plastic bag and threw it in his bicycle basket. Hulan regretted that she would have to leave her revolver behind, but with the way they'd be traveling, she wouldn't be able to take it.

While Hulan dressed in her own musty greatcoat, closed up her house, and put her bag in the basket of her bicycle, David untied Madame Zhang's grandson's coat, shook it out, and put it on. It was a tight fit, but between it, the old blue cap that Hulan had found packed away in a closet, and the woolen scarf that she wrapped around his neck and partway up his face, he was at least partially disguised.

As soon as they lifted their bicycles over the old stone threshold, the sedan's engine started. David and Hulan mounted the bikes and slowly began pedaling down the street. The car made a U-turn and followed them, making no pretense at discretion. "Stay close, David," Hulan said over her shoulder as she began to pump faster, then swerved down one of the side alleys. The sedan kept right with them. Suddenly she turned down a narrow alleyway the car could not fit through. David chanced a look over his shoulder to see two men in plainclothes jump out of the car and begin cursing. David and Hulan pressed on, trying never to slow for pedestrians who strolled through the narrow labyrinth of alleys.

David felt that they had disappeared into another century. There were no cars or even motor scooters here, only the soft *whoosh* of bicycles and the gentle ring of their bells, the sound of children at play, the melodious call of merchants hawking their wares. Across the city they rode, keeping within the narrow confines of the *hutong* alleys. When they came to a dead end, Hulan asked directions. When someone noticed that David was a foreigner, Hulan explained, "Oh, the stupid big nose got lost. I am helping him get back to his hotel. It is our responsibility to show friendship to Americans whenever we can, even if they are backward and stupid." When they got to major intersections—which came with frightening regularity—David pulled his scarf up, focused on the asphalt before his front wheel, and tried to keep to the middle of the stream of bicycles crossing the road.

They had two stops to make before meeting Beth Madsen. The first was at Hulan's parents' apartment. While she went up, David waited on a side street, tinkering with the spokes of his bike, desperately hoping that no one would approach him.

The maid let Hulan in. Hulan said, "Please, I wish to be alone with my mother. Do not disturb us." Without another word, the maid backed out of the room. Jinli sat in her wheelchair, as she always did, staring out the window.

"Mama, it is Hulan. I am going away for a few days. Don't worry about me." Hulan leaned over and gave her mother a gentle kiss. "I love you, Mama."

Then Hulan went to the desk. In the bottom drawer she found

her mother's papers in a yellowed envelope. Hulan took her mother's identity card, tucked it inside her coat, and—without looking back— left the apartment.

David and Hulan continued their journey across the city. A couple of blocks from the Sheraton Great Wall, they pulled over again. Hulan took off her greatcoat. Underneath she was dressed as usual in fine pastel silk. She brushed off her clothes and ran her hands through her hair. "Do I look all right?"

"You're fine," he reassured her.

A few minutes later, Hulan emerged from the alleyway, turned onto Xinyuan Road, and pushed through the doors of the Kunlun Hotel. She walked through the lobby and down one of the shopping arcades to a travel agency.

"I'd like to book two seats on the next flight to Chengdu," she said in Chinese.

"Please sit down, madame," the woman said. "Would you like to arrange a scenic tour?"

"No, I just want to get there on the earliest flight. My mother is very ill."

The woman regarded Hulan. "You can't be Sichuanese. Your Beijinger accent is too good."

"I have lived in the capital many years now. My work unit is here, but my family still lives in Chengdu."

The woman checked through the flight schedule. "Is this evening at six satisfactory?"

"Absolutely. Two seats."

"Two seats?"

"I said this already," Hulan said impatiently.

"I shall need to see your identity cards."

"Pshaw! You don't need identity cards to travel in China anymore. You haven't needed this for ten years."

The woman tapped her fingers on the desk as though summoning a waiter in a restaurant. "I want to see your . . . "

Hulan reached into her pocket and quickly flashed her mother's papers. Then she opened her wallet, took out two hundred-*yuan* notes, and placed them next to the woman's hand. "My husband has his card at home." The woman's fingers tapped a few more times, then she swept the money off the surface of the desk and into her lap.

"The names?"

"Jiang Jinli. My husband is Zai Xiang."

After a few more tense minutes, Hulan left the travel agency with two tickets to Chengdu in hand. She met David down the alley, where they once again mounted their bikes, rode parallel to Liangmane Road, chose the middle of the block to cross busy Dongsanhuanbei Road, thereby avoiding the camera at the intersection, then made their way to the pathway along the canal past the Sheraton Great Wall to the little shop for kitchen goods that David had passed each day on his early-morning jogs.

Beth Madsen, dressed in a thick red wool coat with shiny gold buttons, paced nervously along the bank. David pulled to a stop next to her. "Beth," he whispered. When she turned, she saw a larger-than-average Chinese soldier with most of his skin covered by layers of wool cloth to protect him from the weather. David pulled his scarf down to show his face. "It's me, David Stark."

"David? What are you doing out here?"

"I need your help, Beth. I'm in trouble."

Beth looked over his shoulder to where Hulan was standing next to her bike. "What's this all about?"

"They're trying to kill us."

Beth Madsen laughed. When he didn't join in, she turned serious. "You're not kidding, are you?"

He shook his head.

"Go to the American embassy," she suggested.

"I've been there."

Beth stared at him intently, then turned, walked a few steps away, and watched as an old man poled his boat along the canal. "I thought, a drink. Maybe, you know . . . "

"Beth, please . . . "

Beth straightened her shoulders, then turned back to face him. "If I'm going to help you, I need to know what I'm getting into."

Quickly they told her as much about what they knew as he felt she could grasp. When they reached the end, Beth said, "But if half of what you say is true, they'll be looking for you."

"That's what I'm counting on," David said. "They're thinking we're going to try to hide, and we are. But we're going to hide in plain sight."

While he outlined his strategy, Beth regarded Hulan. The Chinese woman met this scrutiny evenly. At the end of his description, Beth thought for a moment, then said, "Okay, but let's do it quick before I lose my nerve."

Again Hulan shucked off her coat, looked at David one last time for reassurance, then the two women set off. David would wait here for fifteen minutes, then make his way down one of the alleys to where it met the main thoroughfare. If all went well, Hulan would arrive a few minutes later in Beth's car, and they would drive straight to the airport. David scrunched down on his haunches as he had seen so many Chinese men do and looked out at the canal. The same old man David had seen on his morning runs was loading baskets onto his boat. Watching this man going about his everyday business calmed David.

The two women had a long walk back to the hotel. By the time they passed through the side entrance, Hulan was shivering from the cold and from the fear she felt when she saw the two plainclothes policemen who watched the comings and goings of guests. But they must have been instructed to look for a Caucasian man or they were duped by seeing Hulan with a Caucasian woman, for they paid no attention to the women but kept stamping their feet to keep warm and puffing on their cigarettes.

As soon as they got inside Beth's room, the American sighed. "I think I held my breath the whole way," she said, trying for a light conversational tone that came out more as a quaver. Beth giggled nervously, then opened the closet and pulled out an Armani pantsuit of fine gray wool and a silk blouse. Unself-consciously, Hulan stripped down to her underwear and slipped on Beth's outfit. It was a little big in the hips, but otherwise it fit perfectly. To complete the ensemble, Beth added a velvet trimmed headband and a pair of Bally flats. In just five minutes, Hulan had changed from a Beijinger to a wealthy overseas Chinese.

Beth gathered together a few other clothes and stuffed them into a plastic shopping bag from the Kempinski Department Store across the way. She picked her red coat up off the bed and handed it to Hulan. "Here, take my coat, too."

"You've done enough," Hulan declined politely.

"If you don't mind my saying so, this isn't a time to show your Chinese manners. Just take it."

A few minutes later, when they walked back out the side entrance, the two policemen again ignored them. Beth raised her hand and her driver pulled the Town Car up to the steps. As the two women slipped into the backseat, Beth gave instructions. A couple of minutes later the driver stopped at the designated meeting place. David was nowhere in sight.

Hulan knew the best thing to do was to circle around and hope that he showed up shortly. Instead, she envisioned the worst: David was injured or dead. This thought propelled her against all reason out of the car. "If I'm not back in five minutes," she told Beth, "don't wait! Go back to your hotel and forget this ever happened." Beth, whose skin had taken on a pale green tint, nodded. Hulan turned away and hurried down the alley, which led to the canal. David hadn't moved from his spot on the bank.

"David, are you all right?" she asked, her voice tremulous.

He turned to face her. He seemed unconcerned that he had missed their rendezvous. "What do you see, Hulan?"

"David, we have to get moving!"

"Just tell me. What do you see?"

Hulan looked around. "A gray sky. Some houses. A couple of shops. A canal." She tried to appease him with these simple answers, but the danger of their situation got the better of her. "Come on! This isn't the time to take in the sights! We've got to go!"

He ignored her commands, saying, "The canal. Where does it go?"

"I don't know. I suppose it connects with others, maybe it pours into the Grand Canal or the port at Tianjin."

"And you still don't see it?"

"No, David, I don't," she said in frustration.

"Every morning I've come out here to run. Every morning I've watched that man load baskets onto his boat. Do you see him over there?"

"Yes."

"You didn't mention him."

"David!"

He creaked to a standing position, shook out his legs, and crossed to her. He turned again to face the canal, put one arm over her shoulder, and with the other pointed. "A boat, a man, a basket, a canal. It's how they moved Henglai to Tianjin without being seen. They hid him *in plain sight.*"

It was an important discovery, but Hulan was too scared to care. She grabbed David and their parcels and led the way to the car. The driver didn't question anything but drove straight out the toll road to the airport. When David and Hulan got out, Beth said, "Good luck." Then she closed the door and the Town Car pulled away.

The next hour would be the trickiest if David's plan was to work. They were traveling as Chinese but dressed as Americans. While David watched their few bags, Hulan queued up in the busiest line she could find, hoping that the clerk would be too harried to focus on the names on the tickets or the woman who stood before her. Wordlessly Hulan handed over the tickets. To Hulan's relief, the woman behind the counter never even looked up but just typed the names into the computer, issued seat assignments, handed the tickets back to Hulan, and chirped, "Next."

As always, the airport was filled with soldiers. They were young men, most of them from the countryside and unaware of politics, but their presence had a physical effect on David. Beads of sweat broke out on his forehead despite the waiting room's chill. Hulan took his hand in hers and said under her breath, "All we have to do is get on the plane." David wiped his brow with the back of his hand. "I don't think they'll look for us here. At least not yet." But she said this only to calm David, for she knew that all it would take was just one of her colleagues to walk into this waiting room for her to be recognized. She and David had committed no crime, but that didn't mean anything. People disappeared in China all the time. People were executed in China all the time.

The flight was called. Hulan handed the tickets to the attendant. When the woman said something to Hulan in Chinese, she pretended she didn't understand. "Have a good flight," the woman said, switching to English, then tore the tickets without looking at the names.

As soon as the plane took off, David felt the tension ebb from his body, knowing they would be safe for the duration of the flight. In just a few short hours his whole way of living had changed. He'd always valued the fact that he lived by his brain. He was skilled at logic, linear thought, conservative analysis. Now he seemed to be operating purely on instinct and intuition.

He thought over what he'd done. Leaving Los Angeles without telling anyone what he was doing was crazy enough, but evading the police in China was another matter altogether. He could practically hear the unctuous tones of some Chinese official explaining to some bureaucrat at the American embassy that China could not be responsible for an American who went off on his own, that the government had the China International Travel Service just so foreigners wouldn't get themselves into trouble, and that the government would do everything they possibly could, but how exactly were they supposed to find one lone man in a country of a billion persons?

And while that government official blabbed on, David could already be dead. He imagined his own demise. Would he be conscious as his internal organs melted into pulp? Would he be staring into the eyes of the killer as his intestines were pulled from his belly? Or would he be totally oblivious—walking down the street one minute, a bullet in his brain the next?

When David put his own welfare aside and thought of Hulan, wild desperation bubbled up inside him. How could he have let her come back to China? What would happen to her if she was caught by Zai or even Watson? Those people had no compunctions about killing, and if something happened to Hulan, David didn't know what he would do.

It was close to nine when the plane landed. As David and Hulan walked across the tarmac, they were once again gripped by fear.

Would they be arrested as soon as they entered the terminal? But police and army activity at the small provincial airport was practically nil. No one seemed to be looking for David and Hulan, and they blended in with the other foreign travelers. Since they had nothing to pick up from baggage claim, they simply walked out of the terminal and pushed into the crowd beyond the barrier. They were assaulted by locals offering taxi rides. Hulan settled on a young woman whose English was fair.

In the car, the driver asked where they wanted to go. David told her to take them to the best hotel. The driver nodded, put the car into gear, and began another hair-raising drive through a strange city. When the young woman behind the wheel ascertained this was their first visit to Chengdu, she gave a brief history of the city. It was also known as Brocade City, for in the ancient times Chengdu had been a stop along the Silk Route for that fabric. The driver knew of several brocade factories, which she would be happy to show her guests tomorrow. Chengdu was also known as Hibiscus City because of the abundance of that flower. However, the two foreign guests had arrived too early in the season to see them in bloom.

Even in the dark, Hulan and David could see that this main road, South Renmin, was lined with small hotels, restaurants, and shops. Closer to the city, they drove past two large construction sites. The gate for one said BROCADE CITY VILLAS. Inside, David could see what looked like Orange County tract housing. The driver said, "These are the best villas in the city. For foreigners. If you want, I can bring you to this villa park tomorrow. Maybe you will buy one." Across the street, a huge apartment complex—also for foreigners—was going up. A series of billboards advertised three-bedroom penthouses, pools, a golf course, and tennis courts.

As they crossed over the Jin Jiang River, a tributary of the powerful Min Jiang, which would eventually join the Yangtze, the driver pointed to the hotel. On the roof of the Jin Jiang Hotel were huge electric signs in gold, orange, and blue advertising the hotel, shops, and products of the region. Twinkling lights festooned the trees in the motor court, where several young men in bright red uniforms jumped to attention to open doors, carry David's and Hulan's parcels, and escort the travelers to the front desk. The lobby was all highly polished marble and sparkling crystal. At the center of the room was a six-foot-tall bouquet.

Just as at the airport, there were no guards and no army personnel in evidence. Perhaps for this reason they had no difficulty in arranging for a room. In fact, to Hulan's eyes, the man behind the desk affected an ostentatiously casual demeanor at the presence of this mixed-race couple.

With considerable pomp, the bellboy showed them to the hotel's best suite, which included a sitting room with a piano, white brocade-upholstered furniture, a skylight, a bathroom with a sunken tub big enough for six, and a bedroom with a lush red canopy over a gilt-encrusted bed. David bestowed a generous tip—an increasingly popular custom in China—on the young fellow, then locked the door behind him. "This is too expensive," Hulan said, looking around at the lavish decor.

"Hide in plain sight," David said. "I don't think anyone will be looking for two desperadoes in the Princess Suite or whatever this is. Besides, if we're going to go out, we might as well do it in style. Do you still like room service?"

22

FEBRUARY 13

Panda Brand Deer and Bear Farm

The next morning they slept till eleven. When they finally awoke, the temptation to stay in that bed, in that place forever, was great. Languidly, Hulan pulled herself out of bed and tottered off to the bathroom. David flipped on the television to CNN, hoping to hear news of the current status of U.S.-China relations and if it was still safe for him to be in the country, but the network was airing an international sports segment. David turned it off, threw off the bed-clothes, and walked to the window, where he stood naked looking out over the city. The sky was cloudless, and David could feel the sun's rays through the glass, but the air itself was thick from the numerous factories that spewed orange-brown chemicals from their smokestacks. The people on the streets below—vendors selling fruit from baskets, pedestrians on their way to work, a few old people doing tai chi in the park by the riverbank—were dressed for this more temperate climate in bright lightweight sweaters.

Hulan emerged from the bathroom wrapped in a terry-cloth robe, her hair twisted up in a towel. "Lots of hot water," she said. "It feels great." And it did. Despite their tenuous situation, the good night's sleep and the warmth of the air assuaged their fears just enough that they decided to go down to the restaurant for brunch. The dining room was huge and colorful. At the far end of the two-story room was a floor-to-ceiling sculpture of a local mountain replete with craggy rock, hanging plants, and waterfalls. Giant umbrellas in magenta, orange, red, yellow, and turquoise hung from the ceiling. The mezzanine was decorated with pillars, wrought iron, crystal chandeliers, potted palms, and crisply appointed tables, while the ground floor was sumptuous in earth tones and white linen.

On a series of long buffet tables, trays and chafing dishes brimmed with Chinese and American food. David found himself passing up the scrambled eggs, pancakes, and French toast. Instead he piled his plate with noodles, dumplings filled with pork and garlic, *hom don*—hard-boiled salted egg—and fresh pineapple and watermelon. From the condiment table, he procured large dollops of chilied turnip, spicy bamboo shoots, and pickled radish. All of this he washed down with steaming hot cups of jasmine tea. The meal was rich, spicy, and deeply satisfying.

After breakfast, they wandered through the ground-floor shopping arcade, where David purchased and changed into a new set of clothes. Now they were finally ready to face the day.

One of their biggest mistakes, they realized now, was not getting the exact location of the Panda Brand farm, but when they'd last spoken with Guang Mingyun, they were concerned only with saving Spencer Lee's life. That was only yesterday morning and so much had changed. Hulan stopped by the concierge desk and was told that the farm was located in Guanxian City. "However," the concierge said, "the Dujiangyan Dam may be a more rewarding experience for you. Panda Brand does not cater to Westerners, and the dam is very dramatic." But at Hulan's gentle insistence, he gave the directions to the farm.

To get there, they would need a car, and Hulan would have to be the one to rent it. She left the hotel and waited at the corner for the traffic director, who stood on a podium in the intersection, to signal a direction change, and for an old woman, who was responsible for pedestrians, to blow her whistle for the all clear. Hulan crossed South Renmin Road, walked down a block past smelly public bathrooms to

the Minshan Hotel, where she used her mother's identification
papers to rent the car. She arrived back at the Jin Jiang's motor court
with her enthusiasm severely dampened. "I haven't driven in twelve
years, David, and even that was in Los Angeles. I don't know if I can
do it."

But an hour later Hulan had negotiated her way straight through
the middle of town—passing department stores, hostels for pilgrims
about to set out overland to Tibet, the railway station, and a colossal
statue of Mao, under which was carved a slogan, "Realize the Four
Modernizations; Unify the Motherland; Vigorously Develop China."
As she drove, they talked about how they should present themselves
once they reached their destination. Just this single morning they had
shifted personas a couple of times. In the hotel, they were American.
Hulan had rented the car as a Chinese. In the car, David wrapped his
muffler around his face and hoped that the other drivers, the traffic
directors, and the old women with their whistles would not take
notice of him. But once they got to Panda Brand, David would not
be able to pass as a Chinese.

"Maybe I should pose as your interpreter," Hulan suggested.

"Okay, but then what am I? A businessman, a doctor, a tourist?"

If he were a tourist, then why wouldn't he be accompanied by an
interpreter and driver from the China International Travel Service? In
Beth's Armani suit and with a change in attitude, Hulan could pass
herself for an overseas Chinese. But then why was *she* there, where
was she from, who were her relatives, what did they do in America,
and what did she do in America? All of these questions they needed
to be prepared to answer without hesitation. They hoped that this
constant shifting, this constant movement, would keep anyone from
making an accurate identification of either of them. But the fear of
being caught kept David and Hulan very focused.

By two, they'd left the hubbub of the city behind them. The sky
was a radiant blue, and David and Hulan rolled down their windows
to let the warm air flow in around them. Within a half hour they
were driving past fields lush with winter greens that spread out from
the highway to the horizon. Here and there, peasants bent to their
labors. Some pulled weeds, some clipped at errant suckers. Still others

carried buckets of water slung from poles across their shoulders. With great care, the water was ladled onto individual plants.

Which was not to imply that Hulan and David's journey was peaceful. If anything, the drivers on this road were worse than those in Beijing. The highway had four lanes—two in each direction. The outside lanes were unofficially designated for pedestrians, bicycles, tricycle carts, wheelbarrows, hand-pulled wagons of every size and variety, and beasts of burden. Most of these conveyances were loaded down with produce.

The two center lanes were devoted to automobiles, great trucks carrying scrap metal, produce, and gasoline, buses packed with humanity and with goods of every sort strapped to the roofs, and motor scooters whose drivers tempted fate as they wove in and out of traffic. Everyone passed any and everything he or she could. Typically cars swung left out around an obstacle and into oncoming traffic. Sometimes—and it happened more often than David would have liked—two cars abreast would do this maneuver, pushing the one farthest to the left into the oncoming "pedestrian" lane.

But for all this tumult the actual pace was relatively slow. Hulan kept at a steady twenty or twenty-five miles an hour except for those moments when she would push the car to seventy or eighty. So, although Guanxian City was only thirty-four miles from Chengdu, it took almost two hours to reach. Leaving the City of Brocade, they passed through the villages of Xipuzhen, Pi Xian, Ande, and Chongyizhen before hitting the outskirts of Guanxian, known—as the concierge had said—as the home of the famous Dujiangyan Dam and irrigation system. This system, Hulan explained, was known to all Chinese, for it had been in use for more than two thousand years.

On they drove, following the banks of the Min Jiang, finally reaching Guanxian proper. Prosperity had hit this town hard. The whole area was caught in a vortex, catching up one or more centuries in just a matter of years. Old-style farmhouses—low stone edifices with tile roofs—were dwarfed by the new multistory office and residential towers that rose next to them. Near the river, new plantings had yet to soften the brutal cuts into the landscape made by the construction of a series of villa parks similar to the one David and Hulan had seen when they first arrived in Chengdu. Hulan had never been here before, but she surmised that this town had always been a resort of sorts. Now that the Sichuanese had real money, they were buying homes and apartments for weekend getaways. She suspected that truly wealthy businessmen, who could afford a car and driver, might even make this commute daily.

David and Hulan began seeing advertisements for Panda Brand Deer and Bear Farm. From billboards pink, powder blue, and soft yellow cartoon animals (but no pandas) beckoned all to come visit them in their wonderful home. Hulan followed the signs to a residential neighborhood, drove under a high gate that read PANDA BRAND DEER AND BEAR FARM and FREE AND OPEN TO THE PUBLIC in Chinese, Korean, and Japanese, and into a parking lot filled with tour buses.

Hulan and David followed more signs leading down a lovely tree-lined pathway to the "observation area." To their right were low houses hidden behind high stone walls. To their left, they could see into open pens where a small herd of deer grazed. They passed a guide in a uniform and a perky blue hat hurrying her charges back to their bus. But after this tour group, the lane was deserted except for a few molting chickens and a couple of kids on bicycles who ignored the farm for the everyday sight it presented. The two investigators climbed a set of stairs and crossed over a small bridge, which served as the observation deck above the pens. They continued farther into the complex, turned a corner, and came upon two side-by-side enclosures for the bears.

The pens were open, clean, and home to perhaps thirty Asiatic brown bears, more popularly known as moon bears for the white marking that resembled a crescent moon on their chests. Seeing humans, the animals, as a mass, lurched to their feet. Immediately, David and Hulan could see that these animals had no corsets, no drains, or any other foreign objects attached to them as they swayed over to just under the overhead bridge. Looking down upon their round heads, David saw that they were much smaller than he expected. They looked like pudgy ten-year-old boys—short, plump, with goofy faces that looked up at the visitors longingly. The bears balanced on their hind feet and begged for handouts.

Hulan and David retraced their steps and entered the souvenir shop. The room was large enough to hold several tour groups at once. Despite the obvious popularity of the place, the manager saved energy—a mandate throughout the country—by keeping the lights off. So, although fluorescent fixtures hung in pairs from the ceiling, the only illumination came from the waning daylight that filtered through the windows.

Along the perimeter of the room were glass display cases behind which young women waited to serve customers. In the middle of the room, a few final tourists gathered around a long table where they could pick up, fondle, and smell ginseng or deer musk. Several full sets of still-fuzzy deer antlers lay atop these other remedies. The other two walls were bordered by low couches and tables where customers could sit, sip tea, sample the wares, and bargain for the best price. Just as Guang Mingyun had said, the Panda Brand Deer and Bear Farm did not openly sell bear products in any form. Again and again David and Hulan asked if there was any bear bile for sale, each time trying variations on their question. David complained of liver problems. Hulan said she needed bile for her mother, who had been ill many years. David said he wanted to take some back to America to give as gifts. But each woman they asked insisted that there was no bear bile for sale there. It was against the law.

At five minutes to five, the stragglers from the last tour group left. Once the others were gone, Hulan approached another saleswoman and said that a friend in Beijing had suggested they come here for bear bile. "She was mistaken," the clerk answered tartly. When David offered a bribe, no one took it. Then the manager came out and began locking up. "It's time to go home," he told Hulan in Chinese. "You can come back another day."

Reluctantly David and Hulan left but lingered by the car to watch as the clerks filed out. Most left in groups of three or four, throwing their sweaters over their shoulders, swinging lunch pails, gossiping and laughing. A final group stepped out into the parking lot and stood together talking. The manager closed the door behind him, said good night to his employees, then set off down the walkway that led past the deer and bear pens. Three of the women gave last waves, mounted their bicycles, and pedaled away.

One young woman remained. She was dressed in pale pink shorts, a skintight white vest, flesh-colored knee-highs, black patent-leather high heels that had seen better days, and a black leather jacket, which she left open. She wobbled across the cobblestoned parking lot to David and Hulan. "I know where you can get bear bile, but it will cost you," she said.

"How much?"

"For directions, a hundred dollars U.S. For the product, you will have to do your own negotiating."

"One hundred dollars is a lot of money," Hulan observed. It was almost a third of the average annual income in her country.

"I will not bargain with you," the woman responded with a toss of her hair.

"You'll take us there?"

"I said directions, a hundred dollars."

"What if you're not telling the truth?"

"I work here every day. You can find me tomorrow."

David pulled out his wallet and handed the money to the young woman. The budding entrepreneur counted the bills, folded them, and squeezed them into her pocket. Only then did she give the directions to the Long Hills Bear Farm, which, she explained, was also owned by the Guang family.

After the woman had disappeared down one of the alleyways, Hulan sighed. "Can you drive?" That was the last thing David wanted to do, but hearing the fatigue in Hulan's voice, he took the keys. Fortunately, he had several side streets to navigate before he reached the main road. Still, it came faster than he wanted, for suddenly there he was, trying to keep alive and not kill anyone else. At first he drove slowly and cautiously. After five diesel trucks passed him, he picked up the pace. When a man with a pushcart strolled into the automobile lane to pass two old women without even looking back over his shoulder to see what was coming, David tapped the horn for a few half-hearted trills. When a bus spewing black exhaust slowed just long enough to allow a woman to throw up out the rear window, David crossed the center line, put his foot to the floor, laid his hand firmly on the horn, and got around the offending vehicle. Once back in his lane, he turned to Hulan and grinned.

After another hour, when they reached the small village of Yingxiuwan, David turned off the main road and crossed a bridge over the upper reaches of the Min Jiang. The road narrowed and automobile traffic all but ceased. Still, pedestrians wandered along the side or down the middle of the road. From here, David and Hulan followed the Pitao River, a tributary of the Min Jiang. The car's engine groaned as the incline grew steeper. By now, David was almost wishing for the zaniness of the main highway as the road turned into slithery gravel and deep potholes. To their right, a deep ravine cut into the rhododendron-covered mountains, their tops cloaked in mist. Even up here, every inch of soil was put to good use. There were terraces, of course, but more impressive were the tracts of land sometimes only a few feet wide that were planted with cabbages, bok choy, and onions.

Twilight was just falling when Hulan yelled, "Stop the car!" David pulled over to the edge of the ravine. "Look!" she said excitedly. "Look down there!"

David leaned across her and peered over the cliff. He saw the river and some men working along the bank. Behind them, an imposing building—low, compact, windowless—sat bleakly and totally out of place in this almost idyllic environment.

"Do you know what that is?" She didn't give David a chance to answer. "It must be the Pitao Reform Camp. It's the place where my father was sent."

"Let's take a closer look."

"I don't think we should."

"We're up here. They're down there," he reasoned. "I think we'll be okay."

They got out of the car and stood together on the edge of the precipice. Inside the yard of the camp, where not one blade of grass grew, they could see several men in dull gray uniforms breaking boulders into rocks. Others packed these rocks into baskets, slung them onto their backs, and carried their heavy loads through the front gate and down to the riverfront. Another group of men stood in a row in the water, some only up to their ankles, others up to their waists. Although Sichuan Province was much warmer than Beijing, the waters that rushed by came from recently melted snow. The men with the baskets set down their burdens and began passing the rocks from man to man out into the river.

"What are they doing?" David asked.

"If this were somewhere else—near a stretch of cultivated land, for example—I would guess they were doing some kind of diversion or irrigation project. But look, those rocks must be washing away in the current. They aren't *building* anything. They're just keeping busy."

"It's hard to imagine your father and Guang doing that kind of work."

"And Uncle Zai, too, even though he was here later," Hulan added. "Oh, David, what a waste!"

"It was all right in front of us, but we couldn't see it. Guang's ties to Sichuan, the bear farm, this place. Think of the years Guang and Zai must have plotted. And your father . . . "

"Right," she said. "Everything must have started here."

23

LATER

Long Hills

By the time Hulan and David reached the landmark the young woman at the Panda Brand facility had described—a pair of stone pillars marking a dirt road on the left—darkness had enveloped them. They bounced over the rutted road, which led down into a canyon. The headlights danced crazily into groves of dense bamboo. They came around a corner and almost had a head-on collision with a black sedan that shimmied within inches of David and Hulan's car and sent them skidding off the road and into a low ditch.

"What was that?" David exclaimed.

"I don't know. Are you all right?"

David nodded. "And you?"

"I'm fine, I think." They waited a moment, feeling shaken, then Hulan asked, "Who was that? Do you think we should follow him?"

"He's already got too much of a head start. Let's find the farm first." David put the car in reverse and with much squealing of tires and billowing dust edged back onto the gravel road. A few minutes later they came around another curve, and the road opened up. Ahead of them, in the beam of the headlights, they saw a couple of low buildings enclosed by a fence and a sign that read LONG HILLS

BEAR FARM. David stopped the car and the two of them sat staring ahead into the darkness.

"I wish I had a weapon," Hulan said.

"I wish you did, too, but I'd settle for a flashlight."

By opening the car doors David and Hulan seemed to shatter the silence. When they shut the doors, they were again plunged into inky blackness. They waited for their eyes to adjust.

"Ready?" Hulan whispered.

"Yeah."

They met at the front of the car and crept forward. Hulan gently pushed open the gate. Its creak seemed louder than the car doors' slam.

"Let's look out back first," Hulan suggested softly. David nodded and followed her between the two buildings. As soon as they reached the other side they could hear deep breathing and could smell the bears. A few more tentative steps and they came to the first cage, which stood several feet above the ground on four posts. Beneath it, excrement and old food that had fallen through the mesh rose up in a pile a good two feet high. Inside the cage, a moon bear looked at them and groaned. This sound roused the animals in other cages.

As they edged forward, David and Hulan saw several cages, each with a moon bear. The animals had no room to stand or even sit up. They all wore metal corsets around their middles. Some of them had gangrenous infections that festered and oozed pus from beneath their corsets; others seemed to be suffering from dementia.

"Is there something we can do for them?" David asked.

There was no mistaking the impatience in Hulan's voice as she said, "What? How? We're in the middle of nowhere, David. Come on, we'd better see what's inside."

The first building was locked, but from the sounds of movement and heavy animal sighs inside, they determined that it must house more bears. Then they walked to the second building. It appeared to be a storage shed of about fifteen by fifteen feet with several window-size openings. David poked his head through one. He could smell the warm aroma of fresh hay mingled with the feral odor of more bears, which he could hear breathing deeply. But he couldn't make out anything else. The door easily opened and they entered. But the room—with only starlight to illuminate it—was pitch black. Then, just ahead of them and to their left, they saw the small orange glow of a cigarette's tip as someone inhaled.

A voice in English said, "I have been waiting for you."

Hulan was not surprised to hear her father. "Baba," she said.

"Yes, it is I." Then a match was struck and a kerosene lantern lit. In its flickering light, David saw Vice Minister Liu, dressed not in a sharp Western suit but in the clothes of a peasant. A pistol dangled casually in his hand. David knew nothing about guns, but this one looked to be of a large caliber. Liu smiled. "It took you so long to get here. But now that you have arrived, are you surprised?"

"No," Hulan answered. "I think I suspected you after the bomb . . ."

"Hulan!" David's voice was rough.

"I tried to tell you and you laughed the idea away," she told David, not taking her eyes off her father. "Then there were so many other things. What happened with Spencer Lee's petition, how the execution papers were so easy to find in Section Chief Zai's office, how the vice minister told us Zai was in Tianjin, then seeing the Pitao camp."

"But you didn't follow your instincts," Hulan's father admonished gently.

"Oh, Ba . . ."

The regretful sound in Hulan's voice erased the smile from her father's face, which twisted with rage. In that moment, the horrible reality of their situation hit David. They were alone with this man miles and miles from anywhere and anyone. Father and daughter began to speak, but David deliberately tuned them out to concentrate on how they might escape. The room had only the door for an exit. If worst came to worst—and David had no illusions that it wouldn't—he might be able to push Hulan out of harm's way either out the door or behind one of the eight bear cages that were set two to a wall. But how long would that protect her? A minute? Five? And then what?

"But why the triads?" Hulan was asking her father. "I see now I didn't know you, but I always thought you held them in contempt."

"When I hear you like this," Liu mused, "I think, My daughter is not so stupid. She is slow maybe, but not stupid. You are right. I abhor the triads."

"But you made some connection with the Rising Phoenix during the ministry's past investigations," she surmised. "That's why you'd never let Section Chief Zai take his evidence to the courts."

"They offered me money," Liu said, jutting his chin. "I took it. Then, when this opportunity came along, I thought, Here are people who can transport our shipments and distribute the product in the United States. We had a very good relationship . . . "

"Until?"

"The others wanted to make more money. Those boys and the father went behind my back and made a deal. So I killed the boys. But I also wanted to send a message. And I did. But I think you and Attorney Stark figured this out."

"David did, yes."

Liu turned his virulent gaze to his daughter's lover. "Tell me, *David*"—the sound of his name spoken in such a patronizing tone sent a chill down the American's spine—"how did I do it?"

"You needed information first," David said. "You knew that your partners had made some kind of a deal with the Rising Phoenix. Were they planning to cut you out entirely?"

Hulan's father nodded, then said, "Go on."

"Henglai was smaller, so you probably overpowered him first. Those boys must have been surprised. You were their partner."

"They thought I was a weak old man. They were wrong."

"Billy was a tough kid, so you focused on Henglai. You tortured him with—what?—cigarettes?" When Liu said nothing, David went on. "You didn't need to kill Billy at all. He could have passed on your message. But by then you were carried away."

"But my method," Liu said irritably.

"The beetle," David answered quickly.

"Correct. It was so easy to put a little of the powder on a cloth and hold it over their mouths and noses. But then . . ." Liu shook his head in distaste. "It was unpleasant, watching the blisters form on their lips and nostrils, listening to their screams, waiting for the stomach hemorrhage that would finally silence them." He mutely relived the memory, then inquired in an interested voice, "And where were they killed?"

David and Hulan didn't know. Liu grunted. "A warehouse, but who cares?"

"Afterward, you took Billy Watson to the park," David continued. "You wanted him to be found, and you wanted him to be found where his father could see him."

"If the top beams aren't straight, the bottom ones are crooked also," Liu recited. "Do you have that saying in America?"

"No."

"But you understand the meaning."

"I think so. Like father, like son?"

"Exactly. And the son had to be destroyed to make the father see his mistakes. This betrayal . . ." Liu's jaw clenched. "This betrayal was Watson's doing. He thought *he* was the big man. He thought that just because he had the ranch that he was taking the biggest risks. He thought, I have the two boys, I have the Rising Phoenix, why do I need old Liu? But the whole thing had been *my* plan. I was in charge. It was a hard lesson, but Bill Watson learned the truth." Liu stared at David with cold black eyes. "Now tell me about Henglai."

"The canal, am I right?"

As Liu nodded, the lantern's light glinted off the lenses of his glasses. These two *had* appreciated his work.

"You delivered your second message," David continued. "You wrapped up Henglai and placed him in the water tank in place of the shipment of bile that the others had arranged for."

"I'll tell you," Liu said, "putting that boy in there was no easy task. I am not as strong as I once was, and that boy was just dead weight." He cackled at his pun, then said, "I wanted the Rising Phoenix to understand who they were dealing with. I couldn't let them cheat me."

"So you ruined their shipment of immigrants."

"It didn't have to be that way," Liu said apologetically. "All they had to do was throw the body overboard."

"But they didn't," David said.

"Who can explain the stupidity of others?"

"They weren't that stupid. They knew we were coming."

Liu grimaced. "You give them too much credit. No, I think they simply panicked in the storm. The *Peony* was adrift and moving into U.S. waters. What else could they do but abandon her?"

David chose not to pursue that, saying instead, "You also took care of Spencer Lee."

"That was unfortunate," Liu said, then explained himself. "I was ready to continue my partnership with the Rising Phoenix. Even the dragon head agreed we should continue our shipments. But after the arrests in Los Angeles, things became more difficult. Someone had to fall, and we all agreed that the boy was expendable. I signed a paper," Hulan's father confessed. "I used Zai's stamp. There is no artistry there."

"Why bear bile, Ba? Was it because of Mama?"

"After your mother came back from Russia, I tried many things to help her. I finally heard about Dr. Du."

"Is he a part of this?"

"Of course not." Liu cleared his throat and spit in disgust. "He's an old fool, but he has a lot of knowledge and he likes to talk. He's very free with information, as I'm sure you found out."

"The government was sending him out to talk about medicines made from endangered animals," Hulan recalled from their interviews with Du. "They had even sent him on some raids here in Sichuan."

"You see? He talks too much. He'd brag about these things, too, whenever I took your mother to see him. When the time came to find a farm, I knew where to look."

"And in Henglai you found someone who could be very useful to you," Hulan said. "Did you seek him out?"

Liu lazily waved his gun back and forth. "To tell you the truth, Henglai came later. First, I had the Rising Phoenix and we did a few insignificant jobs together to build trust."

Liu fell silent, waiting for David and Hulan to inquire about those other "jobs." When they didn't, he asked, "Haven't you wondered,

Attorney Stark, how so many people could leave China on a freighter from a major port without attracting the attention of Chinese authorities?" David didn't respond. Liu sneered, "Let's just say I used my influence to make sure people would look the other way." He paused, then added, "Oh, there are so many things I'd like to tell you . . ." As Liu's voice trailed off, David realized that the other particulars could come later, if there were a later.

"No," Liu continued, "all this happened because of Billy Watson. You know by now that he was a hooligan. One day he is brought to my office for some minor offense. He's sitting there telling me about his father. I had met the ambassador, of course. I thought, Let's bring Big Bill Watson in here and see what happens."

Liu again turned his attention to his daughter. "You know how Americans are. They are so brash and think they own the world. He says to me, 'Maybe we can work things out.'"

"He offered you a bribe," Hulan deduced.

Liu nodded. "But I didn't want his money. I said, Let's meet for lunch at the Black Earth Inn."

"When Nixon Chen said 'your boss' comes here, he meant you," Hulan said.

"Don't interrupt me! I am talking!" Liu chided his daughter. He paused to gather his thoughts, then said, "On that first day I am thinking, Who knows how this will turn out? Soon we are having lunch every week in a private room. Then Billy is coming and bringing his friend Henglai. The first time we all meet everything comes together for me. Henglai! Guang Mingyun's son!"

"You knew him in the camp," Hulan said.

As Liu said that indeed he had, David thought he heard something outside. Neither Hulan nor her father had seemed to notice.

"Let me tell you something," Liu continued. "Guang Mingyun was someone I went to for help after I got out of Pitao. We had been through a lot together, but he chose to look the other way. Since that time I watched him, and from the ministry that was very, very easy. I saw him with his airplanes and satellites. I saw him with his munitions factory. I saw him open Panda Brand. So when I met Henglai at the Black Earth, my first thought was of Panda Brand. By that time, I had been thinking about exporting bear bile for many years and I knew that company very well. Now suddenly the time was right, the people were in place, and we had access to the product."

"The others didn't resist?"

Liu snorted. "The Watsons were greedy. And Guang Henglai? He is a Red Prince. He has lots of money, but he is bored. At first it is a game for him: Find people on the inside at Panda Brand, steal the packaging and bile."

"But to cheat his own father?" David asked.

"Guang Mingyun is so busy making money, he pays no attention to his different businesses. That makes it a simple matter for Henglai—or someone else—to take advantage. Eventually Guang Mingyun suspected something, but by then we already had this place."

The more Vice Minister Liu talked, the more David and Hulan could see how his obsessions had corrupted him. Yes, he told them, he wanted to get rich. Who didn't these days in China? That's why it had been so easy to recruit couriers. Liu had suggested that Billy and Henglai find help at the Black Earth, since people there were always looking to make a deal—legal or otherwise.

The scheme had been perfect until his partners got greedy. "They should never have tried to cut me out," he repeated as though that explained how he could have gone on a rampage that had resulted in the deaths—either by his own hand or those of the Rising Phoenix— of seven people. David ticked off the list in his head—Guang Henglai, Billy Watson, Cao Hua, Noel Gardner, Zhao Lingyuan, Spencer Lee, and Peter Sun. David and Hulan would soon be added to that bloody tally.

"Clean blade in, red blade out," Liu intoned. He stood and began to pace before the window openings on his side of the shed. "This is how Mao told us to deal with our enemies. And I did, with the help of those Rising Phoenix scum. The whole time I am thinking this brings back the purity of the old days. When I think of that time, I cannot help but remember the three of us together. Mama, Baba, daughter. I needed my daughter to come home to complete our family. I needed her where I could keep an eye on her. Hulan has known this for many years."

Hulan shivered but didn't speak.

"But then, Liu Hulan, my own dear daughter, I see that my actions might bring me the greatest happiness of my life." Liu stopped in front of one of the openings and nodded to himself at the memory. David thought he saw a shadow pass outside. "Revenge is a glorious action. It is deliciously pure."

"I suppose, then, we might find Ambassador Watson's body here?" Hulan asked.

"No, you just missed him."

"The car on the road? He's not dead?"

"The ambassador and I were waiting for you for many hours. He is such a boring and predictable man, don't you agree? But you're right. He left. He wanted to get back to the embassy in Beijing. He thinks he'll be safe there." In his usual way, Hulan's father waved his hand, as though dispersing a bad smell, only this time, he held a gun in it. "Why would I *kill* him? The other punishments are so much greater, don't you agree?"

"He'll have diplomatic immunity from the crimes committed here in China," Hulan said.

"I think your father's referring to murdering Watson's only child," David suggested.

"Yes, of course, there's that," Liu agreed amiably. "But even better, he must face the boy's mother every day, knowing that he is responsible for her misery. And when she finds out that her husband is guilty . . . Does she know this already? Is that why you're here? Oh, how I would love to see the look on his face." He conjured up this image and allowed himself another laugh. "But no, I wasn't thinking of the ambassador. I was thinking of you."

David took a step forward, hoping that Hulan's father was so caught up in his story that he wouldn't notice. But the bears— already groaning and tossing their heads from side to side as they picked up the humans' emotions—became even more agitated. When two of the bears threw themselves against the bars of their enclosures, the vice minister's gun instantly came up. His aim was steady and directed at David's heart. He began to pace again.

"The truth is, when I assigned you to the investigation of Guang

Henglai, I did it because—well, what can I say?—I didn't think you would get anywhere. Naturally, Ambassador Watson did not want the case to proceed either. So when I received orders from high above to pull our department back from the case, I thought all was going according to plan. But I hadn't counted on those imbecile immigrants on the *Peony*! When they didn't throw the body overboard, that obviously complicated things for me."

David believed they didn't have much time left. A pitchfork leaned against the wall behind Hulan's father, but it may as well have been on the far side of the moon.

"Then your lover finds the body on the *Peony*," Liu said. "I cannot begin to express to you how I felt when I heard this news. Then when I received orders that the case must be reopened and that we—two great countries—must work together, my future suddenly spread out before me as clear as could be. You see, I had never forgotten that day in the *hutong*. I never forgot what you did to your mother."

"Hulan didn't do anything," David said. He heard the pistol's crack and felt the searing burn as a bullet entered his arm. The impact lifted up his body and hurled it against the shed's back wall. The bears roared. Hulan screamed and moved toward David.

"No! Stay where you are," her father said, swinging the weapon back in her direction. Liu grudgingly dragged his eyes to the American, who sprawled against the wall, his hand over his wound. "There are many ways to die, Attorney Stark. Quickly with a bullet. Or slowly. I tried to make it painless for you once in Beijing, but it didn't work out. So be it. We are here now. And I want you to understand this. You know nothing about Hulan, nothing about me. I suggest that you keep quiet and your death will be merciful."

Liu slowly backed up, coming to a stop against one of the shed's windows. His attention returned to his daughter. He took a fatherly tone, the one he had always used when talking to her about family obligation, tradition, and customs. "As you know, revenge is a duty for all Chinese people. Like the debt we owe our parents, it must be paid. Like monetary debts we accrue, they must be settled. It may require many years or many decades, but a Chinese of honor will exact revenge. I have waited patiently, Liu Hulan, and now that time is here."

Liu raised his pistol to his daughter's head. Hulan straightened her shoulders. Then, from his position on the floor, David saw an arm reach through the window opening, quickly come across Liu's neck, and hold him in place. The surprise caused his gun to waver. Hulan knocked it from his grasp. At the same time, another hand came out of the shadows and pressed the muzzle of a revolver against Liu's temple.

"It's over," Section Chief Zai said.

24

STILL LATER
Long Hills

For a moment, all was quiet, then Zai spoke. "Hulan, you know what to do." When she didn't move, he ordered, "Inspector Liu, pick up the gun."

She did and aimed it at her father. Zai's lips were close to Liu's ear. He said softly, "I am going to come inside. You stay where you are. Understood?" Liu nodded. Zai slowly loosened his grip, disappeared for a few seconds, then stepped through the door.

"My old friend, welcome," Liu said bitterly.

Zai lifted his revolver to keep a bead on Liu. Hulan dropped her father's gun, looked around, found David, and rushed to his side.

"I'm all right," David said. He looked up at Zai. "You followed us. The car outside Hulan's house . . ."

"And many others," Hulan's mentor said, nodding. "I knew you would eventually come to Chengdu. I waited for you at the airport. From there it was simple. Hulan is a professional, but she wasn't looking for me to follow her and I have more experience."

"You let us come down here." David lifted his good arm. His gesture took in the shed, the bears, Liu.

"When you drove off the main road, what could I do?" Zai then addressed Liu. "I think this was your main mistake. This place is out of the way, but the position . . . It is not what we learned in the army."

"What are you talking about?" David was indignant. Hulan put a hand on him to calm him.

"This camp is down in a canyon and very remote," Zai explained. "I couldn't trail you then. You would have seen me. But from the main road I could watch without being observed myself. I followed your headlights as you made your progress. If you had gone very far, then I would have driven in. But when the lights stopped here, I knew I should walk. My arrival would be more of a surprise."

"You knew everything," Liu concluded.

"A long time ago," Zai said sadly. "We have, after all, known each other many years."

"I wanted you to pay and Hulan, too . . . "

"Liu, how many times did I try to tell you?"

The conversation had taken a turn. David felt Hulan pull away from him. She stayed very still at his side, listening.

"I know what I saw," her father was saying. "I know what I heard. My daughter destroyed her mother, my wife."

"No!" The syllable cut sharply through the room. "It was your own back-door ways that destroyed Jinli. You have never wanted to hear the real story, Liu. But this time you will. What happened to Jinli was *your* fault."

"Never! It was you and Hulan!"

"I was there," Zai shot back. "I saw it happen. Remember, we were together at the Ministry of Culture. I knew you were into schemes even then. I'm not talking about the ways you tried to get films made. We all did what we could in those days to bring honest stories to the people, not just propaganda. But you were my friend, and when others came to report that you had taken a bribe, that you were taking kickbacks from the workers, or that you were having an affair with Secretary Sung, I ordered them out of my office. They despised you for your crimes and I did nothing."

"Ba?" Hulan sounded very young.

"It's all lies," her father said.

"It is the truth, Hulan," Zai said. "You were a small child. You saw only your mama and baba. You didn't *know* what was happening."

Hulan looked confused.

Zai turned back to his old friend. "But I did and so did others. As the Cultural Revolution waged on, I knew it would be harder to protect you. Soon I began to hear rumors that the workers wanted to kill you. I refused to accept the reality. That is something I will have to live with for the rest of my life."

Zai hesitated before going on. "Then one day Jinli came to the ministry. The vultures saw their opportunity. They circled around her. They recited your crimes. Let me tell you, Secretary Sung was the worst of all."

Liu agreed. "She was such a pretty girl, but she had venom in her heart."

With her father's acknowledgment, Hulan suddenly realized that all the fond memories of her childhood had been false.

"They were holding me back, accusing Jinli and me of being fornicators, too." Zai's voice dipped as the images came back. "I can see Jinli on the balcony now, backing away, backing away, until she hits the railing, loses her balance . . . As she flailed, she looked about for help and no one stepped forward. Then she fell to the courtyard below."

Zai looked up and saw Hulan across from him, tears streaming down her face.

"They said if anyone touched her, they, too, would learn to fly," Zai continued. "We both remember how things were in those days. Those people spoke the truth, and no one wanted to risk death. Jinli lay in the courtyard for four days while I went to get you. Four days! Such a long time! But the people were so harsh, so unforgiving. These cruelties were common. Usually victims were just left to die, but I couldn't let that happen."

"When you were coming for me, she was lying there alone?" Hulan asked. "Ba, where were you?"

Liu sank to the floor. His skin had gone pale.

"Your neighbors already had him in the *hutong*," Zai said.

"For four days?" Hulan asked. Her training didn't allow her to believe that simple answer.

For the first time since Zai's arrival, Liu spoke directly to his daughter. "No, I was not in the *hutong* the whole time."

"You were with Secretary Sung," she guessed.

He shook his head. "I had already tired of her. There was another woman, a tea girl from the ministry." He looked directly at Hulan now. His eyes were tormented. "And what you said in the *hutong* . . ."

"All that you heard—every word Hulan spoke—was a lie designed to save your life," Zai said. "But more than that, I wanted the gossip to travel back to the Ministry of Culture. The people took pity on Jinli, and I was able to call for an ambulance. I sent her to Russia, where her money could buy her decent medical care *and* safety. I sent Hulan into exile—away from her family, away from her homeland. The rest you know."

"Everything she did . . ." Liu's body began to shake, and he couldn't complete the sentence.

"Your daughter was like the Liu Hulan of legend," Zai finished for him. "She martyred herself to save you and her mother."

Liu uttered a low guttural sound. Then he moved quickly, scrambling across the floor to the gun Hulan had dropped. He picked it up and stood.

"Put it down," Zai said, his aim still steady.

Liu wasn't listening. He stared at his daughter. "I'm sorry," he said. He tried to say something more but couldn't. Before anyone could move to stop him, he raised the gun to his head and fired.

25

FEBRUARY 14–MARCH 14
Home

For David, several days went by in a blur of pain and narcotics. He was admitted to a Western-style hospital in Chengdu, where he endured lengthy surgery to remove the bullet and reconstruct the bones in his arm. David had lost a lot of blood, but the doctor assured Hulan that he would recover completely. The best thing he could do now was stay in bed and rest.

On that first day in the hospital, Hulan was sitting on the edge of David's bed, waiting for him to regain consciousness and watching a local newscast when she heard about Ambassador Watson. "Despondent over his son's death, the United States ambassador to China committed suicide this morning at the official residence," the reporter announced as on the screen Watson's body was wheeled from the official residence. This was followed by shots of Elizabeth Watson getting into the back of a limo and Phil Firestone making a statement lamenting the loss to America and China of such a fine man.

Hulan put through a call to Zai, who, after the events at the bear farm, had ordered men to the embassy to arrest Ambassador Watson—they would worry about diplomatic immunity later—but they were too late. After leaving the farm, Watson had driven back to Chengdu and taken a flight back to Beijing, where his wife confronted him about Billy's death. Unable to accept her husband's lies, she killed him. Zai himself had flown up to meet with her, but the murder had occurred on embassy grounds, making it an American problem. Knowing this and wanting to protect his boss even in death, Phil Firestone acted swiftly, arranging for Mrs. Watson to accompany her husband's body to Washington, where he would be buried with full honors in Arlington National Cemetery. Hulan had relayed all this to David as soon as he awoke.

David began to heal. Hulan came to the hospital every day with tin containers of soup. Together they watched the story unfold on television. On the International Hour on CNN, David and Hulan watched the president eulogize his old friend, then go on to make a broad policy statement about the continuing conflicts with China. He hoped that these would be resolved, but if they couldn't, he—like Big Bill Watson, who throughout his life had stood up to bullies domestically and internationally—would take a tough stance.

"Turn it off," David said.

Unlike the U.S. government, Chinese officials chose to use the case as an object lesson. Ironically, it was unlikely that the Chinese people would believe the account of Liu's actual suicide, having heard so many political falsehoods in the past. Still, one quarter of the world's population watched as the iron triangle closed around other couriers found at the Black Earth Inn, the young woman who worked at the Panda Brand souvenir shop, as well as several others who'd been involved in the packaging, sale, and transportation of the bile.

For Liu's official eulogy, a document written by committee that would define how he and his family would be perceived for the next fifty years or so, the government dredged up all manner of unsavory revelations from the decadent lifestyle of his grandparents through Liu's corruption at the Ministry of Culture, and ending with the murders and smuggling. In accordance with tradition, Liu's descendants were also examined. While on a personal level Hulan might never get over the events at the bear farm, her role there protected her from disgrace now. In fact, there had already been a brief flurry of stories in the media recalling the brave deeds of the revolutionary martyr Liu Hulan and drawing parallels between her life and the inspector's.

"To have two suicides of such prominent people should attract someone's attention," Hulan said one day after reading a particularly florid account in the *People's Daily*.

"Yes, if anyone's paying attention," David had responded. But no one was.

On the morning of February twentieth, any chance that the full story might emerge was lost as another story of far greater significance was announced. Hulan came to the hospital and turned on the television to see a simple black-and-white photograph against a blue background with the characters for "Comrade Deng Xiaoping Is Immortal" displayed beneath it. (Later, they discovered that Deng had died the previous morning. The government, Hulan explained, had postponed the announcement to curtail spontaneous public demonstrations.) China entered a period of mourning. Word came down that the Lantern Festival, the final festival of Chinese New Year, should be downplayed this year.

On February twenty-third, doctors pronounced David well enough to fly to Beijing, but procuring seats proved difficult. Deng was from Sichuan Province, and many people from his village had been invited to the memorial in the capital. Hulan used the combined clout of the MPS and her status as a member of one of the Hundred Families to obtain airline tickets.

On February twenty-fourth, Deng's family and a few top officials met for a private funeral. Deng Xiaoping had always said he wanted a frugal and private service. His wishes were observed up to a point. His wife, children, and grandchildren cried over his body. Hulan—like hundreds of millions of others—watched in television close-up as Deng's daughter kissed her father's waxen cheek one last time. Later his body was driven by Toyota minivan past thousands of Beijing's citizens along the Avenue of Perpetual Peace past the Forbidden City and Tiananmen Square to Babaoshan, the cemetery reserved for revolutionary heroes, where he was cremated. Deng had also said he wanted to live to see China regain sovereignty over Hong Kong. This wish, too, could only be partially fulfilled; some of his ashes would be sprinkled in Hong Kong Harbor.

Hulan's recent notoriety won her an invitation to the memorial service attended by ten thousand people—an auspicious number to the Chinese—in the Great Hall of the People. At 10 A.M. on February twenty-fifth, whistles and horns on cars, trains, boats, factories, and schools sounded all across China for three minutes to mark the beginning of the service. Hulan took her place with other Red Princes and Princesses on the ground floor of the Great Hall. A few rows ahead of her, she saw Nixon Chen and Madame Yee. A few rows in front of them, she glimpsed Bo Yun and a couple of others she'd seen at Rumours.

Everyone stood to listen to President Jiang Zemin read the eulogy. Like Hulan's father's, it was a carefully worded document, one that would be studied for years to come. In it, Deng was remembered for surviving three purges and for creating the market socialism that had brought so much change to China. The Cultural Revolution, when Deng had suffered so, was proclaimed a "grave mistake." The bloody massacre at Tiananmen Square, for which Deng proudly accepted responsibility, was mentioned, but Jiang's words were cautious.

As Hulan listened, she couldn't help but wonder about President Jiang's future. On the street, people sometimes referred to him as "Flowerpot," because he had become as common as a flowerpot at ribbon cuttings and other photo opportunities. He also had a penchant for singing American movie tunes and reciting passages from the Gettysburg Address to entertain visiting dignitaries. Were these the actions of a "paramount leader"? Did he qualify as the "first among equals"? Would there be a power struggle during this fall's Fifteenth Communist Party Congress or would it take a year or two for his detractors to get organized? Jiang was the commander in chief of the world's largest army, but did he have the support of the generals? No one knew the answers yet, but like a Chinese opera there were still many acts to come.

Hulan was still not quite sure why she had come there. She supposed it was seeing Deng's daughter tearfully kissing her father on television the day before. For all of his political accomplishments— and failures—Deng must have been a good father. He must have loved his children very much to elicit such a public show of emotion from them. After a lifetime of wishing and trying, Hulan had been unable to forge a similar bond. So she stood in the Great Hall of the People mourning less for Deng than for the absence of love from her own father.

David would have liked to stay in Beijing, but he had a lot of unfinished business in Los Angeles. Before he left, he and Hulan had one last dinner with Zai, who'd just been appointed vice minister. Despite his new title, he looked much the same. His jacket was worn and his shirt was frayed at the collar and cuffs. He spoke haltingly about Hulan's father. He knew his friend's history of corruption but had seen no reason to be suspicious until their trip to Tianjin. After Liu assigned his daughter to the Watson case, Zai concluded that his friend had to be involved. "After Cao Hua's death, my main concern was for your safety," Zai told Hulan. "I wanted you out of the country. I hoped you wouldn't return."

Hulan began to mist up, and they decided to drop the subject, but later in the evening when Zai excused himself to go to the men's room, David followed. "Hulan's father talked about people high up who ordered him to reopen the case. They—whoever *they* are—must have known about him. Who told them? Was it you? Was it *your* opportunity to get revenge on Liu?"

Zai looked very tired. "He was my oldest friend. Where he was concerned, I followed a one-eye-open, one-eye-closed policy almost my entire life. Even after everything that had happened in the past, I would have done nothing to harm him, until I believed that Hulan was in danger. That I could not stand."

"Then how did they know?" David asked. Zai just shook his head.

On March first, sixteen days after the events at the bear farm, David—with his arm in a sling—was back at Beijing airport in a private waiting room. Vice Minister Zai, as yet unaccustomed to dealing with the media, trudged through a speech for the benefit of the local press. His words were translated into English for a few stringers by a young woman from the Language Institute of Beijing. David scanned the faces of Zai, Guang Mingyun, and others from the Ministry of Public Security who had turned out for this official farewell. Out of the corner of his eye, he saw Beth Madsen walk by the window that separated this room from the rest of the terminal. She was either leaving Beijing or coming in on another of her business trips. If she was departing, then they'd probably be on the same flight. At his side, holding his hand, was Hulan. They had said their most intimate farewells at her home, knowing that at the airport their behavior would be circumscribed by formalities.

Vice Minister Zai ended his remarks. The assembled crowd applauded. Then he stepped forward and presented David with a plaque showing the Great Hall of the People with gold characters etched on each side. The two men shook hands. Then it was Guang Mingyun's turn. "I am grateful for what you did, even though the outcome has reflected badly on my son's memory." He handed David a package wrapped in plain brown paper and tied with string. "This is just a small token. Please do not embarrass me by opening it now." They, too, shook hands, then Guang Mingyun faded into the crowd.

Zai cleared his throat and said a few last words in Chinese. The others nodded and drifted away so that only Zai, David, and Hulan remained. "Again, we are thankful for your help," the older man said. "China is a good country, but sometimes we make mistakes."

"As do we," David acceded.

"Yes, none of us can avoid human nature. In these events neither China nor America was completely clean or completely dirty. People died who did not have to. I think particularly of Investigator Sun and Special Agent Gardner. We should honor their memories by remembering our ultimate success. I hope we can work together in the future to stop corruption and other types of crime. I have much still to do here, and I'm afraid you will be going home to many hard tasks. But I believe we have made a good start."

"Thank you."

"Thank *you*." Zai looked around. "I will keep the others away."

With that, Zai left the waiting room and stood outside the door, leaving David and Hulan alone.

"This won't be for long," he said.

"I know."

"You'll come soon."

"I will."

"You promise."

"Absolutely."

"If you don't, I'll be back for you."

She smiled. "I'm counting on that."

When it was time to board, David had a hard time letting her go. As he walked down the jetway, he paused and turned to look at her one last time. She was standing—dry-eyed—by herself. Nearby, an old woman swept the floor. A few young men in army uniforms rushed by eager to begin their furloughs. A handful of businessmen scuttled past, talking on cellular phones. David waved to Hulan and turned away.

After takeoff, David opened the package Guang Mingyun had given him. David didn't know what he'd expected, but it certainly wasn't a computer disk. He held it thoughtfully for a couple of minutes, balancing it in his hand. Once the pilot turned off the seat-belt sign, David got up and walked to where Beth Madsen was working on her laptop. The seat next to her was vacant.

"May I?" he asked.

"Sure." After he sat down, she nodded at his cast. "You're more or less in one piece, I'm happy to see. Can I ask what happened?"

After David told her and thanked her for her assistance, she said, "I've never been so scared in my life, and I didn't *do* anything."

"Your help meant a lot to us. I don't know what we would have done . . ."

"It's over now. That's the main thing." Then, seeing the look on his face, she asked, "Or is it?"

"That's why I came over here. I have another favor to ask of you."

He handed her the computer disk. She closed her file and inserted the disk. There were no passwords or secret codes. Instead, the disk had spreadsheets listing shipments, future delivery dates, and payment schedules for nuclear trigger devices made by the Red Dragon Munitions Company, a division of the China Land and Economics Corporation, and sold to a consortium of generals in the People's Army. Hitting an icon brought up another spreadsheet showing how the consortium had arranged to resell the triggers to several countries and individuals.

"Do you know what this is?" David asked.

Beth Madsen ejected the disk and handed it back to David. "I don't want to know, and I don't think you do either." Then, affecting a carefree manner, she said, "Now let's see if we can find a flight attendant to pour us some champagne. I think I need it."

By the time David saw Madeleine Prentice and Rob Butler at the U.S. Attorney's Office, they'd both already been briefed about his activities in China. He gave them the disk and they never mentioned it to him again. But within a few days, David could see its impact in several small pieces buried deep in the newspaper and in cryptic faxes from Hulan. A new flurry of arrests had been made on both sides of the Pacific. Of those in China, Hulan thought David might recognize the name of General Li, who, until his fall from power, had served on the Central Committee. He was the grandfather of Li Nan, the Red Princess Hulan and David had met that night at the Rumours nightclub.

David was unfamiliar with the names of the men arrested in the United States. Most of them were not American citizens but hailed from places in the world where terrorism was rampant. However, there were a handful of native-born crackpots who had also placed orders through Chinese middlemen to buy the nuclear triggers. To date, Guang Mingyun's name had been kept out of the press. David suspected that it would never appear.

All this David apparently observed with only passing interest, since he was busy with his own cases. Madeleine had given him the go-ahead to prosecute Hu Qichen and Wang Yujen. Armed with the information Spencer Lee had chanted during his death ride, David subpoenaed Lee Dawei's financial records from several banks in

Southern California and was able to piece together an intricate money-laundering scheme. David then went to the grand jury and had come away with an indictment. Immediately after the dragon head's arrest, the entire organization started to disintegrate. Now David spent his days interviewing witnesses who willingly stepped forward. He had worked toward this moment for many years, but he had no illusions. The Rising Phoenix had suffered a blow—perhaps even been defeated entirely—but in the vacuum another gang would seize power.

On March thirteenth, David invited Jack Campbell to run with him the next day around Lake Hollywood. In the morning, the FBI agent—dressed in a warm-up suit—met David at the gate that led into the lake property. As they stretched, Campbell kidded David about trying to run with a bum arm, but the younger man answered tersely that it helped his recovery to keep the blood moving. Then, to ease the tension, David clapped the agent on the back, jogged in place for a few steps, and went back to his stretches.

They started out at a leisurely pace. It was still early morning and only a few people had set out ahead of them. The air was fresh and the lake reflected the blue of the sky. David waited until he could verify that no one else was on the path, then he shoved the agent against the fence. David held his cast just under Campbell's chin to pin him in place. The look of surprise on the FBI agent's face was quickly replaced by a laugh. "What the fuck! You're pretty handy with that thing."

"Tell me what this was all about!"

Campbell attempted a shrug. "What's to tell?"

"This was never about endangered animals, drugs, illegal immigrants, or the triads. So how about the truth?"

"The truth? Can't do that," Campbell said lightly. "You don't have the clearance."

David jammed his cast against Campbell's chin. "I think I *earned* my clearance."

"You're sounding pretty tough for an AUSA, but, hey, I'm the one with the weapon."

A small smile played across David's lips. "I don't think so."

The agent reached behind him for the gun he kept holstered at his waist. His eyes widened when he realized it was gone.

"I took it while you were stretching."

"I didn't think you had it in you. You've got balls, Stark. I'll give you that."

"Let's try it again."

But Campbell wasn't ready to cave in that easily. "What about the other runners?"

"I'll worry about that when they come. Until then, start at the beginning, and no lies."

"The beginning . . ." Campbell said thoughtfully. "I guess that would be with Guang Mingyun. He was up to his elbows in those nuclear trigger shenanigans. Could we prove it? Absolutely not. So we get a break. Here's this big operator and his only son is murdered. *You* find the body. Guang wants the killer found—*at any cost.* Do you know what that means? *He came to us.* Guang knew his son was up to no good, but he was willing to take the risk that whatever we uncovered might cause him to lose face." Campbell paused, considered, then asked, "What does it matter now, David? We got the bad guys."

"Finish it!"

"So he comes to us, like I said. We have a practical government, David. We're a country of merchants. We always have been. We say, This is gonna cost you. What do you have to trade?"

"The triggers."

Campbell nodded. "He tells us he's noticed some improprieties in one of his businesses." As Campbell said this, a memory of Hulan's father rushed into David's brain. At Long Hills, Liu had said that anyone could take advantage of Guang Mingyun. Indeed, while his back was turned, his son had begun cheating him. At the same time, someone else had horned in on the Red Dragon trade. "Guang says he's willing to give us names if we help him," Campbell continued. "As a gesture of good faith, he tells us where and when a shipment of the triggers will be delivered. Those arrests were made while you were flying to Beijing the first time, but the people were all low level. But see, Guang has already promised he'll give us the big guys—generals in the People's Army no less—if we find his son's killer. A deal like that doesn't come around very often."

"So you sent me to China to get the deal rolling."

Campbell held up a hand. "Now wait. You're getting ahead of things. We know that Guang's a prickly guy. We also know that we'd rather do business with a capitalist like him than some unknown down the line. We're thinking ahead. We have been for a long time. What's going to happen after Deng dies? Will the generals take power? Will some conservative wacko emerge from the Central Committee who's got a bug up his butt about capitalism and democracy? We've got analysts who weigh these things and here's what they tell us: Guang's bringing wealth to the country. He's got support from the people. Man, this guy's consolidated power all along the Yangtze. He's driven by money, that's something we can understand. So, back in Washington, they think Guang's not such a bad guy to have in our camp. We've certainly been in bed with worse. To put it bluntly: We've got a vested interest in China. Guang Mingyun is someone we understand. We speak the same *language*. Only one thing's going to hold him back: the People's Army. We help him find his son's killer and we help him bring down the strongmen in the army. All this may not happen today or even a year from now, but down the line, we'll expect tit for tat."

"All for a price."

"Exactly."

"Part of that price was Noel."

"Yeah, I know," Campbell said with regret. "But, Stark, he knew what he was getting into. It's a risk we take every day."

"What about Watson?"

"Power corrupts." Campbell shrugged. "These things happen."

"So you knew."

"We knew *something*." Campbell held up his hands again and spoke earnestly. "You understand that when I say 'we' that doesn't necessarily mean me or even the Bureau. I just do what I'm told." His hands dropped as he said, "Let's just say that what happened came from the highest levels of government."

David also remembered hearing that same phrase in China.

Everything the president of the United States and all those officials in China had said these last few weeks had been bait used to ferret out the ambassador, Vice Minister Liu, and the generals—each guilty of their own crimes—and to keep Guang from reneging on his deal. All the rhetoric, all the threats, had been nothing more than a political smoke screen. Those people who made up Campbell's "highest levels of government," whether here or in China, had toyed with David's and Hulan's lives with complete dispassion and the certainty that they would never be revealed.

"We were pawns," David said bitterly.

"You wanted the truth. There it is."

"Hulan?"

Campbell tried a nod, but David was right there with his cast.

"Remember getting the security clearance for your AUSA job?" Campbell asked. "We knew about your involvement with a known Communist."

At this, David released the agent in disgust and strode away. He turned back in anger. "How long did you know?"

"What does that matter now?"

"It matters to me. How long did you personally know about me and Hulan?"

"I guess from our first case. The Bureau gave me a file. You looked like a good guy, but one never can tell."

"You *played* with our lives," David said in anguish.

"It was for a greater good, Stark. We've picked the right side for once. You're a part of that."

There was a time when an argument like that would have worked on David, but no longer. He took one last look at the man he had once called his friend, turned, and continued his run alone.

Hulan stood at her kitchen window, waiting for the water to boil and looking out on the innermost courtyard of her old family home. Spring was just beginning and the temperature had finally started to rise. In the garden, the wisteria vine that an ancestor had planted more than one hundred years ago had begun to bud. Glossy green leaves were gradually opening on the jujube.

The kettle whistled. Hulan poured the hot water into a teapot. While it steeped, she set some peanuts, watermelon seeds, and a few salted plums in little dishes. With her tray ready, Hulan stepped out into the garden. She lingered for a moment under the colonnade and savored the tableau before her. Sitting under the twisting branches of the jujube were her mother and Uncle Zai. The man who had stood by Hulan's family through good times and bad perched just opposite Jinli on a porcelain stool. The tilt of his head as he spoke to Jinli implied deep intimacy. Hulan crossed to them now. As she did, Uncle Zai self-consciously pulled his hand away from Jinli's. Hulan set her tray on a low stone table and poured the tea. The three of them sat in companionable silence, enjoying the warmth of the sun.

After David's departure, Hulan had moved her mother and her nurse back to the *hutong*, where the two of them had taken up residence in one of the bungalows that faced onto the garden. Jinli seemed unaware of her husband's absence, let alone his death. Rather, she had experienced increasing moments of coherence, sometimes even engaging Hulan in conversation for five or more minutes at a time. Mostly her talk was of childhood memories—of the time she hid from her amah behind the spinning room, of the gardenias that her mother liked to float in bowls of water throughout the house, how her uncles had practiced their juggling and tumbling right here in this courtyard until their mother chased them out. At those moments, Jinli's voice, although soft and unaccustomed to speech, was as beautiful as Hulan remembered.

There was so much Hulan could do for her mother now. Hulan had her own money, of course, but her father had left behind an estate appropriate to a patriarch of one of the Hundred Families. No land or buildings or stock, just cash. That some of it was profit from her father's scheme troubled Hulan, but the Ministry of Public Security—under the advisement of Vice Minister Zai—had refused to confiscate any of it. This left Hulan with more than enough money to provide for her mother's care, to begin restoring the buildings of the compound, and to put some aside for—

"*Eeeah*," a voice called out. "*Ni hao ma?*" Neighborhood Committee director Zhang Junying stepped out onto the veranda.

"*Huanying, huanying,*" Hulan said in welcome, moving to meet her neighbor before she came all the way into the courtyard. "Come inside the house, auntie. Have you eaten? Do you drink tea?"

Madame Zhang looked longingly over Hulan's shoulder to where the other two were sitting. "Your mother is looking very well."

"Oh, she is very tired." This traditional answer, though untrue, showed Hulan's respect for her mother's life of devotion, duty, and hard work.

Hulan took the Neighborhood Committee director's elbow and led her back into the kitchen. "Sit here, auntie, where you can still see the garden and we can talk without disturbing the others."

"Very well," the old woman said coolly, understanding that she was not wanted.

"Come, come, auntie, this is not a day for hard feelings. This is still new to Mama. We must give her time."

"She shouldn't get too comfortable here, you know. Pretty soon they'll come through and mark our homes 'to be demolished.' Then the bulldozers will arrive and we'll all move away. I say, Let's go before they kick us out like old dogs! We'll go someplace modern. Get a dishwasher."

"We won't have to do that, auntie. They won't demolish our *hutong.* Our paramount leader lived only a few blocks away. No one will destroy his neighborhood."

"But Deng's dead."

"His home will become a pilgrimage site. The government will want to keep everything just as it was during his lifetime."

"Um," the old woman said thoughtfully. Then she clapped her palms on her widespread knees to signal a change in subject. "No matter what happens I must continue my duties as Neighborhood Committee director."

"Of course," Hulan agreed.

"And as such I have come to visit you today." She hesitated, hoping Hulan would confess of her own accord and save her from this accusation, but the young woman only sat there, her hands folded calmly in her lap, her eyes focused on her mother in the garden. Madame Zhang cleared her throat. "I have not seen you bring home female products in many weeks, nor have I seen their remains in your trash." Hulan did not deny this. "You know our one-child policy," the older woman continued. "You have not applied for a pregnancy permit. You also know how our government feels about children outside of marriage . . . "

Without shifting her gaze from her mother and Uncle Zai as they sat under the jujube, their heads together as they recalled some happy memory, Liu Hulan reached out and patted the old woman's hand. "You worry too much," Hulan said. "It is almost spring and the harshness of winter is over. It is time for us all to begin new lives in China."